a dark matter

a dark matter

A NOVEL peter straub

First published in Great Britain in 2010 by Orion Books,
an imprint of The Orion Publishing Group Ltd
Orion House, 5 Upper Saint Martin's Lane,
London WC2H 9EA

An Hachette UK Company

10 9 8 7 6 5 4 3 2 1

A CIP catalogue record for this book
is available from the British Library.

ISBN (Hardback) 978 0 7528 9182 8
ISBN (Export Trade Paperback) 978 0 7528 9183 5

Printed in the UK by CPI Mackays, Chatham ME5 8TD

The Orion Publishing Group's policy is to use papers that are natural,
renewable and recyclable and made from wood grown in sustainable
forests. The logging and manufacturing processes are expected to
conform to the environmental regulations of the country of origin.

www.orionbooks.co.uk

For Judy and Ben Sidran

Is there an emptiness we all share?
                    Before the end, I mean?
Heaven and earth depend on this clarity,
                    Heaven and earth.
Under the gold doubloons of the fallen maple leaves,
The underworld burrows in,
                    Sick to death of the light.

—CHARLES WRIGHT, *Littlefoot*

at first

A Few Years Back, Late Spring

The great revelations of my adult life began with the shouts of a lost soul in my neighborhood breakfast joint.

I was standing in line at the Corner Bakery on State and Cedar, half a block down the street from my pretty brick townhouse, waiting to order a Swiss Oatmeal (muesli) or a Berry Parfait (granola), anyhow something modest. The loudest noises in the place were the tapping of laptop keys and the rustle of someone turning newspaper pages. Abruptly, with a manic indignation that seemed to come from nowhere, the man at the head of the line started uttering the word *obstreperous*. He started out at a level just above ordinary conversation. By the time he found his rhythm, he was about twice that volume and getting louder as he rolled along. If you had to settle on one word to yell over and over in public, wouldn't you pick something less cumbersome? Yet he kept at it, spinning those four lumpy syllables every possible way, as if trying them on for size. His motive, for nothing actually comes from nowhere, soon became obvious.

Ob*strep*erous? ObSTREPerous? OBSTREPEROUS? Ob-strep?-ER-ous? OBstreperous?

Lady, you think I'm obstreperous now? This is what he was saying. *Give me another thirty seconds, you'll learn all about obstreperous.*

With each repetition, his question grew more heated. The momentarily dumbfounded young woman at the order counter had offended him, he wished her to know how greatly. The guy also thought he was making himself look smart, even witty, but to everyone else in the shop he had uncorked raving lunacy.

His variations were becoming more imaginative.

Ob*stree*perous? Ob*strap*erous? ObstrapOROUS?

To inspect this dude, I tilted sideways and looked down the good-sized line. I almost wished I hadn't.

Right away, it was obvious that the guy was not simply playing around. The next man in line was giving him six feet of empty floor space. Under the best of circumstances, people were going to keep their distance from this character. Eight or nine inches of white-gray hair surged out in stiff waves around his head. He was wearing a torn, slept-in checked suit that might have been ripped off a cornfield scarecrow. Through a latticework of scabs, smears, and bruises, his swollen feet shone a glaring, bloodless white. Like me, he had papers under his elbow, but the wad of newsprint he was clamping to his side appeared to have lasted him at least four or five days. The puffed-up bare feet, scuffed and abraded like shoes, were the worst part.

"Sir?" said the woman at the order counter. "Sir, you need to leave my store. Step away from the counter, sir, please. You need to step away."

Two huge kids in Southern Illinois sweatshirts, recent graduates by the look of them, jammed their chairs back and marched straight toward the action. This is Chicago, after all, where big, athletic-looking dudes sprout out of the sidewalks like dandelions on a suburban lawn. Without speaking to anyone, they came up on the homeless guy's flanks, hoisted him by his elbows, and transported him outside. If he had gone limp, they would have had a little trouble, but he was rigid with panic and gave them no more difficulty than would a cigar store Indian. He went stiff as a marble statue. When he

4

went by, I took in his blubbery lips and brown, broken teeth. His bloodshot eyes had a glazed look. The man kept saying, *obstreperous obstreperous obstreperous,* but the word had become meaningless to him. He was using it for protection, like a totem, and he thought as long as he kept saying it, he was out of danger.

When I looked into those flat, unseeing eyes, an utterly unforeseen thought jolted me. The impact felt like a blow, and brought with it a cryptic sense of illumination as brief as the flaring of a match.

I knew someone like that. This terrified man with a one-word vocabulary reminded me so vividly of someone that he might have *been* that person, now in the act of being ejected onto Rush Street. But . . . who in the world could it have been? No one I knew was anything like the damaged character now staggering forward and back on the sidewalk beyond the great windows, still whispering his totemic word.

A voice only I could hear said, *No one? Think again, Lee.* Deep in my chest, something big and decisive—something I had been ignoring and thrusting out of view literally for decades—stirred in its sleep and twitched its leathery wings. Whatever had nearly awakened tasted, in part, like shame, but shame was by no means all of it.

Although my first response was to turn away from whatever was causing my internal tumult (and turn away I did, with as much of my native resolve as I could summon), the memory of having witnessed an inexplicable illumination clung to me like a cat that had jumped onto my back and stuck its claws into my skin.

The next thing I did involved a typical bit of unconscious misdirection—I tried to believe that my distress was caused by the register girl's stupid language. Maybe that sounds snobbish, and maybe it is snobbish, but I've written eight novels, and I pay attention to the way people use words. Maybe too much attention. So when I finally stood in front of the young woman who had told that ruined creature that he "needed" to leave her "store," I expressed my unhappiness by ordering an Anaheim Scrambler, which comes with smoked bacon, cheddar cheese, avocado, and a lot of other stuff including hash browns, and a corn muffin, too. (Alas, I am one of those people who tend to use food as a way of dodging unwelcome emotions.) Anyhow, when did people start framing commands in terms of neediness? And how long had people in the restaurant business been calling their establishments "stores"? Couldn't people see the ugliness and inaccuracy of this crap? The creature within me rolled back into its uneasy sleep, temporarily lulled.

I parked myself at an empty table, snapped open my paper—the *Guardian Review*—and avoided looking at the big front windows until I heard one of the staff bringing my tray to me. For some reason, I turned around and glanced through the window, but of course that wretched, half-sane character had fled. Why did I care what had happened to him, anyhow? I didn't, apart from feeling a sort of generic pity for his suffering. And that poor devil did not remind me of anyone I knew or had once known. For a couple of seconds, a kind of misguided déjà vu had come into play. Nobody thought of déjà vu as anything except a momentary delusion. It gave you an odd buzz of recognition that felt like occult knowledge, but the buzz was psychic flotsam, of no value whatsoever.

Forty-five minutes later, I was walking back to my house, hoping that the day's work would go well. The minor disturbance in the Corner Bakery hardly counted even as a memory anymore, except for the moment when I was sliding my key into the front-door lock and saw once again his glassy, bloodshot eyes and heard him whispering *obstreperous obstreperous.* "I need you to stop doing that," I said out loud, and tried to smile as I stepped into my bright, comfortable foyer. Then I said, "No, I do *not* know anyone even faintly like you." For half a second, I thought someone was going to ask me what I was talking about, but my wife was on an extended visit to Washington, D.C., and in the whole of my splendid house, not a single living thing could hear me.

Work, unfortunately, was of no use at all. I had been planning to use the days my wife was gone to get a jump-start on a new novel then known as

Her Level Gaze. Never mind the total lameness of the title, which I intended to change as soon as I came up with a better one. Atop my oversized desk, a folder bulging with notes, outlines, and ideas for chapters sat beside my iMac, and a much smaller folder beside it held the ten awkward pages I had managed so far to excrete. Once I started poking it, the novel that had seemed so promising when still a shimmer of possibility had turned into a slow-moving, snarling animal. The male protagonist seemed to be a bit slow-moving, too. Although I did not want to admit it, the main character, the young woman with the disconcertingly level gaze, would have eaten him for breakfast in a single bite.

At the back of my mind was a matter I did not actually want to think about that day, a far too tempting suggestion made some years ago, God, maybe as many as five, by David Garson, my agent, who told me that my publisher had, who knows how seriously, proposed to him over lunch that at least once I should write a nonfiction book, not merely a memoir, but a book *about* something.

"Lee," David said, "don't get paranoid on me, he wasn't saying he wanted you to stop writing novels, of course he wasn't. They think you have an interesting way of seeing things, that's their main point here, and they think it might be useful if just once, and I mean *just once,* Lee Harwell could turn this reader-friendly yet challenging *trait* of his onto some event in the real world. The event could be huge, or it might be something smaller and more personal. He added that he thought a book like that would probably do you some good in the marketplace. He has a point there, actually. I mean, I think it's an extraordinarily interesting idea. Do you want to consider it? Why don't you just mull it over for a couple of days, see what occurs to you? I mean, just as a suggestion."

"David," I said, "no matter what my intentions are, everything I write winds up turning into fiction, including my letters to friends." Yet David is a good guy, and he does look out for me. I promised to think about it, which was disingenuous of me because in fact I already had been turning over the possibility of doing a nonfiction book. An unpublished and unpublishable manuscript I had come across on eBay a couple of months earlier, a kind of memoir by a Milwaukee homicide detective named George Cooper, seemed to crack open an old, officially unsolved series of murders that had much interested my friends and me when we were in grade school and high school. Of even greater interest to me right now was that these "Ladykiller" homicides appeared to have an at least tangential connection to a dark matter that involved these friends of mine, including the amazing girl who became my wife, though not me, in our last year in high school. But of that I did not wish to think—it involved a young man named Keith Hayward who had been, it seemed, a sick, evil child tutored in his sickness and evil by a truly demonic figure, his uncle. All of that was in the sort-of memoir Detective Cooper had written out in his cursive, old-school hand, and even as I put the story together I was determined to resist the gravitational pull it worked on me. The immense theological question of evil felt too great, too complex to address with the tools and weapons I possessed. What I knew best had only to do with stories and how they proceeded, and a mere instinct for narrative wasn't enough to take on the depths of the Hayward story. That my wife and our friends had come in contact with creepy Keith Hayward also put me off.

At the usual hour of one-thirty, hunger pulled me into the kitchen, where I put together a salad, warmed up some soup, and made half a sandwich with pumpernickel bread, Black Forest ham, coleslaw, and Russian dressing. Dinah Lion, my assistant, who would otherwise have been present, did not come in on Mondays, so the isolation of morning remained intact. Dinah would be gone for the next ten days or so, also, in an arrangement we had worked out with my accountants that was going to let her join her parents in Tuscany at half pay in exchange for some juggling with the vacation she normally took in August.

For some reason, the second I sat down before my solitary little meal, I felt like weeping. Something vital was slipping away from me, and for once this sense wasn't just a fantasy about the novel I was writing. The huge wave of sadness building up within me was connected to something more critical than *Her Level Gaze*; it was something I had lived with for much longer than I had my foundering book. Tears steamed up into my eyes and trembled there. For an excruciating moment, I was in the ridiculous position of grieving for a person, a place, or a condition that remained hidden from me. Someone I loved had died when we were both very young—that's what it felt like—and I had committed the dim-witted crime of never stopping to mourn that loss until just now. This must have been the source of the shame I tasted before I started ramming scrambled eggs, avocado, and cheddar cheese into my mouth. *I had let this person disappear.*

At the thought of the breakfast I had forced down my throat in the Corner Bakery, my hunger curdled. The food on the table looked poisoned. Tears slid down my face, and I stood up to turn toward the counter and grab some tissues. After I had wiped my face and blown my nose, I bagged up the half sandwich, covered the salad bowl with clingy film, and slammed the soup bowl into the microwave, where I could be counted on to forget about it until the next time I opened the thing. Then I made an aimless circuit of the kitchen. The book I had begun writing seemed to have locked me out, which I usually take to mean that it's waiting for some other, younger author to come along and treat it right. It would be at least a day before I could face my desk again, and when I did I would probably have to dream up some other project.

Her Level Gaze had never been right for me, anyway. At heart, it was a tidy little story about a weak man and a woman like a jungle animal, and I had been dressing it up as a kind of postmodern love story. The book really should have been written by Jim Thompson sometime in the mid-fifties.

A grim, heavy tide of grief went through me again, and this time it seemed that I was mourning the death, the real death, of all my childhood and youth. I groaned out loud, baffled by what was happening to me. A treasure house of beauty and vitality, all of this drenched yet hard-edged sense of pleasure, sorrow, and loss, had vanished, been swept away, and I had barely noticed. My parents, my old neighborhood, my aunts and uncles, a whole era seemed to call out for me, or me for it, and in rapid succession, as if in a series of frames, I saw:

the way a snowfall had looked on a December night in 1960, the big flakes tumbling softly as feathers from a measureless black sky;

a lean hound coursing through the deep snow at the bottom of our sledding hill;

the shredding lacquer on the tops of our sleds, and the chips and dents in the long, cool runners;

a glass of water shining from within on my mother's best white tablecloth.

Circling half blind with tears around the marble counter in my Chicago kitchen, I saw the stunning, inelegant west side of Madison, Wisconsin, the place where I had grown up and which I had escaped pretty much as soon as I could. My amazing girlfriend, now my wife, Lee Truax, had fled with me—we drove across the country to New York, where I went to NYU and she waited tables and tended bar until she could enroll at NYU, too, and cause a great fuss and commotion wherever she went. What was speaking to me, though, was not our college years and the East Village, but Madison's west side, so different then and so much the same, the place where Lee Truax and I had met as children and gone to school with all of our troubled, gorgeous friends.

Then I saw them all, our friends, who had needed to be convinced I was not a jerk because my father was a professor at the University instead of being absent or being nothing, really nothing, like theirs. For a moment their faces shone as clearly as the glass of water that had burned itself into my memory atop my mother's prize white tablecloth . . . their young faces tilted toward the Eel's fine-tuned heart-stopping face. Although they called me Twin, meaning hers, I never really looked like that. And in the next moment, before I could fully take them in, a curtain slammed down like a prohibition. Bang! *No more of that for you, bud.*

"Please," I said, then "What's happening to me?" What a baffled moment, filled with what terrible pain—the pain of *what I had not done,* of *what I had lost because I had not done all of that which I had not done.* Whatever it was, I had no idea, I knew only that *I had not done it.*

Then, as if on a giant screen before me, I saw the moving lips, the unshaven face, the torn horrible feet, and I heard the ragged, almost mechanical voice sucking on the four syllables that represented safety to a ragged soul. At that moment, shut out from a realm I long ago had been happy to abandon, I wished I had a totem, to protect me from Madison—the peeling glaze on the Flexible Flyer; the coursing hound; the sound of lockers banging shut in a high-school hallway; the precise way light from the windows in Room 138 fell across the Eel's face and Dill Olson's at the beginning of our senior English class, giving them a gorgeous, washed-out glamour.

Looking for release, I switched on the radio, tuned as is generally the case to NPR. A man whose name I had temporarily blanked out even as I recognized his voice said, "The really unexpected thing is how melodious Hawthorne sounds when you read him aloud. We've lost that, I think, the idea that the sound of writing is important, too."

And Nathaniel Hawthorne turned the key; Hawthorne gave me entry to the lost realm. Not the idea of reading him aloud, but that of hearing his words recited: the sound of his writing, as the man on NPR said. I knew exactly how the Hawthorne of *The Scarlet Letter* sounded, because I had once known a boy who had the ability to remember everything he read, and this boy often quoted long passages from the Hawthorne novel. He also liked to throw into ordinary conversation the crazy words he had discovered in a book called *Captain Leland Fountain's Dictionary of Unknown, Strange, and Preposterous Words.* (He had once told me he found it extremely odd that while nostology was the study of senility, nostomania had nothing at all to do with old age but simply meant a serious case of homesickness.) His name was Howard Bly, but we, our little band, all called him "Hootie." For some reason, all of us had silly nicknames. The kid couldn't help memorizing everything he read. When a string of words entered through his eyes, it printed itself on some endless scroll in his brain. Although I certainly wish I had this capacity, I don't have the faintest idea of how it works, nor did it seem particularly helpful to Hootie Bly, who was not at all literary.

When we were seniors at Madison West and he was seventeen, Hootie looked about thirteen or fourteen, small, blond, pink-cheeked, and cherubic. He had eyes the ceramic, cerulean blue of dolls' eyes, and his hair flopped over his forehead like bangs. Think of Brandon De Wilde in *Shane,* put a few years on him, and that would be Hootie. People tended to love him, if only because he was so beautiful and didn't say a lot. He wasn't smart, like the Eel, my girlfriend, Lee Truax, but neither was he stupid or slow—it was just that Eel was *really* smart. Hootie was not aggressive or forward or pushy in any way. I guess he was born with natural modesty. That doesn't mean he was passive or wishy-washy, because he was not.

This is what Hootie was like: When you look at a group photo, particularly a picture of a bunch of people doing something like hiking across a meadow or hanging out in a bar, you can always spot one person who stands mentally off to one side, enjoying the spectacle before him. Digging things, as Jack Kerouac would say. Sometimes Hootie liked to just lie back and, well, *dig* what was going on around him.

I can say this about Hootie Bly, that he was good through and through. The guy didn't have a mean-spirited or cruel cell, never mind a bone, in his body. Unfortunately, because of his size and the way he looked, people who were not as good-hearted—bullies, jerks—sometimes went after him. They enjoyed picking on him, teasing him in a way that went beyond teasing, sometimes actually shoving him around, and at times we who were his best friends felt we had to step in to protect him.

Hootie could speak up for himself, though. The Eel told me that when a truly ugly and unpleasant fraternity boy insulted him in a grungy State Street coffee shop named the Tick-Tock Diner but called the Aluminum Room, Hootie gave the asshole a murky look and baffled him with a quote from *The Scarlet Letter:* "Art thou like the Black Man that haunts the forest round about us? Hast thou enticed me into a bond that will prove the ruin of my soul?" Less than a minute later, the UW student widened his insult to include Hootie's parents, who, the kid knew from having seen all of them in the place, owned Badger Foods, the little triangular grocery store two blocks down on State Street. Hootie came back at him with another bit of Hawthorne. "What a strange, sad man is he! In the dark night-time, he calls us to him, and holds thy hand and mine, as when we stood with him on the scaffold yonder!"

The fraternity boy, the same sick, twisted Keith Hayward I had recently been reading about in Detective Cooper's unhappy memoir, apparently charged toward him, but was held back by his roommate and only friend, Brett Milstrap, who did not want them to be thrown out of the Aluminum Room before the (probable) arrival of this gorgeous blond girl they coveted so greatly that just the sight of her sipping a cup of coffee could keep them warm and happy for three or four days. Meredith Bright was her name, and like Hayward and Milstrap she played a huge role in the story I began trying to figure out over the next weeks and months. She must have been one of the most beautiful young women ever to appear on that campus. The same would have been true if she had gone to UCLA instead of UW. Meredith Bright detested Keith Hayward and thought nothing of Brett Milstrap, but the first time she laid eyes on Hootie Bly and Lee Truax, she was enchanted by them. For a number of reasons.

It would be fair to say that the whole long, crazy story I wound up trying to unearth began when Meredith Bright, seated alone in the Aluminum Room's last booth, lifted her eyes from her copy of *Love's Body,* gazed down the length of the counter to spot Hootie and the Eel, and rocked them both by smiling at them. But before I get even farther ahead of myself, I have to go back to where I was and explain a few more things about Hootie and our little group of friends.

I said that hearing one of those comfortable NPR voices talk about the experience of hearing Hawthorne read aloud was all I needed—all I needed, that is, to understand the intense, unexpected deluge of emotions that had been chasing me around the room since I had looked into the blood-shot eyes of Mr. Obstreperous as two fullbacks from Carbondale toted him by on his way to the exit. I had fought so tenaciously against the sudden sense of recognition that unmediated images and passages from my childhood had streamed back to me in a painful flood. The reason for my doomed tenacity was that Obstreperous reminded me of Hootie, who had spent four decades in a Wisconsin mental hospital, communicating entirely in individual words from Captain Fountain and, maybe when feeling particularly nostomaniacal, sentences like "Hast thou enticed me into a bond that will prove the ruin of my soul?" *The Scarlet Letter* and the Captain's obscure gewgaws: that isn't craziness, it's fear, the same kind of absolute terror that turned Obstreperous into a muttering statue.

I wanted to know more about that fear. Now that I had opened up this seam, it came to me, I wanted to follow it right to the end. Once I understood the causes of Hootie's paralysis, I thought, a layer of reality that had been closed to me for nearly forty years would at last become visible.

But it wasn't all about me, not by a long shot.

Off and on, over the decades since the mid-sixties, this hidden world—the whole question of the wandering guru named Spencer Mallon, what he had accomplished, what he had not, what he still meant to those who had loved and admired him—had troubled me, more than troubled me, aroused an ongoing doubt and misery that stuck to me like a shadow whenever the whole issue swung back into view. Part of this continuous disorder was rooted in the silence of a single human being. She wouldn't talk to me about it, and neither would the others. They shut me out. I mean, I don't want to go overboard about something that happened so long ago, but was that really *fair*? Everything was fine, everything was chummy, and just because I didn't want anything to do with this Mallon faker, they closed ranks against me. Even my girlfriend, who was supposed to look like my twin!

You know what happened? Like a dumb kid, I thought I was, I *told* myself I was, sticking to my principles, when actually the whole business of this amazing man who had been to Tibet and seen someone cut off someone else's hand in a bar, who talked about the *Tibetan Book of the Dead* and a philosopher named Norman O. Brown, who was besides that tied in to ancient magic, all this stuff kind of scared me. It sounded like total bullshit, but it also seemed far out of my league—because, who knows, there might have been some reality in it, after all. I think I was afraid that if I met this guy, I might have to believe in him, too.

The Eel knew exactly how I felt, that's how smart she was. She understood that my reaction was a lot more complex than I was willing to accept, and that I was backing away from a fear she found second rate to begin with made her lose a crucial degree of respect for me. Given that I had no interest in pretending to be a college student and had therefore stayed at home the first time my friends all went to the Aluminum Room, I had two chances to make things right: I could have come along to the Italian restaurant where they first heard Mallon's spiel, and I could have made up for my lapses by joining everyone at the second Mallon-séance, in the Henry Street apartment that turned out to be where Keith Hayward and Brett Milstrap lived. Those were my two chances. But after I said no the second time, the door slammed shut, and I was left alone outside, where I had deliberately gone and placed myself.

While they were all trailing after Mallon, I took long walks by myself and wound up, some of the time, shooting lonely hoops at a grade-school playground. Or trying to. I remember missing fifteen free throws in a row, one after the other. On the big day itself, Sunday, the sixteenth of October, 1966, I just stayed in my room and reread Thomas Wolfe's *Of Time and the River,* a novel I loved to distraction because it seemed to describe me, Lee Harwell, exactly, a sensitive, lonely, brilliant young fellow obviously destined for literary success, or if not me *exactly,* at least the person I'd be if I'd gone to Harvard and traveled around Europe, O lost, O soulful, word-crammed wanderer on this earth, a stone a leaf an unfound door.

For two whole days, I had no idea where she was. When I did get some information, it was infuriatingly circumscribed. This was, precisely, all that I was allowed to understand: in one way or another, under circumstances forever closed to me, things had exploded. There had been a gathering, a meeting, perhaps some sort of ceremony, and at this event everything had gone spectacularly to hell. A boy had not only been killed, he had been hideously mutilated, ripped to shreds. One of the inevitable rumors about this cataclysm had been that the dead boy seemed to have been torn apart by enormous teeth. During the months that followed, over in fact the next four decades, the one person I still knew from those days who had been part of Mallon's ill-fated entourage, my wife, had refused even to try to explain what had happened to them all.

For a week or so, she just clammed up. The only details she was willing to share with me had to do with the conduct of the police during the subsequent investigations, the confusion and rage of her useless father, her impatience with our teachers and fellow students, her despair about poor Hootie. After things had calmed down a bit and the mystery of Hootie's location had finally been clarified, Eel tried on at least two occasions to visit him at the Lamont Hospital, where it turned out he had been all along. The first time she spoke to someone there, whoever it was (apparently, descending to such details was a waste of time) forbade her to come out: Mr. Bly's condition was too grave, too precarious. A month later, she tried again. This time, the gatekeeper invited her to visit the hospital, and it was Hootie Bly who turned her down. Using words borrowed from Hawthorne, he refused even to see her. Ever. His refusal stayed firm throughout our senior year, and I guess finally Lee gave up. After we took off for New York, she never mentioned him again.

From time to time I thought of that smiling, blue-eyed kid and wondered what had become of him. He was still important to me, and I knew that he must still have meant a great deal to my wife, who eventually ceased to be the Eel and became widely known, in certain circles, under the name

16

she was born with. I wished him well. After six months, I thought, eight months, he must have left the hospital and picked up his life again. He probably moved back in with his parents. On their retirement, he would take over Badger Foods, maybe liven it up a little. Or get out of Madison, marry a girl who looked a lot like him, work in an office, and raise two or three blond, cherubic children. People like Hootie Bly were *supposed* to have uneventful, essentially unexamined, but deeply appreciated, truly lived-in lives. If the world didn't turn out well for them, the rest of us didn't have a chance.

Hootie's true fate remained a mystery to me until the summer of 2000, when on a rare vacation together my wife and I went to Bermuda. I tend not to take vacations, and my wife prefers to visit places that she already knows, where she has both friends and something to do. She spends a lot of time at conferences and board meetings, and she has a busy, useful, completely admirable life. Marriage to a novelist can be as lonely as being one yourself, without even the companionship of imaginary people. I am happy that Lee has created such a fulfilling life for herself, and I enjoy those few times when we go somewhere together for no reason other than to relax and walk around. (Of course I always bring my work, and Lee travels with her own gadgets.) So we were having a nice lunch at a place in Hamilton called Tom Moore's Tavern, and across the room I saw a man of about my age with blond hair going gray, a good tanned face full of character, seated at a table with a very appealing woman who looked a good deal like him. If my wife were not present, despite her age the blond lady would have easily been the best-looking woman in the room. The former Eel remains completely unaware of this, and she gets irritated if someone points it out, but no matter where she happens to be, Lee Truax is always the most beautiful woman in the room. I mean that. Always.

The well-off, affable man across the room could have been the grown-up, prosperous Howard Bly, if Hootie had made all the right choices and enjoyed a fair bit of good luck. "Honey," I said, "Hootie Bly could be sitting across the room from us, and he looks great."

"It's not Hootie," she said. "Sorry. I wish it were, though."

"How can you be so sure?" I asked.

"Because Hootie's still in that hospital. The only thing that's different about him is that he got older, just like us."

"He's still there?" I asked, aghast. "In the Lamont?"

"That's where he is, the poor guy."

"How do you know?"

I watched her measuring her fish with her fork, then severing a morsel she moved carefully onto its tines. Other people seldom notice this, but my wife eats in a very particular way. I always enjoy watching her go through the necessary rituals.

"I have my ways," she told me. "From time to time, people communicate with me."

"That's all you're going to tell me, isn't it?"

"This conversation is about Hootie, not who told me about him."

And that was that. Her refusal to speak returned us to the familiar ancient silence, where I had no right to ask for information because I had chosen first not to prowl around the university campus, then, more condemningly, not even to meet, much less adore, Spencer Mallon. My friends, even the Eel, they all but worshipped this guy. I should say, especially the Eel. Who do you think she thought she was protecting by refusing to name her source?

That's enough of Mallon, at least for a while.

■

Of the five people in our little band from Madison West, three had serious problems with their fathers. At the time, I thought this explained a lot about their attraction to Mallon, and I still do. Going by what my friends told me, Spencer Mallon might have been designed by committee to be hypnotically appealing to a bunch of adventurous seventeen- and eighteen-year-old kids who had, one way or another, been wounded by their bad-news dads.

He certainly spoke straight to my friends, he roped them right in. He *seduced* them—that's what it comes down to. And because they had been hypnotized and seduced, they followed this character out into an obscure meadow owned by the university's agronomy department and cheerfully went along with whatever it was that proved to be so ruinous to them, every one.

The Eel's dad was no prize to begin with, but after crib death took her little brother in his sixth or seventh month, I don't remember, he fell apart, spectacularly. Carl Truax had earned a few patents that proved he had been an inventor once, and most days he dragged himself out of his foul-smelling bed to put in a few hours in the backyard shed he called his "workshop." By the time his daughter was in her senior year, he had stopped pretending to do anything out there but drink. When the day's first bottle became no more than a fond memory, he took off on his round of crummy taverns and bars, scrounging for a couple of dollars he could spend on more alcohol. How guys like that manage to get money is utterly mysterious to me, but good old Carl almost always managed to raise enough to see him through his day's drinking and still have a few bucks left over. Sometimes he brought home a present to appease the only other person who lived in his hovel, his amazing daughter, the person who, when he was home to eat dinner, cooked it for him and did her best to keep the hovel clean and sanitary. Her attitude toward her father generally vacillated between a dry rage and a furious contempt.

Just before Dilly Olson came up with the brilliant idea of hanging out in places like the Tick-Tock to pose as UW students and get invited to fraternity parties, the ploy that led them straight to Keith Hayward, Meredith Bright, and Mallon, Carl rolled in with a poster he had won in a poker game at the scuzziest dive in all of Madison. It was of a famous Cassius Marcellus Coolidge painting called *A Friend in Need,* depicting half a dozen dogs dressed like humans playing poker. He was sure she'd love it. A cigar-smoking bulldog was using a rear paw to pass the ace of spades under the table to a yellow mongrel, wasn't that the cutest damn thing you ever saw?

The Eel detested this sentimental piece of shit, but three of the boys, who were reminded of themselves, fell in love with *A Friend in Need* and talked about it nonstop for days. They had the run of the hovel and therefore constant access to the masterpiece because about a week after the death of her infant son, Carl's wife and Eel's mother, Lurleen Henderson Truax, took off without softening the shock of her absence with advance warning or a farewell note. Four days after the baby's burial, when her husband was on his rounds and her nine-year-old daughter at school, the Eel's mom crammed some stuff into a cheap suitcase from St. Vincent de Paul, ducked out of the hovel, and disappeared. Lurleen had her own problems, plenty of them, and the Eel missed her in the complicated way you'd miss a hive of bees that produced great honey but seemed intent on stinging you to death one day.

After her mother's vanishing act, the Eel, Lee Truax, raised herself. She made herself do her homework, she shopped and made meals, she helped herself with her homework and put herself to bed at night, and she figured out that whatever you did had long-term consequences. She learned that people tell you all about themselves by the way they act and the things they say. All you had to do was pay attention. People opened themselves up, put everything on display, and never knew they were doing it.

Although not gay, the Eel decided early on that because boys always ran things and gave the orders she would prefer to look like a boy rather than a girl, so she took out the good scissors and gave herself a Mo Howard bowl cut, and started going around in blue jeans and plaid shirts. Dressed like that, under her weird haircut, she looked like the Platonic ideal of a tomboy. As long as you took the time to look at her with the same concentration she gave you, all of this somehow made her incredibly cute. If you just casually, lazily took her in and let your eyes roam elsewhere, you would probably think she was on the plain side. You might even take her for a boy.

Hootie loved her, God knows I loved her, and if the other two guys in our group did not bring exactly the same kind of emotion to their relationships with her, they felt close to her in a comfortable, uncomplicated way—

almost as if she really were another boy their age, albeit one they wished to protect. They did their best to protect Hootie, too, so it wasn't because she was female. Half the time, I think they almost forgot that she wasn't just another boy. I had been tremendously fond of these guys, and I trusted them absolutely. They were the people with whom I spent most of the day and hung out with at night, the people I talked to on the phone after school. Once Boats Boatman and Dilly Olson understood that I was not a snob, despite the disadvantage of actually living in a house that was pretty ritzy by their standards, plus having an intact set of parents, they relaxed around me and started treating me the same way they treated themselves, with a rough, affectionate good humor. Like Hootie, like my wife in her particular way, these two young men had been ruined, I thought, by whatever Spencer Mallon had caused to happen out in that damned meadow.

Going back a step, I could also say that their wretched fathers had trashed their lives by scarpering off, which made them vulnerable to peripatetic wisdom merchants like Mallon. Nobody ever says this, but in the sixties these frauds were all over the place, especially in towns with college campuses. Sometimes they were homegrown, academics who jumped off the rails and used their classrooms as pulpits, but just as often they wandered in from nowhere, preceded by a little bubble of promissory excitement built up by acolytes who had been converted during the guru/philosopher/sage's last visit. Generally, they stuck around for a month or so, sleeping on their admirers' couches or spare beds, "borrowing" their hosts' clothing, accepting free meals and free drink, sleeping with the hosts' girlfriends and other female admirers. Everybody owned everything, according to them, so naturally they had a right to all of their followers' possessions. Ownership was a morally suspect concept. Spencer Mallon told the Mallon-ites that "everything is everything," which extended the usual nonpossessive mind-set into the cosmos. Even when I was seventeen I thought all this was claptrap, a variety of nonsense particularly friendly to predators. But I was raised in a reasonable home by reasonable people.

Jason Boatman, whom we called "Boats" for two obvious reasons, was being raised almost entirely by his mother, Shirley. We all liked Shirley Boatman, and she liked us back, especially the Eel, but it was no secret that the slight drinking problem she had before her husband deserted her had blossomed into something much more serious after that. Shirley was a long way from Carl Truax's passionate surrender to alcohol, but she drank a beer with breakfast and nipped at the gin bottle all afternoon. By nine o'clock at night, she was so deeply in the bag that she usually passed out in her chair.

Seven years before Spencer Mallon's arrival in Madison, Boats's father, who had been running a struggling boatbuilding enterprise in Milwaukee and commuting back and forth three or four times a week, announced that he had fallen in love with a twenty-year-old apprentice boatbuilder named Brandi Brubaker. She had come to him from the UW boathouse, like a lot of his underpaid assistants and apprentices. He and Brandi would be renting a place near the boatyard on Lake Michigan, and in the future his visits to Madison would be to continue his work for the rowing team and to see his son.

The visits to his son soon petered out to once a month, then stopped altogether. His business picked up, and probably he had less time to give to his old family. Cunning little Brandi had soon produced a pair of twins, Candee and Andee. They were "adorable." Boats lost whatever interest he had once had in boats and boat-building, and would happily have traded his father for any of the others', even Dilly Olson's, who had run off ten years earlier, never to be heard from again.

At seventeen and eighteen, Jason Boatman was a pretty good-looking kid until you put him alongside Dilly, who made him look furtive and shifty. That he actually was kind of furtive and shifty did not trouble those of us who had been his friends since grade school. Before his father abandoned him, Boats had been fairly outgoing, cheerful, and easy to read. He was skinny and on the tall side, the kind of nice, friendly kid who goes along with what everybody else wants to do. After his father left, he buried his sense of humor and became morose. He didn't talk as much, and his shoulders slumped. He walked around with his hands in his pockets, staring at the ground, as if looking for something he had lost. Boats completely gave up on school. In class, he sat nearly sideways at his desk and gave the blackboard the suspicious look you'd have for someone you suspected was lying to you. His dominant mode was mild grievance. If you went to his house, instead of hello he'd say something like "About time you showed up." He stopped reading books and participating in sports. His conversation became taciturn, almost reluctant, except for when he complained. Complaint brought out a recognizable version of the Boats we remembered from grade school, observant, voluble, wholly present. These arias centered on our teachers, the books they assumed we would read and the homework they assumed we would tackle each night, the weather, the brutality of athletes, the sloppiness of the school janitor, his mother's blurriness as the evening wore on. Boats and the Eel could swap drunken parent stories like a saxophone player and a drummer trading fours. But no matter how far-ranging his laments over the state of the world, Boats never spoke of his father. Every now and then, apropos of nothing, he shook his head and muttered, "Brandi Brubaker," coughing up the name of his father's new wife like a hairball.

The other great change that befell Jason "Boats" Boatman after his father split involved a ferocious concentration on shoplifting. He started thieving on a heroic scale. It was like a binge, only it never stopped. What do you call that, a spree? Boats went on a lifelong thieving spree. Back in the fifth grade, all of my friends now and then swiped things like candy bars, comic books and paperbacks, and school supplies from the neighborhood shops, but there was no consistency or pattern to it. None of us did it all the time, and I did it less than most. Sometimes, Eel or Dilly Olson couldn't afford to get the new notebook or ballpoint pen some teacher wanted to see on our desks, and the only way to get the required object was to go around to the stationery store and swipe it. Boats acted exactly the same way up until about a month or so after his father took off. Then wherever he went, he dipped into stores and ransacked whatever he could, he stole everything he could carry out on his person. He gave us so many sweaters and sweatshirts that some of our parents got suspicious. (Not the Eel's father, of course.) Shirley Boatman could see what was going on, and she warned Boats that one day he'd get pinched and have to go to court. The warning had no effect.

Eel told me, and it made a lot of sense even then, that he used all these shoes, socks, underpants, UW T-shirts, erasers, notebooks, pencils, staplers, and books to feed a howling emptiness within him. When Mallon came along and scooped them all up, he now and again deputized Boats to nab various items for him. According to Mallon's theories, Boats wasn't stealing anything, he was just redistributing it. Because everything was everything, nobody, especially shop owners, owned any of the property they imagined theirs. It always struck Eel and me as funny that if Boats actually believed in Mallon's theories, he would stop stealing on the spot. As far as he was concerned. the whole point of theft was that whatever you slipped under your coat really belonged to someone else—that's why putting it under your coat made you feel better. The sense of a fleeting superiority helped feed the emptiness within. But of course everything that entered that cruel space was instantly consumed.

I have mentioned that going over to State Street to hang out in the Aluminum Room and pretend to be UW students was Dill Olson's idea, and this was typical of Donald Olson's role in our little band. Don Olson would have been a leader wherever he went to school: he was one of those kids who possess a natural, built-in authority that seems rooted in a deep personal decency. The way he looked undoubtedly added to this already considerable personal authority. During grade school, he was always taller than the rest of us, and by his senior year in high school he had topped out at six-two. His height would have been insignificant had it not been in a sense magnified or spotlighted by the effect of his deep dark eyes, crisp dark eyebrows, high-cut cheekbones, mobile and expressive mouth, smooth unblemished olive complexion, rather longish dark hair that fell nearly to his collar, and effortlessly immaculate posture. He always stood as straight as a marine, but gracefully, as if nothing could be more natural than perfect posture.

If Dilly Olson had used his handsomeness for gain, if he had demonstrated an awareness of its effect and pleasure in that awareness, if he had betrayed any trace of self-love, he would have been ruined—in a different way, I mean, than he was, in effect, ruined by the course of his life. Instead, he seemed to have no idea that he was incredibly handsome, or to feel that his obvious good looks were irrelevant to the real business of his life. What that real business might be was still an unknown quantity. If we had lived in New York City or Los Angeles, someone would almost certainly have come along to suggest that Dill Olson become an actor, but we lived in Wisconsin, and no one we knew had ever become an actor or, for that matter, any other sort of artist. We saw a lot of movies, but the people who acted in them were clearly the products of some other, more elevated realm. They were remote from us, those actors. Even the air they breathed was another substance than the workaday stuff we inhaled.

Unlike me, Dill did not read books as if they, too, were meant to be inhaled and thereafter to inform your thoughts and actions. He never got lost in a book, he was not academic or scholarly in any sense, and it seemed that he could never follow the path that Lee Truax and I had set upon, that of going to college and feeling our way into our futures through the usual means of exploring a curriculum. He could not afford college anyhow. His mother and her stuffy and alcoholic new boyfriend, a credit union officer whose dearest wish was that Donald Olson leave home for good, had let him know they would not pay for college tuition.

That Dill would get some ordinary office job or become a clerk in a shop seemed impossible, unjust, and the draft board, otherwise eager to devour young men just like him, had already declined his services because of a faulty valve in his heart: in a moment of boredom and despair, he had tried to enlist, naturally without telling anyone, and been declared 1-Y, medically

25

unfit until such time as grade-school students were issued guns and helmets, which surprised the army recruiters as much as it disappointed him, briefly. As time went on and the demonstrations grew louder and more frequent, Dill learned enough about what was going on in Vietnam simultaneously to be distressed by the war and grateful for his draft status.

Actually, the conflict in Vietnam gave him a cause that helped take his mind off the depressing subject of what he would do after he graduated. Madison West forbade any form of outright political expression as a matter of policy, and our principal, a World War II veteran, would probably have done his best to expel any student bold enough to organize or participate in an antiwar gathering on school property. We didn't need our own, though, because we could fall into the speak-ins, teach-ins, marches, and crowd scenes that were always taking place on and immediately around the university's campus. By 1966, Madison was well on its way to the aggrieved, rolling boil of 1968, and all the protests and marches gave Dilly lots of opportunities to meet college girls at the same time that he genuinely protested against the war.

And Boats cared about the war, too, because he feared being snatched up by the army the day he graduated from high school, but he was far more interested in college girls and fraternity parties.

Unless I'm wrong about this, part of Mallon's appeal to Dilly Olson lay in his attitude toward Vietnam. Mallon made it clear that he thought the war was necessary at that specific time—he seemed to have a semi-religious feeling about violence, which he saw as a kind of birth—although he implied that his final goal, attainable through a certain occult ceremony, involved using a sacred violence as a means of so transforming our earth that the war in Vietnam would end of itself, like a weed deprived too long of water. The fire would devour the fire, the hurricane devastate the rampaging typhoon. It was something like that, anyhow. After all this destruction would come a rebirth, the dimensions and nature of which were to be explored joyfully by Mallon and his chosen few. I have to give that fraud this much, that he told Dilly, Boats, my wife, and his other three followers, Meredith Bright, Keith Hayward, and Brett Milstrap, that the great transformation and rebirth might last only a second or two, also that it might take place only in their minds, as the opening of a fresh vision, a truer, more essential way of seeing things. Despite the damage he caused to every one of these kids, I have to respect his honesty on this point. Like every other phony sage and prophet wandering through campuses in the mid- to late sixties, Spencer Mallon promised an end to time and a new apocalypse; unlike most of the others, he admitted that the end of time might last only a moment, or take place only in the throwing open of a mental window. I hate the man, I think he was a phony who got lucky in the worst possible way, but I have to respect this evidence of what feels to me like wisdom. If not wisdom, a conscience.

■

My girlfriend—Lee Truax, the Eel—and her companions went to the Tick-Tock Diner, called the Aluminum Room for the odd, reflective, tinfoil-like material covering its walls, and in that unlikely little dump a stunning blond girl named Meredith Bright welcomed the Eel and Hootie into the end booth where she sat alone with a copy of a book called *Love's Body* by Norman O. Brown (one of Spencer Mallon's guides and teachers, in this case literally). Down at the front of the diner, terrible Keith Hayward and his roommate, Milstrap, regarded the scene in jealousy and disgust. (It should be noted that even at this first meeting, both my wife and Hootie found Keith Hayward oddly unsettling.) True to her time if not her type, Meredith had some expertise in concocting horoscopes, and it turned out that she had wheedled Mallon, her guru and lover, into letting her draw up a horoscope, or maybe a series of horoscopes, I'm not sure how this works, to determine the astrological signs most desirable in his followers. According to her calculations, the group required a Taurus and a Pisces, exactly what Eel and Hootie were, to accomplish its ends. Less urgently, they also needed a

Scorpio and a Cancer, Dilly's and Boats's signs. So they were doomed from the start, all of them. It was in their stars.

I'm sure this was genuine: I don't believe Meredith cooked up a phony chart after encountering my friends in the Aluminum Room. Although to me such recognitions cannot but sound delusional, I believe that Meredith Bright understood that Eel and Hootie satisfied her crucial astrological requirements the minute she spotted them staring up at her from the bottom end of the counter. I think of how innocent they must have looked, how tremendously innocent they actually were, and how appealingly innocent they must have seemed to Mallon, who devoured innocence wholesale. Having guessed what she needed only to confirm, Meredith summoned Eel and Hootie before her with a beckoning look, and after asking for their names, she did the same for their astrological signs. Bingo! On the money! And what luck, a Taurus and a Cancer were sitting right down at the end of the counter, what do you know, they must all come to an eight o'clock gathering, two nights hence, in the lower room at La Bella Capri. Please. Pretty please, with sugar on the top. Meredith Bright actually said that.

Because they could not have resisted any such invitation from the world's most desirable woman, they immediately agreed to show up in the downstairs dining room of the State Street Italian restaurant they had known all their lives. The Eel asked me to come along, Dilly tried to cajole me into joining them, but I had not gazed into the bottomless, speaking eyes of Meredith Bright, and I said no. It was not even as though they were still pretending to be UW students, because Meredith Bright had understood from the first that they were in high school. My friends and my lover, for Lee Truax and I had been sleeping together since our fifth date, tried but failed to sell me on the mystery and glamour of Spencer Mallon (as described by Miss Bright).

And the next time we were alone, Eel asked me, "You really don't want to go? It'll be so cool, it'll be so interesting! This Mallon guy won't be like anyone you've ever seen before. Come on, sweetie, don't you want to meet a real, I don't know, magician? A traveling wise man who has something to teach us?"

"The whole idea of a traveling wise man makes me sick," I said. "I'm sorry, it just does. So no, I'm not going to sit downstairs at La Bella Capri and listen to this guy's b.s."

"How do you know it'll be b.s.?"

"I know it'll be bullshit because it can't be anything else."

"Well, Lee . . ."

This was really poignant. Her inability to speak, her lingering silence, expressed a kind of hopelessness no one wants to see in his girlfriend, his close companion, his beloved and intimate friend. She was telling me that not only had I missed the point, it seemed likely that I would never understand. Then she asked:

"Do you mind if I go?"

At that second, I could have rewritten her future. Right there. Mine, too. But it wasn't in me. She so much wanted to waste her time sitting at the feet of this peripatetic con man that I could not object. It should have been harmless; the only consequence should have been the memory of a tedious and confusing hour or two. I said:

"No, I don't mind, you should do what you want."

"Yes," she said, "I should."

She went, and they went, and arrived early, and took a side table and ordered a pizza and gobbled away while the real university students arrived, among them Brett Milstrap and the disconcerting Keith Hayward, who sneered at them as he and his roommate commandeered a table near the front. Soon, the clubby downstairs room had filled up with students attracted by whatever they had heard about the evening's star attraction. At ten after eight, a ruffle of conversation and laughter from the top of the staircase drew the attention of all, who swiveled their heads toward the arched, cavelike stucco entrance at the foot of the stairs to observe the grand entrance of Meredith Bright, a lush, darkly beautiful young woman later introduced as

Alexandra, and Spencer Mallon, who, accompanied by his stunning acolytes, entered the downstairs room in a flurry of beautiful faces, rough blond hair, a safari jacket, and weathered brown boots, "like," Hootie Bly told me later, "a god."

I formed a clear mental picture of this being only fifteen years later, in 1981, when having gone alone to the first showing that day of *Raiders of the Lost Ark,* I saw Indiana Jones, in the person of Harrison Ford, striding through clouds of dust and sand. A safari jacket, a dashing hat, a weathered face neither young nor old. Out loud, I said, "Good Lord, that's Spencer Mallon," but no one heard me, I hope. The theater was two-thirds empty, and I was at the end of the row third from the back, surrounded by vacant seats. Much later, in a rare moment Lee described Mallon's face as "vulpine," so I altered the Indiana Jones model a bit, but not by much.

Within seconds of his appearance in the entry at the foot of the stairs, Mallon separated himself from the adoring women and led them to the foremost table, whirled a chair back to front, parked himself on it astraddle, and began to talk, ravishingly. "For anyone else," an awed Hootie told me, "the way he talks would be like singing." It wasn't that the guru chanted, rather that his voice was surpassingly musical, capable of tremendous range, and distinguished by the beauty of his timbre, I guess you'd call it. He had to have had something, God knows, and an extraordinarily beautiful voice can be very persuasive.

Mallon described wandering through Tibet; he talked about *The Tibetan Book of the Dead,* in the mid- to late sixties virtually the Bible for phonies. In Tibetan bars, the Eel and Hootie told me, Spencer Mallon had twice—two times!—seen one man sever the hand of another, seen the blood rush down the length of the bar, and seen the man with the hatchet snatch up the severed hand and throw it to a waiting dog. It had been a sign, a signal, and he had come to explain its meaning.

After they finally opened up a little, both Hootie and my girlfriend reported that despite the severed hands and streams of blood it had been like listening to music, except music that had meaning flowing through it. "He made you see things," both of them said, although when not in the guru's presence they found it difficult to describe his message. "I can't repeat any of that stuff," Hootie told me; the Eel said, "Sorry, but if you weren't there, there's no way I can make you understand what he said to us."

Then she added, "Because he said it to *us*, get it?"

She was deliberately excluding me, depositing me on the far side of a line she had drawn in the sand. They had been singled out, my four friends, they had been elevated to a height so great I was scarcely visible anymore. Mallon had signaled them to remain after the UW students left, and when they and the two girlfriends, as spectacular as magicians' assistants, remained alone in the lower room, for once without Hayward and Milstrap, the sage told them they would help him at last achieve something, a breakthrough, I'm not sure what he said about it, but it was going to be a breakthrough anyhow, the culmination of all his work to date. He thought, he hoped so. The vessels had shattered, he said, and divine sparks flew through the fallen world. The divine sparks yearned to be reunited: and when they were re-united, the fallen world would be transformed into a glorious tapestry. Per-haps they would be privileged to witness the transformation, in whatever sense, whatever manifestation, and for however long. The little band from Madison West felt essential to him, he *needed* them . . . It was like that, a sense of immanence, urgency, promise.

"Trust me," he said, perhaps to all of them, but specifically to Dill. "When the tide rises, you shall be by my side."

Olson told this to me in a private moment, and I did not think he was boasting: for once, Dilly seemed to be at peace with himself. I suppose that was when I started to get scared. Or maybe I mean alarmed. What did this mysterious guy mean, anyhow, by "When the tide rises"? What tide, and how would it "rise"?

Before they separated, he told my friends to meet him two nights later, and gave them the address of the Gorham Street apartment of Hayward and

Milstrap. During the next two school days, my friends were quivering with excitement, and after I had twice refused my girlfriend's invitation to join them in diving down the rabbit hole, I was excluded from their accumulating expectancy. They had joined shoulders against me. I'd missed my last chance. But of course I did not at all want to pursue them into the rabbit hole. What I did want to do was to persuade Eel, at least, that she and they were being exploited by a handsome fraud who may have said he was interested in causing great transformations through occult means but was undoubtedly after earthier goals.

In fact, even before the Gorham Street gathering, the guru's reputation had begun to shred. The beauty named Alexandra, one of Mallon's companions on his first outing, came up to Hootie in the Tick-Tock (where they now went every afternoon, straight from school) and tried to warn him from associating with the man. Too bad—by then Hootie loved his hero, and Alexandra's tales of his amorality and double-dealing hurt him, on Mallon's behalf. Hootie thought she must have been inventing most of her story; that somehow Spencer had brought this huge-eyed, wild-haired, gypsylike dame to hysterical tears impressed the dickens out of Hootie. And that Mallon should have been kicked out of a fraternity house or two sounded like either an exaggeration or an actual lie—someone was lying anyhow, he thought, probably the fraternity boys because they were angry that Mallon had moved on. When the ranting woman warned Hootie that Mallon would probably try to move in with one of his group, he flushed with excitement and hoped it would be him! And in fact, not long after the Gorham Street meeting, Spencer Mallon did wind up spending a couple of nights in the basement of Badger Foods, the Blys' little corner grocery store.

Not that I was aware of Mallon's location, because I was not. The Eel, with whom I had spent nearly every school and weekend night for a year and a half, continued to sit next to me in class, but otherwise acted as though she had embarked on some luxury cruise that I had declined, inexplicably, to share with her. At night, she barely gave me five minutes on the telephone.

I had missed, all but literally, the boat, and the Eel was so entranced with the details of her voyage she had little time left over for me.

All I knew of the Gorham Street séance was that my girlfriend had wound up being seated at a long table beside Keith Hayward while Mallon held forth. "He was great, but you wouldn't understand, so I'm not even going to try," she told me. "But boy, I'm never getting that close to Keith Hayward again. You know, that guy I was telling you about, with the thin face and the wrinkled-up forehead? And acne scars? He's seriously bad news."

Had he tried to pick her up? At least for those with eyes, the Eel was so cute that I could hardly have blamed him.

My question angered her. "No, you idiot. It's not what he did, it's what he *is*. That guy's scary. I mean, *really* scary. He got mad at something—well, Spencer called him out for staring at his girlfriend, that Meredith, who doesn't deserve him, by the way—and he didn't like being called on it, not at *all*, and I don't know, I guess I grinned at him for getting pissed off, and then he was pissed off at *me*, and I looked at him, and the guy's eyes looked like black holes. I'm not kidding. Black puddles, with horrible, horrible things swimming around way way down. Something's wrong with Hayward. And Spencer knows it, too, but he doesn't see how sick that asshole really is."

I thought that she was probably right about this, at least in a way. The Eel had clearer, quicker insights into people than I did, and undoubtedly she still does. In Rehoboth Beach, Delaware, she once performed a delicate service for her favorite organization, the American Confederation of the Blind, that completely stunned me when she later described it. What she did there amounted to psychic detection, and it was absolutely successful. In any case, I learned from Detective Cooper's memoir how rightly Lee had read Keith Hayward, and now it terrifies me that she should have spent five minutes in his company. At the time, he didn't sound too dangerous, just off balance, desperately unhappy, probably introverted and bitter about it. A lot of people are like that, and many of them would have struck the seventeen-year-old Eel Truax as disturbed; Keith Hayward, on the other hand, was as sick as she described him to me, Mallon, and everyone else in their group. Only Hootie really took her at her word, and of course no one paid any attention to what Hootie thought.

■

At the Gorham Street gathering, Spencer Mallon told his followers two stories, and I will set them down here as they were told to me.

Story #1

A few weeks into a new academic year, Mallon was spending a couple of weeks moving between fraternity houses and student flophouses near the University in Austin, Texas. Although nothing of an unusual or illuminating nature had as yet taken place, he'd been sensing the immanence of some extraordinary event. (And in fact, something quite extraordinary did happen, though it did not play a part in the story he wanted to tell.) On the morning in question, he walked out onto the hot, stony sidewalks on East 15th Street and strayed toward his favorite coffee shop, the Frontier Diner. Soon he became aware that a man in a suit and a necktie was tagging after him on the other side of the street. For some reason, perhaps the formality of his wardrobe, the man made him feel unsettled, almost threatened. He could not deny that part of his unease was the completely irrational feeling that despite appearances this man was not in fact a human being. Mallon ducked into a side street and moved quickly to the next intersection, where he found the man waiting for him, still on the other side of the street.

Mallon thought he had no choice: he marched across the street to confront his pursuer. The man in the gray suit retreated, frowning. By the time Mallon had crossed the street, the man had somehow managed to disappear. Mallon had not seen him dip into a shop or behind a parked car, he had not seen him do anything at all. One second, the man who only appeared to be

34

human (he thought) had been walking backward with a look of displeasure on his face; the next, he had been absorbed into the pale brick of the building behind him.

If only for a second, had Mallon glanced away?

Around he turned, and on toward the coffee shop he continued. After he had rounded the corner and returned to 15th Street, he sensed a commotion taking place behind him, and, nerves prickling, looked over his shoulder. Half a block away, the not-quite-human figure in the gray suit came to an abrupt halt and stared straight ahead.

"Why are you following me?" Mallon asked.

The being in the suit pushed his hands into his pockets and shrugged. "Has it occurred to you to wonder what else might be following you?" But for its oddly mechanical quality, his voice sounded almost perfectly human.

"Do you have any idea what a useless question that is?"

"Take care, sir," the figure said. "I mean that sincerely."

Mallon whirled around and strode, though he did not jog, to the diner. All the while, he had the feeling that the man was behind him, although whenever he looked back, his pursuer was nowhere to be seen.

Inside the diner, he moved straight down the length of the counter past the booths, ignoring the empty seats. Marge, the waitress, asked him what was up.

"I'm trying to shake somebody," he told her. "Can I go through the kitchen?"

"Spencer," she said, "you can walk through my kitchen anytime."

Mallon came out into a wide alleyway where a cluster of garbage cans stood against the wall to his right. One of them, silvery where the others were dark, looked as though it had been purchased that morning. An unlined yellow index card bearing a few written words had been taped to its shiny lid.

He knew that the card had been left for him. Although a toxic fog seemed to hover about it, he could not force himself to walk away without reading the words. He peeled the card away from the gleaming lid and raised it to his eyes. In blue-black ink that still looked wet, the words on the card read, QUIT WHILE YOU'RE BEHIND, SPENCER. OUR DOGS HAVE LONG TEETH.

Story #2

A year later, Mallon had wandered to New York, a city he seldom visited, and soon he found himself with little money and less to do. The Columbia University students whose promise had seemed so great when he began working with them had proved to be incurious dilettantes. A helpful admirer had provided him with a forged student card, and while the last of his money ran out, he spent his days in the library roaming through the literature of the arcane and occult. When in his research he came across a particularly helpful volume, he looked to see if it had been consulted in the past decade; if it had not, he withdrew it from the library, informally.

Prowling through the stacks one day, he seemed to catch an odd light filtering into the long shelves of books. The light appeared to come from somewhere near the library's central core. At first he paid it no attention, since it was faint and intermittent, no more than an occasional half-seen rosy pulse. An odd spectacle for a library, perhaps, but odd things often happened at Columbia University.

When the pulse became brighter and more distracting, Mallon began to move through the stacks, looking for its source. It is important to note here that none of the graduate students roaming the stacks observed the pulsing, orange-pink glow. The glow led him across the stacks in the direction of the elevators, growing more vibrant as he went, and finally brought him to the closed metal door of a carrel. There could be no doubt that the carrel was the source of the glowing color, for it streamed out over the top, around the sides, and beneath the bottom of the metal door. For once in his life, Mallon was uncertain of his mission. It seemed to him that he had drawn near to the defining mystery of his life—the great transformation that alone could give to his existence the meaning he knew it must possess—and the sheer importance of what he had come upon paralyzed him.

Two students coming down the narrow passage outside the carrel looked at him oddly and asked if anything was wrong.

"You maybe see a trace of color in the air around that door?" he asked them, referring to the pulsing, wavering waterfall of radiant orange-pink light that streamed toward them.

"Color?" asked one of the students. Both of them turned to look at the door to the carrel.

"Something bright," Mallon said, and the waterfall of radiant light seemed to double in intensity.

"You need to get some sleep, bro," the young man said, and the two of them left.

When they were out of sight, Mallon summoned his courage and gave the door a feeble rap. No response came. He rapped again, more forcefully. This time, an irritated voice called, "What is it?"

"I have to talk to you," Mallon said.

"Who is that?"

"You don't know me," Mallon said. "But unlike everyone else in this building, I can see light pouring out of your carrel."

"You see light coming from my carrel?"

"Yes."

"Are you a student here?"

"No."

Pause.

"Are you on the faculty, God help us?"

"No, I'm not."

"How did you get in this library? Are you on the staff?"

"Someone gave me a fake student card."

He heard the man in the carrel scrape his chair back from the desk. Footsteps approached the door.

"Okay, what color is the light you see?"

"Kind of like the color of cranberry juice mixed with orange juice," Mallon said.

"I guess you better get in here," the man said.

Mallon heard the clicking of the lock, and the door swung open.

That's it? The story ended when the guy opened the door?
You'll see. Everything stops when you open the door.

About a week later, on Saturday, October 15, 1966, the eight of them—Mallon, the Eel, Hootie, Boats, Dill Olson, Meredith Bright, Hayward, and Milstrap—went out to the agronomy meadow at the end of Glasshouse Road, climbed over the concrete barrier, and went through a rehearsal that seemed to satisfy Mallon. That night, they all trooped off to a party at the Beta Delt house, home to the fraternity Hayward and Milstrap belonged to. I wasn't invited and heard about it only later. That night, I finally got through to the Eel around midnight, and she had reached a stage of drunkenness well past incoherence. The next day she was too hungover to talk to me, and that evening, she and all the rest of that doomed bunch followed Spencer Mallon back to the agronomy meadow.

Then there was only silence; there came rumors of a "black Mass," of a "pagan ritual," nonsense like that, given heat by the disappearance of one young man and the discovery of another's hideously mutilated corpse. Brett Milstrap had vanished from the earth, it seemed, and the cruelly mangled corpse had been Keith Hayward's. For a while, policemen stalked through our houses, through our school, everywhere we went, asking the same questions over and over. In their wake came reporters, photographers, and men with dark suits and tennis ball haircuts who hung around the edges of the action, watching and taking notes, whose presence was never explained. Lee stayed at Jason's house for a week or two, refusing to speak to anyone but Hootie and Boats and those who could force her to talk to them. Mallon had fled, all three parties agreed on that point, and Dill Olson had followed in his wake; Meredith Bright had taken off at a dead run, packed up her clothes, and camped out at the airport until she could get a flight back home to Arkansas, where police questioned her for hours, day after day, until it was clear that she had almost nothing to tell them.

The police never did catch up with Mallon and Dilly, who evaded questioning without even really trying to: after recuperating for a short time in Chicago (actually, in the same Cedar Street apartment I bought many years later, located in a building across the street from my present house), they hit the campus trail as a double act. Mallon took Dill *over,* he somehow *incorporated* him, of course with his victim's full cooperation. Olson loved Mallon, too, as much as my girlfriend and Boats did, and I guess he was content to follow his idol around the country, doing whatever he was asked to do. My information about Dill Olson's fate came from Lee, who had some sort of intermittent, flickering, but nonetheless reliable connection to him. I was never to know any of the specifics about this, of course, as I had missed the boat, definitively, and so had been spared the mysterious experience that came to define their lives. There was a magic circle, and I stood beyond its periphery.

Here's who was inside the circle, and this is what they wound up doing:

Hootie Bly, we learned, had become a permanent resident of the psychiatric ward at the Lamont Hospital, where he spoke only in quotations from Hawthorne and outbursts of unknown words from Captain Fountain's dictionary.

Before graduation, Jason "Boats" Boatman left school and became a full-time professional thief. Was that enough, could that have been enough for him?

Dilly Olson had surrendered his life to the man he had unofficially adopted as his father, and this was what he gained from his surrender: a secondhand imitation of a life, a weary existence as the magician's apprentice, subsisting on scraps that fell from the master's hand, being clothed in the master's cast-offs, and sleeping on strangers' couches with the brokenhearted girls his master discarded. Years later, Lee told me that Mallon had retired, but Don Olson was carrying on as the mage's replacement, or the new, improved model, or something similar. He had learned a lot in the intervening years, he had digested the *Tibetan Book of the Dead,* the *I Ching,* and the works of Giordano Bruno, Raymond Lully, Norman O. Brown, and God knows who else, and the trade of traveling guru, after all, was all he knew. But still. When I think of the heroic boy he once was . . .

Of Meredith Bright and Brett Milstrap I knew nothing, but presumably they each had a story to tell, should I be able to find them.

And of course the final figure left standing within the circle was my wife, Lee Truax, the most beautiful woman in any room she happened to enter, blessed with intelligence, courage, excellent health, a stunning house, a wonderful career as board member, counselor, and troubleshooter to the noble ACB. Her husband loved her, however imperfect his literal faithfulness, and the basis of his not inconsiderable success, his breakthrough book, *The Agents of Darkness,* had been his attempt to deal with the unfathomable event in the meadow and could therefore be seen as a tribute to the woman to whom it was dedicated. (Nearly all of his books were dedicated to his wife.) Thanks to this husband, myself, she had and always would have enough money never to worry about her finances. However, Lee Truax had been afflicted, too, cruelly, and although her affliction had first made itself known only in her early thirties, since when it had darkened and deepened, she had understood immediately that its origin had been Mallon's great event in the meadow.

■

There they were, my wife and onetime friends, still in their sacred circle; and here was I, on the outside, after all the intervening decades still baffled by what had happened to them.

A well-known voice on NPR had brought Hawthorne to me, and after Hawthorne, Hootie Bly, still interred in that damned mental hospital. Because of Hootie, everything else had flooded in. The lean hound coursing through the snow, the peeling lacquer on our sleds, the whole townscape of Madison's west side, a glass of water shining like the epitome of everything that could not be known, all that eluded definition . . . The faces of those who had been my most intimate friends, who had shared everything with me until the moment I refused to follow them into discipleship: their beautiful faces blazed before me. Half of their incandescence was what we had meant to each other, and the other half came from precisely what I had never known, never understood.

Why had they, each in his or her own way, not only jumped off the rails but jumped into such distorted lives? For a second, the room wobbled and everything in my life seemed at stake.

I needed to know: as soon as that recognition struck me, I knew that I feared whatever might turn up in the effort to know what had really happened out there in the meadow. Yet, *I needed to know,* and my need was stronger than the fear of whatever might crawl out of the knowledge I might turn up. All this time, I admitted to myself, I had been jealous of them for whatever they had *seen* out there, no matter that it had screwed them up, each in a different way.

Her Level Gaze had just withered away beneath my hand, and although I had become fascinated with Detective Cooper's fearsome revelations about the Hayward family—Two dark stars! Direct genetic transmission of a dreadful psychopathology! And this poor old brutal detective, taking his secrets to a beer-sodden grave!—I didn't really want to give a year or more of my life to writing about it all.

Honestly, I thought it was beyond me. My agent and my publisher were making tactful noises about a nonfiction book, but as I stood in my kitchen and wiped startled tears from my face the last thing on my mind was the possibility of writing about my lost world, my lost ruined friends, and whatever my wife might have hidden from me. (Hidden to protect me, even.) No, I realized, I didn't have to write about it. In fact I really did not want to put this warm and breathing material, only just glimpsed, through all the familiar, sometimes laborious gestures demanded by writing. Right then, all of that effort felt mechanical and factory-like, industrial. What I glimpsed had sped away into invisibility, like a white hare tracked through deep snow . . . I wanted the experience of following the ever-vanishing hare, not the experience of turning the pursuit into writing.

So, fine. Maybe I didn't have a book. What I did have, a project that had come wrapped in necessity, felt infinitely better.

The first thing I did, once I had calmed down sufficiently to use a keyboard, was to e-mail Lee in Washington. It was her past as well as mine, and if I intended to open a curtain she had insisted on keeping closed, she deserved to know about it. For the rest of the afternoon, instead of pretending to work I caught up on my Netflix movies (*Wall-E* and *The Dark Knight*), and about once an hour checked my cell phone for e-mail. I did not actually expect Lee to reply immediately, but at 6:22 my time, 7:22 hers, she responded by telling me that it would be interesting to see how far I got. (Lee uses various speech recognition systems, and while her early attempts resulted in a lot of typos and mistaken words, by now her messages are generally free of errors.) And she was writing back so quickly, she explained, because she had just learned something that might be useful to me. Donald Olson had run into some trouble a couple of years ago, and in fact she had heard that he was just being released from jail in a day or two and would undoubtedly be grateful for a place to stay on his first few nights of freedom. If I liked, I could meet him for lunch somewhere in Chicago, and if he passed muster, invite him to use our guest room. It would be all right with her, she assured me.

I e-mailed back, thanking her for the information about our long-ago friend, and said that if she truly would not mind, I would probably do as she suggested. How, if I dare ask, had she learned of Olson's situation? And how could I get in touch with him?

You know I have my sources, she wrote back. *But don't worry about writing to Don. I gather that he prefers to get in touch with people rather than the other way around.*

I'll wait to hear from him then, I told her. *How are things going, anyhow? Are you enjoying yourself?*

Busy busy busy, she wrote back. *Meetings meetings meetings. Sometimes the mills grind exceeding small, but I have a lot of ACB friends in the DC area who seem willing to listen to me complain. Please let me know what happens with Don Olson, will you?*

I typed, *o.c. o.c.,* using our ancient code that meant of course, of course.

Then for a couple of days I read, watched movies, took walks, and waited for the phone to ring. One day it did.

hootie's blues

Two or three years after everything happened, and I had learned all that I was ever going to know about what had befallen my friends out in the university's agronomy meadow and was just about to start a new book that would have nothing to do with any of this, at that moment of odd psychic drifting when a hundred little notions wake up and start humming, the possibility of a story came to me. It only indirectly concerned the main story of Mallon and my friends, which had been given to me in a series of fragments. Even back at the beginning I knew that I never really wanted to turn all of that into either straightforward fiction or the kind of neither-this-nor-that called "creative nonfiction." This would be a story poised right on the narrow wall between fiction and memoir, and based on a number of things confessed to me by Howard "Hootie" Bly during the period when he was living down the street from me in the formerly ratty Cedar Hotel. In the last months of his residence at the Cedar, Hootie met the love of his life and future partner, and together they moved to an affluent northern suburb. We had spent a good deal of time together, Hootie and my wife and I, as had Hootie and I separately, and eventually, in bits and pieces strung out over many of our private conversations, he told me what had happened on October 15, the day before the great event—the day of the "rehearsal."

With only a few small changes, I thought, I could make something interesting of Hootie's funny, unresolved tale. It was about preparing for something forever out of reach. For once, the idea of working so close to the literal truth excited me, so I set aside my new novel and spent about three weeks writing what I called "Tootie's Blues." "Tootie" was Hootie, of course, Spencer Mallon was "Dexter Fallon," Dill Olson was "Tom Nelson," and so on. When I had finished it, it did seem pretty good to me, but I had no idea what to do with it. I forwarded it as an attachment to David Garson, but he never said a word about it. I thought he was, in his way, being polite. The only alternative I saw was that it had vanished into deep cyberspace. Either way, the chances of the long story's publication in The New Yorker seemed nonexistent. Then I dragged its folder from my desktop into my "Stories" file and forgot about it, mostly.

At the time, I didn't realize that I gave up on the story so easily because its publication had never been the point. Writing it was the point. I wanted to write it—I wanted to inhabit the seventeen-year-old Howard Bly's point of view—because in that way and no other would it be possible for me to join Eel and the others for at least a part of the journey I had refused to take. Imagination gave me access to some of the experience the rest of them had shared. The hospital parts of the story were based on what I saw on my visits to the Lamont with Donald Olson, formerly the heroic Dill.

When I got up the nerve to give Hootie a copy, he took two or three days to read it and came back with a little tucked-in smile that I did not know how to read. He sat down and said, "Man, and I thought Mallon was a magician. It's like you were there, right there with me."

So here Howard Bly is speaking, pretty much as he did to me, of the way the early part of his life kept penetrating his long second act, the decades he spent in that hospital. Even more than most people, Hootie was marinated in his own history. I think he knew that he had to wait until he caught up with himself before he could begin to catch up with the people he so lovingly thought of during his long days on the ward.

The names have all been restored to their original forms. I trust I do not have to cite the provenance of the eccentric words in the first paragraph.

Neither agomphious nor arctoid, neither creodont nor czigany, Howard Bly knew himself a lonely, imperfect being ever scrambling to imitate the manners and habits of those he loved and admired, not to mention worshipped, as was the case with Spencer Mallon. God knows, he needed the man, the more than man, the *heroic marvel* Mallon was.

Which was exactly how Captain Fountain's book came in. Captain Fountain transformed Howard Bly's life by the simple mechanism of demonstrating to him the existence of a secret code that if fully understood would surely reveal the unknown and hidden structure of the world, or at least of what was called reality.

He had come across the great tome while rooting through an old box in the store's basement. By this time Troy and Roy, who would surely have ruined everything, were a problem no longer, having been drafted the previous year and sent to Vietnam, where all their top-secret games of soldiering and snipering no doubt came in handy, at least until Roy got killed.

The contents of the box made it clear that they belonged to Troy. A rusty knife, a squirrel's tail, old arrowheads, a broken compass, pictures of naked women torn from glossy magazines. (Roy would have had more nudes and a couple of broken Zippo lighters.) Jammed up against one side of the box was a slim white hard-backed volume that Troy Bly had undoubtedly purchased in one of his rare bouts of self-improvement. He had wanted to expand his vocabulary, doubtless because an advertisement had convinced him that females were sexually aroused by big words. Hootie didn't care about that. He didn't believe it either, at least as it applied to the girls at Madison West. Anyhow, he did not want to make out with any of the popular girls at his school. Sometimes, although he could scarcely admit it to himself, he thought about holding the Eel in his arms, about lying down in the grass with the Eel. Holding and being held. The Eel's lips on his. It was shameful, yes, he knew that, his friends would find him disgusting, and Eel's "Twin" would be enraged; hurt, too, which was much worse.

Howard never imagined that the words in Captain Fountain's book would cause the Eel to desire him. He thought the Captain's book greater by far than a sex potion. The flat, flinty shimmer of the words on the page caused him to fall in love, for he had stumbled upon a kind of ultimate security blanket: a vocabulary known only, he imagined, to priests of an unknown and secret order.

O morigerous [obsequious],
morology [nonsense],
morpheme [a word reduced to its basic element],
morphology [dealing with the structure of plants and animals],

O nabla [ancient Hebrew harp],
nacelle [small boat],
O nacket [tennis ball]!

Meredith Bright . . . Meredith Bright loved him because he looked like an angel. She had whispered this information into his blushing ear at the finish of the Gorham Street assembly, placed one long cool hand against each side of his face, leaned smiling in so that her own face became a billboard golden and lavish, and in a soft voice that sank trembling into the pit of his stomach and flew out to the endings of his nerves, told him, *Hootie, you look just like a beautiful porcelain angel, and that's why I love you.*

No one would understand his feelings for the Eel, not even the Eel, but being totally in love with Meredith Bright made sense to everyone. Also, they all knew that she liked him. Along with the Eel, Hootie was one of her favorites. Of course Spencer Mallon was Meredith Bright's special favorite, he was the man she had chosen in the way she would choose a movie star like Tab Hunter or a famous singer like Paul McCartney, and the two of them got in bed together and did sex things—over Hootie's heart crept a certain secret picture that made him feel as though he were melting like a snowman on a warm day. In the secret picture, Howard Bly lay on a narrow bed squeezed between Spencer Mallon and Meredith Bright. As they clasped each other, their arms wrapped him in a double embrace. His face pressed against Meredith Bright's ripe and blossoming bosom, and Spencer Mallon's flat, muscular chest pressed against the back of his head. Down below, something was happening that he could not define or describe but came wrapped in images of great storms and blowing curtains.

In rushed:
    lallation [baby talk]
    lalochergia [use of obscenity to decrease tension]
    murrey [dark red]

Closely followed by:
    mugient [bellowing]
    mymy [bed]
    prushun [boy who desires to have sex with an adult male]

And:
    pruritic [causing hysterical itching]

This, too, became a part of the secret hidden behind the obscurest of words, not to mention at the heart of sacred texts. And within Spencer Mallon, whom Hootie loved as he had never loved before. Which was one reason his "story" about following him down a hotel corridor to two doors and having to guess which one was his had been so unsettling. If you were right, there was

Spencer Mallon, right in front of you—taking care of things. But if you picked wrong . . . had he ever told them what happened if they picked the wrong door?

(*You were eaten by a tiger.*)

Long ago, Howard Bly had seen someone eaten by a tiger. He needed to see no more. One of them was to inhabit the country of the blind, Spencer had said, and it should have been him, Howard Bly. In the place he lived, there was nothing to look at anyway.

Because of Spencer Mallon, Howard Bly had a special hatred of doors. For hours on end, the attendant named Ant-Ant Antonio Argudin crouched hidden behind a door marked PERSONNEL ONLY where he smoked his stinky cigarettes, only guess what, Howard never once knocked on it. And guess what again? Howard Bly had lived in the hospital for forty years, he knew what was behind the PERSONNEL door, and it didn't scare him. A dull green room with broken-down furniture and an ashtray nobody was supposed to use . . . an ugly table with a coffeemaker, magazines lying on another old table. Men's magazines. Magazines for men. Howard had seen them, but he hadn't looked. That was where they went, the attendants—Ant-Ant, Robert C. (for Crushwell), Ferdinand Czardo, Robert G. (for Gurnee), and Max Byway—when they wanted to be by themselves.

On the sixteenth of October in the year 1966, Mallon had succeeded in opening his door, and what happened after that was so terrible that Howard had encircled himself with the sacred stones of his words, and they had kept him safe in the midst of the reeking-storming-down-pink-orange light. Until a huge and fatal orb made of sentences had knocked everything out of Howard Bly's head and sent him spinning cock-a-hoop through a hundred stories that comforted him, mocked him, tortured him, babied him, and showed him the only way he could continue.

■

Now. Enter Spencer Mallon, seated on a carton in the store's basement, swinging his legs beneath him and leaning forward on an arm so ropey the muscles cast shadows. Wiping a sleeve across his eyes as he muddled unseeing into the Game Room, fat old Howard Bly had no problem at all in seeing them as they had been on that day. Tall, athletic-looking Dilly-O on the floor, leaning against a low wall of boxed canned goods, his knees hugged to his chest, his head drooping over. Dill's dark hair, longer than that of the others, swung forward over his ears to frame his young tough's face. Between his lips, a cigarette from a pack of Viceroys lately stashed behind the cash register sent up a straight, unruffled column of white smoke.

Dilly-O, you were like a god! You were!

In a UW rowing team T-shirt, dirty white painters' pants, and tennis shoes, Boats squatted on the floor, staring at Mallon, hoping for some indication of what they were to do that day. With his newly awakened senses, little Howard was painfully aware of how greatly Boats wished to become Spencer Mallon's favorite disciple.

■

Spencer Mallon leaning over, staring at his legs moving back and forth like pistons . . . He wiped a hand over his face, then ran it through his perfect hair.

"Okay," he said. "Things are getting intense. Meredith drew up a chart, and it tells us that the optimal time and date are only two days away. Seven-twenty p.m., Sunday, the sixteenth of October. We'll still have the light, but no one else should be around."

"Around where?" asked Boats. "You found a place?"

"The university agronomy meadow, on the far end of Glasshouse Road. Good site, excellent site. Tomorrow afternoon I want us to go out there for a rehearsal."

"Rehearsal?"

"I want us to get it right. Some of you knuckleheads hardly know how to listen."

"When you said 'chart,' " asked Boats, "did you mean some kind of navigational chart?"

"Astrological," Mallon said. "Based on our group. Time and date of birth are when we first got together at La Bella Capri."

"Meredith did an astrology chart?" asked the Eel. "About us?"

"She's an experienced astrologist."

He grinned at his followers. To Howard, the man's inner desperation immediately shrank to a more tolerable level.

"I still feel a little weird about relying on that thing, to tell you the truth, but Meredith was absolutely confident of her results, so we're aiming for seven-twenty two nights from now. What about four o'clock for our rehearsal? Everybody cool with that?"

They all nodded. Only Howard, it seemed, felt that Mallon was still uneasy about the use of astrology.

"Will Meredith come to this rehearsal?" Howard asked.

"She damn well better," Mallon said.

Laughter followed this remark.

Mallon said, "I want you to partner up tomorrow. It could get wild out there."

"What do you mean?" Boats asked the question for all of them.

Mallon shrugged. "Hey, on the other hand, these things usually go nowhere. And that could happen, too."

"You've done this a lot?"

Momentarily, discomfort erased Mallon's anxiety. "What do you think my life is about? But this time, okay, this time I think I'm closer than ever."

"How can you tell?" asked Boats, with a silent, stricken echo from Howard Bly.

"I can read the signs, and the signs are all around us." His discomfort arose again and affected his posture, his expression, even the angle of his legs.

"What do you mean, signs?" asked Boats.

"You got to keep your eyes open. Look for the little things that don't belong."

With a shock of surprise, Old Howard, who had moved onto a chair in the Crafts Room, realized that if Boats and Dilly-O were ever to get together now, they would not, not ever, not really talk about what had happened in the meadow—because they would never be able to agree about it. He almost wished one of them, maybe Boats and Dill together as of old, would drive up to Madison to see him. After all this time, which yet had gone by in a moment, he would find a way to talk to them.

"There's something I should say to you. Something I should have realized a long time ago." Mallon snapped his mouth shut, looked down at his dangling legs, then looked back up and gazed at each of them in turn. Howard's stomach froze, and though he did not know it, so did the Eel's.

No, no, no, Howard thought.

"When our ceremony is finished, I'll have to leave. Whatever the results are. And remember, the whole thing might turn out to be a total bust. One of the things that could happen is . . . nothing at all."

"But if something does . . ." said Dill.

"Then I'll *have* to get out of town!" Mallon emitted a grade-A Mallon chuckle, rueful and charmingly self-amused. To two of his young disciples, it seemed contaminated by self-consciousness. He was looking at himself in a secret mirror.

"Look," Mallon said, "there are no instruction manuals for what we're trying to do."

He tried to grin, and at least to Howard Bly succeeded only in making himself look sickly. "But you know that everything is everything, am I right? As long as we take care of each other, nothing bad is gonna happen."

It was getting worse with every word, Howard thought. Looking around, he saw that only the Eel seemed to be as stricken as himself. The other two were lapping up Mallon's reassurances in the old way.

"Everything is everything," said Dill.

What does that mean, exactly? Howard asked himself.

Spencer Mallon was looking straight at the Eel, and the Eel was trying not to show discomfort.

Oh, my Spencer, my darling my dearest, don't be this person, be yourself.

"Once in Kathmandu," Mallon said, "I heard a gorgeous woman with an amazing, smoky voice sing a song called 'Skylark.'"

This part, really, this part was almost too much for Old Howard, it damn near cut him off at the knees.

Mallon was still staring at the Eel. "We were in a funky little bar with a tiny bandstand. What she did with 'Skylark' made me break down and weep. And what a beautiful song that is anyhow. When the set was over, I went up to talk to her, and after a little while she went home with me. I made love to that woman until the sun came up the next day."

"How nice for you," the Eel said, amazing Howard with this display of cool.

He straightened his back and put his hand on his heart. "Eel, you're my skylark. You're going to rise up singing, you'll sail up into the blue, singing one long, continuous song that'll hypnotize everyone who hears it."

The Eel said, "Don't talk to me that way."

The Eel was capable of producing tears, who would have thought?

■

The previous afternoon, as he found himself remembering, Hootie Bly had bopped on over to the Tick-Tock Diner in the company of his darling friend Eel. But when they arrived within the State Street shoebox of their favorite campus hangout, Meredith Bright's bright hair and face did not shine from the reflective walls. Neither did she occupy any booth or counter seat. Considering the reassuring possibility that Meredith might after all drop in at any second, they took two seats at the bottom of the counter, near the window.

They ordered cherry Cokes, all they could afford. Moments later, a skinny guy with furze on his cheeks and a russet whisk broom sprouting from his chin slid out of the third booth along the wall and plunked himself down beside young Howard. A second and a half of memory search identified this being as one of the college students who had shown up for both the gathering at La Bella Capri and the meeting on Gorham Street.

"Listen," he said, leaning forward on his elbows and speaking in a conspiratorial manner intensified by the arm sliding over Howard's shoulders, "I don't know why I'm doing this, it's not like you're going to be grateful or anything, but I gotta tell you—be careful around your friend Mallon."

Howard said, "What do you mean?"

"Mallon is not a guy you can trust."

Aggressively, the Eel asked, "Why not?"

"Okay, if you're going to make this difficult." The bearded boy turned away.

"Hold on," said the Eel. "I just asked, that's all."

The boy swiveled back. "I'm trying to do you some good, all right? Mallon is a con man. He comes over to our place, he takes a couple of records, a bunch of shirts, and when you tell him you don't like it, he says, 'Everything is everything,' like that's some kind of answer."

"So what does he get out of being here?" asked Eel.

"Sex," he said. "In case you hadn't noticed."

The Eel inhaled deeply and blinked a couple of times.

The boy grinned. "Plus, the opportunity to spread his bullshit around and act like a hero. A guy cuts his hand off in Tibet, and that makes you a philosopher? Maybe, if you're a lunatic. Besides, I doubt any of that stuff ever happened. Think about it, that's all I'm saying. And keep him out of your room, or wherever you live. The guy's a thief."

"We don't have to worry about that," Eel said. Her voice was hard and oddly brittle. "When he's with us, Boats does all his thieving for him."

"Hey, if that makes you happy." The boy shrugged. The way he held his mouth made the rufous broom on his chin jut straight out. Then he jumped off his seat and, with a hint of haste that suggested offense, returned to the booth.

"I didn't say it made me *happy*," Eel confided to the Howard that had been.

"Actually, what does he do when he isn't with us?" asked little Howard.

"He goes hither and yon," said Eel, for some reason sounding a little bitter. "Last night, for example, he went to the Falls for dinner. I know, because he took me with him."

Unable to contain his dismay, Howard said, "Spencer took you to dinner at the Falls?"

The Falls was one of Madison's best restaurants, right up there in the top two or three. Until this moment, the young Howard had supposed that none of his band, like himself, had ever as much as seen the inside of the place.

"I was going to tell you," Eel said, shifting around on the stool. "It was all right, once I started to feel comfortable."

It was strange, Howard thought: he had never seen the Eel look less comfortable than right now.

"What did you eat?"

The Eel shrugged. "Some fish. He ordered a steak."

"Why did he take you out for dinner? How did that happen? He's staying in my basement, for God's sake."

"He had a fight with Meredith, or something, so he asked me. I said sure. What else would I say? I'm sorry you're jealous, Hootie, but that's what happened."

"I'm not jealous," Howard said, staring down at the jaunty straw leaning against the side of his half-empty glass. "How did you get your dad to let you go?"

"He didn't even notice I was gone."

"All right."

"I mean, all our dads are screwed up, but yours is the best of the bunch."

"Obviously, you don't have to live with him," Howard said, remembering the morning's outburst of rage and indignation over the absence of a single family-sized bag of Lay's potato chips from a box supposed to contain a dozen. That Spencer Mallon had opened the box and pilfered the bag of chips made Howard feel sick to his stomach.

A great part of Howard Bly yearned for the simplicity of the days before the arrival of Spencer Mallon, when nobody stole bags of potato chips from the basement, nobody came creeping into the building at all hours and padded downstairs half drunk to fall asleep on a mattress that had to be shoved out of sight every morning. It seemed now that Spencer Mallon had also managed to mess up his relationship with the Eel, a matter of grave importance.

"So what did you talk about?"

"He didn't really want to talk. He said I made him feel better."

"That's ridiculous," Howard said, horrified because he was beginning to suspect why it might not be.

Eel startled him by bursting forth with a sequence of words and sentences that flew by so quickly he could barely make them out. "Do you get the feeling that Spencer isn't really himself lately? I don't know what to think about him anymore." Something vital and submerged flicked across the Eel's face. "I'm totally confused. I'm not very happy. What happened to Meredith, for example? But why am I asking you? You're useless." Then, as if the insult had been immediately forgotten, that blazing face turned to his. "If you ask me, he's an asshole."

"I think he's scared of something," Hootie said. "Maybe he's worried this whatever-it-is isn't going to work."

"What if it doesn't? He's been messing around like this for years." And there it was, coming into flower before him, the bitterness Howard had noticed earlier. "If you ask me, the only great upheavals that are happening in this country have to do with Vietnam and civil rights. Spencer Mallon didn't have a thing to do with either one."

Hootie could say nothing to this.

"And you know what? The guy isn't even any good at what he does. He came here to get a bunch of smart college students around him, and who does he wind up with? Four dumb high-school students, plus two, only two, frat boys, and there's something wrong with both of them, especially Keith Hayward."

"You forgot Meredith Bright," Hootie said. "And you're not dumb, Eel. Come on."

"Okay, he wound up with three dumb high-school students, two sickos, and a blond who completely bought all of his bullshit."

"Look, Eel," said Howard, hoping above all to revive their old sense of conviction. "You and I believe in him, we really do. Okay, Dilly wants Mallon to adopt him, and Boats wants to be his bodyguard forever, or something like that, but we're *different*, aren't we? We're the reason Meredith came back to the Aluminum Room—she wanted to talk to us! To *us*! And Dill and Boats, they're super-impressed by Spencer, he's like the answer to their prayers or something, but you and me, we just love him. We don't even look at him the same way they do. I see you look at him, Eel, I know. You'd do anything he asked, isn't that right? *Anything.*"

The Eel nodded, suggesting emotions too complex for Hootie to read. For a second he even thought the Eel might cry, and utter terror filled him.

"What happened, anyhow? Was he mean to you in the restaurant?"

Eel jumped down from the stool. The discussion had ended.

■

And on the day after the tense gathering in the basement, Howard thought he saw one of the agent-creatures that had followed Mallon through the streets of Austin.

As if emanating from his pores, the acrid stench of a bad dream had floated alongside him, darkening everything before him. Shadows deepened. Water seemed to gush from the tap, his toothpaste tube to swell in protest as he squeezed. His mouth tasted more of blood than Colgate. Back in his bedroom, the poison within him infected the view from his window, that of a barren street stretched like an eggshell over a roaring void.

It was Saturday, thank goodness.

Howard shoved his legs into a pair of jeans, thrust his head through the neck of a bright red Badger T-shirt, and slid his feet into moccasins. The rehearsal was to take place that afternoon, and a restlessness compounded of fear and impatience caused him to grab a cruller and a half pint of milk from their cabinets and sail through the side door before he had bitten into the pastry. Slanting down from State Street, Gorham Street offered the same spectacle of unopened shops and empty parking places in front of closed stores.

Oozing through his pores, his terrible dream contaminated whatever struck his eye. Fat snakes lurked in the deep shadows of the gutters. The cruller, which should have been sweet, crispy on the outside and as yielding as cake within, crumbled in his mouth like plaster.

For hours, it seemed, he had dreamed of Keith Hayward driving through a desert at night. Beside the road grew scrub punctuated by occasional tall cacti. Hot air devoid of moisture blew from the dream over the dreamer. A college boy as good-looking as the Swedish exchange students who sometimes dropped into the Aluminum Room lounged in the passenger seat of the red sports car. Improbably, his name was Maverick McCool. If you were named Maverick McCool, especially if you looked like a Swedish exchange student, girls, even girls like Meredith Bright, probably hung out on the sidewalk, praying for you to walk past your window.

The abrupt intrusion of Meredith Bright into his reverie brought with it the information that the red car was her Skylark. Keith Hayward should have been forbidden even to touch Meredith's car. From the shock of this revulsion had come the real horror of the dream, the knowledge of what was in the trunk.

Keith Hayward had murdered Meredith Bright, dismembered her body, stuffed her remains into two black garbage bags, and crammed the bags into the Skylark's modest trunk. Unaware of their freight, Maverick McCool smiled at something said by monstrous Keith Hayward. That Hayward had already murdered a number of other people and intended to go on accumulating victims for a long, long time spoke from every part of the image in Howard's mind—and the smiling passenger was to be the next victim! Poor McCool! A grimy, frigid wave of horror had snapped Howard into wakefulness. In his panic, his first impulse had been to get to the phone and call Meredith Bright. Howard swung his legs over the side of his bed, and before he pushed himself upright, realized that he did not know her telephone number. He fell back panting on the bed, feeling as though he were trying to blow the terrible dream out of his body and into the morning air.

From nowhere in particular, the phrase *serial killer* seemed to enter his mind. With it came memories of headlines and TV news stories about the Milwaukee maniac called "the Ladykiller." How many women had he murdered and, according to the police chief in Milwaukee, turned to *bloody rags*? Five? Six? *This is a man who murders women and turns their corpses into bloody rags,* the detective had said, whatever his name was, Hooper, Cooper, something like that. *Do you imagine that we would ever allow a monster like that to run free?* Unfortunately, they had allowed him to do exactly that, so run free he had, the monster, piling up more corpses until he died of old age or retired to Florida.

Up ahead, a figure turned the corner onto Gorham Street and became a half-seen silhouette in the glare of the sunlight.

Terror thrust its roots into Howard's guts. Keith Hayward had just walked into the dazzle at the top of Gorham Street and now, quick as a ferret, begun to move toward him. Too frightened to step back, Howard awaited the fiend's attack. He opened his mouth to scream.

A second later, the downpouring light revealed that the man advancing upon him was not Hayward, but someone far more frightening, one of the "dogs" Mallon had warned them about. In terror so great he could not so much as moan, Howard shuffled backward, stumbled over his own feet, and dropped to the sidewalk, hard. Pain flared in his left hip, and his buttock felt as though it had been struck with a sledgehammer. Gasping with pain and fear, he propped himself up on an elbow and realized that no one stood in front of him.

On the sunlit sidewalk, a footstep sounded. Gray trouser legs and two polished black wingtips. The knees bent as their owner leaned over. Howard looked up into the face of an unremarkable man in his mid-thirties with a cap of thick but very short dark hair. Flinty amusement shone in his pale blue eyes.

Howard held out his right arm, half expecting the man to pull him to his feet. The man bent closer and mouthed the words *Sorry, kid.* Howard dropped his arm and tried to scoot backwards, but his feet were still tangled, and his right ankle throbbed. The man stooped down and settled his hands on his knees.

"Did something frighten you?" His voice was low, soft, and not quite human.

Howard nodded.

"You should probably pay attention to that," the man said. The reedy metallic quality at the center of his voice made it sound as though it were projected from somewhere inside him rather than created in his throat.

"Were you in the girls' bathroom at Madison West?" Howard asked.

"I go where I like," the man said, again sounding as though some other smaller man within him was talking through a megaphone. "Close your eyes now, son."

Terrified, he obeyed. For a second the air directly before Howard Bly became as hot as the wind from his dream desert. The sound of footfalls mutated into something softer that padded away, clicking.

No, he thought at the time; in the hospital, pretending to look at the first page of an old paperback of L. Shelby Austin's *The Moondreamers* found in the Game Room, the old Howard shook his head at his stupidity.

Ant-Ant Antonio glanced up from one of the jigsaw tables, and old

Howard Bly gave him an empty-headed look and said, "Portmanteau redivivus." If Hayward had cut Meredith up according to plan, he could have stashed her body in a *portmanteau,* but he would have to be *redivivus* to do it now.

"Mr. Bly, you da m-m-man," Ant-Ant told him.

Because Ant-Ant expected him to nod, Howard nodded.

Although he had imagined he was going to tell Mallon everything, that afternoon young Howard failed to describe either his nightmare or the sudden appearance on the sidewalk of the "agent." His hero's customary lordliness could not quite conceal the heightened flutter in his nerves and bloodstream. Howard remained convinced that only he and Eel had observed their hero's anxiety. Did that mean they had to protect him?

At the same time, he'd had to protect himself, too, from Keith Hayward. Okay, Hayward hadn't murdered Meredith Bright. All the same, Howard thought, something inside him had so darkened and shriveled that he could easily become one of those guys who traveled around the country murdering strangers. Or one of those demons who lurk like spiders in the webs of their terrible apartments, and dart out to pick off their victims. Back when they were all in fifth or sixth grade, they had paid as much attention as the grown-ups would allow to the Ladykiller.

Young Howard wanted to control the mixture of fear and revulsion Keith aroused in him. The idea that his suspicions might put Hayward on alert made him feel as though hot tar was being pumped into his stomach.

■

When everyone who wanted to take part in the rehearsal had met, as instructed, at the busy corner of University Avenue and North Francis, on the edge of the campus but not on it, Howard had placed himself as far as possible from Hayward, who began their march by sticking close to Mallon and jabbering away like a monkey.

Brett Milstrap hung in there on his other side, now and then tossing in a comment. Milstrap looked amused. In fact, Milstrap always seemed to be amused around his roommate. Basically, the guy was using Hayward to prop up his own ego. The Eel had once told Hootie that Milstrap looked like a student who had just cheated on a test, which was pretty brilliant, Hootie thought. Even the yellow polo shirt and khaki pants he was wearing, classics of the preppy wardrobe, could not disguise the falsity at the center of his being. And he *loved* being creepy in his own special way, you couldn't miss it. No wonder he was Hayward's best friend.

On the other hand, Spencer's willingness to tolerate Keith Hayward's company just baffled Hootie. The frat boy's inner illness seemed so obvious that Howard wondered if Mallon simply wished to keep an eye on him. Maybe he was trying to neutralize this horrible killer-in-the-making. In that case, what was supposed to happen to the rest of them when Mallon took off?

The thought of Mallon's desertion made Howard want to reel across the sidewalk.

After a couple of blocks Hayward must have tired of trying to impress Mallon, because he turned to Milstrap and pretended to say something in confidence while Mallon continued on ahead. Carrying shopping bags filled with stolen materials, Dilly-O and Boats strolled along behind. The Eel, who trusted Hayward no more than Howard did, sent him a half smile, half grimace that told him he was not alone in his loathing of their mutual enemy. He sped up, patted the Eel on the shoulder as he went by, and slipped in next to Mallon, who turned from intense conversation with Meredith Bright and looked down at him.

"Do you have a question?"

"Why didn't you take Meredith's car?"

"I guess *all* of us couldn't fit in," Meredith said.

Mallon ignored her. "We have to stick together now. I think that's part of the whole deal."

"Is this meadow far away?"

Mallon smiled. "Maybe a mile and a half."

"All right," Howard said, aware that Meredith Bright was taking in this conversation with a look of impatience on her face.

"I sense you have something else in mind," Mallon said.

Meredith Bright turned her head from him.

"Do you want to talk about it in private?"

Hootie nodded.

Mallon whispered something to Meredith, who, looking annoyed, slipped back behind them, but not far enough to join the Eel.

"So what's your problem?" Mallon asked him.

He snapped back into focus. "I had a nightmare about Keith," he said, and abruptly realized that he did not want to tell Mallon the whole of his dream.

"Aha," Mallon said.

"I know you can't really tell anything from dreams," he began.

"Hootie my boy, you have a lot to learn."

This, Howard thought, was going to be like swimming upstream. "Okay. I dreamed that he murdered people. I know that doesn't mean he really does, but I had the dream in the first place because I think something's wrong with him."

"I guess so," Mallon said. "You and the Eel keep bringing it up."

"There *is* something wrong with him," Howard insisted.

In the Crafts Room, pretending now to be interested in the second page of *The Moondreamers,* the older, fatter, gray-haired Howard nodded.

"S-Sure lovin' that book, aren't we, Howard?" said nosy Ant-Ant, cruising by.

"Quacksalver," Howard shot back, informing ignorant Ant-Ant Anthony that he was a charlatan.

"I know," Mallon told the angelic boy-Howard who had relished the nickname Hootie. "And you know I know, Hootie."

"He's sick inside," Howard said. "I think he likes to hurt people." He decided not to amplify this remark with references to dismembered bodies and the trunks of cars. If he ever got around to Maverick McCool, Mallon would laugh him right back to State Street, and he would be too embarrassed ever to talk to his hero again.

"Sometimes, Hootie, you amaze me."

"So you know, too," he said, fighting not to show how deeply his hero's condescension had wounded him. "Why do you let him stay with us?"

"We need warm bodies. With Keith, we get a two-for-one deal, because Milstrap goes wherever he does. Oh, the guy's different, I know that. Don't you remember what I said to him at our gathering?"

"He's worse than you think," Howard said, miserable that Mallon refused to take him seriously. "I can't stand being in the same room with him. I can't stand *looking* at him."

Mallon gripped Hootie's upper arm, walked him across the sidewalk, and pushed his shoulder up against a plate-glass window. For a half second of sudden panic, maybe less, Howard imagined that he had seen Brett Milstrap inside the shop gazing at them through the big windows. It was impossible—side by side with Hayward, Milstrap came sailing by at just that moment, deliberately ignoring them.

Mallon bent down and spoke directly into his ear. His voice was soft and rapid. "I have taken Hayward's problems into consideration and will do my absolute damnedest to use them tomorrow evening."

"Use them?"

"For *us*. Don't you think what is inside that wretched kid exists also in the hidden world?"

Young Howard could not speak. Old Howard felt his eyes prickle.

"We want to let it give us the privilege of seeing what it's all about. It'll be contained, it'll be held—I have spells for binding and unbinding, they're ancient, they're well tested, they do what they're supposed to do, these spells. I think there's a good chance that exposure to this force could reach out to Keith and fix him."

Young Howard shook his head; the old Howard pressed his hands to his eyes, like Mallon on Gorham Street. "He can't—"

"For the first time in his life, he'll get a good look at this crazy force whipping around inside him. Don't you think that would change a man?"

"Have you ever seen anything like that happen?"

Mallon straightened up and looked ahead. Some thirty feet away the group had come to a halt. Meredith and the little band were looking back at them. Hayward, whispering to Brett Milstrap, had turned his back.

"We're holding things up," Mallon said. Howard thought he meant *Let's not leave Meredith alone up there.* They began moving forward again.

Mallon's voice had returned to its usual register, and it was filled with all his old authority. "Not exactly, no, but I've seen things like that."

"What's the weirdest thing you've ever seen?"

Mallon's eye cut toward him again, and Howard said, "Don't tell me that stuff about seeing a man's hand cut off in a bar."

Spencer Mallon placed a hand on the side of his face and squinted ahead. Keith Hayward stopped whispering to his roommate and turned a dark glance upon them.

"The weirdest thing," Mallon said. He smiled. "Usually, the closest you get is the feeling that something *almost* happened—that the veil trembled for a second, and you came close to seeing what was on the other side. Or that some extraordinary force was hovering just out of sight, almost close enough to touch, but you weren't good enough to hold it there, or strong enough, or concentrated enough, or that something else in the room screwed things up. That's what happens most of the time."

Mallon looked up the block to the others, most of whom were now looking back with undisguised curiosity. Dill seemed almost on the verge of anger. Mallon swept his fingers through the air, telling them to keep moving forward.

"But four, five years ago, when I was in Austin, this strange thing happened. And *that* was absolutely the weirdest place my investigations ever took me. It was around the time the agent left a note for me on the garbage can, remember? I said that something extraordinary happened there, but I didn't get specific."

"I remember," Howard said, offended that Mallon might think it possible he had forgotten.

"Also, I didn't mention that I was living with this girl, Antonia. Looked a little like Alexandra, remember her from La Bella Capri? Antonia was the first woman I ever knew who considered herself a witch, a Wiccan. So one day Antonia and I are lying around on her bed. It's about five o'clock in the afternoon, and we're supposed to get up and meet some people, only she says, *Why don't you and I try to do something here?*

"We went into the living room and stood side by side on her rug, naked. She's burning some laurel and myrtle and cypress in a bowl, and she dipped a little oil of something or other into another bowl, a big one, with some other dried herbs crushed up into it. She lit seven candles. Then she sang something, I have no idea what, but it sounded exactly right. 'Okay,' I say, 'what do we do now?'

" 'Just give it your best shot,' Antonia said.

"Because I didn't expect anything to happen, I began to quote the first thing that came to mind, a passage I had memorized a couple of days before from Campanella's *Universalis Philosophiae.* I *do* know Latin, you know. And Greek. Anyhow, I'm rattling away in the Roman Empire's good old mother tongue, something about inhaling the Spirit of the World and hearing planetary music, and I notice that this dense, powerful odor is coming from the burning herbs—actually, it smells like sex plus death, if that makes any sense! Eros and Thanatos, the old Greeks called it. I'm getting turned on all over again, *very* turned on. Words are still pouring out of my mouth, and all of a sudden it is clear to me that what I'm doing is another form of sex, sort of a whole body sex. Antonia is moaning away beside me, and I'm right at the point when I don't think I can hold out a second longer, and then it's like the floor drops away beneath me, and I'm not in that room anymore.

"I'm on a dark plain. Fires are burning on the horizon. The sky is red. It all happens so fast, I don't have time to be scared. Then I understand that *something is there with me,* only I don't know what is. I can't see it, I just know it's close. This huge, monstrous *being* is big, it's invisible, and it is really, really interested in me. I can hear it turning around to get a look at me, and all of a sudden I'm so scared I practically faint . . . before I can blink, I'm back in Antonia's living room. She's kneeling on the floor, bent over. It looks like she's praying to Allah. Which wouldn't have been a bad idea, come to think of it. There's a strong, strange smell in the room, like old blankets and cold ashes.

"I asked her if she was all right, but she didn't answer. I bent down and rubbed her back. She lifted her head, and it's covered with blood, her whole face is bloody. Turns out, she just had a bloody nose, but it looked like she'd been knifed, or beaten up. I asked if she was all right all over again. She shook her head. 'What happened?' I asked. I even asked, 'Did you see it?' "

Spencer laughed, apparently at his own foolishness.

"What did she say?" Howard asked.

"She said, 'Get the hell out of my house, and never come back,' that's what she said. You have to admit, Hootie, it was a truly weird experience."

"You don't know what happened to her?"

"She had her own trip, that's what happened to her, and she couldn't handle it. Right now, you're thinking, 'Why would he want to do that again? Wasn't it terrible enough for him?' Right?"

"Well . . ." Hootie said. "Wasn't it?"

"It came from me, don't you get it? I *produced* what I saw—an image of pure sexual force. Okay, it looked pretty dark, but the woman with me was a *witch,* for God's sake! Don't you think she added in some kind of potion to keep me under her spell? It didn't work, and it bounced back on her, that's all. In our case, right now, I think something a lot more *comprehensive* is going to happen." Mallon settled his hands on Howard's shoulders, and lowered the handsome shield of his face to within inches of the boy's.

In the Crafts Room, the fat old Howard Bly turned to the wall to keep the attendant from seeing him weep.

"Hey, everybody," said sadistic Ant-Ant Anthony. "Check out Mr. Vocabulary B-Boy. He's having q-quite a d-day. Aren't you, Mr. B-Bly?"

Decades back in time, Spencer Mallon was saying, "And let's face it, Hootie. Although you may not know it, I'm finished here—it's all over, more or less." His breath smelled like freshly cut hay. "*They flee from me, that sometime did me seek,* in case you've ever read Thomas Wyatt. That's all she wrote, apart from the fun all of us are going to have over the next day and a half."

"Fun?" Howard asked.

"Just you wait. I have a little surprise arranged for all of you. I'm going to make your dreams come true." He grinned and ruffled Hootie's dead-straight hair.

For the rest of the walk to the agronomy meadow, Howard Bly had to deal with the questions Boats and Dill fired at him.

He said: "It's not important what we talked about."

He said: "What I wanted to know, I found out. He doesn't trust Hayward either."

He said: "But yeah, I trust *him.* He's really trying to learn new things, you know."

He said: "Yeah, it's a little scary. He's seen some really weird stuff."

He said: "No, I have no idea what the surprise is."

Looking back down the sidewalk in frustration, he caught sight of an outright impossibility. Ten yards back, Brett Milstrap stood in the middle of the sidewalk, trying to wave all of them back. He did not look like a student who had just cheated on a test, he looked weary and despairing in his bright yellow shirt and khaki pants. He seemed to be both the age he really was and decades older. The only problem was, Brett Milstrap was now walking up University Avenue side by side with his roommate and only friend, Jack the Ripper. Hootie swung around to check and found that along with

71

the rest of their party, the roommates had turned the next corner and were no longer in view. The same was true of Boats and Dilly. Apparently, Milstrap had doubled back in one hell of a hurry to head off the expedition from the rear. It made no sense at all.

The Eel leaned around the corner and urged him to pick up the pace, for God's sake.

"Hey," Hootie said, and looked back over his shoulder to see that the imploring figure had disappeared. "Is Milstrap up there?"

"Right up front with his best buddy."

The group embarked on a series of smaller roads new to Hootie and his friends. The houses grew farther and farther apart. Eventually they reached the slightly wider and more substantial Glasshouse Road, where residences disappeared altogether. Arrowing straight toward a long flat greensward that had to be their destination, it was Madison's most disreputable street. All the businesses rejected by the city's more conventional sectors seemed to have settled here. RUDY'S TATTOOS was flanked by two run-down rightward-tilting bars with rows of motorcycles propped outside. Continuing on both sides down to the end of the street stood Pedro's Magic Emporium, Monster Comix, Capital Guns, Badger Pawnshop, Badger Guns, Scott Myers School of Martial Arts, Knife And Blade World, Hank Wagner's Pistol Range, Scuzzy's Midnight Lounge, Whips 'N Chains, Betty's Boudoir, stores with signs proclaiming LEATHER: ALL LEATHER and WEAPONS SALE OR RENT, and an unnamed store with a streaky, unclean display window papered with magazine covers depicting naked men and women. These businesses occupied small, one-story buildings roughly the size of the Aluminum Room but shabbier. At the far end of Glasshouse, two bars, THE DOWNBEAT TAP ROOM and HOUSE OF KO-RECK-SHUN, faced each other on opposite sides of the street.

Just past the street's blunt end lay an enormous, shimmering swath of green that looked as though it had come from a world altogether more generous and expansive. When Howard looked at it, he thought for some reason of what Mallon had said about his high school and imagined him standing on the meadow's green carpet with his arms wide, declaiming in ancient Greek.

By common though unspoken agreement, the group moved to the middle of the street. For most of its length, the journey down Glasshouse Road felt like a trip through a ghost village. Low, dim music floated from the biker bars, along with a barely audible buzz of conversation. Although lights burned in the windows of the gun shops, customers neither entered or emerged. Hank Wagner appeared to have taken the day off from target shooting, and no one was stocking up on dirty magazines. In one of the biker bars behind them, a growling voice uttered a fragrant curse. With a sound like the snapping of wood, something broke. Several dogs, or things that sounded like dogs, began to mutter in dog language. The little group drew more tightly together, with Spencer Mallon and Dilly-O, watchful and listening hard, at their head. "Don't look back," Mallon said. "*Don't look back.*"

Hootie found himself bracketed between the Eel and Keith Hayward, who had drifted up out of nowhere. Hayward's hand fell on his shoulder like a metal claw.

"Does silence give you the runs, baby face?" Hayward whispered.

Hootie jerked away, shuddering.

Then voices filled the air, and the sound of booted feet striking pavement. A lot of motorcycles roared into life. The little group in the middle of the road froze, then quickly began drifting to the right, away from the uproar of the motorbikes.

"Let's step along here," Mallon said, sounding more nervous than he probably wanted to appear. "We want to get up on the sidewalk." He reached out for Meredith Bright and yanked her to his side.

With Mallon in the lead, the little group scrambled onto the sidewalk. Hayward had rushed up behind Howard Bly, who was at first aware only of the thin, ravaged face lowering itself toward his right shoulder, exhaling breath so sour it seemed to have been twice recycled. A skinny arm encircled with stiff dark hair like bristles snagged his waist. Hootie's mind went white with revulsion.

"Widdle Hoo-dee scaiwed, widdle Hoo-dee aw fwightened of the big, bad motowcycohs," Hayward hissed.

In a panic of loathing, Hootie struggled against the bony arm pressing him into Hayward's body, and felt it drop away of itself. Hayward had lost interest in him, and now he was thrusting himself past Meredith and toward the front of the group. Heading elsewhere, the roaring of the motorbikes faded behind them. Howard became aware of some kind of scuffle taking place up on the sidewalk outside the House of Ko-Reck-Shun. Mallon, Meredith, Dill, and now Keith Hayward kept him from seeing it. He gathered up his courage in both hands and moved toward Mallon's free side, Hayward's touch seeming to burn through his clothing. Howard could hear the Monster (the Eel's name for him) braying his stupid laugh, *haw haw haw*, as he went around the side of the group, wondering what could be so terrible that it amused Keith Hayward, wondering also why the Eel was nowhere in sight. When Howard reached Mallon's safe side, both questions were answered. The Eel stood rigid with shame and rage on the sidewalk outside the seedy House of Ko-Reck-Shun, being upbraided by a spectacularly drunken old man who had obviously just come out of the bar.

It took Howard Bly a moment to realize that the ruined old man was Carl Truax, the Eel's father. If his clothes were not yet in rags, they were shapeless and filthy with grime, and his whiskery cheeks folded in toward his wet mouth and flickering tongue. He was trying to shout, but his voice rose only to a squashy, wobbling stage whisper.

"Lee, damn you, what you doin' way the hell over *here*? You're supposed to be in school!"

In a voice as small and hard as a walnut, the Eel said, "It's Saturday, you moron."

Howard Bly could nearly have fainted—such humiliation, such courage!

"I'll drag you home and slap you silly. I'm your father, father a the famous goddam *Eel,* and I'm goin' show the *Eel* who's boss. Leave you black an blue, make you bleed from the ear holes, thass right, you hitch your sorry ass over here and lemme—"

"You're too drunk to do anything to anybody, Mister, and you're certainly not going to injure the *Eel,* now or ever again," Mallon broke in. "Now shut up and either go home or back inside. The choice is up to you."

The old man skittered toward him, muttering, "Choice is up ta me, fuckin right, you fuckin asshole." He aimed a wide, looping punch at Mallon's head, and Mallon easily ducked away. His ruined clothes fluttering about his skinny body, Eel's father shambled around in a circle, lowered his head, and tried a sloppy one-two combination that came nowhere near his moving target. Keith Hayward was still braying *haw haw haw.*

Mallon dodged another weightless blow and gave the Eel a look of pure handsome perplexity. "I don't want to hit the guy."

"Knock him out, I don't give a shit," the Eel said.

"Fuck this," Dilly-O said. He rushed into the fray, came up on the old man from behind, and caught him under the arms. Then he spun him across the sidewalk, shoved him through the yawning door, and propelled him back into the bar.

"First time anyone was ever thrown *into* that place," said Brett Milstrap.

"You know it? You been to the House of Ko-Reck-Shun?" asked Mallon, keeping an eye on the doorway. Lazy, drunken laughter sounded from the interior.

"Well, once, yeah," Milstrap said. "I was really drunk, and these guys took me there, and I think somebody maybe tied me up . . . ?" He closed his mouth and made blackboard-erasing motions with his right hand. "Whoa."

"Should have gone to Scuzzy's instead," said the Eel, demonstrating if not full recovery from the embarrassment at least the desire to tough it out.

"Are you kidding? We *came* from Scuzzy's."

"How do you feel, really?" Mallon asked. "If you like, we could take your father home, make sure nothing happens to him."

"He'll get home fine by himself. He just won't remember any of this."

"You have to be a little shook up," Mallon said. "Come on."

"No, *you* come on," the Eel said. "I want to see our meadow."

"Then take a look at it." He swept one arm toward the concrete barriers and the end of the street, making a comedy of presenting all of them with the shimmering swath of grass on which Howard had imagined him reciting ancient Greek.

By turning to look in the direction Mallon was pointing, this enlarged version of the little band was declaring itself, it occurred to Howard, ready for whatever expansions of consciousness might be in the offing. It was brave—brave all the way round. It was amazing, how Mallon managed to stack all these layers in his comedy, his gesture of giving them the meadow.

In the Crafts Room, tears spilled from Howard's eyes as he, too, regarded the dazzling meadow where their lives had submitted to such gorgeous ruin. He saw it whole, and he saw it pure, for in his imagination the meadow had been untouched by everything that had touched *them*.

The meadow before them, that sun-struck meadow in the last moments when it was no more than an irregular field owned by the UW Department of Agriculture . . .

■

The agronomy meadow, in effect an enormous and complex grassland, was bounded on two sides by state highways, on its distant far end by a dense wood owned by the forestry department. Near the highway that swooped by far off to their right, a long row of metal devices like sun reflectors had been slanted over little squares of variegated grasses. Immediately behind the shining reflectors stood a line of red wooden boxes with their lids propped open. The shimmering grassy space of the meadow, perhaps twenty square acres altogether, spread out over the ground like an enormous blanket, rising up here and there into little folds and peaks and corrugations, elsewhere disappearing into deeper folds or swales that might have been made by man but long ago had been absorbed into the meadow's fabric.

"I see why you picked it," Meredith said.

"Oh? Why did I do that?"

"You tell him, Hootie," Meredith said, and placed a cool white hand on the back of his sweaty neck. "You and Eel, you're good at seeing things."

Hootie cast a sideways glance at the Eel, who was fidgeting with impatience. "Because we could hide in one of those valley things." He thought about standing in one of the little valleys. "Then you'd have to look up at the hillside, except it's too low to be a real hillside. You want us to be looking up. Spencer, did you really go to West Point?"

Mallon laughed in surprise. "I did, yes, Hootie, I did. I'm proud to be able to say that."

"But didn't you say that you went to the University of California at Santa Cruz?" asked the Eel, now looking indignant instead of impatient. "Where you met the guy who wrote *Love's Body*?"

"Is there some reason we are dicking around like this?" Hayward asked.

"You doubt him?" asked Meredith, so pale that she seemed almost bloodless.

"All these questions," Mallon said. "Let's save that spirit for when we can really use it. Don't waste energy in the doubt game."

"Why does doubt have to be a game?"

"Eel, don't you see . . ." Meredith was unable to speak above a whisper.

Mallon silenced her with a glance. "Doubt undermines good energy. Above all, Eel, you don't *want* to doubt me. Right now—a moment from now—we are going to walk into this stupendous meadow together, and we must be united, one force, because none of this is going to work unless every

77

element in our chain, down to the *molecular* level, is directed unswervingly at our common goal. We have to be like a *laser* beam, guys—to smash through the consensus perceptual level, that's what it takes. Do you think you're here by accident?"

When he looked around at his circle of followers, fixing each one with his stare, Spencer Mallon appeared, if only to Howard Bly, to be a couple of feet taller than anyone else.

"Keith, are you here by some kind of random selection? Brett, are you?"

Hayward shook his head. "Uh uh, no way."

Milstrap said, "Whatever you say, boss." Balanced on one leg, his hand on his hip, Milstrap was completely restored to his unpleasant self. Hootie wondered what had gone wrong with him, and how it had been set right so quickly.

"You two, Meredith, and the kids here, you bring us into balance—get it, Eel?"

The Eel swallowed.

"Know what I studied at West Point? Among other things, *chemistry*. This may amaze you, Eel, but at heart I am a scientist. At Santa Cruz, besides philosophy I studied psychology. Also a *science*. Data, data, data—you spend thousands upon thousands of hours doing research with lab animals, and then you interpret your data. The second I heard about the four of you, I knew you'd be perfect for this experiment of ours.

"And now, Eel, if you and your friends are ready, if all of us are ready, we will walk into our meadow and find our perfect valley. I'll tell you what, prove I'm right—you show *me* where it is."

With considerably more mockery than the first time, he swept his arm toward the meadow, inviting Eel to demonstrate the perfection of his research methods. This was going to be as much an experiment as those involving the sun reflectors and wooden boxes that marched down the right side of the meadow.

"Hell, I'll do it," said Dilly. He strode up to the nearly waist-high concrete barrier that marked the end of Glasshouse Road, swung his shopping bag over the barrier, then slipped over it one leg at a time. Following closely behind him, Boats vaulted over, bag and all.

"Come on, Eel," said Dill. "Let's show him where it is."

Clumsily, the Eel swung over the concrete wall. Even more clumsily, Hootie came after, and while he was brushing concrete dust off his shirt, Mallon leaped atop the barrier, then jumped down, all in one graceful gesture. He extended a hand to Meredith, who settled her blue-jeaned rump on the top of the barrier and swung her legs over in tandem.

Keith Hayward tried to imitate Mallon's effortless agility. He nearly fell off the barrier, but caught himself in time to jump down. Brett Milstrap went over in the style of Dilly-O, one leg at a time, but less nimbly. He muttered, "Scraped the family jewels." When Boats and Keith Hayward started to laugh, Hayward cut himself off in mid-bray and glared at the younger boy.

"Let's show him what we're here for," Dill said, ready to start.

He gestured to his friends and led them toward the heart of the meadow. Grasses and wildflowers tangled at their feet. Various shades of green stretched out before them, folding into low berms covered with sprawling, untidy ranks of Queen Anne's Lace and tiger lilies. The meadow seemed larger once they had entered it. Somewhere in the distance, bees hummed in the motionless air.

Howard glanced at Mallon, following along behind them next to Meredith Bright. His earlier anxiety seemed to have disappeared. He was smiling to himself, and he looked both pleased to be in the meadow with them and genuinely curious to see if, unaided, his youngest followers could locate the site he had chosen. Keith Hayward and Brett Milstrap lounged along eight or nine yards behind, muttering. Hayward caught Hootie's eye and gave him a glance so smoky, threatening, and resentful that the boy at once whirled around, as if jabbed with a pointed stick.

If he turned around again, Hayward would be staring at him still, and that would be too disturbing—like looking down into a dark body of water and seeing something large and ill defined shifting around in there. He and Dill were right at the front of the little column proceeding through the meadow, which was fine with him. Boats and the Eel came along a couple of feet behind. After a wider gap, Mallon and Meredith Bright walked along ahead of Hayward and Milstrap, who lagged and dallied like disaffected schoolchildren.

Dilly hesitated, and Howard pointed to a clump of tiger lilies that covered the beginning of a fold in the landscape. As the fold continued across the meadow, the vegetation surrounding it grew thicker and more varied—black-eyed Susans, brambles, lupines, and wild roses like tough miniature baseballs.

"Damn it, Hootie, Meredith was right," Dilly-O told him. "You are really good at seeing things."

"That's sort of brumous to me," Howard replied, "but if you're looking for someplace where you can be out of sight, this one's better than the one you were thinking about. Right, Eel?"

"Bingo," said the Eel.

"I wasn't thinking about some other place, I was just *thinking*," said Dill. "You know what I mean, don't you, Spencer?"

"Go in there and tell me if it's right," Spencer said, finessing the question. "Did you say 'brumous'?"

"Um, hazy," said Howard Bly, beginning to blush.

Weeds and wildflowers disguised the entire length and height of the swale. From the Glasshouse Road end of the meadow, it appeared to be merely an overgrown ripple in the land. Narrow and shallow where the group entered, it gradually deepened and widened out as they proceeded. When they had come to a point slightly past midway, the grassy wall to their left rose nearly to the top of Howard's head, and the thick combination of grasses and weeds growing all along the soft ridge concealed them all. To their right, the opposite ridge had sunken into a low, concave rill of land where the grasses had burned brown. The cars speeding along the distant highway were moving dots of color.

The Eel and Dill looked up at Mallon. He was glowing like a torch.

"Once we get in there," he said, "we might just change the world."

■

Mallon asked Dill to take the white paint and paintbrush out of the bag and use them to mark out a circle approximately six feet in diameter on the brown, patchy earth that covered the long, low rise before them. "Boats, give him a hand. I want that circle to look pretty damn circular, if you know what I mean. The circle is the most perfect form in nature, and ours isn't going to work right if it's shaped like an amoeba."

"Where do you want it?" Dill asked.

"It has to be where it has to be. All of you, look over the ground and find the circle. *Find the circle.* It's already there. We're just going to paint over it so we can be sure we find the right place tomorrow night. So start looking, everybody—you'll see it in the dead grass, you'll see it in the dust, look long enough and it'll jump out at you. If you can find this place without me leading you to it, you ought to be able to find the circle."

Dill said, "You want us to look . . . ?"

"I'll give us all a minute. When the minute is up, everybody is going to point at the place where they found the circle. All right, start looking."

Old Howard stared into the pages of L. Shelby Austin and remembered looking for something nobody would ever be able to find. On the patchy ground, no circle waited to be discovered. Spencer was wrong, young Howard admitted to himself. Maybe not about everything, of course not about everything, but in this one instance, that of the imaginary circle, he was out to lunch. There it was, irreducible fact. The fucking circle did not exist. He *still* thought that was true. Nothing in L. Shelby Austin could change his mind, not that L. Shelby Austin, author of *The Moondreamers,* gave a damn. Howard remembered looking over at the Eel, and being unable to see if her faith was strong enough to support belief in the magic circle.

It could have gone either way. The Eel was putting on a tremendous show of concentration, furrowed forehead, squinty eyes, tense shoulder muscles, the whole deal.

Far back in time, Spencer Mallon cried, "Time's up!"

Three arms shot out, his, Dilly-O's, and Keith Hayward's, their index fingers by some miracle all pointing at roughly the same patch of ground. Half a heartbeat later, everyone else, Howard Bly among them, jumped on board, and four other arms flew out straight before their dishonest owners.

Meredith Bright squealed, "I see it, Spencer! It's right there!" Young Howard thought, *She wanted to see it, that's all*; for the hundredth, the thousandth time, the fat old Howard in the Game Room thought, *She was faking it, just like me.*

Triumphant, Mallon ordered Dill and Boats to paint the white circle upon the existing one they had located through what he called "psychic divination." The two boys pulled the small cans and the wide brushes from their bags, pried the lids off the cans, and set about trying to describe a decent circle on the untreated ground. The dead and dying grass soaked up the paint but left a white shadow bright enough to be seen. The earth, however, refused to take the paint and instead clotted the brushes. Mallon told them to pour it out. If they needed more, they'd bring it tomorrow. Stepping slowly backwards toward each other, pouring thin white streams from their cans, Boats and Dill traced out a reasonably acceptable circle they completed by turning side by side and drizzling the last of their paint onto the ground.

"Perfect," Mallon said. "Now get the ropes."

The boys took the ropes from the bags and looped them on the ground in front of the circle. They would serve, Mallon said, chiefly as symbols of confinement, but should actual roping be called for, he would depend on the boys to do their best. They looked nervous and uncertain, but they nodded.

"Candles," Mallon said. "Matches."

Dill and Boats dipped into their bags and produced a white wax candle and a box of kitchen matches for each participant, Mallon included.

Mallon arranged his party here and there in the grassy dell according to a pattern he had worked out in his mind and confirmed, he said, in texts of ancient magic. At the center of the pattern, he stood facing the fuzzy white circle, his back to the overgrown rise. Ten feet apart, Boats and Dill stood before him on each side, like watchful bodyguards. From a position well to the left of Boats, Howard, Eel, and Meredith Bright gazed at Mallon and the circle, the Eel and Meredith for some reason seeming to be so uncomfortable with their proximity they kept edging apart; so easy together they seemed to form a separate party of two, Hayward and Milstrap took a similar position to Dill's right. Once they had taken their places, they were to strike their matches and light the candles. Today, they would pretend to execute this step.

"After the candles are lighted, we will maintain silence for as long as I think is necessary," Mallon said, "When it feels right to break the silence, I will begin to recite something in Latin. It will be whatever comes into my mind. You won't understand a single word, and that's perfectly fine. Concentrate anyhow, pick up whatever you can. You are part of the raw material, too, and I am going to need your total involvement. So listen hard—listen as though your life depended on it. Because it might!"

This also required rehearsal. Pretending to hold up a lighted candle, Howard Bly watched his hero and tormentor stand as still as a driven post and mutter a rushed string of words he would not have comprehended even had they been audible because they were in a language spectacularly dead. As ordered, he concentrated as hard as he could without closing his eyes. After a couple of minutes, Howard began to feel that their little group had been joined by a number of strangers. It was no more than a feeling, but the feeling was too strong to ignore or dismiss. Because the strangers were invisible, they became more present to him after he closed his eyes. One by one, then in groups of two and three, they wandered up and encircled Mallon and his followers. Howard could *feel* this happening: it was like gradually being surrounded by more and more ghosts. But these presences were not ghosts. In exactly the same way, the fat little candle he held slightly above his head had begun to burn, for he could *feel* the flutter flutter flutter of its small, bright flame. Though invisible to the open eye, it was a real, not a ghost flame.

In the same way that he saw the wavering candle flame, Howard knew that the strangers all about them were not human. He had seen one of their kind on Gorham Street. The Eel had seen one in the girl's bathroom at Madison West. The creatures had been waiting for Mallon and his group on Glasshouse Road, but instead of trying to scare them off, they had spooked them into going toward the meadow. Now they resembled (it came to him) humane, upright dogs: dogs in handsome but outdated human clothes, deerstalker hats, Norfolk jackets, swallowtail coats, smoking jackets, bowlers, homburgs. About half of them seemed to be Weimaraners, but a good many bulldogs and Irish setters appeared in the crowd. Some of them smoked cigars. They looked a great deal like the dogs in the Eel's great painting, except that they seemed melancholy and irritable, not relaxed. They made Hootie extremely uncomfortable, for among the ranks of those who had made the dog-things so grumpy was himself, who alone could see them.

And why would the creatures drive them toward the meadow in the way sheepdogs drive their herd? Howard could read the answer in their watchful attitude: the agents, as Mallon called them, wanted to see how far they'd get.

Mallon had no idea that the dogs had gathered round. His anxiety seemed to have left him completely, and he appeared to be both utterly at ease and so charged with excitement as to be on the verge of trembling. The radical incompatibility of these states caused the young Howard to fear that Spencer Mallon might split in half, or float away from him, never to return.

Just as this appalling notion flew into his mind, the young Howard Bly caught a strangeness in his peripheral vision—a movement like that of a white scarf blown across the meadow. He moved his head to look more closely and for a second or less had the impression that he was seeing something small, white, and agonized, not a scarf, twist itself off of the brown grass some four feet to the right of the white circle of paint and gyrate upward until it snapped into invisibility. Around it, the atmosphere had flared: the landscape appeared to bulge as the white shape flew past. So quickly had it come and gone, he questioned whether he had seen it at all. Then he realized that of course he had seen it, in his way, and that the tormented white scarflike thing had been in flight from whatever had caused the world to ripple and bulge as it followed in pursuit. The wretched white thing had *flown through*, it had *escaped* into this world.

Immediately, there came a second recognition, that the invisible but real flame had guttered out and the dog-creatures had left them—all at once, their invisibility had become absence. For a moment, this absence felt more threatening than their presence.

Mallon lowered his arms and told everyone that they had done everything they could for that day. He thought the rehearsal had gone well, in fact very well. He did, too: Howard could still feel the man's suppressed excitement beating away beneath his cool exterior.

"Everybody, go home and have a good dinner, if that's in the picture for you. Then comes the surprise I promised you. Hootie, Eel, Boats, Dill? This is your night to go to a fraternity party. Keith and Brett have made it possible for all of us to attend the Beta Delt bash tonight, and it's gonna be great. Free beer, live rock 'n' roll, three girls for every boy, three boys for every girl. Except you, Meredith! Big big fun guaranteed for all. Keith and Brett, we all thank you for making a dream come true. See what I mean, Hootie?"

"Yeah," Howard said. "Amazing." This was another world now, he thought, one he hardly knew at all.

No one else, it seemed, had seen the tormented white scrap fly over the dead grass. No one but he had sensed the presence of the agents or held a candle with an invisible flame. *So what did I do, I believed it was me,* the old Howard said to himself. *Hootie said to Hootie, what you saw back there was nothing but yourself, and Hootie believed what he said.*

Dill returned home for dinner. Howard and the Eel went along home with Boats, whose mother was still sober enough to cook one of their favorite meals, macaroni and cheese. She slopped the yellow mush onto their plates, placed before them a bowl of potato chips and cold bottles of Coca-Cola, and watched them eat, chain-smoking Parliaments and smiling at the way they bolted their food. Boats's mom had always been fond of the Eel.

"Hey, where's your boyfriend at?" she asked. "You guys are usually pretty tight."

"Yeah, well, he dumped us," Eel said. "He's just so above it all and *skeptical,* he's gonna miss everything, not that I care even a little bit, God knows."

"Yeah, sure," said Boats's mother. "Okay. So are the rest of you going to a party tonight, or just hanging out, as per usual?"

Boats's mother, Shirley Boatman, had once been very pretty, and the aggressive question had a wistful undertone.

"Maybe a little of both," Boats said.

"You guys should party it up a little more. Where is it, anyhow?"

Boats and the Eel continued eating. His mother popped ice cubes out of the tray in the freezer and freshened her drink with two inches of Seagram's and an equal amount of 7 Up.

"Hey, you don't have to worry about me spoiling the fun or anything." The ashy tip of her cigarette dropped into her glass and disintegrated when it struck an ice cube. She stirred the drink with a finger, and most of the ashes disappeared.

She took a drag on the cigarette and blew out a column of smoke that angled above the table and over their heads. "Who's throwing this shindig, anyhow?"

"It's just some kids. And Mom?—only old people say 'shindig' anymore."

Filling a sudden silence, Eel said, "All I can tell you is, this party's on Langdon Street."

"Langdon Street. When I was a girl in high school, we all talked about going to fraternity parties, but none of us ever did. Our parents wouldn't have let us, for one thing. My mom and dad? They woulda nailed my bedroom door shut. All *I'm* gonna do is say—don't drink too much, and don't make a fool of yourself. Eel and Hootie, I'm talking to my son here. You two'll do fine, I know."

"And what, you expect me to act like an idiot? Gee, Mom, thanks a bunch."

"You want to know what I *expect*? Mainly, Boats, I *expect* you to keep your hands in your pockets. Don't take anything that don't belong to you. It's not like sneakin' candy outa the A & P. It takes money to belong to a fraternity. Once they're in, they watch out for each other."

"Whatever you say, Mom," Boats said.

"Just remember—if you get into trouble, you have to get out of it by yourself." She turned to Howard Bly. "And Hootie, your mom said it was fine for you to eat over here tonight, but she doesn't want you to stay out too late. And she asked me if I knew anything about someone staying in your basement at night."

The three boys looked at her in shock. To little Howard Bly, it was as if adored Spencer Mallon had been revealed to be the white thing that twisted in torment up and away.

"Uh-oh," Shirley said. "Look, I don't know what's going on, and I don't *want* to know what's going on, but if that pervert you all love so much is sleeping in your basement, you'd better get him outta there, pronto."

That evening, Howard was unable to take Spencer aside when they gathered outside the Beta Delt house, which was not actually on Langdon

Street but down a walkway between two other fraternity houses. A wooden, listing structure badly in need of a new paint job, it stood on the far edge of a small asphalt parking lot with a private drive servicing it and two other, equally undistinguished houses. The back of the house led directly onto a wooden deck over Lake Mendota and a long, unstable pier.

Hayward and Milstrap ushered Mallon and the group through the front door and into a lounge or living room with battered and abraded leather furniture arranged around a cold fireplace. A boy in a Hawaiian shirt, shorts, and sandals looked up from a game of solitaire and yelled, "What the hell is with these *kids*, Hayward?"

Hayward said, "Kitchen help."

"You should be kitchen help, you asshole," said the boy.

Howard was able to speak privately to Spencer only after Hayward had led them downstairs and into a large empty room with a bandstand at one end and a bar at the other. When two young men summoned Hayward and Milstrap from an arched doorway, Howard turned to Mallon and described his dilemma. He was fearful that Mallon would either get angry or refuse to move out of the basement, and he kept hesitating and mixing up his words.

No problem, Mallon said. He had not intended to go back to the store that night, anyhow—he'd crash at Meredith's. He'd had a little trouble in that direction, but everything was copacetic again. Women, you know, they're all a little crazy. By the way, there was no reason to tell all of this to the Eel. Okay?

In that direction? Crash? Copacetic? Was this guy speaking English? "Okay," he said.

He wanted to say: Forget about tomorrow, forget the whole thing, my love, you may know you're being watched, but you don't know what you're up against. Pay attention to what they told you. Quit while you're behind.

How could he say these things to Spencer Mallon? It was impossible. For a moment little Howard Bly hovered on the brink of attempting to do

88

that which was not possible to do, and at the end of that moment all choice was stolen from him. The two frat boys who had conferred with Keith and Brett were ordering them into a single line. The boys watched them file through the arch so closely they might have been trying to memorize their faces. Howard was aware that they paid special attention to the Eel and himself. While Milstrap ushered the group into an empty kitchen, Howard looked back and thought he saw Keith Hayward shove folded bills into his pocket.

Milstrap told them that they had been brought in early to avoid inspection at the door. Mallon and Meredith were fine, of course, but as far as the Beta Delts were concerned, the high-school students had been hired as kitchen help. When this turned out to be an ordinary party, just beer, no food, well, sorry, but kiss my ass, okay? So Hayward had forgotten to tell the kids. Big deal, right? Officially, they were supposed to wait in the kitchen until midnight, then go out and start cleaning up the BD Room back out there. In reality, they could wait until the BD Room got really noisy—maybe fifteen minutes after the band started playing—and after that do whatever they liked. If they were nice to the Beta Delts, the Beta Delts would be nice to them. And by the way, the beer was free. Have as much as you like, just don't puke or pass out.

Mallon and Meredith Bright left with Hayward and Milstrap. For a little less than an hour, the Madison West students flopped around undisturbed in the kitchen. Then a din of voices arose in the party room, a guitar began to play blues over a shuffle rhythm, voices male and female amped up into party mode, and the little band slipped out of the kitchen and filtered into the BD Room. The lights had been turned down. Gyrating, bouncing bodies filled the room. Instantly, the crowd separated them.

Howard realized that he had never been to a party even faintly like this, and neither had any of his friends. In high school, big parties took over entire houses, and you could always escape to a quieter, less crowded room or go out on the lawn. You listened to records and hoped somebody had managed to bring beer. Here, everybody had been jammed into one room, and they were all yelling and screaming. The band was the loudest thing he had ever heard in his life: he felt the bass reverberating in his chest, and the sound vibrated as it passed through his body. Everybody, even the dancers, carried big plastic cups full of beer, and beer splashed onto people's clothes and all over the floor. Loud, hard, utterly joyous music echoed off the walls and drilled into his ears. Trying to get to the bar, Howard moved down the edge of the dance floor, weaving through the crowd and squeezing past people who never noticed he was there. When finally he made it to the bar, the Eel was standing right in front of him, reaching up to take two of the sixteen-ounce cups from the boy working the taps. It was one of those unexpected times when he became achingly aware that the Eel was a girl, a real girl, instead of a tomboy so successful that he thought of her as just another guy, more or less. Even worse, she was stunning. Astonishingly, as if to console him for the bone-deep ache that accompanied this perception, the Eel turned around and gave him one of the cups filled to the top with foaming beer.

He moved to the side and caught sight of Dill dancing with a great-looking girl with long, straight blond hair, huge eyeglasses, and wonderful white legs. Dill was grinning like an idiot. Then the crowd closed in front of them, and Howard saw leering Keith Hayward whisper into another student's ear. The feeling that Hayward had been talking about him filled Hootie with revulsion, and instantly he whirled away.

He and the Eel clung together for half an hour, chugging beer and letting the music pound into them. When he was drunk enough to forget about his inhibitions, Howard spun into the crowd and began to dance by himself, wildly, throwing his arms about and bobbing to the beat. Laughing, a college girl moved aside to give him room, and in seconds she and another girl were bopping around in front of him, being both his partners and his audience. A squat guy with hairy arms moved up alongside the girls and started making corny rowboat gestures, then held his nose and pretended to drown. He was a friend of Hayward's, but Howard couldn't remember how he knew that.

Someone passed him another sixteen-ounce beer, his third, and he squirted some of it through his nose, laughing at the cornball guy who was a friend of Keith Hayward's. Oh, yeah! They had been talking together, that was how he knew.

His hands on the waist of the blond girl, Dilly grinned at him and pumped one fist in the air. When Howard copied the gesture, the cornball guy grasped his hand and spun him around, making him laugh all the harder. Most of his beer slopped onto the ground. For a second, he caught a glimpse of the Eel babbling away to two guys who looked like football players. The Eel made him laugh, and he laughed a delicious Eel-laugh, watching a compact man in a gray suit weave across his field of vision.

Unstrung by shock, Howard's legs dissolved beneath him. Before he had time to melt into a puddle on the wet floor, someone caught him around the chest and pulled him upright. His legs returned, though they felt like stilts.

The music went rubbery. He thought it had been indistinct for some time, though he had failed to notice the moment of decay. The individual dancers had turned into blurs. Whoever was in front of him lowered him into a chair. Eel's football players stepped on by, though the Eel was not with them. Then he, too, was traveling down the hall, and being assisted through the doorway into a dimly lighted room with mattresses and huge soft pillows instead of sofas and chairs. The cornball guy with hairy arms settled him down into one of the gigantic pillows and was just stretching out beside him when Spencer Mallon swooped down, spun the guy off the pillow, sank a booted foot into his stomach, and helped Howard scramble to his feet. "Hope you're enjoying your first fraternity shindig, Hootie," he said, and walked him back toward the throbbing party room.

"Only old people say 'shindig,'" Howard informed him.

In the enormous room down the hallway, the band was taking a break. The crowd had refocused on the bar, from which it radiated out along both sides of the room and knotted together again in front of the bandstand.

Howard realized that Spencer Mallon had set him free and wandered, not quite so unsteadily as before, over to a sagging old couch pushed against the wall and sat down next to a drunken boy wearing madras shorts. The drunken boy looked him over and said, "Shane, come back! Come *back,* Shane!"

Inspired, Howard told him that only old people said that. Then he looked across the room and forgot all about the boy in the madras shorts.

On the other side of the empty dance floor, a man in a gray suit was bending over the Eel, who was sprawled out over a baby blue beanbag chair criss-crossed with duct tape. A fraternity boy touched the man's arm, but he paid no attention. The boy grasped his elbow and yelled something. Without seeming to move in any way except to straighten up by a few degrees, the man in the suit caused the frat boy to flail backward across the beer-stained, cup-strewn floor, flapping his arms until he collapsed into a messy tangle of el-bows, knees, and feet. Two other fraternity boys had noticed the backward flight of their brother, who presently lay on the wet barroom floor, apparently bleeding a little from his nose and eyes. One of those who had seen the man deflect his brother had the vast chest and squared-off head of a football player; the other was simply so large he looked impervious to assault. These two turned to the dog, the agent: the killer angel, in Hootie's drunken estimation. He wanted to say, *Leave that guy alone, you don't want to screw with him, no mat-ter how big you are.* They were going to die, Hootie knew, they'd be torn to bloody shreds. Terror so unmanned him that he closed his eyes.

When he opened them, the two giant Beta Delts were picking up their stunned, bleeding friend, and the creature in the suit had disappeared like the unseen beings who had overseen their rehearsal. Hootie wondered if he ac-tually understood anything at all.

When he remembered that Spencer was going to leave them the next day, sorrow again overtook him. The Beta Delt in the madras shorts said something about babies and walked away. Through his tears, Howard saw a blurry Eel slide up to blurry Boats and grip his shoulders. Like him, she was in tears, which were shed, he understood, for the same reason.

Mallon said:

One day, probably far in the future and certainly when you least expect it, you will find yourself in some totally impersonal, anonymous space, and the most important choice of your life will be before you. You'll be on a business trip, or on vacation, getting off an elevator or walking into a hotel lobby. It could be anywhere, but let's stick with these nice, neutral possibilities. And it won't happen like this, but let's say it does. Let's say . . . let's say for some reason you know I'm in Nepal right then, or you know I'm in the hospital. Or you know I'm dead! For whatever reason, I'm gone, I can't be there, but there I am anyhow. You see me walking across the lobby, or getting off the adjacent elevator. Can't be him, you say to yourself, Spencer can't be here, and yet despite all the reasons to the contrary, it's me, all right, and you know it. So the question is, what am I doing there? Because you can sure as hell see that I'm doing something, I'm not just out for a stroll, I'm going somewhere. And the next question is even more important: Why did you see me? Did I just wander into your field of vision by accident? How likely is that? No, there's a reason you saw me, and it's gotta be something pretty important.

So you take off after me—you don't say anything, you just follow along to see where I'm going. Because I'm not just going there, I'm taking you with me—it's your goal, too, not just mine. And the second you start following me, I step up the pace and make it harder for you to do what you have to do.

Is it clear that all this is a kind of parable? Parables don't mean one thing and one thing only, you know, which is the reason people still argue about them, two thousand years later.

I walk you around the block, I duck down alleys, I go into stores and leave by the back door, but you manage to stick to my tail no matter what I do. In the end, we're back in that hotel lobby, so you could say our destination is the place where we started. I get there before you, and when you make it into the lobby, you see me get-

ting into an elevator just before the door closes. You watch the needle swing up and see it stop on the fifth floor. Did I get off there, or did someone else? There's no time to debate about it—the next elevator comes down and opens its doors, and you jump in and push five and the Close Door button before anybody else can get on. The elevator chugs upward, going slower than seems possible, but finally it gets to five, and the doors slide open, and you charge out, trying to look in both directions at once. I'm way down to your right and at the end of the hallway, just turning a corner. You break into a run, because you don't want me to vanish through a doorway without you seeing which one it is.

A door slams shut the second you make it to the bend in the corridor. You barrel around the corner and realize that I must have disappeared through one of the first two doors on the inner side. There are doors on the street side, too, but if I had used one of those you would have seen it closing.

All right, this is the point at which you have to make a choice. But now you face a dilemma. The meaning of your choice became clear to you about a second after you turned to face those two doors, and an immense amount is riding on your decision.

If you knock on the door to my room, I'll open it and invite you in for a long talk. As long as you like. You will have done exactly what you should, and your reward is that you can ask me anything you want—I'll answer all the questions that you've wondered about, all the questions that have plagued you. And believe me, there'll be a lot of questions—once you've had time to think about everything we've done and are about to do, you'll be overflowing with questions. The answers you get will be the explanations you have needed, in fact really hungered for, all your life.

But you realized a second ago that if you pick the wrong door some terrible personal catastrophe will happen to you. This dreadful recognition came to you right out of the blue—guess what, there are consequences to making the wrong decision, and in this case those consequences could be really horrible. And what makes this deal even worse is that the catastrophe will happen not to you personally, although it's still going to be personal, all right, but to someone you love. If you make the wrong decision, something terrible is going to happen to some person you care for with all your heart. Could be a crippling stroke, a hideous mutilation in an auto accident; could be a horrible lingering death, with screams of pain and shit all over the sheets.

Then you will have to make the choice. How much are you willing to gamble? Let's say that you have a feeling about which door is the right one, a sort of gut instinct. Can you trust that instinct?

Tough, isn't it?

But this story ends when you open the door. It doesn't matter if you managed to guess which room is mine, which door I closed behind me. You put your hand on the door handle, you knock, it's all over. End of story. By choosing one, you chose the other, too. Do you understand why? Those two consequences are joined at the hip, they're Siamese twins. Even if you picked the door with the lady behind it—all questions answered, all explanations given, your life solved for you—it's still true that you gave the tiger permission to jump. You gave your assent to catastrophe, you invited tragedy and horror to walk right in. You got lucky, that's all.

Mallon said:
Every secret mission requires a good thief.

Mallon said:
Trust me. When the tide rises, you shall be at my side.

Mallon said:
One of you shall inhabit the country of the blind.

Mallon said:
I think you will rise up singing, you will sail up into the blue. Singing one long, continuous song so beautiful that it will entrance everyone who hears it.

Mallon said:
Words create freedom, too, dear Hootie, and I think it is words that will save you.

donald olson

Chicago, Early Summer

Sprawled out in a high-backed stool, Don Olson had commandeered the entire lower half of the long bar at Mike Ditka's. While his left arm barricaded his drink, his right index finger jabbed the air. He kept his head turned back toward the bartender. The bartender was ignoring him.

"There he is, the guy I was telling you about. You read a book called *The Agents of Darkness*, didn't you? Eighty-three, right? Year it came out? Cover of *Time* magazine?"

"Good memory," I said.

Stationed in front of the two men at the far end, the bartender appeared to be engrossed in passing celery sticks through a stream of cold water. This was going to be even more terrible than I had feared. I wished I had never talked to the guy. The people at the tables were shifting their eyes between Olson and myself. The guys at the far end stared straight ahead. They might have been watching television, but what they were watching, with increasing wariness and alarm, was the former Dilly-O.

"I asked you a question, my friend. Does the name Lee Harwell mean anything to you?"

"Sir," said the bartender, "in 1983, I was eight years old."

"How fleeting is the bauble, fame," Olson said. "Come over here and give your daddy some sugar."

So now this guy was my daddy? The odors of sweat, unwashed flesh, and tobacco intensified as I drew nearer, and I held my breath while I embraced my old friend. Salt-and-pepper stubble covered Olson's cheeks. The stench was part of the reason everyone else had fled to the other end of the bar. The rest of it would have been whatever he had said or done. Olson gripped me a couple of beats too long before releasing me.

"Let me buy you a drink, man, hey? That sound like a good idea?"

"Good enough," I said, and asked for a glass of pinot grigio.

"Pinot for my buddy, and another margarita here. Hey, Lee." A slap on the shoulder. "You gotta know—I really appreciate this."

He leaned back, grinning. "Should we maybe grab a table?"

"Let's," I said, and saw the bartender's shoulders drop an inch or two.

"Which one you like? That one?" Olson was pointing at one of two empty tables at the back of the room.

I was trying to reconcile the scruffy, hard-used man before me with both his eighteen-year-old self and the man Jason Boatman had once described to me in the lobby of the Pfister. Olson looked exactly like a man who had just walked out of prison. The yardbird bravado made him seem inauthentic, potentially dangerous.

"That one's fine." I felt an instinctive need to keep Olson pacified.

The entire room relaxed when we sat down at the back table.

Olson faced the door, keeping a watch out for something that was never going to happen, and the other patrons went back to their conversations, their burgers, their laughter. A small, brown-haired, and extraordinarily good-looking female waiter brought our drinks on a gleaming tray and set them down with a flicker of a glance for me, nothing for Olson. She evoked the memory of forties movie queens like Rita Hayworth and Greer Garson.

She also evoked another memory, sharper, more immediate, and charged with feeling.

"This is a great place, right? I thought you'd like it."

"I like it fine," I said.

"You've been here before, I suppose."

"I think so."

"Places like this are so common in your experience, you don't remember if you were here before?" Olson's eyes flicked away and for a moment inspected the bar's entrance. Then his attention snapped back to me.

"I was here once before, Don. About a week after it opened. We came for dinner."

"They serve good food in this place, right?"

"Their food is dandy. It's ducky. It's swell."

"Okay, I get it. Hey, can I get you anything? An appetizer, maybe?"

Ditka's was on East Chestnut, five blocks south of my house on Cedar Street, not so close that Olson's arrival felt like an intrusion—apart from all the ways in which it felt precisely like an intrusion.

"Come on, let's split a shrimp cocktail." Here he gave another sharp, brief glance at the doorway, but whatever he was dreading or waiting for failed to appear.

"Look, I never got around to having lunch," I said. "And now it's almost four. Let's have a late lunch or an early dinner, does that sound good? On me, please, Don. I know you've had some hard luck lately."

"Today my luck is good. Tell you the truth, though, I could eat a cow."

"Then you picked the right place."

He waved to the waitress, and when her blue-gray gaze found him, performed a mime of reading a menu.

She came to our table with two big gull-wing menus, and Don Olson, alas, folded his hand around her wrist. "What's good here, honey?"

She jerked her hand from his grip.

"What do you think I should order?"

"The Da Pork Chop."

"Da Pork Chop, that's like the specialty of the house?"

"Comes with cinnamon apples, green peppercorns, and au juice."

"That's the baby for me. Start me off with the Fried Calamari. Extra crispy, can you do that for me?"

I ordered a blue-cheese burger and a second glass of wine.

"Another margarita, too, honey. Corona back. Did you ever read a book called *The Agents of Darkness*?"

"I don't think so."

"This is the guy who wrote it. Forgive me, I'm Don Olson, and this is my friend Lee Harwell. What's your name? It has to be as pretty as you are."

"My name is Ashleigh, sir. Excuse me, but I'm going to punch in your order now."

"Hold on, please, Ashleigh. I want to ask you an important question. Think it over, then give me your honest response."

"You have thirty seconds," she said.

Olson checked the entrance, lifted his chin, and closed his eyes. He raised his right hand and pinched his thumb against his index finger. It was a parody of careful discrimination, and it was awful to behold.

"Does a person have the right to turn his friends' lives into entertainment, for money?" He opened his eyes, his hand still raised in that snuff taker's position.

"You don't need permission to write a novel."

"Get outta here," Olson said.

Ashleigh twirled away.

"Ten years ago, that little slut would have gone home with me. Now she won't look at me twice. At least she didn't want to look at you, either."

"Don," I said, "your heart isn't in this. You checked out the door maybe five or six times since we sat down. Is there someone you're afraid will come in? Is someone following you? Obviously, you're on the lookout."

"Okay—when you're in the slammer, you learn to keep an eye on the door. You get a little jumpy, a little paranoid. Couple of weeks, I'll be back to normal."

He made another quick check of the entrance.

"When did you get out, anyhow?"

"I took a bus up here this morning. Know how much money's in my pocket? Twenty-two bucks."

"Don, I don't owe you anything. Let's be clear about that."

"Harwell, I don't *think* you owe me anything, could we be clear about *that*? I just figured, maybe you'd be willing to help me out a little, you and your wife. She was always great, you were always a good guy, and you're about a million times better off than anyone else I know."

"Leave my wife out of this."

"Oh man, that's harsh," Olson said. "I loved the Eel."

"So did everybody else. What do you mean, help you out a little?"

"Let's save the business for after lunch, all right? I'm thinkin' about when we were all on top of the world, our little bunch. And you and the Eel were 'the Twins.' Because you sure did look a lot alike, you gotta give me that."

"I wish you'd stop calling her 'the Eel,' " I said.

It was as though he had not heard. "Man, she must have been one of the great tomboys of all time." For the first time since we had taken the table, Olson seemed able to step aside from his obsession with the door and fully inhabit his half of the conversation.

I remembered something that dampened my sudden flare of anger. "In the old days, when I wanted to piss her off, I called her Scout."

Olson's face creased into a smile. "She was like the girl in, you know, that movie . . ."

I found that I remembered nothing about a movie I had held perfectly in mind a moment before. Lately, these mental vacancies and erasures seemed to be happening with an increasing frequency. "The one with that actor . . ."

"Yeah, and he was a lawyer . . ."

"And Scout was his daughter . . ."

"Damn," said Olson. "At least you can't remember, either."

"I know it, but I don't know it," I said, frustrated but no longer in a bad temper. Our shared failing had put us on a common footing; and this evidence of Olson's aging had served, however paradoxically, to evoke the forthright and appealing young man Dill had been. Full of sweetness, the past bloomed before me.

Simultaneously, we said, "*To Kill a Mockingbird.*" We burst out laughing.

"I have to ask," I said. "What were you charged with?"

For a second, Olson glanced up at the ceiling, exposing a skinny, wrinkled neck that looked like some inedible organic vegetable in a health food store. "I was charged with and convicted of committing crimes of gross indecency with a young woman. The alleged victim was eighteen years old and engaged in an informal program of study with me. For a couple of years, I'd been working with the erotic occult. I started out with a group of ten or twelve, it shrank to maybe six, you know how that goes, and in the end it was just me and Melissa. It got so we could prolong the act like to *infinity*. Unfortunately, she mentioned this feat to her mother, who went completely nuts and got the university involved, which wound up with the Bloomington vice squad hauling me out of my sweet no-rent sublet and dragging me off to the station."

At this point, Olson's eyes again moved from my face to the doorway.

"Indiana turns out to be the most self-righteous state in the Union."

Don Olson once again returned to me, his old friend, and the conversation, this time without the effect of bringing a lost era back to life.

"You were in an Indiana state prison?"

"I started out in Terre Haute, then I was sent to Lewisberg, PA. After six months, they sent me here, to Illinois. Pekin. They like to keep you off balance. But I can do my work in prison the same as anywhere else."

The calamari arrived. We began spearing pieces of fried squid and popping them into our mouths. Don Olson leaned back in his chair and groaned with pleasure. "God, real food again. You have no idea."

I agreed: I had no idea. "What did you mean, your work? What could you do in jail?"

"Talk to other prisoners. Show them another way to think about what they had done and where they were." Olson resumed eating, but did not let it interfere with his explanations. Bits of fried squid and batter occasionally sprayed from his mouth. His glances at the entrance punctuated his sentences. "It was like social work, actually."

"Social work."

"Plus the old hoodoo mojo," Olson said, rippling his fingers before him. "Without you got the sizzle, you can't sell the steak."

Ashleigh returned and picked up Olson's plate without getting near enough to be reeled in. Returning with a small but heavily laden tray, she slid our plates before us with the finesse of a croupier.

Olson cut into the massive pork chop and brought a glistening nugget to his mouth. "Whoa," he said, and chewed for a bit. "Man, these guys know how to cook a pig, uh huh."

He stopped grinning long enough to swallow. "When we all fell in love with Spencer Mallon, the Eel was right there, alongside Hootie and Boats and me. Why *you* weren't, I never understood. You stayed away, but you must have heard all about it."

"Not really," I said. "But that's part of the reason I asked you to come here."

Olson waved at the waitress for more drinks and took the opportunity to check out the doorway again. "Way I look at it, you kept yourself out back then. In fact, way I remember it, you were sort of pissy about what we were doing."

"I didn't see the point of pretending to be a college student. Especially for Hootie, for God's sake! And your 'guru' smelled like bullshit to me." For a second or two, I watched Olson eat. Then I cut the giant burger down the middle and took a bite from the dripping half-moon in front of me.

"Mallon put a curse on all of you, my wife included."

Olson's wandering eyes snapped back to my face, and there he was again, fully present. It was like turning on a big battery, like watching a statue come suddenly to life.

"Jesus, you're still weird about this. It still puts a hair up your ass." He shook his head, smiling. "And do you really think there's any difference between a blessing and a curse? I'd be amazed if you did."

"Come on," I said, a little taken aback by his sudden intensity. "Don't give me that Mallon horse shit."

"Call it what you like," Olson said, concentrating now on his new margarita. "But I'd say the same principle applies to me. And to the Eel."

"Her name is still Lee Truax."

"Whatever."

I took a moment to work on the giant burger while keeping an eye on Don Olson. I tried to work out how far he was willing to go.

"I suppose Mallon's blessing is the reason you went to jail."

"Spencer's blessing allowed me to do exactly what I wanted for the past forty years, not counting jail time."

Something struck me. "Pekin's a federal prison. How does a sex offender wind up there?"

"He probably doesn't." Olson smiled an off-center smile. Another glance over my shoulder. "Come to think of it, probably wasn't Melissa Hopgood got me sent away. Let's call it a financial miscalculation."

"The IRS?" Tax fraud sounded too boring for the man who had once been the heroic Dill.

Olson made a big deal of savoring his mouthful of pork. I saw him come to a conclusion a moment before he swallowed. "The error was, the mechanism we used to create extra money was pretty fuckin' dubious."

He grinned and raised his hands: *Hey, you got me.*

"Melissa knew this kid. Turned out the kid was a sort of big-time facilitator. From a big, serious family. Lot of money flowing into the country, lots of money flowing out. If I could help him with a distribution issue, I'd make enough to get off the road and settle down somewhere. I thought I'd maybe write a book."

He winked at me. "The stuff about erotic magic was all straight truth, by the way, and Melissa did go and blab to big fat Maggie Hopgood about all the orgasms she was having, but she threw in some stuff about the distribution setup, and that's why the boys dragged me away in the cold, cold mornin'."

"A drug deal."

"Let's just say, my get-rich-quick scheme didn't pan out. From now on, I stick to honest labor and the kindness of friends."

"Is this where we get to business?"

Don Olson racked his knife and fork. His plate now held only a bone, a knot of gristle, and brown smears. "A minute ago, you said you were still curious about Spencer and the old days."

I said nothing.

"You tried to get the Eel to tell you what happened that day in the meadow?"

I held my silence.

"I'm not surprised. It's a hell of a topic. You guys must have spent a lot of time with the police."

"They were interested in what I might have heard about Keith Hayward. If he had enemies, stuff like that. All I knew was that my girlfriend hated his guts. Which I wasn't about to say."

"Hootie hated him, too."

"Later on, did Spencer ever say anything about Hayward?"

Now it was Olson's turn to let a question hang in the air.

"I did a little research, and some pretty interesting stuff turned up. Do you remember hearing about the Ladykiller, back around 1960?"

"Hayward couldn't have been the Ladykiller," Olson said, firmly. "He had a whole different bag."

"I'm not saying he was. But he had a connection to the murders, and I have the feeling that he had at least some kind of effect on whatever happened out there in the meadow."

"Ask that gorgeous Miss Thang for the check," Olson said. He looked up and regarded the ceiling for a couple of seconds. "To get me back on my feet, I need, hey, a thousand dollars." He grinned. "Of course, the amount is up to you."

"On the way to my place we can stop at an ATM. And yes, the amount is up to me." I waved at the waitress and pretended to scribble in the air. She brought the check, and I handed her a credit card. Olson leaned back in his chair and crossed his arms over his chest. He never took his eyes from my face. It must have cost him something to keep from eyeing the entrance. After I added a tip and tore off the receipt, I stood up and stared at the floor for a little while. Olson continued regarding me.

I met his gaze. "I'll give you five hundred."

Olson stood up without taking his eyes off mine. Smiling an annoying lopsided smile, he moved toward the entrance with a sloping, sidling walk that insinuated a trace of criminality and an underlying degree of physical strength. It seemed a kind of unspoken rebuke. Several of the remaining patrons kept their eyes on Olson, making sure he was really leaving.

The bright dazzle of Chestnut Street seemed lighter, less ponderous than the atmosphere we had just left. "What did you do in there before I showed up?"

"Shook 'em up a little," Olson said, grinning at the memory.

"So I gather."

"When my first margarita came up, I had me a little taste and said, 'In the joint you can get any kind of drug you can name, only it's like tequila was wiped off the face of the earth, which is pretty fuckin' strange when you consider how many Mexican motherfuckers are doing time.' Then I started talking about you, but the damage was done."

I steered my companion north onto Rush Street, and for a couple of minutes Olson fell silent to inspect both the people around them and the spaces between the people. Being outside, I saw, increased his sense of threat. Chicago's usual gridiron charge and swerve occupied the sidewalks. Olson did not excite notice until we paused for a traffic light, when several people moved away from his odor.

"I didn't expect so much hostility out here in the land of the free."

"A shower and a change of clothes will fix that. I'm amazed you can't smell yourself."

"On the bus everybody smelled this way."

Two more blocks took us to the Oak Bank, and I stopped in front of the ATM machine. Before I could pull out my wallet, Olson whispered, "Let's go into the lobby, okay?"

He was nodding like a bobblehead doll. Transacting our business out on the street ramped up his anxiety.

"We're in no danger here."

"Must be nice to feel that way," Olson said.

I took him into the lobby and led him toward the row of ATM machines. A bearded kid with a backpack was punching numbers into the machine at the far right, and a guy who looked like he might once have been a college lacrosse player—broad back, short hair, starched blue shirt, pressed chinos—was withdrawing money from an ATM near the center of the row. I moved toward the machine two openings to the lacrosse player's left, but Olson stepped in front of me and, like a sheepdog, guided me to the last machine in the line.

"You have no idea how many ways people can figure out your ATM number just by watching you. Trust me."

I extracted my card from my wallet. Olson posted himself like a bodyguard at my shoulder. I brought the card to the lip of the slot and paused. "Hmmm . . ."

Olson stepped back and twisted his neck to look at me.

I pushed my card in and immediately pulled it back out. Olson made a show of looking away while I tapped in the code numbers. "I wish I knew why I said I'd give you five hundred bucks."

"I'll tell you, if you really want to know."

While the screen asked me what I wanted to do now that I had its attention, I swung around sideways and raised my eyebrows in silent demand.

"Because I asked for a thousand."

While bills shuttled out of the ATM, he tilted his head, propped his left elbow in the palm of his right hand, and snapped his fingers.

Olson folded his twenties and fifties into the front pocket of his jeans. "People tend to act in certain specific ways. Spencer had it all figured out. You always ask for twice as much as you really want."

■

A few minutes later, the two of us turned into Cedar Street. After a quick, darting inspection of the terrain, Olson remarked that I sure did live on a beautiful block. Past the restaurants bordering Rush Street, handsome row houses and residential buildings extended eastward beneath the shelter of great trees toward the bright blue immensity of Lake Michigan. For some reason, he stepped off the sidewalk and began to walk toward a semicircular asphalt drive curving up toward the glass entrance of a tall apartment building that, although contemporary in style, fit in perfectly with the comfortable affluence of its surroundings. I had spent a significant portion of my life in that building.

I asked Olson where he was going.

Puzzled, Olson looked back over his shoulder. "Isn't that where you live?" He jerked a thumb at the apartment building.

"No. What makes you think so?"

"Some kind of instinct, I guess." He looked sharply up at me. "To tell you the truth, I once spent some time in that building. A girlfriend of Mallon's let us stay there when she was out of town. But I swear, that's not the reason. I had this *feeling* . . ." Olson brought a hand to his forehead and peered up at me. "Usually, I'm right about stuff like this. Not this time, huh?"

I shook his head. "I lived in that building for twelve years. Moved out in 1990. That's where I wrote *The Agents of Darkness* and the three books after it. I wonder how you . . ."

"I'm not a complete fake," Olson said, appearing to be confused about some central point. "But if you moved out in 1990, why are we here?"

"I moved right across the street, to number twenty-three." I pointed at my four-story brownstone with a shining red door and two rows of clean modern windows on the upper floors. Despite the competition offered by its handsome neighbors, I had always considered it the best-looking building on Cedar Street.

"You must be doing pretty good," Olson said. "What apartment did you live in over there?"

I struggled against the impulse to conceal information from him. "Nine A. It was a nice place."

"Same apartment as the one Mallon and I borrowed from the girl. Nine A—right down at the end of the hallway."

"Now you're starting to freak me out. I first heard about the building from my wife." I took out my keys as we moved toward my red door.

"Why are you being so generous with me?" Olson asked, maddeningly. "Forget that shit about getting half of what you ask for. You didn't have to give me five hundred bucks, and for sure you don't have to let me into this house. It's not like I expect you to give me everything I want."

"Is that right?"

"I just got out of prison, man, we were never really *close* close friends, and you're gonna let me walk into this amazing house?" He tilted his head to look up at the brick facade and its rows of shining windows. "You and the Eel live here alone? With all this space?"

"We live alone."

"Only now even she isn't here."

I could not help it, I flared out. "If you're afraid to come in, go across Rush and check into the local flophouse." I pointed down the street and across the busy avenue, where a yuppie bar seemed to be supporting a sagging residence hotel for derelicts, identified by a big Jetsons-in-Miami neon sign as the Cedar Hotel.

"I'm not afraid of your *house*," Olson said. This, I understood, was almost but not quite the literal truth. "And believe me, I've stayed in that fleabag more times than you can imagine. But what the fuck do you really want from me?"

I inserted the long key into the enormous lock, then swung the red door open onto a wide vestibule with rosewood walls, a Shiraz rug, and a Chinese vase filled with fleshy-looking calla lilies. "For one thing," I said, offering the first rational thing that came to mind, "I'd like to hear about Brett Milstrap." This statement, which I had uttered without benefit of any sort of thought or consideration, startled me. If I had paused to think about it, I would have said that I had long ago forgotten the name of the second fraternity boy who had been in Spencer Mallon's adoration circle.

Infuriatingly, Olson stopped moving just before he would have walked through the door. "When am I supposed to have met Brett *Milstrap*?" Incapable of restraining himself, he looked down to the corner we had turned and retraced our steps: the conflict between his urgency to escape into the house and his reluctance to enter it froze him to the cement stoop. This was maddening to behold.

Shaking his head, Don finally walked across my threshold. For a moment he glanced into the living room, then up at the angular staircase, attempting to adjust, I supposed, to the nature of his surroundings. The staircase and the gleaming warmth of silver and polished wood in the living room probably invited and repelled him in equal measure.

"How many rooms you got in this place?"

"Twelve or fourteen, depending on how you count."

"Depending on how you count," Olson muttered, and began to place his feet on the intertwined long-stemmed tulips woven into the central runner.

"Tell me," I asked from the top of the stairs, "were your encounters with Milstrap accidental, or was he looking for you?"

"Everybody thinks I have all these answers. Which I don't, by the way."

The staircase opened into a roomlike mezzanine space furnished with a desk, a handsome leather chair, cut flowers in a straight-sided vase, and bookshelves flanking the side of the staircase in its ascent to the third floor. A dim, book-lined hallway led into the depths of the house.

"If you ever get in trouble," Olson said, "make sure your lawyer arranges house arrest."

Olson leaned against the top of the railing, narrowed his eyes, pursed his lips. A wave of goatish body stink floated from him as if misted through a secret valve.

"While you're taking a shower, I'll find you some clothes. Drop what you're wearing in the hamper. By the way, what's your shoe size?"

Olson looked down at his battered, mud-colored sneakers. "Ten and a half. Why?"

"I believe this might be your lucky day," I said.

■

Half an hour later, a renewed Donald Olson padded into the ground-floor living room with the delicacy of a cat. I gathered that as well as showering he had washed, conditioned, and mildly gelled his hair, removed his stubble, moisturized his cheeks, and in a number of other ways improved his scent and appearance. The result was amazing—Olson seemed to have transformed himself into a younger, happier, and more handsome version of himself. A portion of this effect was due to his clothing, a blue button-down shirt slightly too large for him and green khakis bunched at the waist and rolled an extra turn at the cuffs. Below the cuffs appeared a pair of lightly brogued cap-toe shoes made from what looked like soft, buttery leather, of a brown so pale they were almost yellow. Apparently impressed by these splendid shoes, Olson smiled and pointed down.

"That's hand-tooling, right?"

"If they were saddles, I guess you'd be right. You can have them."

"Man, you're giving away your *shoes?*"

"My feet went up a half size a couple of years ago. There's a box of my old shoes you can go through."

Olson fell back on the sofa and extended his arms to his sides, his legs out before him. He looked like a furniture salesman. "What comfort. And my room, man. I couldn't ask for anything nicer than that room." Legs outstretched, he lifted both of his feet and contemplated the gorgeous shoes. "Say I walked into a top-of-the-line shoe store, how much would these babies set me back?" He lowered his feet to the carpet and leaned forward, prepared to be astonished.

"How much did they cost? I don't really remember, Don."

"Give me a ballpark number."

"Three hundred." I could not remember how much the shoes had cost, but it was probably twice that.

Olson waggled a foot in the air. "I didn't know you could even wear that much money on your feet." He lowered his foot and spent a moment on a self-inspection: smoothed the fabric covering his thighs, held out his arms to regard his sleeves, ran his fingers down the row of shirt buttons. "I look like a guy with a house in the country and a flashy sports car. A *vintage* sports car—like what Meredith Bright used to drive! Remember that little red car? With that big chrome swoosh on the sides?"

"I never saw her car," I said. "I never even saw Meredith Bright."

"You really missed something, man." He guffawed. "Meredith Bright wasn't half bad, either. Back then, she looked like the most beautiful girl in the world. The most beautiful girl *possible*."

"Do you know what happened to Meredith Bright? Could you help me get in touch with her?"

"Meredith wouldn't add much to your project."

I jerked myself upright. "What is she doing now?"

"She's the wife of a senator. Before that, she was married to the CEO of a Fortune five hundred company. When they got divorced, she took him for thirty million dollars, plus an estate in Connecticut, which she sold to buy something a little bigger in Virginia or North Carolina, I forget, wherever the senator is senator from. He's a Republican. She wants him to be president."

"I'll be damned," I said.

"No, *she* will. It's like something got *into* her." He glanced at the wall beside him, then shifted his body to take it in more directly. The paintings on the wall seemed to have distracted him. They were by Eric Fischl and David Salle, who had been young art stars back when I bought the paintings. I would not have thought Don Olson would be particularly interested in them.

"Got into her back then, you mean?"

"Yeah. Before she started on her career of sucking the life out of rich guys, or whatever the hell it is she does." He shifted around on the sofa, trying to figure out a way to describe what had happened to Meredith Bright. "You know how people sometimes have a kind of internal temperature, an internal *climate*? Meredith Bright has the internal climate of a vampire. That's the best way I can say it. She makes you see the whole idea of demonic possession in a whole nother way. And we *loved* that woman, man, we were crazy about her. She's scary, man."

"I guess her husbands didn't think so."

"Millionaire senators and CEOs got different standards for a wife than other people. If the package looks really classy, they don't care if she's a zombie vampire. And this woman can pretend like a motherfucker."

"Boatman once said to me your whole group was ruined by what happened in that agronomy meadow. It looks that way to me, even though Meredith Bright is sort of a special case. Do you think you were ruined?"

"Of course I was ruined. Look at my life! I need your help to get back on my feet. I just got out of jail. It was Menard, by the way, the prison in that *Fugitive* movie. Menard Correctional Institution."

I nodded but said nothing.

Olson snapped his fingers. "That waitress at Ditka's, what was her name? Ashleigh? You know who she reminded me of? The Eel."

"I know, yes," I said. "Me too. Except Ashleigh isn't as beautiful as your friend the Eel. You should see the way she looks now."

"No offense, but she's the same age we are."

"Just wait," I said, and left the room, using a gesture that would tell a dog it would earn a treat if it sat down long enough. A few minutes later, I returned with a black-and-white photograph in a simple black frame with a foldout stand at the back. I handed it to Olson.

"This was taken about a year ago. I'd show you more, but my wife hates having her picture taken."

"Again, Lee, no offense, but . . ." Olson was leaning against the back of the sofa and holding the photograph in both hands. "Wait."

He sat up, placed the photograph on the tops of his knees, and bent over to peer at it. "Wait a second here."

Olson was shaking his head and grinning. "Here's this little gray-haired woman, but . . . it sort of sneaks up on you, doesn't it? She's amazing. Beauty like that, where does it come from?"

"Sometimes in restaurants, or on airplanes, I see these guys staring at her as if they're asking themselves, *How the hell did that happen?* Waiters fall in love with her. Cops fall in love with her. Cabdrivers fall in love with her. Baggage handlers. Doormen. Crossing guards."

"She's really . . . stunning. Once you see it, you can never miss it again. She still looks like *herself.* The gray hair doesn't matter, she has a couple of lines on her face, they don't matter. She still looks like the Eel, only she grew up into this amazing woman."

Olson was still staring down at the photograph of Lee Truax, the former Eel, her luminous face tilted up to gather or shed sunlight apparently produced from within. "Anyhow, your wife gets out and about, I gather? She does a lot of traveling? That works out okay?"

"Are you asking me about something else now, Don?"

"Well, isn't she . . . is she blind?"

"Blind as a bat," I said. "Has been for years now. It never actually slowed her down. It doesn't even get in her way very much. If she happens to need help, there's always some cabdriver, or doorman, or passing cop, to give her a hand. She could raise a dozen volunteers just by holding up that stick leaning against the chair. She calls it her distaff."

Olson shivered. "Really?"

"Yeah. Why?"

"A distaff is supposed to be this harmless thing you wind wool around, but . . . Oh, never mind. Now, I guess, it just refers to things connected to women. You knew that."

"Of course. I'm sure it's a reference to something she saw back in the meadow. That's why she went blind, you know—because of something she saw. Or because of *everything* she saw. It happened gradually. Over about ten years—roughly 1980 to 1990. She said it was being kind to her, taking so long to become complete."

"*I* saw a distaff," Don said, a little reluctantly. "On that day. Just for a second."

He pushed himself up from the sofa and moved to the windows at the front of the house. Hands in the pockets of the khakis, he bent forward and looked out at Cedar Street. "You got anything to drink here, by the way? Been a long time since lunch."

"Follow me," I said, and brought him back into the kitchen. Last in the row of gleaming cabinetry, down from the refrigerator and immediately above the glass-fronted wine fridge, the liquor cabinet contained dozens of bottles arrayed in ranks.

"And a very merry Christmas to you, too," Olson said. "Do I see some fancy-schmancy tequila back there?"

I poured him a juicy, cognac-like tequila and gave myself a beer. It was a few minutes past six, at least an hour before I would ordinarily permit himself to take alcohol. At a level not quite conscious, I supposed that Don Olson would be more forthcoming if he put away some tequila.

We carried our drinks to the slab of the kitchen table and sat facing each other, as my wife and I usually did. Olson gulped tequila, swished it around in his mouth, swallowed, smacked his lips in appreciation, and said, "Hey, it's not like I want to be ungrateful or anything, but I feel like an imposter in these clothes, man. Blue button-down shirts and khakis might be a great look for you, Lee, but my own personal style is a little edgier, I guess you could say."

"You'd like some new clothes."

"That's what I'm saying, basically."

"We could go to a couple places down on Michigan Avenue. No reason you should feel uncomfortable."

"Man . . . you're like a saint. No wonder the Eel married you."

I let that one go, irritating though it was.

■

On we talked, and later went shopping and had a simple dinner of fish and pasta and talked some more, and I had the odd thought that I was becoming better friends with the former Dilly than we had been in the years when we had seen each other every day.

Olson's abrupt departure on the evening of October 16, 1966, had felt like a wound, all the more painful for being so absolute. There had been something about a rising tide, apparently, but I had assumed this vague prediction to apply to Boats. Unexpectedly, Boats had been left behind, reeling with shock and loss like the rest of the survivors. According to three eyewitnesses, Meredith Bright had bounded harelike through the scraps of orange-yellow fog drifting across the meadow, scramming back into the safety of what we assumed to be her privileged life. At least, her disappearance made sense of a kind. Hootie was another matter. Howard Bly, like us a child of West Madison, had vanished into a world at once eerily utterly unknown and dreadful to contemplate.

This history, and more, formed the substance of the endless conversation between Donald Olson and myself that went for days on Cedar Street. I knew perfectly well that nothing was stopping me from disappearing into my office five or six hours a day, and that I was taking a deliberate break from work (something my wife had only rarely succeeded in getting me to do), yet I could tell myself that spending time with Olson amounted to research of a kind. And it was somehow as though my wife had given me permission to poke around in the only locked room in our marriage—the only one I knew about, anyhow.

On the fourth evening of his stay, Don Olson gave striking corroboration to her conviction that Keith Hayward was a dangerous character. What Don said about Hayward also backed up Detective Cooper's theory that the murdered boy was related to the Milwaukee villain known as the Ladykiller.

"Hootie and your wife used to tell Spencer that Hayward was even worse than he imagined, which was pretty funny anyhow, because how did they know *what* he thought? Besides, they were only going on impressions and intuitions."

"But you had some kind of proof?" I asked.

"Well, it wasn't proof, but it looked crazy enough to spook me."

"What was it?"

"A place, a special place Hayward set up. I wandered into an antiwar rally behind the library and saw him mooching around, trying to pick up girls. He wasn't getting anywhere, let's put it that way. Every girl he went up to shot him down. After he struck out four or five times, he got pissed off. Even that tells you a lot about the guy, doesn't it? He didn't get depressed, he didn't get unhappy, he got angry."

"The girls refused to follow his script."

"That's right. And he *changed*—his face got tight, and his eyes shrank. He looked around to see if anybody was watching him. Never saw me, thank God, because I'd parked myself in a pretty inconspicuous spot. I could tell he had some kind of secret. So when he took off up State Street, I just puttered along behind him.

"The guy marched straight up to Henry Street, where he turned left and zoomed on by the Plaza Bar and right into this vacant lot that had three old sheds, like small garages, at the far end. As soon as he stepped into the lot, he pulled his big ball of keys out of his pocket, and he let himself into the last little shed. Even back where I was, I could hear him slam the door and lock it. Then I waited a couple of seconds and hustled across the lot to look into the little windows in the door."

I had some ideas about Hayward's idea of amusement, but I asked, "What was he doing?"

"Talking to a knife, that's what he was doing," Don said. "And singing to it. *Singing.* He was standing in front of a table, picking up this big knife, kind of fondling it, and putting it back down. The whole deal struck me as really creepy. Who sings to a knife? In a locked shed?"

"Hayward was a disturbed guy, that's for sure. I've been looking through some . . . No, I can't talk about it yet."

"Hey, Chief, that's up to you." Don slumped in his chair and pushed aside his plate. We had lingered at the irregular slab of dark-gray stone that served as the kitchen table. "Is it too late for a nightcap?"

"You know where the bottles are."

Olson slid out of his chair and began to move toward the liquor cabinet.

"Oh, hell," I said. "Get me another beer out of the fridge, will you?" I felt an underlying heaviness tugging at my voice.

"You got it."

Olson handed me a beer and sat down again. His story had excited him, and he would be damned if he would go to bed: Donald Olson was still only a few days out of jail, he was dressed in new clothes, and he had his mitt around a glass of the finest tequila he had ever tasted.

"How's the Eel?"

"Excuse me?"

"Is her conference going well? Or whatever it is?"

"It is, yes. In fact, she told me she's going to stay in Washington for another week. There's plenty for her to do there."

"She knows I'm here?"

"Yes. You can stay a while longer, if you like. There are a few ideas I want to explore, a couple of things I'd like to suggest."

"Okay. And here's some actual good news I was saving up. From now on I won't have to sponge off you anymore."

"You scared up some money? How'd you do that?"

"Called in a few favors. Maybe you could give me a hand setting up a new bank account, arranging for a checkbook, stuff like that?"

"How much are we talking about?"

"If you really want to know, five K."

"You raised five thousand dollars with a couple of phone calls?"

"A little more, actually. If you like, I can pay back your five hundred."

"Maybe later," I said, still amazed. "In the meantime, let's get you down to the bank tomorrow, deposit that money."

■

The next morning, I walked Olson to the Oak Bank and used my long acquaintanceship with its officers to ease the process of setting up a checking account in the amount of $5,500 for my houseguest. Three separate checks had been made out by persons I'd never heard of: Arthur Steadham ($1,000), Felicity Chan ($1,500), and Meredith Walsh ($2,500). Olson wound up with a temporary checkbook and five hundred dollars in cash. When I declined to accept any money, Don tucked half of the debt into my breast pocket.

I thought Olson would write checks until they started to bounce. The credit card company was going to get burned, because Don would see the card as nothing more than cash in instantly available form. To establish credit, he would pay his first month's bill. After that, everything was uncertain.

Feeling like the midwife to a criminal career, I accepted Don's offer to buy me lunch at Big Bowl, the Chinese restaurant near the corner of Cedar and Rush. After we ordered, Olson surprised me. "You're going to ask me to drive to Madison and visit Hootie Bly with you, aren't you?"

The chopsticks nearly jittered out of my hand.

"Let me go you one better. How would you like to talk to Meredith Bright? Meredith Bingham Walsh, as she is now."

"What are you saying?"

"If you're interested, I can probably arrange for you to meet Meredith. Hootie isn't going to say anything that makes sense, but Mrs. Walsh might give you something useful. I don't know, I'm just guessing here."

"The vampire married to the senator? How can you do that?"

"It's a long story," Don said. "I think I amuse her. She sent me one of those checks." He watched me as he sliced a soup dumpling in half and lifted one of the halves out of the bowl. "I guess you're really *into* finding out what happened out there in that meadow. It's like you think everyone saw the same thing, like all of us had the same experience. Is that what you think?"

"I guess I did, yes. Once. But not anymore."

"What changed your mind?"

"A couple of years ago, I ran into Boats on the sidewalk outside the Pfister. This was even before I started getting interested in the Ladykiller." An extremely specific memory returned to me. "He was carrying a suitcase. *Uh-oh,* I said to myself. *He's really still at it.* That suitcase probably had a lot of other people's cash and other people's jewelry inside it. Plus whatever else he felt like stealing."

"You gotta give him this," Don said. "Man has a hell of a work ethic."

"Seen one way, I guess. Anyhow, we recognized each other and he felt like talking, so we went inside and sat in that lobby bar, that lounge. With the big tables, and all the staircases? I thought he'd be nervous, but he said it was actually a very safe place for him to spend the next half hour or so."

Olson laughed, and said, "Good plan."

"So we were sitting there, just talking like two normal guys, and I realized that he might actually tell me something about that day. Back then, he barely even looked at me in the hallways. Hootie was in the bin. Lee refused to say anything. And you were off God knows where."

"Right down the street, at least for a while."

"Anyhow, when we were in the Pfister's lounge, I brought it up. 'Didn't you talk about this with your wife?' he asked, and I said, 'Well, I tried.' 'No way, huh?' he said. Then he said that a lot of time had passed, and he might be able to tell me something. 'It was horrible, though,' he told me. And he said you were the only other person he had ever spoken of this with."

Olson nodded. "Four, five years ago, in Madison. He has a little hideout there, a crummy room near the stadium, and he just waited for me to come through town. We got together after one of my initial meetings with the students, like that one you didn't go to at La Bella Capri. He was shook up—couldn't get it out of his mind. That picture."

"A tower of dead children, he said. With little arms and legs sticking out."

"And some heads, too. Did he cry, when you were talking?"

"He cried with you, too?"

Olson nodded. "It was when he tried to tell me that most of the dead kids were sort of folded over. 'Like tacos,' he said. And after that, he couldn't keep it together anymore."

"Amazing. That's just what happened with me. 'Like tacos,' and boom, he's in tears, he's shaking, he can't say another word for about five minutes, he just keeps making these 'I'm sorry' gestures with his hands."

"Hell of a thing to see," Don said. "But he didn't see much else."

"No. Just a big tower made of dead children. And a lot of blinding red-orange light, light the color of Kool-Aid, streaming in."

"That's what I said to *him*! He's such a thief, he steals other people's words. Anyhow, that light was really foul. Streamed in on us like through some crack in the world. One of the worst smells ever. I'm sure we all went through that. Unfortunately for you, I never managed to see a lot. There was one thing, though."

"Yes?"

"Well, two things, actually. The first one was this dog, standing up inside a little room with a rolltop desk. He was wearing a dark-brown suit, two-tone shoes, and a bow tie. You know how guys with bow ties can sometimes give you this *look*, like you just farted and they hope you'll go away before they have to ask you to leave? Pity and contempt. That's the way he was looking at me."

"Oh, that poster," I said.

"No, not that poster Eel's dad gave her. He wasn't anything like those dogs. He wasn't cute, not at all. This guy was sorry to see me, and he wanted me to go away."

"But there was something else, too."

"Jesus, have a little patience, will you? I'm getting to it. Mallon grabbed me by the elbow and yanked me away, but just before he pulled on my arm I saw that the dog was trying to hide something from me—things I was not supposed to see. These things were more like men, but bright, almost shiny, as if they were made of mercury or something. And they scared the shit out of me. One of them was a woman, not a man, a woman like a queen, and she had this stick in her hand, and I knew that the stick was called a distaff. How I knew I had no idea, but that's what the thing was called. The whole thing scared the shit out of me. It terrified me. No, it *horrified* me, it filled me with *horror*. If Spencer hadn't yanked me sideways, I would never have been able to move."

"You told this to Boats, didn't you?"

"Yeah. He was a lot more interested in his dead children. He asked me if I thought it could have been real. I said, 'It was probably real somewhere, Jason.'"

■

That evening we made several necessary telephone calls, and after that secured reservations at the Concourse Hotel. The following morning, we drove 150 miles north to Madison. For 140 of those miles, we were on I-90 West, for most of our journey a highway with little to recommend it but simplicity and ease of use. Exits for villages and small towns, mileage signs, and billboards appeared, but the towns themselves did not, nor did the restaurants, motels, and roadside attractions advertised in the billboards. From the highway nothing was visible but the few farmhouses and fewer hills that punctuated a wide, flat landscape of fields and trees. For long stretches, three or four cars moving in a huddle fifty yards ahead were the only other vehicles in sight.

Don Olson said, "Slow down, damn it. You're scaring me."

The speedometer revealed that I had been stepping along at eighty-eight miles per hour. "Sorry." I took my foot off the accelerator. "It snuck up on me."

Olson caressed the top of the dashboard with a bony hand. "Man, everything you have is beautiful, isn't it? Me, I got nothing at all. That's fine with me, by the way. I had your stuff, I'd be worried sick about trying to protect it."

"You'd adjust after a while."

"How fast does this old baby go, anyhow?"

"Around two o'clock one night, I was all alone on the highway. Bombed out of my skull. I got it up to a hundred and thirty. Then *I* got scared. That was the last time I ever did anything like that."

"You hit a hundred and thirty when you were drunk at two in the morning?"

"Stupid, I know."

"It also sounds very, very unhappy, man."

"Well," I said, and offered no more.

"Spencer used to say, everybody runs around looking for happiness when they ought to seek joy."

"You have to earn joy," I said.

"I've known joy. Long time ago." Olson laughed. "Spencer once told me the only time he experienced absolute joy was in the meadow, just before everything exploded."

Olson was still sitting sideways, facing me, one leg drawn up onto the car seat, almost grinning.

"This is out of left field, I know."

"All right," Olson said.

"Did you ever sleep with Lee when we were all back in high school?"

"With the Eel?" Laughing, Olson held up his right hand, palm out, as if taking an oath. "For God's sake, no. Me and Boats and Hootie, we were all madly in love with Meredith Bright. Give me a break, man. You'd have to be a rat to go after another guy's girlfriend. I had more principles than that. Anyhow, I always thought you and the Eel were doing it on a daily basis, more or less."

I must have displayed rubber-faced amazement. "I didn't think anybody knew that."

"I didn't *know* it . . . but I sure had the feeling that, you know."

"We tried so hard to—"

"It worked, man. Nobody in our school knew that you and the Eel were having more sex than the rest of us combined, faculty included."

That was probably true, I supposed. Lee Truax and I had progressed to actual intercourse on our fourth (or according to her, our fifth) get-together—encounters too informal to be called dates. At a party during our freshman year, we, by then long an informal couple, had wandered into an empty bedroom and followed our history of kisses, touches, partial disrobings and revelations, to its natural conclusion. We were stunningly, amazingly lucky. Our first experiences of sex were almost totally pleasurable. Within weeks, the mutual discovery of her clitoris led to her first orgasm. (Later, we referred to this day, October 25, as "the Fourth of July.") And we knew from the first that this miracle depended for its survival upon silence and secrecy.

At times, as our erotic life receded over the course of our long marriage, I permitted myself to speculate that my far-wandering wife may have taken a number of lovers. I forgave her for the pain this possibility caused me, for I knew that I, not she, had inflicted most of the heavy-duty damage on our marriage. When we were in our mid-twenties, Lee had mysteriously left me, demanding "space" and "time by myself." Two months later she reappeared, without explanation of where she had been or what she had done. She said she loved and needed me. The Eel had *chosen* me again.

And then . . . ten years later, my prolonged, on-and-off infidelity with the brilliant young woman who had agented *The Agents of Darkness* and thereby permanently changed my life had, I now thought, broken my marriage. That, that was what did it. The affair went on too long; or it should never have ended. Maybe I should have divorced Lee and married the agent. In my world, such recombinations happened all the time: men were forever leaving their wives and trading up, then divorcing and trading up again—editors, authors, publicists, publishing executives, foreign rights people, agents, all in a perpetual roundelay. I had been, however, too stubborn to leave my wife. How could I compound the betrayal I had already committed? That single act would have turned us into clichés—an abandoned wife, a newly successful man who had dumped his longtime spouse for the sexy younger woman who had aided that success. It was impossible that we should become such cartoons.

Yet the essence of our marriage had been broken.

Or maybe, I thought, this was the essence of our marriage: that we had come through so much pain, not just then but other times, too, and managed to stay together and love each other in a tougher, deeper way.

At the worst times, though, I wondered if our marriage had not been broken from the beginning, or from near the beginning, probably around the time I was pretending to be a scholar and Lee Truax tended bar in the East Village. Well, no, that was out of the question. One of the reasons I cherished Lee Truax was that she had stuck with me, she had hung in there.

Madison and Milwaukee

In spite of everything, it always feels good to get back to Madison," Olson said.

"I haven't been here for thirty years," I said. "Lee has, though. A couple of times. Apparently, it's changed a lot. Really good restaurants, a jazz club, whatever."

At the intersection of Wisconsin and West Dayton Street, I stopped at a red light and put on my turn signal. Down West Dayton, I thought I could make out the entrances to the hotel and its garage.

The light turned green. I swung the big car around the corner and aimed for the entrance to the garage. "Hey, did I bring that book I signed for Hootie?"

"Do you know how boring it is to answer the same question over and over?"

"I asked you that before?"

"Twice," Olson said. "You must be even more nervous than I am."

■

After we checked into our rooms on the fourteenth floor and unpacked, I called the Lamont Hospital and spoke to the staff psychiatrist with whom I had spoken that morning. Dr. Greengrass said things still looked good. "All I can say is, keep things on an even keel and everything ought to be fine. It's remarkable, but Howard has been showing us some fine progress over the past eight or nine months. Despite all these years he's been in our community, I might almost say . . . Of course, with his family all gone, and no friends on the outside except yourself and Mr. Olson, his situation isn't likely to change all that much, is it?"

Although I was not precisely sure what the doctor was talking about, I agreed. "He's been showing progress?"

His laughter surprised me. "For most of the time he's been in our facility, Howard has had very specific language sources. I wasn't around in those days, but from the case notes made soon after his admission in 1966, it seems all of his vocabulary came from some extraordinary dictionary."

"Captain Fountain. Good God. I'd almost forgotten about that."

"As you will appreciate, the decision to limit himself to a particularly obscure vocabulary represented a means of controlling the terror that brought him to us. His parents felt they had to consign him to medical supervision. From what I gather, they made the right decision. Most of the people working here, medical staff and attendants, had no idea what he was saying ninety percent of the time. You have to add to this that to keep him from being a risk to himself and the other patients Mr. Bly needed to be heavily medicated. We're talking about the period from his year of intake, 1966, to about 1983, roughly. At that time, the doctor in charge of his case judged him ready for a reduction in medication, which in any case had become far more sophisticated. The results were quite gratifying."

"He began to talk? To use a standard vocabulary?" For several reasons, that would have been extremely good news.

"Not exactly. After the adjustment in his medication, Mr. Bly began to speak in long, beautifully formed sentences and paragraphs, bits of dialogue, and so forth. We eventually discovered that almost everything he said came from the Hawthorne novel *The Scarlet Letter.* Captain Fountain provided the remainder."

"He used to quote from *The Scarlet Letter* back in high school," I said.

"Does he remember everything he reads?"

"Yes. I think he does."

"I ask because he seems to have added a book he just finished reading. It was lying on a table in the Game Room. A kind of a romance novel, or maybe what is called a gothic. *The Moondreamers,* I think. By L. Shelby Austin?"

"Never heard of it," I said.

"Neither had I, but it's had an excellent effect on your friend. Howard's become much more expressive."

"Does he know we're coming?"

"Oh, yes. He's very excited. Very nervous, too. After all, Howard hasn't had a visitor for thirty-one years. This morning, he spent hours deciding what to wear for you. And it's not like he has much of a wardrobe! When I asked him how he felt, he said, 'Anabiotic.' "

"The Captain."

"Fortunately, when Howard was admitted, his mother included his copy of Captain Fountain's book in his box of belongings. She thought we would find it useful. To say that we did would be to understate. For a long time, it was the only way we had to understand him. Over the years, the book now and again vanished from view, but it always resurfaced. I keep it in my desk now, so it won't get lost. Do you know the word *anabiotic*?"

"Never heard it before."

"It's an adjective, of course, and as nearly as I remember, it means 'thought to be dead, but capable of being brought back to life.' Your visit means a lot to Howard."

■

Unfamiliar with mental wards, I had been imagining some Gothic stone pile from a Hammer film, and when the sturdy brick facade of the Lamont Hospital came into view at the end of a winding drive my first reaction was relief. Four stories high and comfortably broad, the building suggested warmth, competence, and security. Rows of handsome windows in ornamental embrasures looked out upon a wide expanse of parkland threaded with paths and green cast-iron benches. "Do you think this place can actually be as nice on the inside as it is on the outside?" I asked.

"Don't hold your breath," Olson said.

Inside, a short flight of marble steps led up to a well-lighted hallway lined with shining pebble-dash windows set into massive black doors. I had been expecting a desk and a receptionist, and I spun around, reading the black legends hand-lettered on the windows. ACCOUNTING. BUSINESS. RECORDS.

Seeming muted by his institutional surroundings, Don Olson caught my eye and wordlessly pointed out the door marked ADMISSION & RECEPTION. "Thanks," I said, to break the silence.

Unwilling to be point man, Olson inclined his head toward the door.

Inside, four plastic chairs against a pale blue wall faced a long white counter where papers had been clamped into clipboards with ballpoint pens awkwardly attached on lengths of hairy string. A stout woman with bangs and thick glasses looked up at us from a desk behind the counter. Before I reached her, she turned away to say something to a pretty, sharp-featured South Asian woman, Ceylonese or Indian, who promptly stood up and vanished through a door at the rear of the office. Next to the door hung a large framed photograph of a red barn in a yellow field. The barn looked as though it had not been used in a long while.

"Are you the people for Dr. Greengrass, or is one of you our new admission?" she asked, flicking her eyes to Don Olson.

"We're here for Dr. Greengrass," I said.

"And you're here about Mr. Bly. Howard."

"That's right," I said, marveling at how much information Dr. Greengrass shared with his staff.

She beamed. "We all love Howard."

The pretty Asian woman came back through the door with a thick manila file in her hand. "Don't we all love Howard, Pargeeta?"

Pargeeta gave me a questioning glance. "Oh, we're all crazy about the guy." She sat down and peered at her monitor, excluding everybody.

Undaunted, her companion reached up to push one of the clipboards toward me. "While I inform Dr. Greengrass you're here, please take the time to fill out and sign these liability forms. Howard is so excited about your visit! He couldn't figure out what to wear, it was such a big deal for him. I let him borrow one of my husband's shirts, and it fit him perfectly. So compliment him on his shirt."

I signed the form without reading it and passed the clipboard to Don Olson, who flipped to a fresh page and did the same.

"Now please take a seat against the wall, and I'll call the doctor."

We sat down and watched her make the call. Pargeeta frowned at her computer monitor and flicked a few keys.

"Are you two in Howard's extended family?" the woman asked them.

"In a way," I said.

"He was so cute, the way he asked me to help him. He said, 'Mirabelle turned to him and asked, "John, is that a new shirt? I love seeing you in new things." ' "

"That was from this *Moondreamers* novel?"

"You can always tell when Howard falls in love with a new book. It's the only thing he'll quote from for a long, long time."

Pargeeta sighed and stood up again. She vanished through the door next to the picture of the abandoned barn.

"Nice photograph," I said.

"Thank you! One of our patients took that picture." A wistful expression crossed her face. "A few days after the photo went up, she killed herself!

The poor woman told Dr. Greengrass that when she saw her picture hanging in here, she realized nobody in the whole wide world had ever understood her and nobody ever would. He raised her medication, but not by enough, is what Pargeeta said. Not that she's an expert."

I could think of nothing to say to this.

During this moment of subtly charged silence, a man in clear plastic eyeglasses and a coat as white as his hair burst through the door at the back of the office. He was rubbing his hands together, grinning, and glancing from me to Olson and back again. Pargeeta came through a couple of seconds later.

"Well, well, this is a fine day, welcome, gentlemen, welcome. You are, I take it, Mr. Harwell and Mr. Olson? Of course you are. All of us here are very pleased to see you." He came around the end of the white counter, still trying to make up his mind. In the end, he made the right guess and reached for my hand.

"In your case, Mr. Harwell, it is a special pleasure. I am a great admirer, a *great* admirer."

This probably meant, I knew, that he had read *The Agents of Darkness.* My real fans tended to say things like "My wife and I read *The Blue Mountain* out loud to each other." It was always rewarding to hear from someone who had enjoyed something I'd written, however, and such is my disposition that praise seldom seems misplaced.

I thanked the doctor.

"And you must be Mr. Olson." He grasped Don's hand. "Also a pleasure. So you knew Howard well, back in the sixties?"

From behind the counter came Pargeeta's dry, sardonic voice. "In case you hadn't guessed, this is Dr. Charles Greengrass, our chief of psychiatry and chief of staff."

He whirled to stare at her. "I didn't introduce myself? Really?"

Pargeeta swung herself into her chair with the economy of a dancer.

She glanced up at Greengrass for a moment only. "They knew who you were, Charlie."

I caught myself beginning to speculate about the relationship between this young woman and Dr. Greengrass and declined to go any further than I already had.

"Gentlemen, forgive me, please. As Miss Parmendera reminds us, this is indeed an exciting moment. Very shortly, we will be going up to the ward to visit Howard, but first I would like to have a little chat with the two of you in my office. Would that be satisfactory?"

"Of course," I said.

"This way, then." He turned away and led us back into the wide corridor with its shining lights and black doors. Before passing out of the office, I glanced over my shoulder and saw Pargeeta monitoring our departure with a smoky, sardonic eye. The woman beside her, who had been quivering with silent laughter, instantly froze into immobility. I closed the door, then hurried a little to catch up with the other two.

"Pargeeta Parmendera?" Olson was asking.

"Exactly."

"Where's she from?"

"Right here in Madison."

"I mean, what's her background? What is she?"

"You're asking about her ethnicity? Her father is an Indian, and I believe her mother is Vietnamese. They came to Wisconsin in the seventies and met as graduate students."

At the end of the wide corridor, he opened a door labeled PSY-CHIATRY.

"The Parmenderas lived next to us for many years. When my children were small, we often used Pargeeta as our babysitter. Wonderful girl, very adaptable."

"And the other woman, the one with bangs?"

"Oh, sure, that's my wife," Greengrass said. "She comes in whenever poor Myrtle can't get out of bed in the morning." He ushered us into a space similar to the reception office where a wide, extremely ample woman in her forties, her cheeks creased into dimples, smiled up at us from a desk that seemed far too small for her. She wore a shapeless teepee-like dress in a pattern of pink roses, and when she smiled her dimples looked aggressive.

"I'll be in my office for a minute, Harriet. Please hold my calls."

"All right, Doctor. Are these Howard's visitors?"

"Yes, they are."

"We just love Howard," said Harriet, her dimples growing even deeper. "He's what I call a real gentleman."

"Ah," I said.

"In here, please." Greengrass had opened a door behind Harriet's desk.

The doctor waved us to the near side of an oval wooden table with a bowl of peppermint candies placed equidistant from two padded chairs. He took a rocking chair on the table's other side. "Well," he said. "As you have seen, all of us in this institution hold Howard Bly in a good deal of affection."

"So it seems," I said.

"He's our oldest patient, not in years, mind, some of our people are in their eighties now, but in the length of his confinement here. He has seen them come and go, has Howard, and through many, many changes of staff, changes in leadership, he has remained the same sweet, good-hearted fellow you will meet today."

The doctor looked upward for a moment and steepled his fingers before him, as if praying. A tiny, reluctant smile tugged at his lips. "Not that he hasn't had his moments. Yes. We have seen Howard very fearful. On two or three occasions, quite aggressive. He seems in particular to fear dogs. One might call it a phobia. Cynophobia, to be exact. Not that such terms are very helpful. I prefer to think of it as a panic disorder. Thankfully, we have techniques for treating panic disorders. Howard's phobic reaction to dogs has moderated significantly over the past decade."

"You allow dogs in this hospital?" I asked. "Do they wander through the mental wards?"

Dr. Greengrass regarded me over his steepled fingers. "Like many institutions of our kind, we have had excellent results with animal companion therapy. At certain hours, dogs and cats are permitted in certain areas. An animal companion, combined with more conventional therapies, can be quite helpful in bringing people out of themselves."

He smiled at us and gave his head a little shake, conceding a point long ago abandoned. "Howard has refused all offers of an animal companion. Once, before I came here, he attacked an attendant who led a dog into the common room. These days, dogs are not permitted in the common room, and Howard can meander around in there perfectly safely. There have been incidents, however . . ."

Dr. Greengrass bent over his desk and lowered his voice. "Incidents in which Howard happened to find himself in the same quarters as a man with a canine animal companion. No one to blame. Simply strolled in, probably with an open book in his hands, and there it was, right in front of him. A man petting a dog. Result? A high-pitched noise of distress, and immediate flight back to his room, where he closes his door and lies on his bed, trembling. But for Howard's, well, terror is not an inaccurate word, but for his *terror,* he would have been released into a group home five or six years ago. I should tell you that he has refused even to consider the possibility that he will ever leave this hospital."

The doctor gave us a look of absolutely impersonal and scientific curiosity. "You are his first visitors in three decades. Can you help explain what I have just described to you? To put it simply, what *happened* to Howard Bly?"

"It's hard to describe," Olson said, glancing at me. "Along with a few other people, we, a few of us, did something in a meadow. A kind of a rite. A ceremony. Everything became dark, confusing, scary. A boy died. Whatever Hootie—Howard—saw, it frightened him very badly. Maybe a dog, or something that looked like a dog, attacked the boy. I was there, but I didn't see that happen."

"Something that looked like a dog?" asked Greengrass. "What do you mean, a wolf? Something unnatural?"

"You got me," Don said.

"We have files, we keep records. We are aware of the Spencer Mallon incident. It appears that your group succumbed to a mass hysteria. A shared delusion. Howard Bly has been living with the consequences of that delusion for all of his adult life. He has been showing us real improvement, but I would still like to know more about the origins of his pathology."

"We would, too," I said.

"Good. I was hoping to hear from you, Mr. Harwell. Can you offer me any information concerning the root of this patient's drastic panic response to dogs?"

I thought for a second. If there was a root cause, it would have to be that silly painting of poker-playing dogs the Eel's father had brought home one night from a Glasshouse Street bar. But of course, the painting was not the cause. The painting had been no more than a convenience for the terrible circus Mallon had awakened or brought into being.

"Nothing concrete. As yet."

"So you are working on this matter, this enigma."

"It's more like a personal compulsion. It feels like I just simply have to know what actually happened out there. I think it would be beneficial to all of us."

The doctor considered him. "Will you share with me any insights or new information that comes to you in your conversations with my patient?"

I nodded. "If I have anything to share."

"Of course." Dr. Greengrass turned to Don Olson. "Maybe you can answer this question for me. Twice, the first time a number of years ago and the second yesterday, Howard said to me, 'Words create freedom, too, and I think it is words that will save me.' Very striking, I thought, since in a sense it is words that have imprisoned him. Do you have any idea what he was quoting from?"

"It's not from a book. Spencer Mallon told him that, three or four days before the big ceremony."

"Like most oracles, Mr. Mallon apparently spoke in riddles." Dr. Greengrass shook his head. "No offense, but what occurs to me is the phrase 'the bottom of the barrel.' "

Don said nothing. The only part of his face that changed were his eyes.

"Well, now," Dr. Greengrass said. "Let's find your friend, shall we?"

He conducted us into the hall and up a wide flight of stairs. At the second floor we continued on up to the third, where Dr. Greengrass pushed open a set of swinging doors and led us into a combination of office and antechamber. Behind a narrow desk that held only a transistor radio, a buzz-cut man in a short-sleeved white jacket that showed off his bulging arms reached out to switch off a talk show. As we came into the anteroom, he stood up and tugged at the hem of his jacket.

"D-Doctor," he said. "We been w-w-waitin' for you." From a man so physical, the stutter came as a surprise. The attendant took a moment to inspect us. "The two of you are Howard's old friends?"

"Uh-huh," I said.

"D-Don't look m-much like him, d-do you?" He grinned and stuck out a giant hand. "My name's Ant-Ant-Antonio. Thought I'd sort of greet you here. I take g-good care of Howard. Him and me get along fine."

"All right, Antonio," said Dr. Greengrass. "Where is he?"

"C-Common Room, last time I saw him. He'll still b-be there."

The doctor took a fat key ring from his trouser pocket and opened the stout black door next to the little desk.

"I'll c-come in with you," said Antonio. "Maybe I'll . . . Who knows? Howard's b-been kinda emotional lately."

With the attendant following along, we trooped into a long, bright corridor hung with photographs and clumsy paintings on either side of two long bulletin boards blanketed in announcements and flyers. On the left side of the corridor, a series of doors punctuated the artwork. Dr. Greengrass opened the single door on the corridor's right side, which said PATIENT FACILITIES. At the side of a little lounge decorated with framed drawings, another door admitted them to a colorful room nearly the size of a gymnasium that was divided into separate areas by game tables and groupings of sofas and chairs. Other chairs and benches lined the walls. The cheerful colors of the walls and the pattern on the carpet made the room feel like a preschool.

Thirty to forty men and women of widely varying ages sat on the furniture or played checkers at the game tables. One older man was assembling a giant jigsaw puzzle with great concentration. Only a few of the patients looked up to see who had come in.

"Dr. Greengrass," said a tall, smiling blond man with biceps as prominent as Antonio's. He had evidently been waiting beside the door. "We're ready for you and your guests."

"Oh, yes," said Antonio. "Yes, we are."

"This is Max," Greengrass said. "He has spent a good deal of time with your old friend."

"Let's get over there," Max said. "He's pretty eager."

"Where is he?" asked Don, scanning the room. No one before them looked anything like Howard Bly, and none of them looked eager. They might have been filling in the time before lunch at a mediocre resort. Some of them wore pajamas, the rest ordinary clothing: khakis, jeans, dresses, shirts.

"Back there in the corner," said Max, pointing with his thumb.

"Stay here, Antonio," said Dr. Greengrass. "We don't want to alarm him."

With ill grace, Antonio consented, and twirled away to park himself on an overstuffed chair.

Max and the doctor led us through the Common Room, and a low bubble of conversation trailed along through the nests of furniture. When we rounded a wide, bright blue pillar near the far end of the room, Max and Dr. Greengrass parted to reveal a bald, round-faced man leaning forward on the edge of a worn blue armchair. He was clenching his hands over a substantial belly and a plaid shirt slightly strained at the buttons. The round face seemed curiously innocent and untouched. This man did not look anything liked Hootie Bly, but his eagerness could not be questioned.

"Howard, say hello to your friends," said the doctor.

Nodding, the old man glanced from face to face and back again. The baffled expression in his eyes made me feel that we had made a mistake, that this poor old duffer should have been left in peace. Then the duffer broke into an ecstatic smile, nodded rapidly, and did an odd thing with his hands, spreading them wide, then bringing them close together. "Dill!"

"Hi, Hootie," Olson said.

Dr. Greengrass whispered, "He's telling you that he's pulling the word from a longer sentence. He does it to save time."

I watched the man in the armchair turn his rapturous gaze upon me and knew with absolute certainty that we had done the right thing. Again, the fat old man did the strange thing with his hands, isolating a word within a preexisting sentence.

"Twin!" he cried. "Oh, *Twin!*"

He pushed himself upright and on the spot revealed, at least to me, that he was indeed Hootie Bly: the shine in his eyes, the shape of his shoulders, the way he held his right hand at his waist while dropping the left. A complex mixture of happiness and sorrow brought tears to my eyes.

Hootie stepped forward, and, uncertain, we moved nearer to him, too. For a moment both awkward and overflowing with emotion, Don and I each clasped one of Hootie's hands. For a moment, Howard quoted something indistinct about Aunt Betsy declaiming that this was a fine, fine day. Then he threw his arms around Don and rocked back and forth for a couple of seconds. Tears spilling from his eyes, Howard turned to hug me in the same way, rocking with glee.

Hootie let go of me, wiped his hands over his shiny face and, eyes glowing, spoke directly to me. "*Skylark, have you anything to say to me?*"

I glanced at Dr. Greengrass, who raised his hands in a shrug.

Don Olson said, "I guess you didn't know. One day, Mallon told the Eel she was his skylark."

The moment he said the word, I was pierced by the bright, sudden memory of a skylark my wife and I had seen soaring above the garden of a pub in North London.

meredith
bright walsh

Don Olson and I occupied a side table in the Governor's Lounge on the twelfth floor of the Concourse. A delicate-looking young man and an athletic young woman, both blond and uniformed in white shirts and bow ties, were settling trays of hors d'oeuvres into pans on a long table against the wall. Bored as a goldfish in a goldfish bowl, a bartender in a brocade vest drifted to the far side of his circular domain. A fresh margarita sat on a white square of napkin before Olson, a glass of sauvignon blanc before me. At a few minutes before 6:00 p.m., the hotel's shadow fell across the half-empty streets that lay between it and Lake Monona. A shadow had fallen on us, too. We had a lot to think about.

■

The decision to accompany Howard Bly on a stroll through the hospital's grounds had not resulted in the conversation I had hoped would unfold along the curving paths. Instead, our excursion had ended in a messy scramble back to the ward—a disaster that would have resulted in the immediate expulsion and permanent removal of Mr. Bly's two old friends from the hospital, but for his startling last-minute intercession. It had been an awkward couple of minutes or so. Hootie began shouting from the moment he burst into the hospital's rear entrance and felt safe.

Dr. Greengrass exploded from his office yelling for the attendants, who promptly smothered the patient with their bodies, as if his clothing had combusted in the sunlight. "What triggered this?" Greengrass bellowed. "What did you do to him?"

Thrashing on the cold floor, Hootie bawled nuggets from Captain Fountain's treasure chest. "Recumbentibus! Recusant! Regardution! Reddition! Redibition!"

"The two of you have undone twenty years of progress!" Greengrass's voice blared over Howard's outcries. "I want you out of here! Visitor privileges are revoked. Permanently and irrevocably."

Olson and I stepped back toward the rear entrance, glancing at each other in mutual shock.

Greengrass leveled a forefinger the size of a cigar. "You will leave this instant! I mean, *off the grounds.* Don't even think about coming back, you hear me?"

The surprising turnaround began with a sudden, shocking silence from the tiled floor. All attention focused upon the fat little man lying spread-eagled between his keepers. Antonio Argudin and Max Byway relaxed their grip and straightened up, breathing a little hard.

Hootie Bly, the focus of everyone's gaze, including that of Pargeeta Parmendera, who had appeared from some nowhere close at hand, lay perfectly still, hands palms up, the tips of his shoes aimed at the ceiling. His eyes found Greengrass.

"Don't do that," he said. "Take it back."

"What?" Dr. Greengrass moved toward his patient, and Argudin and Byway, still on their knees, inched away. "What was that, Howard?"

"I said, take it back," Howard told him.

"He's not quoting," said Pargeeta. "This is major."

Before anyone else thought to move, she darted up to Howard and knelt beside him. His lips moved. She shook her head, not in denial but to tell him she did not understand.

The doctor said, "There's no need to hold you down, is there, Howard?"

Howard shook his head. Pargeeta stood up and backed away, giving Howard an eloquent glance I could not decode.

"Did you use your own words, Howard? Wasn't that normal speech?"

Howard took his eyes from the doctor's and contemplated the ceiling. "Lost as my own soul is, I would still do what I may for other human souls."

Dr. Greengrass hunkered down. The hem of his white jacket drooped against the floor. He reached out to pat Howard's hand. "Very nice, Howard. Was that from *The Scarlet Letter*? It sounded as though it was."

Howard nodded. " 'Hester,' said the clergyman, 'Farewell.' "

"We've all learned to appreciate *The Scarlet Letter* around here. It's quite a novel. You can find almost everything in that book, if you know where to look. Would you like to get up now?"

"Um," Howard said. "Praised be his name! His will be done! Farewell!"

"Are you saying good-bye to someone, Howard?"

"Um," he said again. "Nay, I think not so."

"You're not so frightened anymore, are you?"

"Nay, I think not so," he repeated.

"Well, let's start with sitting up. Can you do that?"

"How can it be otherwise?" He held his arms out straight before him and waited, like a child, to be assisted.

Irritated, Dr. Greengrass glared at the slow-moving attendants. Antonio and Max jumped forward, and each took an arm and together pulled Bly into an upright sitting position. Greengrass waved them away and leaned in closer.

"Howard, can you tell me in your own words, or in Hawthorne's, it doesn't matter, but I'd really prefer you to speak for yourself, can you tell me what frightened you out there?"

Howard glanced over at us. For a moment, I thought I saw the hint of a smile move across Hootie's face. Pargeeta drew in her breath and gripped her elbows—I had a vague impression of conflicting emotions, but could not imagine what might be troubling her, nor could I be certain that she was in fact troubled. It was an emotional shimmer, a faint, unwilling release of feeling.

"Can you try to tell me, Howard?" asked the doctor.

Howard nodded, slowly. He kept his eyes fixed on us. "It was a face, fiend-like, full of smiling malice, yet bearing the semblance of features that she knew full well."

"Fiend-like," Greengrass said.

"The arch-fiend," Hootie quoted, "standing there with a smile and a scowl, to claim his own."

"I see. Let's stand up together now, shall we?"

Antonio and Max got on either side of Howard and pulled him up onto his feet. Dr. Greengrass stood up, a little more slowly, and smiled at him. "Are you all right now?"

" 'Now that I am back in these comforting surroundings, my distress has almost completely left me,' said Millicent. 'But I do hope to have another outing one day soon.' "

"And now we hear from Mr. Austin's *Moondreamers*," the doctor said. "Another useful text. But before that, we heard from Howard Bly himself, didn't we?"

Howard looked over Greengrass's head and, in an instant, became expressionless, numb, almost flat enough to reflect the light.

"You asked me to rescind my order that these men leave our premises and never return. *Don't do that. Take it back.* That was Howard Bly talking, wasn't it?"

Howard stood before him, disappearing inch by inch.

"I'll let them stay on one condition, that you confirm what I'm saying. Say 'Yes,' Howard, meaning 'Yes, I spoke for myself, yes, I found my own words,' and your old friends can come here as often as you and they desire. But you have to say it, Howard. You have to say 'Yes.' "

Hootie began to blush. He seemed once again to be fully present, though in considerable disagreement with himself. His eyes met the doctor's, and the flush spread across his cheeks, darkening as it moved.

"Take it back."

"You're quoting yourself. Well, that's good enough, Howard. Thank you."

■

In a little while, all had returned to the version of normality familiar to the Lamont Hospital. Antonio Argudin patrolled the wards and the common rooms in search of a patient to terrorize; the jigsaw-puzzle obsessives dwelt upon clouds and sailing vessels; propped on his pillows Howard Bly lay reading L. Shelby Austin's masterwork. Dr. Greengrass sat installed behind his desk, discussing hospital policy with Pargeeta Parmendera and the two visitors responsible for patient Bly's recent breakthrough. Prodded only slightly by his former babysitter, the doctor soon agreed that we should feel free to visit our friend whenever we wished to do so, provided of course that we did not interfere with his hours of rest.

■

Don said, "He's not completely sane, is he? This is an awful thing to say, but I think you have to start there."

"So Hootie did see, or thought he saw, a demon, or the devil, or something like that, and that makes him crazy?"

"You heard him as well as I did. 'The arch-fiend,' he said. And something about the devil with a smile on his face. That would terrify anybody.

149

But people who see the devil popping up on garden paths are not sane, I'm sorry."

"It's funny, but for some reason devils popping up on garden paths sounds a little like Hawthorne to me." It was a little like *The Scarlet Letter*, in fact, but I let that slide. "So you and Greengrass both think Hootie was scared."

"Well, he *was*! You heard him. He was scared out of his mind. Come on."

"I'm not so sure about that. He was making a lot of noise, that's right, but he wasn't screaming, remember?"

"It sounded like screaming to me. What do you think he was doing?"

"You thought he was really frightened, so what you heard was screaming. What I heard was shouting. Hootie wasn't screaming, he was *yelling*. It looked to me as though . . ." I stopped, really unsure of how to put it.

"As though *what*?" Don asked.

"As though he wasn't able to handle all the feelings boiling up inside him. I agree, he did see something. But he kept saying 'Farewell,' remember? I think he was really *moved*, I think his own emotions tipped him over. And I don't think Pargeeta saw him as terrified, either. They had some kind of conversation, something passed between them. And there's something else you should consider."

"Namely?"

"He was disturbed, he was angry. You know what I think? You're not going to like this very much, Don. It's possible that he was talking about Spencer Mallon. Because we were there, he may suddenly have realized that Mallon had put him in the mental ward."

"It wasn't *Mallon*. He would never call Mallon the arch-fiend."

"How can you be sure of that? You haven't seen Hootie since 1966."

"Hootie loved that man," Don said. "You would have, too, if you'd had the balls to come with us."

"If I thought my guru had ruined my life, I don't believe I would still love him."

"It's hard to explain," Don said. "Maybe ruin isn't ruin, maybe it isn't ruinous. And don't call him my guru. We weren't Buddhists or Hindus. He was my teacher, my mentor. My master."

"The thought of a master gives me the creeps."

"Then you have a problem, sorry. But I understand. When I was seventeen I thought the same way you do."

"This is a good argument," I said. "We could probably keep it up for hours, but I don't want to keep defending spiritual arrogance. There is another possibility, that it's linked to this Ladykiller business I was looking into. Actually, we should talk about this."

"Why?"

"Maybe what stirred Hootie up, what he saw out in that garden, was Keith Hayward. Everything seems so *connected* to me."

Attracted by free food and drink, guests from the concierge floors had been crowding into the lounge, claiming most of the chairs, couches, and tables. A stout couple wearing crimson UW sweatshirts now occupied the sofa beside our table. The noise level had gone up, most of it centered on the bar, where few empty stools remained. Bored no longer, the bartender grinned and poured, grinned and poured.

Don canted back his chair until his shoulders met the wall. "What's up with this Ladykiller business? Why do you care about it, anyhow?"

I took a good-sized swig of my wine. "Do you really want to know?"

"Just guessing here, but does the reason have something to do with the Eel?"

"*No!*" (Though it did, in a weird way I did not want to think about. This, however, was why I had suggested Hayward.)

My shout did not cause every head to swivel in our direction. All conversation did not freeze. Some heads turned our way, and the noise level did drop off for a moment. Then everyone swung back into their conversations and their drinks. I took another, smaller, swallow of mediocre wine.

"Sorry. No, it's not about Lee, although she's involved, like all the rest of you. What it is, is—just before you showed up—I realized I wasn't going anywhere with my novel—and I saw a guy in my local breakfast place that reminded me of Hootie—and I was thinking about this cop named Cooper, and I realized I had to, *had to* finally figure out what happened to all of you out in that meadow."

"You mean . . . you think you should be trying to write another novel? Because, I gotta say, that's just what I was—"

"NO!"

Heads, more of them, turned our way once again, and the room fell more nearly silent than previously. The bartender leaned forward to peer through the crowd and give me a look divided between concern and inter-rogation. I made hush-hush movements with my hands. "That thing out there in the meadow is mysterious, it's violent, it's life-changing, it's about a huge, astonishing breakthrough . . . isn't it?"

"Not according to Mallon."

"Because he wanted even more! Mallon was a creature of the sixties. He had a kind of spiritual greediness. He actually wanted to change the world, and in a way, Don, can't you see, he actually did! Only no one no-ticed, and it lasted no more than a couple of seconds. He did it, though. At least it looks like that to me."

Olson looked away, and his eyes went out of focus. He grinned. "I like your point of view, though. Mallon changed the world, but only for a cou-ple of seconds. That's cute. But don't forget that the only people Mallon managed to persuade were four high-school students, two assholes, and one girl who fell in love with him."

"Afterwards, all of you were different. And one of the assholes was dead."

"Brett Milstrap was worse than dead."

"How?"

"I'll try to explain it to you later. If I can, which I doubt. Anyhow, what's this business about Hayward? And who's Cooper?"

"With Hayward, you guys had no idea what you were dealing with. Even my wife and Hootie didn't really know what he was like."

"Is this connected in any way with what I was telling you about—that shed? I didn't say this at the time, it seemed too crazy, but when I was standing there, I had this strong, strong feeling . . . that he had strapped some naked kid to a chair. And the kid was why he brought out his knife."

"Amazing," I said.

I had shocked Don more than he wished to reveal. "You're not saying I was right, are you?"

"You were absolutely right," I said. "The boy's name was Tomek Miller. Only he wasn't in the little room on Henry Street, because by then he was dead. His corpse, what was left of it, was discovered in the ruins of a burned building in Milwaukee. December 1961. Miller was probably Keith Hayward's first victim."

Olson blinked several times and tilted a portion of the margarita into his mouth. After swallowing, he appeared to track the progress of the alcohol down his throat. His body relaxed into his chair, and one arm dropped straight to his side. When he turned back to me, he seemed almost to be smiling. "No kidding."

"I said it was amazing."

He shook his head, as if at a particularly satisfying magic trick. "Man, I wanted to make myself invisible and slip right inside that awful place—because it *was* awful. That's what I wanted to get across to Mallon, how twisted Hayward actually was. I heard him singing to his knife!"

"That knife, I guess from what you told me, was a present from his uncle. Tillman Hayward. Once you know a few things about Tillman, it makes a lot of sense."

"So what do you know about Hayward?"

"During dinner," I said.

■

"Maybe there's a gene for what we call evil," I said. "Some variation on the normal pattern that pops up a lot less frequently than the marker for cystic fibrosis, say, or Tay-Sachs, and most other diseases. Hitler could have been born with it, and Stalin and Pol Pot, and every other dictatorial ruler who set about imprisoning and killing his own subjects, but so would plenty of everyday citizens. Every big city would have about three of these guys, every small city maybe one, and every fourth or fifth little town would have one—people who think other people are lesser beings and like to kill, hurt, injure, at the very least dominate and humiliate them. A bunch of other people would have been twisted into similar shapes by their lousy, abusive childhoods, but we're talking about people who are born that way. They carry that gene, and unluckily for everyone around them, it gets activated. It wakes up. Whatever. That's what you ran into when you met Keith Hayward."

"The Bad Seed," Don said.

"Exactly. The other point of view, which lots of religious people believe, is that from birth every single human being is corrupt and sinful, but that true *evil*, the real sulfurous Satanic *thing*, is timeless, comes from outside, and exists independently from human beings. To me, this always seemed a primitive way to think. It absolves you from responsibility for your actions. A devout Christian would say that I had it all wrong."

We were sitting at a corner table in Muramoto, just off Capital Square on King Street. The bartender at the Governor's Club had recommended the place. He had also suggested that we try the Asian slaw salad, which resembled a haystack. It had been delicious, and so had everything else. Although by this time we had both drunk a good deal of first-class sake, I had taken in more than had my companion.

"Are you a little drunk?"

"Um. Hootie's freakout kind of threw me. Anyhow, I wanted these options to be clear. Is evil innate, and a human quality, or is it an external entity, and inhuman in nature?"

"Let me guess. We vote for option one, don't we, since we are humanists, and liberal humanists to boot?"

"Maybe you are," I said. "Lately, I've been a bit ambivalent. However, with your friend Hayward, yes, it's option one all the way. And not only that, Hayward seems to present a case of evil by genetic transmission. Tremendous psychic disorder gets passed from one generation to the next, along with blue eyes or red hair. Here you are, this is mine, and now you have it, too, welcome to the family. That is, as long as George Cooper got things right, which I think he did."

I used my chopsticks to tweeze from the raised black rectangular surface before me a little delicacy so fresh it almost squirmed.

"Now, George Cooper was who, exactly? A cop, right?"

"Milwaukee homicide detective, twenty-six years on the job. Cooper had the whole Ladykiller thing figured out, only he could never prove anything, and he never had the slightest bit of evidence. Imagine the frustration."

Don's eyebrows knitted, creating three separate furrows in his forehead. "And you know this how?"

"From Cooper himself."

"You talked to this guy?"

"I wish. He died about nine, ten years ago. But I did the next best thing. Because I thought I might be able to use it in a new project, I read his book. Cooper had to do something with his frustration, so he wrote it all down—everything he saw, everything he could put together, all the hypotheticals he'd never be able to prove."

"A frustrated cop wrote a book claiming that Hayward had some kind of family involvement with the Ladykiller? Was it through his father?"

"His father's brother, Tillman. That was really Cooper's focus. He went to his grave without ever having been able to prove that Tillman Hayward was the Ladykiller."

"How come I never heard of this book?"

"Cooper didn't write well enough to get published. He wrote sentences like 'Pursuant to my investigation, the Milwaukee Police Department was always getting in my way as a matter of policy.' Outside of his family, no one but me ever heard of his book. I don't think he even *tried* to get it published. He just wanted to write it—he wanted there to be a record. His daughter found the manuscript while she was cleaning out his apartment after his death."

"You talked to his daughter?"

"No, we did everything by e-mail."

"Excuse me, but how the hell did you ever find out about this book that was never published and no one ever knew existed?"

"About five years ago, I was trolling around on eBay, and there it was. *Searching for the Ladykiller,* an unpublished typescript by Detective George Cooper, retired, of the Milwaukee Police Department. Sharon Cooper, his only child, thought somebody might want to use it for research, so she put it up for sale the only way she knew how. I was the only bidder. Twenty-seven bucks, a bargain. This was a time I wasn't too sure what I should do next, and my agent said something about trying nonfiction. So, the old Ladykiller business came back to me, all those murders in Milwaukee that no one ever solved. I happened to see this listing on eBay, perfect, right? It never occurred to me that the Ladykiller murders could have any connection with Spencer Mallon. After I read it, I got in touch with Sharon, but she couldn't answer most of my questions. Her father not only never talked about what he was writing, he didn't talk about his work at all.

"Cooper was old school, a hardnosed, suspicious, tough old bastard. He used his fists a lot, I bet. Whatever the methods, the guy closed a lot of cases, but this one kept getting away from him. Drove him crazy. He thought about it all the time."

"But he knew that Tillman Hayward was guilty of the murders."

"As much as you could know without actually seeing him do one."

"What made him so sure?"

"It was a gut feeling deal, but Cooper had a *great* gut. He got on to Hayward by cross-referencing train and airplane arrivals and departures from Milwaukee with the dates of the Ladykiller's homicides. Tedious work, but he wasn't getting anywhere with the local suspects. Turns out, this guy Hayward came in from Columbus, Ohio, by train and plane two days before three of the murders, and left by the same means a day or two after. That still left three murders, but Cooper thought that the guy had probably paid cash for the bus, or hitchhiked, or borrowed a car for those visits."

"It sounds a lot like guesswork," Don said.

■

It did, I knew, and to counter that impression I tried to get across the powerful sense of sheer obduracy communicated by Cooper's manuscript. George Cooper was not a man to be lightly swayed, he did not yield to whims, he had no fancies or daydreams. His version of guesswork rode upon endless slogging and a cop's finely tuned instinct. After he had noticed the correlation between Hayward's arrivals and the series of murders, he called upon a network of informers to hear whenever his suspect bought a ticket of any sort to Milwaukee. The call came; he opened a newspaper on a bench in the downtown train station; and when forty people got off the train from Columbus, one of them, a slim fellow in a hat and a pinstriped suit, sent out an electrical current that seared over the top of the *Journal* and sizzled directly into Cooper's waiting brainpan. A pure, mocking lawlessness spoke from the man's very being. This, the detective was certain, was Mr. Hayward. He was the kind of man who liked to look cops in the eye and give them a silvery little gleam. Such men made Cooper's hands clench.

Of medium height, in his mid- to late thirties, handsome but for the salient nose looming beneath the brim of his fedora, Hayward left the train in joking conversation with a square-faced, bespectacled young woman who, Cooper could see, barely knew him. Her limp brown hair hung past her ears like overgrown bangs.

Hayward's new acquaintance, so easily amused, had no reason to fear him. The Ladykiller would never threaten this girl: the truth was, he would probably avoid touching her, unless touching her would help him get what he wanted. The Ladykiller took an attitude toward his victims: if they weren't pretty, they weren't worth the trouble. (Unfortunately, if they were pretty, they were worth all the trouble he could concoct.) Hayward wanted something from this typist, this substitute teacher, whatever she was, and it was probably a ride somewhere.

Cooper folded his newspaper and trailed after them as they filtered through the crowd, paused for the gentleman to make a brief telephone call, then went out into the late afternoon sun. His plain blue sedan, dinged a bit on the driver's side, sat a little way down the street. The young woman admitted Mr. Hayward into her green Volvo, and Cooper leaned on his hood and pretended to gaze in fascination at a welter of railway tracks extending halfway to infinity. When the Volvo drove off, he followed it through the downtown, then west to Sherman Boulevard and into a largely lower-middle-class neighborhood where the woman drew up in front of a two-story yellow-and-brown house on a short, patchy lawn. A worn-looking woman and a scrawny boy shot through the narrow front door and trotted down three concrete steps to greet the murderer. Cooper noted the address and, back at the station, found it in the battered reverse directory. Twenty more minutes of research told him that William Hayward, the resident of the brown-and-yellow house, worked at Continental Can and had two siblings, Margaret Frances and Tillman Brady. Margaret Frances, later known as Margot, had no criminal record whatsoever.

This could not be said of her youngest brother. For a time, Tillman Hayward had managed to skirt classification as a youthful offender despite the complaints of half a dozen neighbors that he had been engaged in suspicious activity. "That boy was up to no good," went the general opinion, though the charges were never more specific. In Tillman Hayward's sixteenth year, his luck changed.

A week after his birthday, young Till was caught shoplifting at a five and dime on Sherman Boulevard: oddly for a person his age, he had been trying to steal glue, nails, a box cutter, and a box of thumbtacks. When the officer dispatched to the scene inquired as to the purpose of these items, the boy alluded to a "homework project," and the officer released him with a warning. Three months later, an absentee landlord spotted a wandering light in a basement window of an empty duplex on Auer Street. The landlord let himself in and managed to snag Tillman by his collar in his flight from the basement steps. This time, the boy was taken to the station, largely to impress him with the seriousness of trespass. Again, no charge was filed.

Further proof that Tillman Hayward knew how to disarm officers of the law came when an outraged homeowner on West 41st Street reported that her beloved marmalade cat, Louis, had just been stolen from her backyard by a teenaged boy she knew to be local. A few minutes later, two policemen got out of a patrol car and stopped a boy trotting down Sherman Boulevard with a squirming bag in his hands. Oh, the boy said, this cat *lived* in that house? He had been sure it had gone missing from a woman just off Sherman on West 44th, and he was in the process of returning it when the officers interrupted him. He knew about the missing cat from the posters taped to the lampposts, hadn't the officers noticed? It was like a plague, all these missing pets.

It would have ended there, had not one of the officers involved, clearly a man of a hard and suspicious nature, inserted a note of warning: *Keep an eye on this kid.*

Before Tillman Hayward disappeared for good from the police records, he had been accused of two more crimes, attempted rape and the receipt of stolen goods. Alma Vestry, the young woman who had accused Hayward of trying to rape her, dropped the charge a day before the case went to trial. The two officers who charged the twenty-two-year-old Hayward with receiving a rack of hijacked mink coats destroyed their own case by proceeding improperly, and an angry judge dismissed the charges. Hayward must have known he had been lucky, for after that point he took care to avoid the attention of the authorities.

Detective Cooper may have been a little crazy. Certainly, he was obsessed, and had been since Tillman Hayward stepped off the train from Columbus. He had discovered nothing that would sway a judge, but Cooper began spending nearly half his working day and much of his off-duty life searching for anything that might incriminate his only suspect. Early in the case, Cooper plucked Hayward off the street and brought him in for questioning, but the man glided through every verbal trap the detective set for him. He smiled, he was gracious and patient, he wished to be helpful. The farcical interrogation lasted two hours and produced no results apart from informing Tillman that at least one Milwaukee detective greatly desired to slam him into a cell. Thereafter, Cooper contented himself with observation.

Both his chief of detectives and the police chief may have thought their star detective had slipped a gear, but they trusted his instincts and for a long time allowed him to focus his energies as narrowly as he wished. When Cooper's fed-up partner requested reassignment, they paired him with another detective and let Cooper work alone. The Ladykiller was Homicide's top priority, and if Cooper's methods had a chance of bringing it to closure, his division and his department were willing to stand by and watch.

Detective Cooper developed an instinct for when Tillman Hayward was going to turn up at his brother's house. Sometimes this intuition compelled him toward the brown-and-yellow house to spot, at ease in pleated suit trousers and a wife beater T-shirt, a furtive, behatted form moving past a window or drifting through the backyard. To Cooper's profound regret, glimpses were nearly all the observation he was permitted. Hayward had excellent instincts of his own. He knew when to hide out in an inner room his brother let him use, he knew when to stay at home. After commandeering an attic room across the alley, Cooper passed twelve-hour, fifteen-hour days peering down at the barren backyard and rear windows in which his target declined to appear.

The old cop felt certain that Hayward used the back door and the narrow alley. From time to time, the detective managed to glimpse a swiftly moving form gliding through the kitchen door and melting into the darkness blanketing the yard. But where was he going, and what were his haunts? George Cooper had visited every bar, tavern, saloon, and cocktail lounge within a mile's radius, had shown Hayward's photo to 150 bartenders. Some of them had said, That guy, sure, see him now and then, comes in like three times a week, then stays away for months. Or: This guy? He likes the ladies, and they like him back.

On a busy night at a Brady Street gin mill called the Open Hand, a bartender glanced deep into the crowd and spotted a familiar nose jutting from beneath a familiar hat. He remembered the detective's request, dug his card out of a drawer, and called to report that the man Cooper was looking for was now in his bar. As this took place in the era before mobile phones, the bartender dialed the number on the card, that of the homicide division at the central station. When he was informed of the call, Cooper happened to be in his dented blue sedan, traveling from his apartment to the attic room, even grumpier than usual.

He swore at the steering wheel, the windshield, and the stunned dispatcher. Still ripping out curses, he wrenched his car into a U-turn and hurtled through four lanes of protesting vehicles. Fifteen minutes before he jerked to a stop in front of the Open Hand, his suspect had escorted an intoxicated young lady to an unknown destination. Fortunately, the bartender knew the young woman's name, Lisa Gruen. Miss Gruen could, of course, not be found at the nearby apartment she shared with another graduate student at UW-Milwaukee, nor did her roommate have any idea where she might be. A few of the patrons had glimpsed Lisa's new friend pouring her into a car, but none of them could remember anything about the vehicle except its color, which was dark blue, black, or British racing green. Flummoxed, fearful that in a day or two Lisa Gruen's corpse would be found dumped on the steps of the Central Library, Detective Cooper spent hours grilling the Open

Hand's increasingly irritated patrons. Some of them remembered meeting "Till," "Tilly," cute name for a guy, a little older and more sophisticated than the bar's usual patrons, but a little rough around the edges.

Late the next morning, Lisa Gruen called the station. What was the big deal? All her friends were pissed off—she had ruined their evening. When Detective Cooper turned up at her apartment, he shook her up. Cooper knew that his size, also his distance from any system of value she understood, made her feel uncomfortable. This was fine with him: Cooper enjoyed the creation of discomfort.

No, maybe she had never met Tilly before, but he was obviously a nice guy anyhow. After the gin had unstrung her, he volunteered to drive her home. Okay, he didn't bring her *straight* home, but so what? He didn't do anything creepy, she was sure of that.

Eleven hours were missing from this young woman's life, and their loss caused her not a moment's concern. What had he done with her: where had he taken her? It was a mystery.

Of course she could not describe his car. It had a steering wheel and a backseat. Around three or four in the morning, whenever, the pain in her head, the dryness in her mouth, and the burning in her guts had awakened her. She sat up and looked out the window. Everything spun and swayed. Then came the really embarrassing part. Her escort opened the rear door, helped her out, and held her waist while she doubled over and vomited. Still drunk, she demanded a few more hours of sleep, and he obligingly assisted her back onto her padded bench. When next she surfaced, it was ten o'clock on Sunday morning. He was asking her if she wanted to go home. She said: Aren't you at least going to offer me breakfast? What a gentleman, he drove to a diner that was way out there somewhere, way west, maybe in Butler— who ever thought Butler had diners?—and bought scrambled eggs, whole-wheat toast, bacon, and strong coffee.

Two days later, one possible answer to the missing hours was suggested by a grim discovery in the parking lot of a Prospect Avenue insurance company. Two foraging homeless men investigated a dusty, rolled-up carpet alongside a Dumpster and found within it the nude body of the Ladykiller's fifth victim. She had been a thirty-one-year-old hotel executive named Sonia Hillery, and photographs later supplied by her husband and parents made it clear that, when alive, she had been competent, intelligent, stylish, and attractive. The Ladykiller had spent hours, perhaps days, working on her corpse, and nothing of what had once defined her remained.

George Cooper wondered: had Tilly Hayward stretched out unconscious Lisa Gruen across his backseat before he snatched Sonia Hillery off the streets? If so, what then? After he overpowered Hillery, he would need to stash her body somewhere while he established his alibi by caring for Lisa Gruen. And if Lisa fed her hangover out in Butler the next morning, Hayward was probably renting some little hideaway in the western burbs, or the small towns west of them—Marcy, Lannon, Menomonee Falls, Waukesha, little Butler itself. He drove west to Butler and showed Hayward's photo in the diner—the waiters remembered him and the hungover, slightly pig-faced blond girl he had been with, but none had noticed his car or anything else of interest. Cooper drove slowly up and down its main street, around its old hotel, and through its few alleyways. Nothing, nothing, nothing. Cooper seethed. It burned a hole in his stomach, that while Tilly Hayward had been stuffing a hungover girl with bacon and eggs, a dead woman on a slab, on a table, maybe a basement floor, had waited for his return.

Cooper's rage pushed him down the highways to Columbus, Ohio, far out of his jurisdiction, where his skills and obsessions served no purpose but his own. An uncooperative homicide chief informed him that everything he had to know about Tillman Hayward, he could have learned on the phone. I had to see it for myself, Cooper told him. See what? What his life is like here. Well, said the Ohio cop, you must have a great appetite for boredom. Mr. Hayward is a good citizen. He led Cooper through the records: married, three daughters, not so much as a speeding ticket on his record, not even a *parking* ticket, and co-owner with his wife of four sturdy apartment buildings. And if you need to know anything more about the man, this fine resident of Westerville, one of Columbus's finest suburbs, was also an exemplary contributor to police charities. Detective Cooper, you would be well advised to turn right around and go home, because there ain't squat for you in Columbus.

Cooper could no more obey this advice than he could dance back to Milwaukee on a moonbeam. After promising to go home soon, he picked up a map at an information booth and drove eleven miles to Westerville, where he made his way to the address he had memorized. He parked across the street and two houses down. It was exactly the kind of house, the kind of street, and the kind of community he most disliked. Everything around him said, *We are richer and more refined than you will ever be.* The windows sparkled; the front lawns gleamed. Borders of flowers brightened every substantial, yet not showy, edifice. Knowing what he thought he knew, the neighborhood made him want to shoot holes in the oversized mailboxes, hand painted with images of barns and dogs and ducks, lining the street.

Eventually, the garage door at the Hayward house floated up, and a pale blue station wagon rolled out. In the backseat, three small girls babbled away, with gestures, all at the same time. The driver, presumably Mrs. Tillman Hayward, was a Hitchcock blonde with smooth golden hair and a neat, symmetrical face. As she drove past Cooper, her icy blue eyes flicked disgust and suspicion at him. Christ, he thought, no wonder homicide was such a booming trade.

Soon after his return to Milwaukee and the barren room where he gazed through binoculars at the Haywards' glum backyard, Cooper observed an apparently insignificant event that in a short while seemed as significant as the discovery of a new disease. A stringy boy of eleven or twelve with dark, muddy eyes and a narrow forehead, Bill Hayward's son, Keith, was sitting in a disconsolate manner, as only a boy of eleven or twelve can be disconsolate, on the battered old dining room chair they moved out onto the patchy grass in the summer. To Detective Cooper, Keith had suggested a kind of displacement, a sense that he was making do within an odd emotional poverty. Cooper had taken in only glimpses, but the glimpses insinuated a life of constant performance, as if Keith were always acting the role of a boy instead of actually being one. Cooper did not know why he felt this way, nor did he entirely trust this feeling. It simmered away on a mental back burner, always present but generally ignored.

Here it was again, though, the feeling within the old detective that although this child was genuinely annoyed about something, he was also engaged in a performance. The performance, it came to George Cooper, had all to do with hurt feelings and injured innocence. He displayed his sense of having been misunderstood as if on a stage. For whom could he have been performing, if not his mother? Keith sighed, flung himself backward on the chair so that his spine bent, his head lolled, and his arms hung like pale sticks; then he threw himself theatrically forward until he sat folded over his knees, with his arms dangling nearly to the ground. In a fine display of resentment, he straightened up and squirmed around until he cupped his cheek in one hand and his elbow in the other.

The back door opened, and everything changed.

The act fell away, and the boy became both warier and more open, beneath the thin top layer of his performance visibly curious about what was about to happen. The person who had emerged from the kitchen of the brown-and-yellow house was not Margaret Hayward, but her brother-in-law and object of George Cooper's closest attentions, Tilly. Cooper's initial response to what he was watching was a tightness in his throat and a constriction of his chest. A true cop, he knew instantly that this scene was wrong.

Then he had it: in front of his uncle, Keith allowed his true self to come to the surface.

In his T-shirt and hat, his pants held up by ropy leather suspenders, Till crouched down next to his nephew and squatted on his heels. Smiling, he knitted his hands together, the picture of a devoted uncle. And that, too, troubled the detective. Hayward still carried with him the gleaming mockery that had spoken so clearly in the train station, but at this moment he seemed more genuine than Cooper had ever seen him. These two people were *communicating.* The way they moved their bodies, the look of their eyes, the subtlety of their gestures toward each other, told him that the boy had done something that, although fine with him, had put him in bad odor with his family. Till was giving the boy advice, and his advice contained an element of subterfuge, of camouflage or fakery. The shine in his eyes, his latent smile made this clear. Also clear was the boy's response. He was practically in transports.

All of this was dreadful, even to Detective Cooper. Or perhaps especially to Detective Cooper. He understood that what he was seeing was not the corruption drama for which it could easily be mistaken, but something worse, a moment of recognition that proceeded naturally and on its own terms to a kind of mentorship. The worst of the worst was an actual moment of mentoring, of advice given and received, involving a great ball of keys that Tillman drew from his pocket and offered to his nephew as, the detective thought, some kind of solution. A key opened an enclosure, and within a large ball of keys could be hidden those that opened the most secret and hidden of enclosures—like flags that said *Here! Here!,* the bits of colored string, bright as flames in the lenses of Cooper's binoculars. Tillman Hayward was telling his nephew about the satisfactions of what could be called a private room.

■

"Sound familiar?" I said. "Keith obviously took his uncle's advice to heart. And long before he set up his table and his knives behind the locked door of that shed you saw in Madison, he almost certainly took possession of the basement of an abandoned building on Sherman Avenue in Milwaukee, about five blocks from his house. He would have been eleven or twelve, and he had begun to kill and dismember small animals, mainly cats, that he captured in his neighborhood."

With a pang that felt oddly like heartburn, Cooper remembered both Sonia Hillery, whose body for days had been beaten, abused, punctured, and abraded, and poor clueless, unattractive Lisa Gruen, who had been given breakfast in Butler's Sunshine Diner, and understood that below him, marked by a colorful bit of yarn, lay the key that opened a clinical private hell in Brookfield or Menomonee Falls, in Sussex or Lannon, one of those little towns. If that boy, Keith, didn't know it yet, soon he would be standing before that terrible fact, gazing in as if in preparation for his own ghastly adult life.

"And, remember," I said, "this Cooper was an old-fashioned bruiser, the kind of cop that used to be called a 'bull.' He'd seen everything, he'd seen and done so much, he barely had recognizable emotions any longer. But what he saw happening between Tillman and Keith Hayward really chilled him. He used the word *evil*."

"But he never managed to put the uncle away. What finally happened?"

"On one of his trips back to Milwaukee, Tillman Hayward was shot and killed behind the Open Hand—that bar where he picked up his beard, that girl Lisa Gruen. For Cooper, Hayward's death was a real blow. He insisted on taking the case, and officially he never solved it, never even came close. It was a disaster for him. He knew exactly who had done it."

"He did?"

"The father of Laurie Terry, one of Hayward's victims, a retired crossing guard named Max Terry. Cooper had shown him Hayward's picture, and the old guy thought he'd seen him somewhere, but he couldn't really place him. Later, Terry remembered that he'd seen Hayward when he dropped into the joint on Water Street where his daughter tended bar. It was a couple of days before she died. This guy with the hat and the long nose was sitting down at the end of the bar, flirting with her, like a million guys did every week. As soon as he remembered, he *knew.* If this guy wasn't the murderer, the Ladykiller, why did the cop show him his picture? At the very least, he was a suspect. So the old guy pulled out Cooper's card, called the station house, asked for Detective Cooper. Detective, he said, maybe I'd like to see that Polaroid picture again, the one of the guy in the hat. Cooper went over to his place, showed him the picture again. Now I'm not so sure, Terry said. What's his name, anyhow? Tillman Hayward, Cooper said. A first-class son of a bitch. Don't you go and do something stupid, now.

"It turned out, Max Terry didn't give a damn what kind of advice he got from homicide cops who hadn't solved his daughter's murder. He began going around to one joint after another, waiting to run into Hayward, and he carried a gun in his coat pocket. Through spectacularly good luck or spectacularly bad, Terry walked into the Open Hand just about a week later and spotted Hayward hanging out at the bar, talking to a couple of girls. Terry didn't think twice. He went right up to his target and said, Hey, this guy I know lost a bet, and now he owes you money. You got the wrong guy, buddy. Ain't you Tillman Hayward? Okay, come out back with me, we'll get everything settled."

In his manuscript, Cooper speculated that Hayward might have been amused by this situation: a little old man trying to run some transparent con on him. He must have smiled, Cooper wrote; he may have been smiling right up until the old man pulled the revolver from his pocket and, without even pausing to take aim, fired a bullet first through his Adam's apple; then, taking a quick step forward as Tilly's hands flew to his throat, up through his genitals and into his guts; and finally, as Hayward slumped down the alley's concrete wall, directly through his right eye, putting an end to all the activity within that busy mind.

"Terry confessed it all to George Cooper," I said. "He told him everything he did, just like I told it to you. Step by step. And all Cooper did was write it down. He certainly wasn't going to arrest the old man. He took his gun away and ordered him to go home and keep his mouth shut. Then he drove to the Cherry Street bridge and threw the gun in the Milwaukee River, figuring it might not be the only one down there. What, is that a high-crime area, or something?"

"Or something," Olson said. "Cooper must have been at least as racist as most cops his age at that time."

"Apart from that one comment, you wouldn't know it from his book. The subject of race never comes up. What *does* come up, on the other hand, is your old friend Keith."

"Our friend," Don said. "Hardly."

"Just as well, since his actual friends don't seem to end up all that happily. Brett Milstrap vanishes into some limbo I can't figure out . . ."

"Not surprisingly."

"Anyhow, the first and best friend Keith Hayward ever had in his life, probably the only real one, this kid named Tomek Miller, wound up tortured and killed in that basement on Sherman Boulevard—that's how we know about the basement. Cooper had nothing but suspicions, but he had plenty of those. Keith's friend Miller probably went through hell before he was killed, and his body was badly burned in a fire. However, the autopsy revealed a lot of recent damage, *fresh* damage, to the remaining tissue and to his bones. Cooper was certain that Till and Keith killed the boy, or Tillman by himself with Keith coming in for the coup de grâce, or whatever, and they burned down the building to destroy the evidence. And almost succeeded.

"Cooper had spotted the boy in that area a couple of times, but he never witnessed anything that could tie him to the building. Which wasn't for the lack of trying. Until the building burned down, Cooper had no idea where Keith had set up his secret place. It could have been in any of twenty to thirty buildings on or near Sherman Boulevard. What really got him was, he had followed Keith and Miller over to that area lots and lots of times, only they always managed to slip away from him before they went to ground. He was pretty sure that Miller was something like Keith's slave. This Miller was a funny-looking kid, small, very pale, with big eyes, a big nose, and hands too large for his body. Cooper said he looked like Pinocchio. A natural target, a kid who would expect to be bullied and mistreated. Around Keith, he acted totally deferential, almost servile. He thought Keith had accepted slavery as payment for being protected. Other kids never messed with Keith Hayward.

"In case you were wondering, Cooper questioned Keith twice. Got nowhere. The kid claimed that he and his uncle bonded over baseball. They both loved the third baseman for the Braves, Eddie Matthews. A great guy, according to the kid. All this drove Cooper up the wall. He looked at Keith, and he saw a junior version of Till. It made him sick."

"No wonder," Olson said.

"The kid said he had no idea what Miller was doing in that basement. Sure, they were friends, kind of, but Miller was basically a nonentity, and nobody missed him much. And the parents! No help at all. They were Polish immigrants who had their name changed for them, basically afraid of everything. Cooper scared the shit out of them. Their son knew Keith Hayward, they'd heard his name, but that was about it. Here are these two shrunken, terrified people, he works in a Polish bakery, she cleans houses, no money, suffering the inexplicable loss of their only child, sitting on the edge of a cheap sofa, scared out of their minds, paralyzed . . . they want *him* to explain what happened, because they sure can't. Nothing makes sense to them, *America* doesn't make sense to them, it took their kid and turned him into a spare rib."

I raised my shoulders and made a what-can-you-do gesture, then returned to my meal. After a couple of bites, I realized that I wanted to ask Olson a certain question.

"Don, do you think Keith Hayward deserved to die?"

"Probably. Hootie and your wife thought he did."

I nodded. "I asked Lee about it once, and she said that Hayward wasn't all bad."

"The Eel *said* that?"

"She also said that she didn't think anyone, if you looked inside them, was ever really all bad. But she added that she still thought Keith Hayward deserved to die. I think so, too . . . Look. If Cooper was right about that kid, Hayward's death probably saved the lives of a lot of young women."

Olson nodded. "I've thought about that."

"So this force comes out of nowhere, out of another dimension, or out of the *ground*, I don't know, and rips this guy to pieces. Can that force be evil? I'd say it was neutral."

"Neutral."

"Maybe one of the women Hayward would have killed, had he lived, would have done a great thing someday. Maybe she, or her daughter, or her son, would have made some great medical or scientific breakthrough, or been a great poet. Maybe it's more remote than that. What if one of the women Hayward would have murdered, or one of her descendants, however far in the future, was going to do something apparently insignificant that would eventually have a huge ripple effect? Killing Hayward would be the means to protect whatever that effect might be."

"So these creatures are protecting us?"

I considered that for a second. "Maybe they're protecting our ignorance. Or maybe we're both completely wrong, and something else altogether killed Hayward, some demonic creature Mallon managed to call up."

"I didn't see any demonic creature," Olson grumped. "And I don't think there was one. What happened to your detective, this Cooper? Seems to me like he dug himself a big hole and jumped in."

I laughed. "Yeah, not that there was anything funny about it. He broke the law, destroyed evidence, and interfered with the entire process. All that was left for him to do was keep an eye on Keith Hayward, which he did, and he let the kid know he was watching him, but he knew he had wrecked his own life. He had come to the end. He couldn't keep an eye on Keith Hayward twenty-four hours a day, and he'd never live long enough to watch the kid's children. That twisted gene, or whatever, was out of reach. He couldn't put an end to it. All his skills had failed him."

"What did he do? Eat his gun?"

"Drank himself to death. Resigned from the department, of course. Turned his weapon back in with his badge. He had another one, a pistol he took off a bad guy, but he never carried it around, never used it. He just liked the idea that it was *there*. Cooper lived in a neighborhood off Vliet Street, and there were bars at both ends of his block. For a couple of years, he basically went back and forth between them."

"He put that in his *book*?"

"For him, that was the end of the Ladykiller case, with the detective who carried the whole thing around in his head going back and forth between these joints named The Angler's Lounge and Ted & Maggie's. He *wanted* to write about that. And he had some pretty interesting things to say about it. Sort of totally bleak. It was like living in absolute darkness. If he'd been anything like a good writer, it could have been amazing."

"Why? What did he say?"

"The only way to approach some of that stuff is to realize that he was drunk when he wrote it."

"Can you remember some of it?"

"I'm no Hootie, but some of it stuck, yeah."

"Lay it on me."

"Okay. He wrote, *It has taken me nearly sixty years to learn that in this life, if it ain't shit, it ain't nothing at all.*"

I managed to summon up another of the old detective's darkness arrows. "In another place, he wrote, *What isn't pain is just a wire hanger. I prefer the pain.*"

I smiled at the ceiling, remembering something, then turned the smile toward Olson. "Toward the end, he said, *Who was I working for, all those years? Was my real boss a wire hanger? The way I live wears reality down.*"

"What was he talking about, wire hangers?"

"All I can think of, there isn't much *to* a wire hanger. It's more like an outline than a real thing."

Our check had come. I surrendered a credit card and signed the slip, and at long last it was time to walk back around the square and return to the hotel. We stood up, waved thanks to the waiter, nodded at the grinning sushi chefs, and began to move toward the door.

We went out into the night's warm darkness, pierced above by millions of stars, and on sloping King Street by the lights in the windows of bars and the illuminated prow of a theater marquee.

Chips of mica glittered in the sidewalk. I waited for Don to come up beside me, then almost sighed.

"I think the lounge is still open," Olson said.

"We'll see." I glanced at my companion. "After all that, I hope I never have to hear another word about Keith Hayward or his god-awful uncle. I'm glad they're dead."

"I'll drink to that."

By this time, Don had lost most of his prison swagger. The crude as-sertiveness that must have protected him in Menard but made him an an-noyance on Cedar Street had faded so thoroughly that I felt I had spent the previous ninety minutes doing nothing more complicated than gabbing with a friend. Olson was even walking almost normally now, with only a trace of the old menacing swerve-and-dip. How, I wondered, had he managed to shake five thousand dollars out of people he barely knew anymore?

11:00 p.m.–3:30 a.m.

A door chosen; a door unchosen and untouched; a question unanswered. These matters, along with others like them, floated through my mind as I undressed and hung up my clothes and brushed my teeth and washed my hands and face and slid into my comfortable hotel-room bed.

I stopped my hand on its way to switch off the tall bedside lamp, then lowered it to the creamy folded sheet, and let my head find the waiting pillow.

The Eel had walked into that meadow without me, and now I could never undo the choice I had made, never untie that knot.

Just now, the light could stay on.

◾

"It's a simple business, really," I had said to Don Olson in the Governor's Lounge late that night. We sat at a table next to the big windows, and lights burned in windows near and distant. Alone in his goldfish bowl, the friendly bartender (who had requested, and been gratified by, our evaluations of the restaurant he had recommended) seemed to have lapsed into a deeply meditative state. On the long sofa at the front of the room, a young couple facing the fireplace leaned whispering to each other shoulder to shoulder, like spies in love.

"I doubt that," Olson said. "Look at you."

"Don't you ever get obsessed with a weird story? Play it in your head, over and over?"

"You're tap dancing. Start with the easy stuff. When did this whatever-it-was happen?"

"In 1995," I had said, surprised to have recovered the date so clearly and so swiftly. "Autumn. October, I think. Lee was called away to Rehoboth Beach, Delaware, on an odd mission, almost as a detective. In the end, she *was* a detective, and she caught the bad guy!"

◾

Lying in my bed, hands folded on my chest, the light spilling into half of the room, I went over the conversation with Olson, word by word by word.

—Called away? Who called her?

—The ACB. The American Confederation of the Blind. Your old buddy, the Eel, is very close to the Delaware chapter. In Rehoboth Beach.

■

It sometimes seemed to me that beautiful Lee Truax had been one of the founders of the ACB's Delaware chapter, but of course she was not. She just knew everybody there. How had that happened? She had helped organize that chapter, that's how, she had worked with the first generation of members to establish their structure, someone had invited her, an old friend from New York, Missy Landrieu, a name I of course remembered only fifty percent of the time, sometimes I barely noticed her friends, it seemed. So although neither she nor they had ever lived in Rehoboth Beach, Delaware (and in fact being self-absorbed and work-obsessed, I had never so much as visited the place), the former Eel had deep roots in that pleasant beachside community where the chapter often met. There she was loved and respected, perhaps even more greatly than she was loved and respected everywhere else in ACB-land. And of course it meant everything to this little local chapter in a small, little-regarded state, the Rhode Island of the Eastern Shores, to have a good friend who was on the board of the national organization. Or a trustee. One of the two, unless they were the same thing, which I thought they were not. The friend from New York, Missy, another trustee or board member, though sighted, not blind, and as fantastically wealthy as a heroine in Henry James, had reached out to the former Eel for assistance in a sticky matter that concerned her particular pet chapter—apart, of course, from Chicago, her own.

This sticky matter had to do with funds that had been disappearing, at the rate of a couple of hundred dollars a month, from the chapter's account. The officers had noticed only when the missing dollars added up to just over ten thousand.

■

It was then an oddity of the Delaware chapter of the ACB that nearly all its officers were women. They decided not to call in the police, but first to turn to the national office for advice. By way of answer, the national office had sent Lee Truax, loved, respected, and wise, out from Chicago to solve this problem before it became public.

They knew the names of everyone who had access to that account. Nine women, scattered all over the region, but most of them in the Baltimore area. What the Eel did, I told Donald Olson in words recalled as I lay in my twelfth-floor bed, was to invite the nine women to the Golden Atlantic Sands Hotel and Conference Center, located on the boardwalk at Rehoboth Beach. By virtue of often hosting ACB conferences both local and national, the Golden Atlantic Sands was familiar to all.

—Which is important to the blind, I remembered saying.

■

"What do you mean?" Olson said. "Everyone appreciates familiarity, though it's me who says it."

■

Ah, I had replied, but if you couldn't see, or could only see a little bit, you'd know how much more comfortable you felt in a place you knew well. You could relax better, because on day one you already had a pretty good idea where everything was, from the drawers in your room and the taps in your bathroom to the elevators, the restaurant, and the meeting rooms.

And that was supremely true of the Eel. In a place as well known to her as the Golden Atlantic Sands Hotel and Conference Center, my wife glided, floated, strode unerringly down the corridors, across the immensity of the lobby, through the multiplicity of rooms identified by plaques, and through larger rooms where rows of folding chairs faced podiums with clamped-on microphones. She moved as if she *saw*, because in places like that she did see, and what she saw was an unerring map printed within her mind and body.

I had witnessed her negotiate conference hotels in Chicago and New

York, had seen wondrous Eel rise from the chair beside mine at the announcement of her name, step back and set out, head high, smiling in acknowledgment of applause, to walk without hesitation around the long, white-draped table and move directly to the podium that she might thank her introducer and utter her first words. She *saw*, that's what her unsleeping husband understood, she saw with a sight of her own.

■

Olson gave me a look of absolute patience and relaxed back into his chair. "She got those nine women together, you said? I bet the Eel was a good detective."

"She got the job done," I said. "First thing she did was meet them all in a little coffee shop on the boardwalk, a place they'd all been a million times before, and say that the national organization had sent her out to ask these prominent members of the Delaware chapter about how to handle a problem that the New York office saw brewing. She wanted to talk to them individually, and the ACB had arranged for her to use the most formal of all the public rooms, called the Director's Chamber, which happened to be the only conference room or facility the ACB had never used."

■

—But, the Eel had told me, the Director's Chamber almost had a presence all its own within it, some unacknowledged being summoned by the luxury even a sightless person could register. When you walked in and stood quietly for a moment, absorbing the atmosphere, you could feel that the walls had been paneled in rich dark wood, that fine old paintings and tapestries hung beneath small soft lights, and that what met the touch of your foot was a glowing Persian carpet.

—Do you understand? The Eel had asked. You could feel *the presence of the paintings*, you could feel *the lamps above them*, it all set off vibrations, changes in texture, subtle variations in air pressure—an old and precious thing affects the atmosphere in a different way from something new and more cheaply made, how could it help it?

Everything causes movement. *But in that wonderful room, so much was going on, you really felt as though an unseen, unannounced presence had been there all along, waiting for you—waiting to take your measure! Naturally, for sighted people this wouldn't even come close to working. Sometimes, it seems like sighted people can hardly see anything.*

—And what she did, I said to my old friend and houseguest, what Lee Truax did, was she sat in there and waited as they came up, one by one, at their scheduled half-hour intervals, knocked on the door—tentatively, uncertainly, their uncertainty increased by what they could feel of the weight and density, the sheer seriousness, of the wood that made up the door—heard her invite them in, felt for the big handle, and walked inside through a forest of unexpected impressions, almost groping their way along through the crowded silence, until Lee Truax spoke again and invited them to take a chair across the table. When they sat, another figure seemed to join them, a figure perhaps from a portrait, someone known not to be present but present nonetheless, an authoritative ghost. And they had to deal not only with her, but with this illusion their minds and senses had created for them. It would be hard to say which of the two was more powerful.

■

I regarded the soft yellow lamplight flattening out upon the folded white sheet and melting into the pale blanket, and saw the thin, shadowy face hovering beside my wife in a richly appointed room. That what I pictured could have no connection to the face imagined by the Eel's disquieted visitors placed leaping flames beneath my gathering unease. They—he and she—had been together in the State Street diner, in the basement of the Italian restaurant, again on Gorham Street, yet again on Glasshouse Road and in the meadow, twice. Twice. Loathsome, loathsome Hayward had been close enough to hold her hand. And when she made space for him, he had come back to her. I knew what had happened in that room, and it was obscene.

■

"One at a time, they knocked and came in," I had said to Olson. "One by one, they sat down across the table. A few of the nine women who passed through the Director's Chamber that day could distinguish light and dark. I think two of them had a vague, blurry, partial vision in one eye. The rest saw nothing but a complete darkness. But no matter what their eyes did or did not report, they could not but feel that another figure, a figure conjured from the materials of the room itself, had been waiting in there for them all along.

This is what the Eel told me.

■

In the necessary lamplight, I remembered the shock of realizing that I had fallen into the old habit of referring to her by her old nickname. How many times had I done it already? Three times, four? If so, the battle was already lost.

—She started gently, the Eel said. The woman opposite her had already sensed that this meeting, this summons, *in fact, was not quite what she had been expecting, and her antennae were up.*

—Tell me about yourself, the Eel requested. Anything, it doesn't matter. I want to hear you talk about yourself. Outrage me. Delight me. Offend me. Horrify me. All I ask is that you do not bore me.

So they began, the women, one by one, feeling their way toward whatever they imagined the Eel wanted. At the start, it was about where they grew up, their mothers, the schools they attended, and how they wound up getting married. This is the way I got involved with the ACB.

—Could you tell me something else? What is there about you that nobody knows?

(That other presence, that shadowy face, flickered with interest and came a little nearer. It knew all about things unknown—things unknown were where it lived.)

—Surprise me, she said. This is why we are here.

—I'm what people call 'straight,' and I have been all my life, I like having sex with men, but right now what I'd most like to do in all the world is lie down with you on top of this table and hold you as tight as I can. Is that outrage enough for you, Lee Truax?

—I've been blind since the age of two, and I grew up in a house with three sighted older brothers. The oldest one was killed by a drunken driver, the second one committed suicide with his girlfriend in the front seat of our family car when they were in high school. The one closest to me, Merle, who should have died like the other two but didn't, used to take me into the field behind our house and make me play with his ugly thing. And worse. My parents, they never thought he could do anything wrong, they thought Merle was the same as Jesus. When I was eighteen, I got married so he wouldn't be able to rape me anymore. Now I have three boys of my own, and the only way I can stop myself from detesting them is by getting out of the house. That's probably why I work for the ACB.

(The shadowy third shivered with delight. Slowly, it snaked a cold arm over the Eel's shoulders.)

—You want to be horrified, Ms. Truax? I can probably horrify you, if that's what you really want. What you're here about, the reason you asked us to meet you at this hotel, has nothing to do with some vague problem the New York office saw "brewing." It's a lot more specific than that, isn't it? The powers that be want you to investigate the sexual harassment going on in this chapter. A pattern of sexual harassment. Or to be more accurate, Ms. Truax, they want you to ask around, discreetly, without ever doing anything that might actually uncover anything sordid, and after a couple of days go back and report that the rumors are unfounded. But they are not unfounded. One of us makes life very uncomfortable for some of the younger women working under her supervision. I've been waiting for someone to come around here looking into this matter, and you're it, and I'm saying, yes, this horrible behavior is going on. But I'm not going to tell you who it is. That's your job, Ms. Truax.

—You want me to tell you something about me that nobody knows? All right, Lee. Why not? I don't imagine you're going to tell the police or anything, are you? This is like a trust exercise. It is, right? I know how this works. And I don't think you'll blame me, either.

(Here the shadowy third tightened its grip on the Eel's shoulders; here, lying between smooth white sheets and too fearful to turn off the bedside light, I closed my eyes.)

—The reason you won't blame me is because you're going to understand what I did, even if you won't precisely see it my way. I lost my vision at about the same age as you, when I was in my early thirties. Well, I didn't exactly "lose" it. I was attacked and blinded by a man I had just broken up with. Robert didn't want me to be able to look at another man, so he made sure I'd never see anything again. I turned him in to the cops, and I testified at his trial, and he went bye-bye. His sentence was fifteen to twenty-five, only he got out in seven. You know what he did? He called my mother and told her he wanted to apologize to me, so could he please have my phone number? He paid his debt to society, he's a changed man, he wants to know he has my forgiveness. Like a dope, she gave him my number.

—The guy calls me up, asks can he come over? No, I say. You make my skin crawl, of course you can't come over. He begs me to meet him, anyplace. Please. I just want to say a few words to you, then you never have to see me again.

—All right, I say, meet me at this café, the Rosebud, and I told him where it was.

—I didn't say the Rosebud was half a block from my apartment. Probably had half my meals there, everybody knew me, everybody knew my story. One of the staff, Pete, the son of the owner, used to take good care of me, make sure everything went all right. Look, I was thirty-nine, still reasonably good-looking, I was told, and Pete was twenty-eight, he probably had some older-woman crush on me. Anyhow, when he led me to my table, he said I looked kind of tense, was anything wrong? Not really, but, well . . . I explained the whole situation, and he said he'd keep an eye on my table.

—In spite of my tension, the meeting went okay. Robert's voice sounded different than I remembered it, a little lower, a little softer. Nicer. That threw me off, a little—I tried to remember his face, but it was just a pink blur. He said he knew he'd done a terrible thing, he understood that no apology could ever be adequate, but it would mean a lot to him if I could at least say that I no longer hated him. It's not as simple as that, I said.

—We go on talking for a while, and Robert has a burger and a cup of coffee, and I have a tuna salad and a Coke, and he's telling me how hard it is to get a job *if you're an ex-con, but he has a line on something good. His parole officer is pretty happy about it. Do I have a job now, what with . . . you know. Yes, I have a job with a foundation, I say, life is all right for me, it's a struggle, but I try not to complain, even to myself. He says he admires me. I say, Listen to me, I don't want your admiration, and I don't want your respect, either. Just be straight about that.*

—Robert got it, he really did, at least he seemed to. After that, things went surprisingly well. He said that we had a deep connection, we had done certain things to each other, he understood that I'd had to go to the police, he understood that he'd put himself in prison, but it was through my agency, which involved a choice. It was interesting to hear Robert say these things.

—At my insistence we split the bill, whereupon Robert asks if I'd mind if he walked home with me, no more. A farewell gesture, he called it. Come on then, I said, make your gesture. If that's what you want.

—Stupid me. Between my place and the Rosebud there's this enormous empty lot that goes down into a big ravine, and after we get about midway past it, he tells me he wants to take a detour, and before I can say anything, good old Robert clamps a hand over my mouth and puts his other arm around my waist, and he drags me into the empty lot.

—No matter how I thrash around, I can't break his grip. The bastard pulls me clear across the lot and down into the ravine, where he throws me down and jumps on top of me with his hands pinning my shoulders. I'm sure he's going to rape me, and I say everything that comes into my mind, mainly a lot of begging him not to do it. It's no use screaming, because no one could hear me.

—Shut up, he said. I'm not going to rape you. I just wanted to scare you so bad you'd know how I felt almost every day during the past seven years. Scared shitless. Being blind can't be as bad as some of the shit that happened me. I just evened the score. Now get up and get out of here. I never want to see you again.

—I sat up and put my hand on a rock I didn't know was there. That rock moved right into my hand.

(The figure crowded in beside the Eel snickered in delight. I was seeing a ghoul with his arm around my wife.)

—YOU never want to see ME again?

(Then—right then—I could feel someone next to me, the Eel said. It wasn't just them, those women from Delaware, who sensed the presence of someone else in that room, it was me, too. And the figure that joined me was nothing like the judge I had been counting on, not at all. It was sick, it was disgusting . . . it was what we call evil because we don't have any better words for it.)

—I was furious! My body acted before my mind could tell it what to do. I swung my arm around toward his voice, and Robert must have turned his head away, because he didn't stop my arm or duck or anything, and before I realized that I was trying to hit him in the head with that rock, I felt the rock smash against something hard. I yelled in shock, but my body kept moving—I slid forward and swung that rock down again, and this time I felt something crack up like an eggshell, and my hands were all wet. I started making some kind of noise, not yelling, not crying, something messier and less articulate than those—I was down in that ravine, for God's sake, and I'd just killed a man who had once been violently in love with me. And you know what? I was glad, violently glad, that he was dead.

(The disgusting figure clutching the Eel shivered in ecstasy, then disappeared, having obtained what it wanted.)

—Someone pounded down into the ravine, and I screamed and struggled to stand up. It had to be a cop, and I'd go to jail for a lot longer than that asshole ever had. A man was saying, My God, my God, over and over, and I realized he wasn't a cop. It was Pete from the diner! He had come out to make sure nothing funny happened to me, and when he couldn't see me on the street, he ran into that enormous lot. Pretty soon, he heard me making that noise, and here he was, my savior!

—Pete got me home unseen, and he got me into my apartment and let me clean up and change into fresh clothes. He put all the bloody stuff in a garbage bag and told me he was going to burn it all after he dragged the body deep into the ravine and covered it up, or put it in a cave, or hid it somehow, so nobody would find it for a long time. And I guess he did a good job, because Robert's body is still down there. No policemen ever came around asking tough questions. I got away with murder. Is that secret enough for you, Ms. Truax?

The next lady said:

—This is funny, it makes me smile when I think about it. The strange stuff that happens in your life! So, anyhow. When I was a little girl, my mother used to take me into her favorite stores so I could shoplift things for her.

Eel had her thief.

■

"She got her to confess?" Don asked, next to the dark windows in the lounge.

"That she did," I remembered saying, all the while feeling, far too near, the beating of enormous wings. "It took her twenty minutes. The woman broke down. She said she only stole a little at a time, and she hadn't really noticed how the amount grew. By now it scared her, but she didn't know how to stop. 'You've already stopped,' Lee told her. 'It's over.' They worked out a repayment schedule, never brought in the police, solved the whole problem in one afternoon. The lady went away shaken but reformed. You know, she had kept on shoplifting through her whole life. Like Boats!"

"Yeah, like Boats," Olson said. "But this lady got caught."

He smiled, then looked upward, distracted by a thought. "What year was this, again?"

"Nineteen ninety-five. October, I think."

"That's interesting. I have the feeling that in October of 1995, Spencer and I were visiting this patron of his, an old lady named Grace Fallow. She was rich, and she liked Spencer to come to her and give consultations. This was way at the end of the time I was working with him."

"Yes, and?"

■

—Yes, and? Meaning, what is this to me?

■

"Grace Fallow lived in Rehoboth Beach. She put us up in a hotel called the Boardwalk Plaza."

■

—Grace Fallow lived in Rehoboth Beach . . . Boardwalk Plaza.

■

"We could have run into her! Wouldn't that have been weird?"

"I guess it would have been, yes."

He frowned at me. "Hey, it was a *coincidence*. We never saw her, and as far as I know, she never saw us. But maybe, you know, she glimpsed him and got caught up in nostalgia. It *was* a pretty exciting time in our lives. And I could be wrong about the date." He paused and looked up and to the left. "Actually, I think I *was* wrong. I think Grace Fallow asked us to pay her a visit in October of 1996, not '95. Yes. I think that's right. It was 1996."

■

—Sure it was, I muttered, using a phrase I had not spoken to my friend in the lounge. In the lounge, I had said nothing; I had merely nodded.

A long time passed before I felt able to turn off the bedside lamp and invite the mind-stirring darkness.

■

The following morning, we went back to the Lamont Hospital and there a stupendous thing took place, but before I explain what it was, we are going to skip over the next four days, each of them packed with events that may have been a shade less stupefying but were pretty astonishing anyhow, at least to all who were present. But on the fifth day, the one to which we are skipping, another amazement, in fact several of them, occurred, all of which began with Don Olson's announcement over toasted bagels and Danish pastry at our usual table in the lounge that Howard Bly, the source of the stupendousnesses and stupefactions noted above, had been told not to expect his friends this day. In response to my question, Olson told me that he had a surprise for me. The surprise involved a quick trip to Milwaukee.

"What's your surprise?"

"You'll find out when we get there. We have kind of a small window here. It takes an hour and a half to drive to Milwaukee, but on an airplane you get there in half an hour. Now, even though I really hate to fly, I booked us cheap tickets on this new no-frills airline, EZ Flite Air. All you have to do is get us to the airport in the next forty minutes or so and pay the money. In Milwaukee, we can rent a car. I figure you'd gain at least half an hour, and unless I'm all wrong you're going to want it."

"What's all the rush?"

"The person we're going to meet can't spare a lot of time."

"And you won't tell me who this mystery person is."

"You're wasting precious minutes," Olson said, wiping his lips with the napkin as he stood.

In five minutes, we were driving to Dane County Regional Airport, and in twenty-five I was standing eighth in line at the EZ Flite Air desk in the bright, wide lobby. I alone had no luggage. All I planned to bring with me, a notebook and a fountain pen, had been slipped into my jacket pockets.

Don Olson, who admitted to being one of those people who exist in a state of near-paralytic fear from the moment a plane's wheels leave the ground to the moment they meet it again, had disappeared into the depths of the terminal to hunt down candy bars and magazines, or whatever else might dull his anxieties. Since it was still fairly early in the morning, I hoped that Olson would not feel compelled to gulp down a couple of whiskies. Or at least that he might hold it to two and no more.

The line crawled forward, moving at the rate of perhaps one foot every twenty minutes. The ticket clerks on the far side of the distant desk spent a great deal of time staring, befuddled, at a monitor visible only to them. They

186

tapped keys and shook their heads and whispered. Eventually the key tap-ping, the whispering, and the head shaking ceased, and another group of passengers were handed their boarding passes and directed toward security and the gates. I settled in to wait my turn.

To kill time, I fieldstripped my pen to reassure myself that it was almost full. What do you know, it was. While I reassembled the pen, a fraught cou-ple with three enormous bags was released from the desk, and I could move another foot and a half. I pushed my hands into my pockets and leaned for-ward to see if my shoes required shining. They did not, yet. I straightened up, inhaled deeply, and sighed. Both of the boys at the desk had flattened their hands over their crew cuts in a posture of amazement and confusion. This was not a good sign. One of the boys tapped a lot of keys and bent toward the invisible monitor. What he saw there caused him to shake his head.

I turned around and looked at the people on the other side of the wide, empty space behind me. College students and other civilians crossed my line of vision, going in and out of the doors, gabbing into cell phones, leaning against pillars and waste bins, standing or sitting on their luggage. Nearly everyone wore or carried a backpack, and almost everyone was under the age of forty. I hoped to see Olson, but the candy bars and magazines must have been on the other side of the terminal. My gaze drifted across a row of disheveled-looking young people arrayed on a line of stationary chairs and stopped to focus upon a slim older man in a black leather jacket, a light-weight black turtleneck, and jeans. This was no ordinary geezer. He looked a bit like an actor. The man's hair, ample, silvery white, and just short enough to escape being a coiffure, swept back from his suntanned, slightly vulpine face to fall past the collar of the jacket. He had prominent, dead-level cheek-bones and deeply set blue eyes and could have been any age between seventy and eighty-five. This imposing, undoubtedly self-invented character was looking directly at me. Evidently he had been staring at me for some time.

That the object of his concentration had caught him at it did not at all embarrass him. He simply went on looking at me, calmly, as if I were an animal in a zoo.

I had no idea why this should be true, but the man's gaze irritated and upset me. Being looked at in this way felt impudent, condescending, like a diminishment. It was uncomfortable to be singled out and *watched*. I wished the man would focus on some other victim. He looked completely self-sufficient. The man's intensely blue eyes were shamelessly trying to lock with mine.

When I spun around to break contact, it felt as if I had dropped an electrified wire. The young men at the counter were now handing baggage tickets and boarding passes to two girls. The line diminished by one, a tall, long-haired man with an ill-concealed bald spot and a six-foot duffel bag that rolled behind him on its convenient wheels like a dog. I advanced another foot. A messy family of two heavyset parents and four even more heavyset kids, dragging a great many heaped-up bags, trudged across the empty space, gathered behind me, and immediately began to argue.

If you say that one more time, I'm going to. I was only trying to. Why don't you ever LISTEN to. Molly, if you don't stop flapping your mouth. I don't have to if I don't want. I don't care if the kids are. Those brats are the whole reason for.

I tried to use the family as cover while checking to see if the silver-haired man was still staring at me. To my relief and surprise, the man was no longer standing in front of the big windows. Then a movement caught my eye and, heart already jumping in my chest, I turned my head and saw, about four feet off to my left, the silver-haired man approaching me. He stopped moving and held up his hands.

"Do you want something from me?" I asked. "What is it? Who are you, Rasputin?"

The family at my back sensed drama and fell silent.

The man smiled. His smile was beautiful. "Aren't you Lee Harwell, the writer?"

Astonished, I nodded. "I am, yes."

"I've read all your books. Please let me apologize. I must have seemed very rude."

"It's perfectly all right. Thank you for explaining."

While this was going on, the young men dispensed another boarding pass and baggage ticket, and I moved into the gap left by the couple ahead of me. The silver-haired man sidled closer. The awful family shoved their bags forward, eyeing the man as if they expected him to perform some feat of magic.

He leaned sideways and rolled his expressive eyes at me. His lips pursed, and wrinkles divided his forehead into furrows. I thought: *There's more. I should have known.* I looked through the terminal, but Olson was probably guzzling tequila in some distant corner.

"I must speak to you," the man said, softly. "Could you please move away with me? This has to be private."

"I'm not moving out of this line."

"It concerns your safety."

Before I could object, my admirer placed one hand on my elbow, another in the small of my back, and shifted me a foot and a half to the side as easily as if I were on wheels.

"Now, hold on there, mister," I said, pulling away.

"I am holding on," the man said, smiling once again, and with the same effortless authority used the slightest pressure in the small of my back to stop me from moving away. He leaned in and whispered, his eyes pinning mine.

"I was staring because I had a very strong premonition about you. You must not take this flight."

"You're crazy," I said. Once more, it seemed that my hand had fastened onto an electric fence, and pure energy pulsed through me. I tried to break contact, but the pressure on my back, which felt like the pressure of a doll's hand, held me fast.

"Please. If you go up to the counter and buy a ticket from those two fools and get on EZ Flite Air 202, the consequences will be drastic. Catastrophic."

"And how do you know that?"

"I *know*. If you fly to Milwaukee you will lose everything." He paused to be certain that this had hit its mark. "Don't you have a car? Drive there, and all will be well."

"All will be well?"

The man's hands dropped away. The sense of release from some profound but invisible energy was as palpable as the sudden cessation of an uproar.

"Think about it, Lee."

"What's your name?"

The beautiful smile transformed the severity of his face. "Rasputin."

The man stepped back. In seconds, he had disappeared.

Two couples and a man who looked like a retired soldier stood between me and the ticket counter.

I looked at the clerks, paralyzed as ever by their cluelessness, and wondered: *What if the whole airline is like these guys?* How many successful flights had EZ Flite Air managed to pull off, anyhow? And where was Don Olson?

As soon as the question had formed, Olson appeared at the edge of the crowded distance into which "Rasputin" had disappeared. Perhaps he had seen that odd and impressive character.

After Don came up to me, bearing copies of *Vanity Fair* and *The New Republic,* on his breath a faint perfume of bourbon, I asked if he had noticed a striking man in a black jacket, silvery hair to his shoulders, and the face of an Apache chief, if Apaches were WASPs. Don blinked and said, "What?"

I repeated myself.

"Maybe I missed him."

"You couldn't miss a guy like that. No one could. It'd be like missing a burning building."

Don blinked again. "No then, I didn't see him. Why? What did he do?"

"He told me not to take this flight."

We were permitted to move another eighteen inches toward the head of the line, where we now stood third.

Olson asked why the man had advised against the flight, and listened to the answer with what looked like equanimity. "What do you want to do?" He seemed, at a level deep within, almost amused.

"I was waiting for you to come back, so I could ask you."

"I'll go along with whatever you say. As long as you say the right thing."

I gave him a look of exasperation. "I hate to say it, but I want to take the car."

"You said the right thing. Let's get going."

I said, "All right," and realized that I could not simply walk off. The family behind me was wrangling again, so I asked the people ahead of me if they were getting on the flight to Milwaukee.

The man of the first couple said, "No, Green Bay."

The woman of the second couple said, "Terre Haute. Why?"

The man who resembled a retired soldier smiled and said, "I'm going a lot farther than these other people."

I asked if he were changing planes in Milwaukee.

"St. Louis."

I turned around to face the couple. They must have weighed a total of at least seven hundred pounds, and they had big, grouchy faces. Their children were waddling in circles, whining. The couple saw me looking at them from a foot away and fell silent in wondering amazement. No one ever talked to them, I realized.

"I'll make this brief," I said. "Are you traveling to, or changing planes in, Milwaukee?"

"Are we what?" asked the wife.

"No," said her husband.

"No *what*?" she asked him. You don't tell him our. He didn't. He doesn't. You don't, you always, you never.

Don and I walked away from the squabbling couple, through the wide empty space, and outside to the parking lot.

"I'm almost tempted to say . . ." Olson began, and I told him not to.

■

Once we got on the long, straight highway to Milwaukee, Olson switched on the radio and tuned it to Newsradio 620 WTMJ, the Milwaukee NBC affiliate, just then and for the next two hours broadcasting *Midday with Joe Ruddler,* a call-in show that very few people called in to, because the host, Mr. Ruddler, formerly a sports newscaster in Millhaven, Illinois, much preferred talking to listening. (Ruddler also fancied SHOUTING, BELLOWING, and RANTING. He liked to refer to his career as a television sportscaster as "When my name was in lights" or "When I was in the BIG LEAGUES.") Don had learned that attending to such programs in his off-hours, or while in transit, provided a bottomless well of local information that often proved useful to him during his residencies in the communities where he plied his unusual trade. Mallon, he said, had done the same.

Joe Ruddler was outraged about his phone bill. On his landline, he had made only five calls, for which the total cost was twenty-two cents. Yet his bill was for the amount of thirty-two dollars and seven cents. How did these CLOWNS manage a trick like that?? Joe Ruddler's outrage flowed out from a self-replenishing fountain.

When we were about forty miles from Milwaukee, Ruddler dialed his voice way down and said, "We just got some grim news here, friends, and I want to take the liberty of sharing it with you. I'm jumping the gun on the official announcement, but to an old broadcaster like myself the news is news, and ought to be reported straight and true in a timely fashion, not sifted and filleted and spun this way and that until black turns into white and vicey-versy."

"No," I said. "It can't be."

"Can't be what?"

"So pardon me for shaking up your day, my friends, forgive me if you can for bringing Mr. Death into our conversation here. We'd prefer to keep him out, I know, but when Mr. Death walks into the room, people tend to give him all their attention, because our Mr. Death is ONE GOSH-DARNED SERIOUS FELLOW. Well, prepare to pay attention, folks.

"About twenty minutes ago, a plane fell out of the sky and crash-landed on a farmer's field near the little hamlet of Wales, not far from highway I-94. There were no survivors, at least no OBVIOUS ones."

"No, no," Don said, shaking his head. "This is . . ."

I shushed him.

"EZ Flite Air Flight 202, on its regular journey between Madison and our fair city, BIT THE DUST, you could say, AUGURED IN, as the fly boys once had it, killing everyone on board, passengers and crew alike. They add up, ladies and gentlemen, to seventeen souls."

Don moaned and put his face in his hands.

"There have been BIGGER air crashes, killing MORE souls, but that's not relevant. Here we have a genuine opportunity for thought, for philosophy, and I think we ought to SEIZE it. Now think of this—seventeen people, turned into crispy critters, bones broken, bodies all smashed up—why THEM? Huh? Right? Are you HEARING me? These people DIED TO-GETHER. My question to you is, did anything unite them BEFORE they met their fates? Did they have ANYTHING IN COMMON? Because they sure do now! If you were to look back into those seventeen fragile human lives, really look, turn a magnifying glass on them, a MICROSCOPE, do you think you'd see some common threads? You bet you would! Jenny knew Jackie in grade school, Jackie used to babysit for Johnnie, Johnnie owed a lot of money to Joe. There'd be a TON of that. But go deeper.

"There is another side to this question. Fourteen passengers died, and three crew members. But SIXTEEN tickets were booked for that flight, and TWO of them were never paid for. TWO PEOPLE decided no thanks,

I'm not gonna GET on good old Flight 202 from Dane County Regional Airport to Mitchell Field, thanks anyhow, but no. They were GOING to take that flight, but they CHANGED THEIR MINDS, both of 'em. Why? I wanna know, I really do. WHY? Huh, right?"

I gave Olson an uneasy, unhappy look and found the same thing coming back at me.

"The question is, what does this MEAN? We're allowed to think about MEANING, aren't we?"

"I'm pulling over," I said. "I can't take this anymore. My hands are shaking, and it feels like my guts are, too." I drove the car into the breakdown lane, turned it off, and slumped down in my seat.

Joe Ruddler roared on. "Because let me tell you this, the truth as I see it is THE TRUTH, period. Full stop. Take my word for it, heck, you can take that to the bank. JOE RUDDLER DOES NOT LIE TO YOU, folks. He CAN'T. Joe Ruddler happens to be too darn simple-minded to do anything but speak the TRUTH, and he's been that cotton-pickin' way his whole durn LIFE! That's what he DOES, he tells THE COTTON-PICKIN' TRUTH! Yowza!

"And this is what I'm here to tell you, my friends. Those two folks that backed away from EZ Flite Air 202 have a DESTINY. Yes, they DO! They were SAVED FOR A PURPOSE. In all LIKELIHOOD, they just suppose they got lucky. Yes, they DID, they SURE did, and do you know why? The reason they got LUCKY is because—"

"Is that," I whispered.

"—they have a DESTINY! Only one thing in the world is more POWERFUL than the possession of a DESTINY. That one thing is MEANING. There is MEANING in their lives, they are wrapped in a MEANING!"

Unable to bear this stuff a moment longer, I struck a button, and the radio went dead.

"Am I in possession of a destiny?" Olson twitched on his seat, as if he had been prodded or poked. "Oh, Christ, look at that."

He jabbed his index finger at the right-hand edge of the windshield, and when I shifted my gaze to look out, I saw for the first time what should have been apparent for at least a couple of minutes, and would have been, had we not been so claimed by loudmouthed Joe Ruddler. Miles away in a distant field, a narrow column of dense black smoke coiled up into the air, widening out as it rose.

"OmyGod," Olson said.

"Oh, my God," I said, a moment behind him. "Oh, Jesus."

"How many people did he say?"

"Seventeen, I think. Which includes three crew."

"Oh. Oh. This is terrible. Did we see any of them, do you think?"

"Not at the ticket counter. Though some of those people way ahead of me must have been . . . I wonder if those two girls . . . And that guy who was going bald . . ."

"Lee, I can't look at that smoke anymore. All right?"

"I feel sick."

"Drive away. Let's get out of here."

I followed orders, and we fled.

Fifteen minutes later, Olson asked, "Feeling better now?"

"Yeah. I am. Weird, but better."

"Same here. Weird but better."

"Relieved."

"*Really* relieved."

"Yeah," I said. "You too, huh?"

"It's like the reverse of survivor guilt."

"Survivor euphoria."

"Survivor bliss."

"Hah!"

"Jesus, man, we could be lying dead back there. Or smashed up, or *burned* up into, what did he say, crispy critters?"

"We almost were. *So* close."

"Missed us by fuckin' inches."

"By millimeters."

Don punched the dashboard, then planted his hands on the roof and pushed up. "Whoa. Is it okay to feel like this?"

"Sure! We're not dead!"

"Those seventeen poor sons a bitches are all dead, and we're still alive!"

"Exactly. Yep. That's it, exactly."

"Being alive feels pretty fuckin' good, doesn't it?"

"Being alive is great," I said, with the feeling of uttering a profound but little-known truth. "Just . . . *great.* And we owe it all to that guy. If he *was* a guy. Maybe he was some kind of angel."

"Your angel, anyhow."

I gave him a questioning look.

"What do we know about him? Two things. He knew who you were, and he didn't want you to die in an airplane crash."

"So he was my guardian angel?"

"One way or another, yeah! For sure! Hey—remember what you were saying about a woman Hayward never got to kill because *he* was killed? Or her child, or her grandchild? A ripple effect?"

I nodded.

"That talk-show guy, Joe Ruddler, was yelling about destiny. It's the same thing, isn't it?"

"Oh, come on," I said.

"Did that guy ask if you were on Flight 202?"

"I think so. Sure, he did. Hold on. No, he just came up and told me he had a precognition that if I took Flight 202, the consequences would be terrible."

"So he already knew what flight you were on."

I slumped a bit. Perhaps after all I would be required to be in possession of a destiny.

"One way or another, it's about you, Harwell. Face it."

I wished Olson had not mentioned my speculations. Most of my joy-
ousness at still being alive had evaporated, though I had a vivid memory of
its taste.

"I'm going to read my copy of *Vanity Fair* right now," Olson said.

He leaned over the back of the seat, fished around in his bag until he
had dug out the magazine he had purchased in the airport, and thumped
himself down again while he riffled through its pages. "Beautiful ads in
this thing," he said, and spoke no more until we reached the exit for downtown Milwaukee, where he told me to get off the highway and drive to the
Pfister.

"I should have known," I said. "You guys think there's only one hotel
in Milwaukee."

"My surprise isn't a guy," Olson said. "When you get to the hotel, go
into the lot."

■

After Don had made a call from one of the phones behind the
concierge desk, we took adjacent armchairs in the Pfister's lobby and watched
clusters of people come down the hallway from the elevators to the newer,
Tower part of the hotel complex, descend the lobby steps, and gather before
the long front desk. They were usually in families. Sometimes small groups
of men bunched up as they registered, punching their friends' shoulders and
laughing open-mouthed at jokes.

"They're all doing something together," Don said. "And they came
here to do it. Are they in some association, some club? Or do they all work
for the same company?"

"There sure are a lot of them," I said. "Are we waiting for this surprise
of yours to come down here? Why don't you tell me who it is?"

"Because that would spoil the surprise. We're waiting for someone to leave."

"So we can follow this person. This woman."

"Nope. Completely, hopelessly wrong. Why don't you just wait?"

I crossed my legs, canted sideways, and leaned on the chair's armrest. If I had to, I could have waited there forever. Whenever we got hungry or thirsty, we could order sandwiches and drinks from wandering waiters. The Pfister was a gracious old grande dame. The studly concierge wore a cavalier's pointed mustache, and the composed and deferential registration clerks would have looked at home behind the desk at the Savoy. Only the sport shirts, khakis, and boat shoes of the guests located the lobby in its time and place.

"I can't believe what's happening with Hootie," I said.

"Neither can Dr. Greengrass and that steamy little Pargeeta."

"You think Pargeeta's 'steamy'? She strikes me as cold and haughty."

"Don't know much about women, do you? Pargeeta's a *freak*. She's so freaky, Hootie turns her on!"

"That's ridiculous."

I remembered seeing an odd conflict of emotions surfacing in the young woman's face when Howard lay on the floor. After Greengrass asked him to speak in his own words, Pargeeta almost smiled. Whatever her feelings had been, they looked nothing like arousal.

"The girls always loved Hootie, man."

"When he looked like the blond kid in *Shane*."

"It's a good thing you write fiction. If you had to describe the real world, nobody would recognize it."

"Face it, Don, you couldn't tell a story straight if somebody put a gun to your head. Mallon was the same way."

"Aww," Don said. "We're having our first argument."

I realized that I was more irritated than I had thought. These Mallon people made up the rules everywhere they went, arrogant, conceited, grasshoppers who depended on everyone else to feed them and clothe them and given them drugs and alcohol and listen to their ridiculous lies and open their legs whenever the Mallons and Mallon-ites wanted . . .

I had a sudden visual flash of the silver-haired man in the airport, and with it occurred a certain dread possibility. Instantly, I thrust it away.

"Calm down," Don said. "I see by your face that you're getting all cranked up. Remember that I'm doing you a favor here. And looky looky looky, I believe our question has been answered."

I followed the direction of his gaze and saw, just now flowing down the lobby steps and earning a smile from the Cavalier, a cluster of people of every age, all of them stuffed into blue jeans that strained over their swollen bellies and ample hams. At their center moved a round-faced young woman encumbered with what appeared to be a loose gauze bandage floating about the top of her head. They were a family, mother and father, uncles and aunts, sons, daughters, cousins, wives and husbands, and even a couple of roly-poly children who darted in and out of the general confusion.

"Is that a melee, or what?" asked Olson. "God, look at her. She's the Queen Bee, all right."

The lively familial scuffle bustled toward the front desk, where it broke apart into singles and couples, allowing Don's Queen Bee to throw out her arms and move at a slow, stately trot toward the desk. Two beefy males of approximately her age moved into position to receive extravagant hugs. The gauze on the young woman's sturdy head was a wedding veil, swept back over an elaborate and lacquered hairdo. Apart from the veil, she wore a gray Eau Claire sweatshirt, the same kind of jeans as the rest of her family, and—a wonderful touch, I thought—well-worn, nearly knee-high cowboy boots with stacked heels and much ridging and stitching. She had come down with her family to greet the arrival of the groom and the best man, his brother.

"Going to be noisy in here tonight," I said.

For a moment, I switched my gaze to a group of four men in crisp dark suits and gleaming shirtfronts who emerged from the nearer, non-Tower elevators and strode past the wedding party, moving toward the Jefferson Street exit at the back of the lobby. These men moved with the quick, gliding pace of dogs intent on their goal, entirely indifferent to the spectacle around them. The curls of white wire running from the ears of the two tall, athletic-looking men in the rear disappeared beneath the smooth collars of their jackets. Pacing just ahead of a thin, watchful-looking man with black-framed glasses who had tucked a black leather folder beneath his elbow, the obvious leader of this pack had perfect CEO hair graying at the temples and a broad, suntanned face with deep smile lines around the eyes. He looked as if he had just purchased the hotel and was heading out to buy two or three more.

Open-mouthed, Don Olson tracked the progress of these men toward the exit. They swept out in a fluid unit, flowing through the self-opened glass door like sharks prowling the sea.

Olson turned to me and tapped my bicep. "Time for the big surprise, bud."

He stood up. I did the same. "So that's who we were waiting to leave."

"Gee, d'ya think?" Olson wove through the lobby furniture, going to the same elevator the four men had just left. I followed a few steps behind.

"The man who owns the world, his lawyer, and his security team."

"You didn't recognize him."

"I don't read the business section," I said.

"That's not the one he's usually in." Olson came up to the single lobby elevator and punched the button with a knuckle. Immediately, the door retracted.

"Okay, I give up," I said. I went into the elevator and watched Olson use his knuckle to punch the button for the fifth floor.

"What's the business with the knuckle? A sanitation issue?"

"You really didn't recognize that guy? He might be our president one day, if our luck runs really bad."

I snapped my fingers. "You don't want to leave fingerprints. It's a trick you learned from Boats."

"Why leave your prints all over everywhere? Use your elbow, not your hand. Use your knuckle, not your finger. Wear gloves. A world like this, privacy disappearing in a hundred little ways, you might as well do what you can to cover yourself. Just ask the senator what *he* thinks about individual privacy. Fine for him, is what he thinks. That guy, him and those like him need so much privacy they want to take most of what we got."

"He's a senator?"

"First term, but give him time. They've got big plans, *huge* plans."

"They? Him and that skinny lawyer guy next to him?"

"Him and his wife."

The elevator stopped on the fifth floor. I followed Olson out as I had followed him in, and when we turned to go down the corridor, something awakened in my memory.

"Is this senator's name Walsh?"

"Senator Rinehart Walker Walsh, of Walker Farms, Walker Ridge, Tennessee."

"Currently the husband of . . ."

"The former Meredith Bright. The one remaining survivor of Spencer Mallon's ceremony-slash-experiment-slash-breakthrough in the agronomy meadow that you still haven't met."

"Apart from Hayward's roommate, Brett Milstrap."

"Well, good luck with that. And you forgot Mallon."

"You mean he isn't dead?" This information shocked me: it was like hearing that the Minotaur still lived at the heart of his labyrinth. A sudden foul taste and a scalding sensation rose from the back of my throat into my mouth.

"Of course he's not dead. He lives on the Upper West Side of New York and he makes his living as a psychic. He's a *great* psychic. Want to meet him? I'll give you his address."

I tried to picture myself ringing Mallon's doorbell, and a shiver of revulsion ran through me. "All this time, that bastard has been alive." I still could only barely believe it. "Jesus. You know, back in the airport, this terrible idea came to me, and I . . ."

Don said, "Pull yourself together, Lee. This isn't exactly going to be a day at the beach, either."

At the end of the hallway he knocked on a door marked "The Marquette Suite."

The door swung open. A tall, cadaverous, black-clad man in his mid-thirties stood before us, already backing away. He had a pronounced stoop, dark hair that dripped over his pale forehead, dark, shiny eyes, and a long, slippery mouth.

"Yes," he said, making a sketchy bow of his slouch. "Donald, of course, here you are, yes." Briefly, he offered Don his limp hand, which Don took, briefly, and dropped without shaking. The man turned his entire upper body to me, and swung his hand with it. His eyes glittered. It was like meeting an undertaker from an old black-and-white movie. "And this must be Mr. Harwell, our famous aut'or. What a pleasure this iz."

I met the man's dangling fingers with his own. They felt cold and lifeless. After a moment of contact, I pulled back my hand.

"I am Vardis Fleck, Mr. Harwell, Mrs. Walsh's assistant. Please come with me into the drawing room."

We were in an entry or anteroom where a large oval mirror in a gilt frame faced a high table with a huge flower arrangement that widened out in a fan of stalks and twigs. Behind Fleck, two doors slanted toward each other in a triangular corner. He glided to the door on the right and swung it open.

"Please," he said again, smiling with his mouth only.

"I hope you're still cooking on all burners, Vardis," said Don. "And that there is peace in the kingdom."

"Never a boring moment when *you're* around, Donald."

He followed us into a wide, functional space with groupings of couches and upholstered chairs around dark wooden tables. A bare fireplace stood in the wall to our right; on the wall to the left, a tall black console displayed a large blank television and an array of drawers around the minibar. Cut-glass vases on two tables held huge, thrusting flower arrangements doubled by mirrors identical to the one in the foyer.

"But I can assure you that I am cooking on every one of the burners that I possess," Fleck added. "Such is the nature of my employment. I wish to add that you are my dear lady's most truly *unconventional* acquaintance. She knows no others who request a monetary contribution upon releasse from priss-on."

With a languid flap of a hand that resembled a broken bird's wing, he waved us to the furniture in front of the fireplace.

"A contribution she was as happy to offer as I was grateful to receive."

"Mr. Fleck," I asked, parking myself on the sofa's rigid and unyielding cushion, "might I ask where you are from? Your accent is very musical, but I'm afraid I can't place it."

"You may, you might," said Fleck. He was bowing slightly and backing toward a baronial door with a cornice and a grand entablature on the left side of the room. An identical door stood in the wall to our right. Behind these would be many others, leading to interlocking rooms. All of the rooms would be as anonymous and impersonal as this one.

"It is an un-usual story, if I may permit myself. I was born in Alsace-Lorraine, but my childhood was spent in Veszprém, Transdanubia, in the Bakony Mountains."

"Fleck is a Hungarian name, is it not?"

The man's smile became almost alarmingly toothy, while his wet-looking eyes remained cold. "Mine is *a* Hungarian name, as you remark." His upper body inclined toward the floor at an even greater angle, and he reached behind him for the knob, swung the door open, and disappeared through it backwards.

For a couple of seconds we heard his shoes pattering away. Then the footsteps ceased, as if Fleck had taken flight.

"You see him often?"

"Without you see Vardis, you don't see Meredith. I think even the senator has to make playdates and dinner arrangements through that guy."

"Does the senator know about your visits?"

"Of course not. Why do you think we had to wait for him to leave?"

"She's a pretty brave woman, whatever you say."

"Because of what she's risking? Meredith Walsh doesn't give a shit about risk, she has the guts of a burglar. Hold on, she's coming."

Audible through the vast door to their left, light footsteps ticked across a wooden floor.

"I thought she'd come from the other side, didn't you?" I asked. Olson put a finger to his lips, staring at the great door as if in expectation of something wondrous or appalling.

When the door opened, the first thought that came to me was, *Well, now I can say that I have seen at least two extraordinarily beautiful older women.*

Coming toward me was a lush, slender woman in a short black dress cut low in front, a handsome jacket of a subtle blue, and black toe-cleavage pumps with three-inch heels. She was taller than I had expected, and her silken, well-shaped legs made her seem almost obscenely young. Her abundant hair seemed to shimmer between light blond and silver-white, first one, then the other, then back again. All of this had an impact, of course, but what made my heart pick up speed and my vision lose focus was her face.

Abandon and control, warmth and teasing distance, deep humor and deep gravity informed her face, along with a hundred other promises and possibilities. Meredith Walsh looked like a woman who could understand everything, and explain it all to you in words of one syllable, patiently. She also seemed to be of no particular age whatsoever, apart from possessing an undeniably attractive maturity that made youth seem like a mere chrysalis. Her stunning looks, her obvious intelligence, her warmth, her sexuality, her humor, these things flummoxed and upended me, and by the time the gorgeous, sexy, witty, grown-up blur that was Meredith Walsh had somehow magically appeared beside my chair, I wanted, in no particular order, to take her home with me, spend hours in bed making love, and marry her. Standing to greet her came more from reflex than a conscious decision. Once I was on my feet, I was grateful she extended a hand instead of leaning forward for a kiss on the cheek: being that close would have been too intoxicating.

"Lee Harwell, this is such a treat," she said. "I'm so pleased that Don made it possible for me to meet you. Please, sit down. We have only about an hour, actually less, but we should be as comfortable as possible during our time together, don't you think?"

She sat where no chair had been, but instantly one appeared beneath her.

"Yes, of course," I heard myself say. "I certainly want *you* to be comfortable."

I found myself taking in the top of her head before it came to me that I was supposed to sit, too. How could Donald Olson ever have come to such absurd conclusions about this woman?

When I sat, her gaze surrounded me.

"What a gentleman you are. No wonder you charmed Vardis so completely. Of course Vardis is one of your most ardent admirers. I wish I could say that I have read your books, too, but a politician's wife leads an absurdly busy life. However, I will get to one of your books as soon as is possible. I will make time for it."

I made the usual self-deprecating noises.

"And Don, you are in good health, now that you no longer have to eat institutional food? You've been staying with Mr. Harwell?"

"He's been amazingly good to me."

"How very nice for you, Donald. Would the two of you care for a drink of some kind? Scotch, vodka, martini, gin and tonic? Coffee or tea, perhaps? Vardis will be happy to prepare anything you might want. I'm going to ask him to bring me some water."

She looked brightly from face to face. We both said water would be fine for us, too. Meredith Walsh turned sideways to punch a button on an elaborate telephone that had come into existence at the moment she extended her hand.

Without picking up the receiver, she said, "Vardis."

In seconds, her creature slid in through the door by which he had exited. Head bent low, hands steepled before him, he listened to the orders and pronounced the words "Three waters, yes." Again, he opened the door without looking at it and backed out.

By this time I had recovered a portion of my sanity and could look at the woman before me with sufficient clarity to see that she had undoubtedly had facial surgery, probably several times. The skin over her cheekbones seemed too taut by an infinitesimal degree, and there were no lines on her forehead or at the sides of her eyes. She was maybe twice the age she seemed to be, I thought, and three or fours years older than me. Everything about her belied these facts.

"You knew each other in high school," she said, and gave us the benefit of her extraordinary eyes. "In fact, as I understand it, Mr. Harwell—Lee, if I might—you were part of that lovely group I met one day in a little coffee shop on State Street. And you're interested in that disastrous evening Spencer Mallon orchestrated out in a meadow."

"That's exactly right," I said. "I avoided this subject for years and years, and after all this time it became something I finally had to work out. Then all of this information about Keith Hayward dropped into my lap, and I began to learn more and more about Mallon and the meadow."

I waited for Meredith Walsh to respond, but she merely looked back at me with the suggestion of a smile.

"I guess my interest in all this is more personal than professional."

She smiled more broadly. "So I gathered. Obviously, I invited you here to help you, as far as I can, satisfy your personal interest in all of us back then. I promised Donald, who has always been extremely discreet about our contacts, to give you an hour when my husband was scheduled to be else-where. Right now, he is or shortly will be speaking at a rally for a local mem-ber of his party, and after that he will meet and greet at a cocktail reception."

A hint of sadness and regret deepened her beautiful smile. *Here it comes,* I thought, preparing myself to be dismissed.

"My husband is an important and ambitious man whom I am going to assist in his quest for the presidency. He knows nothing at all about that cu-rious incident in 1966 or my brief relationship with Spencer Mallon. He never can know anything about that, and the same is true of the press. We went into the meadow, and before we could get out, a young man was mur-dered there. Hideously, I might add. And equally unfortunately, the whole event smacks of magic, of the occult, witchcraft, elements that can never be associated with someone in my position."

"You're telling me that whatever you say to me cannot be used in any-thing I write."

"No, I am not. I don't want to hinder you in the writing of this book of yours. You are a well-known author. If this book adds to your fame, you might be able to give a public endorsement of my husband's candidacy. All I ask is that you conceal my identity and keep it secret for as long as anyone is interested in your story."

"I could probably do that." I was a little taken aback by this cold-blooded swap. "You could have another name, you could be a brunette, a freshman instead of a sophomore, or whatever you were."

"A junior," she said. "But I wasn't a junior there for long. That evening scared me right out of school. Without even bothering to pack more than a very small bag, I dropped out of school and went back home to Fayetteville."

Her luminous eyes called to me, then summoned me in. Apparently, she could do that whenever she liked. "The Arkansas Fayetteville."

"Oh," I said, as if knew all about the Arkansas Fayetteville. "Yes."

"I made enough money from local modeling jobs to move to New York, and in two weeks I was working with the Ford Agency. Never did go back to college, which I regret. There are a lot of great books I'll probably never read—there are probably a lot of great books I've never even heard of."

"I'll send you lists," I said. "We can have our own book club."

She smiled at me.

"Lee, I'm a little puzzled by something. Can I ask you about it?"

"Of course."

"When I talked to Donald this morning . . ."

The door on the right side of the room opened, admitting Vardis Fleck, hunched over a silver tray that contained a silver ice bucket, three small bottles of Evian, and three sparkling glasses.

"And you took a long time, too, Vardis," Meredith Bright said, putting a sharp edge on her voice. "Everybody's operating on some sort of delay this morning."

"I had to attend to some duties," said Fleck.

"Duties? Surely . . ." She caught herself. "We'll discuss your duties later."

"Yess." Fleck used silver tongs to drop ice cubes into each glass, then unscrewed the plastic caps and poured a careful half of each bottle into the glasses. He set the glasses down on red paper napkins he must have pulled from his sleeve and made a quick exit.

"Please let me apologize for my tone," she said, speaking only to me. "Vardis should have remembered that our first obligation is always to our guests."

"Believe me, we hardly feel overlooked," I said.

"But if you take the poor guy's head off," Olson chimed in, "make sure you sew it back on at that same angle."

"Please, Donald. Anyhow, gentlemen. When I spoke to you this morning, Donald, we arranged that you and your friend were going to take a plane from Madison, rent a car at the airport, and arrive here very shortly after the time when I was *led to believe* that the senator would be leaving for his engagement. Now, the senator had *misled* me, and he left almost an hour later than I thought he would, so it all worked out in the end, but still I'm wondering . . . why didn't you get here when you said you would?"

"You haven't been listening to the news, have you?" Olson asked.

"I never listen to the news, Donald," she said. "I hear more than enough about current events at the dinner table. Why, though? What happened?"

He explained they had been warned against taking the flight, which had subsequently crashed, killing everyone on board.

"Isn't that amazing?" she said. "Imagine, all those poor people. You were rescued from a tragedy! Really, the whole thing is just staggering."

Meredith Walsh did not appear to have been staggered, however, and she did not look as though she were responding to news of a tragedy. Instead, she seemed for a moment nearly to be suppressing an upwelling of mirth. Her eyes glittered; her skin acquired a delicious, peachlike flush; she brought her hand to her mouth, as if to conceal a smile. Then the moment passed, and the mingled wonder and sorrow in her eyes and face made it seem an illusion, a cruel misinterpretation of her mood.

"Do you ever listen to Joe Ruddler on the local NBC affiliate?"

"I heard him on our last visit here. The man is a dolt, but he tries to tell the truth."

"We heard about the crash from Ruddler. He already knew that two people had booked the flight and changed their minds at the last minute. He made a big point of saying that those two people were saved for some kind of purpose." Although I did not believe Ruddler's ideas had any validity, speaking them made me feel as if a golden light surrounded me.

"How silly," Meredith said.

"According to him, our lives now have a meaning."

"Meaning like that doesn't exist. If you want to be totally self-centered, fine, be self-centered, but don't pretend that the universe agrees with you."

As she spoke, my sense of being wrapped in a warm golden light dwindled and vanished. I also noticed that the signs of her cosmetic surgery were not as subtle as I had first thought. Nor was she as flawlessly beautiful as she had at first appeared to be—I could detect traces of bitterness in her face. Bitterness was fatal to beauty.

"What *is* interesting about your story," she went on, "is that you were warned off taking the flight. Who warned you?"

"I never even saw the guy," Don said. "He came up to Lee when I was on the other side of the terminal."

Meredith Walsh's powers had not deserted her. Again, the wondrous deep warm playful eyes took me up and swallowed me whole.

"Tell me about it, Lee."

She had created a private game, with only two players.

"He was a distinguished-looking guy. Dressed all in black. Lots of long white hair, chiseled face. I thought he could either be an orchestra conductor or a fabulous con man. He marched up and said he liked my books. He apologized for being rude. Then he said he'd had a premonition that I shouldn't take my flight. If I got on the plane, I'd be risking everything, and would *lose* everything. I asked for his name, and he said, 'Rasputin.' Then he turned around and walked away."

Smiling, Meredith Walsh brought her hands together in a silent clap. "Maybe he was from the future, sent back to save your life! Maybe he was your as-yet-unborn child!"

"Not very likely," I said.

"No, come to think of it, to have a future child you'd have to get a new wife. Lee Truax, the sweet little thing everyone called the Eel, would be well past childbearing age. You did marry the Eel, didn't you, Lee?"

"I did."

"So you share a first name, and if she had changed her last, you'd both be Lee Harwell, wouldn't you?"

"Yes," I said, not happy with her tone.

"Is she well, the Eel?"

I suddenly took in that for some reason Meredith Walsh detested Lee Truax.

"Yes," I said.

"I—and I should say *we,* to include Spencer Mallon, the man we all loved—we did love him, didn't we, Donald?"

"Did we ever," Olson said.

"*We* never saw you, we never met you, though we did hear just a little bit about you. You and the Eel looked so much alike that you were called 'the Twin,' weren't you?"

"I was 'Twin,' " I admitted.

"You must have been adorable. Did the two of you really look so much alike?"

"It seems we did."

"Would you say you're a narcissistic person, Lee?"

"I have no idea," I said.

Meredith's arms and neck were stringy, and her hands had begun to shrivel. In a decade they would resemble monkeys' paws.

"You have to have a healthy narcissism to take care of yourself, to keep on looking good. But you'd also think that a person whose partner resembles him would have to be a little on the cautious side. How long has your wife been blind? Donald didn't really know the answer to that."

I glanced at Don, who shrugged and looked down at the buttery lace-ups I had given him on our first day together.

"Completely blind? Since about 1995, somewhere around there. It's been a long time now. She began gradually losing her sight in her thirties, so she says she had plenty of time to practice. Lee gets out and about, she travels by herself all the time."

"Don't you worry about her?"

"A little," I said.

"You give her a lot of freedom. If I were you, I might be uncomfortable with that."

"I'm uncomfortable about everything." I smiled. "It's my magic secret."

"Maybe you're not uncomfortable enough," she said.

Her eyes were bright but not luminous, her forehead was unlined but not youthful, her smile lovely but not at all genuine. Under Meredith Walsh's regard, detached and cruel and curious, I saw that during the first seconds after she came into the room, I had briefly but thoroughly lost my mind.

"What an odd thing to say, Mrs. Walsh."

"Such a beautiful little girl, with that funny tomboy appeal." Having flashed her claws, she indulged her curiosity again. "The other beautiful child among you was Hootie. Honestly, Hootie was practically edible. A little blue-eyed china doll! How is he doing, after all this time?"

"Hootie was very sick for a long time, but in the past few days he has made amazing progress. He was living in a mental hospital, but now there's some hope he will be able to move into a halfway house."

"He had a real, honest-to-God breakthrough," Don said. "Ever since that day out in the meadow, Hootie could only communicate by quoting from *The Scarlet Letter.* Later on, he added another book or two, but he only used his *own* words when his doctor tried to throw us out."

"Well, well," said Meredith, only superficially engaged. "He wanted you to stay with him, I gather."

"It's actually a wonderful compromise," I said. "Hootie realized that he remembered every word of every book he'd ever read, which meant that everything he could ever want to say was covered! He could pull it all up, too. In seconds, he could identify where everything came from."

"A lovely story," Meredith said. "Lee, don't you ever wish you had joined in, come along?"

"Not really," I said. "I wouldn't want my version of what happened to get between everyone else and theirs."

"If you had been there, you could have kept an eye on your girlfriend."

"Meaning what?"

Meredith Walsh broke eye contact. The way she moved her head and the expression on her face returned to me the vivid image of a harsh and piti-less old woman I had several times encountered in a Turkish street market. She had tried to soften her appearance with a lot of rouge and kohl, and sat half crouched behind a table strewn with bracelets and earrings: a street ped-dler, a bargainer for advantage.

"I don't mind throwing things away," she said. "I don't mind discarding things, destroying things. That's about choice, it's a way to express your pas-sions. Jewelry, houses, expensive cars, the people who call themselves your friends, the people who happen to be your lovers—I've thrown it all away, at one time or another. Without a trace of regret. But do you know what I hate? I hate to *lose* things. Losing is an insult, it's a kind of wound. A woman like me should never lose anything."

She glanced back at me, her cold eyes blazing. "I used to be completely different from the way I am now. Believe it or not, I was once a virtual child. Shy. Gullible. The Eel wasn't like that, was she?"

"No, not really. Though she was very young, too, of course. And in-nocent."

"I remember her innocence. Girls that age are just as innocent as daf-fodils, as mayflies. Me too, even though I thought I was completely sophis-ticated, what with going to bed with Spencer and jabbering away about 'mind games.' Mind games. Spencer should have met our campaign strategist, there's someone who really knows how to play mind games!"

She smiled, though not at us, and not with any warmth.

"Funny, everything we do now is mind games, the point of which is nothing more than knowing how to keep score. There really isn't anything else, once you have things figured out."

She tasted what she had said and found it sour enough to be accurate.

"When did you figure things out? When you married your first hus-band? When you divorced him? When you became involved in politics?"

Briefly, astonishingly, she gathered about her most of her old psychic and erotic force and with a movement of her shoulders and a dip of her head sent it toward me in a rush of heat and expectation. I wondered how this capacity would play itself out over a long campaign.

"How do you think I *married* Luther Trilby? Standing in front of his limousine and batting my eyes? How do you think I *stayed* married to that disgusting psycho pig for twelve years?"

"I see." It was heartbreaking—none of the subsequent horror needed to have happened to her.

"Do you?" she asked, voracious to the last.

"Out there. In the meadow."

I had surprised her, and she did not enjoy surprises. Her face narrowed down around the smallest smile I had ever seen. "Maybe you're not a total idiot. Donald would never have known the answer to that, would you, Donald?" She had to retaliate against someone, and Vardis Fleck was cowering in some secluded chamber.

"I only know what I have to know," Don said. He was unperturbed: Meredith Bright Trilby Walsh no longer had any power to injure him. They had worked through all of that decades earlier.

"Why don't I give you what you came for?" Meredith's voice was flat and steely, and not at all feminine. "After all, that's one of the things I'm supposed to be best at."

"Please," I said, wondering at what she thought she excelled.

| Meredith's Version |

You couldn't begin with the ceremony in the meadow, you had to pick it up much earlier. Pigheaded and arrogant, Mallon had his little heart set on impressing his followers with the razzle-dazzle firework display he was hoping to whip up. Guys like Mallon devour adoration, they gulp down all the love in the room and then whine that there isn't more. It's always all about them, no matter what they say.

And the more talented these guys tend to be, the more damage they cause.

So before you even got to what happened on University Avenue and thereabouts, you had to hear about the early afternoon.

That Sunday was a little rocky from the start. What with it being his big day and everything, Mallon was spooked. That he had a sort of premonition that this time all his work and study and mumbo-jumbo was going to pay off in some brand-new way made him even more anxious. The college students could be counted on to get to their rendezvous on time, but what about those goofy high-school kids? They bounced around like rubber balls, their terrible parents had no idea how to instill even a tiny bit of discipline in their children. The only reason they made it to most of their classes was that they moved from room to room in lockstep, apart of course from days when they all ducked through the exits and fell out of windows and boogied on outta there.

To guarantee their participation in his ritual, Mallon ordered the kids to meet him on the south side of the state capitol at noon, and wonder of wonders, such was their devotion they showed up. He marched them off to the old movie theater on the square, bought them tickets to *The Russians Are Coming, The Russians Are Coming!*, escorted them up to the counter and let them order all the candy, popcorn, and soft drinks they wanted, led them to an empty row, and ordered them to sit down and pig out on their candy. Twizzlers and Good & Plenty for lunch, weren't they lucky? They were to sit through the movie twice, then come out. He would be waiting on the sidewalk, and they'd all walk together to meet the others on University Avenue.

Mallon sat through the hilarious and amazing performance of the theater organist on the great Wurlitzer that floated up from the orchestra pit. The kids cracked up at the way the little bald man flapped his rubbery arms and bowed and swayed while the huge organ mooed and brayed so loudly the walls and the floor vibrated, and when the still-flailing little bald man sank again beneath the level of the stage and the lights dimmed and the curtain rose (all of which the guru himself described to Meredith once they finally got back on track) the great man told the eager kiddies that he had details to take care of, but he'd see them outside in less than four hours. Enjoy the movie!

At which point he rushed out of the theater and with his cock undoubtedly pounding in his moleskin trousers ran right away over to Meredith Bright's apartment on Johnson Street, where he attempted to tranquilize his ever-building anxieties by shedding his clothes and pulling her into her bed. Not that she put up much of a fight. Mallon was then, still and for a little while more, her adored, her mentor, her Master. An excess of tension made him ejaculate too quickly, and Meredith was still such a baby that she blamed herself. As a result, she roused him into a second, far more successful romp, after which he dropped into sleep so profound he drooled on her pillow. Ah, Maestro!

He slept, she stroked his beautiful hair, and read more of *Love's Body*. Twice fucked, Meredith learned that documents create an inherent contradiction between fetishism and magic that leads naturally to thoughts of prefiguration and the recognition that nothing ever, ever happens for the first time. As everything keeps on recurring in an eternal revolution, renewals— like Spencer's!—take place again and again, throughout time. When her lover stretched and smacked his lips, she did her best to effect a second renewal, but Spencer, who was at his most leonine, his cock its most silken and pendulous, his chest its broadest and most manly, his hands their most shapely, thrust aside her willingness and announced that he had to get something to eat before meeting the kids at the end of the second screening of *The Russians Are Coming, The Russians Are Coming!* Sorry, the Master was having one of those I-have-to-be-alone moments, those my-soul-is-mine-alone-and-must-remain-so spells, always enchanting when used against other people.

Left alone, she thought her apartment looked asprawl and unkempt. Without Spencer breathing softly in her bed, *Love's Body* was just little heaps of disconnected sentences. Meredith tossed the book onto a chair. A thrill of distaste prompted her to lean over and flick it to the floor. She tried the TV but found only soap operas, which were far too much like her actual life to be watchable, though some of the actors were extremely cute. (Meredith Bright had never suffered a coma or amnesia, nor had she discovered the existence of an evil twin, but there always seemed to be way too much *drama* going on: boys prostrated themselves before her at least three times a year, boys thought they were being irresistibly original when they strummed guitars beneath her window, boys went crazy right in front of her, and to tell the truth so did girls, often, in one way or another. And as for her parents, forget about it, they even *looked* like the old standbys and authority figures on soaps: corporate CEOs, police commissioners, high-ranking medical staff, and beautiful but treacherous grandparents.) Eventually, she faced up to the nullity of her existence and wandered out to take her time getting to the rendezvous point.

She had gone only a little way off State Street when she began to hear the sorts of noises that she associated with antiwar protests and civil unrest.

Secretly, Meredith didn't even like the word *dissent.* The facts it called forth into the world made her almost ill with revulsion—so messy, so disorderly, so violent! Only when she was irritated with Spencer Mallon could she admit to herself how profoundly uninterested she was in Vietnam, in the whole depressing topic of Negro rights. In Arkansas, almost nobody she knew became rabid on these subjects; why were people so unreasonable in Madison? Why couldn't they just let things sort themselves out, the way things always did?

Voices distorted through bullhorns, voices raised in chants, police sirens, mob sounds, the sounds of booted feet striking the pavement, all of this signaled the nearby presence of chaos she could almost smell without being able to see. Meredith tried to cut around it, wherever it was, while thinking that Mallon was going to love this uproar, he would take it as a sign!

For a while she worked her way west, trying to identify where all the trouble was without actually encountering it. The protest, the demonstration had obviously begun elsewhere than the library plaza between State and Langdon, the usual site of political unrest, though to be honest protests and demonstrations, pickets, petition signings, teach-ins, and strikes took place all over the campus and its surroundings. You never knew where you were going to run into a guy with a megaphone, a sullen mob blocking access to a classroom building, ranks of angry-looking cops facing down boys with beards, and girls spinning around in leotards and Danskins. Or cops on horseback like overseers staring down at a line made up of white Wisconsin hippies in denim jackets and young black men in leather and sunglasses, all of them linking arms and swaying in what she took to be an artificial ecstasy.

After another block, she finally began to notice, then to put together, the evidence of what had taken place. Crumpled and torn posters and leaflets littered both the pavement and the street she could see when she looked one block north. Splintered wood, too, from a table or a sawhorse. Items of clothing lay here and there amongst the scattered papers—T-shirts, sweatshirts, sneakers. Meredith picked up speed, knowing that she was jogging toward confusion and violence. The shouts and uproar grew louder as she moved toward the next intersection, which happened to be one block east of their rendezvous point, the corner of University Avenue and North Charter Street. Then a little crowd of young people, perhaps half a dozen, came bursting into the intersection before her, running hard. Some of them wept as they ran. One of the boys had wound a shirt around his head, and a circular bloodstain blossomed on the shirt. She shouted a question at the running students, but they ignored her in their flight.

The police had attempted to shut down an off-campus demonstration, a take-it-to-the-people effort she could faintly remember having heard about. Instead of yielding or disbanding, the crowd of demonstrators had moved their protest down the street, causing the police to charge, in turn causing the students to run westward down University with the cops coming after them, waving nightsticks. The din coming from the precise place where her group was scheduled to meet filled Meredith with fear and disgust, revulsion and panic. None of her many instincts encouraged her to move toward the corner of University and North Charter, but when she came at last to North Charter, and the appalling din assailed her, she took her courage in both hands, turned north, and made her way through students racing the other way.

It was a stunning chaos. An extraordinary litter covered the street, bags of garbage, long streamers torn from banners, bottles, beer cans, torn books, broken bits of wood. All of it was *in motion*. Some of what appeared to be garbage was, when looked at closely, human bodies around which students with flowing hair and bell-bottom jeans stood their ground and bellowed at enraged policemen in science-fiction protective helmets with face guards, who bellowed back, their nightsticks raised. The young people lying in the street had fallen, toppled by either a blow from a policeman or a push from someone in a tearing hurry, and were struggling to creep away unnoticed. Cops with faces exposed strode amidst the carnage, plucking kids off the street and propelling them into black vans with ruthless mechanical efficiency.

For a second, Meredith caught sight of Hayward and Milstrap on the other side of University Avenue, staring with huge eyes at the pandemonium before them. A huge cop on a monumental black horse rode across the scene with his nightstick raised like a sword, scattering kids like windblown confetti. At the far end of the intersection, he wheeled around and came sweeping back again, putting a definitive end to most of the remaining resistance. In his wake, Meredith looked again across the Avenue and saw that Hayward and his roommate were staring at her and making hand signals to stay where she was, they would work their way toward her.

"There was a huge student protest that turned into a riot on that same day?" I burst out. "How come this is the first I ever heard of it?"

"Hell, man," Olson put in, "there were protests and demonstrations and riots all over the place in those days. It just slowed us down a little. No big deal. Even the *Capital Times* didn't say much about it. Like two paragraphs."

"Because the *Cap Times* wanted to downplay everything antiwar, don't you get it? You guys were in such a bubble, you didn't notice that things were falling apart all around us, and you didn't care that we wound up being way, way off schedule!"

"What schedule?" Olson looked genuinely puzzled.

"Aah! Why do I put up with you?" Meredith yelled. A door opened, and Vardis Fleck's gleaming head poked through the gap. His mistress waved him away.

I remembered a detail from my wife's grudging accounts of the days spent under Mallon's spell before the rite in the meadow.

"Yes, the schedule," I said.

Meredith Walsh swung her tight, furious face toward me and drilled me with an unspoken question.

"You're talking about the time frame you developed by doing a horoscope of the group. You were supposed to begin by . . . I don't remember. Seven-twenty?"

"Exactly," she said. "Donald, do you remember? *He* did, and he wasn't even there! Do you know how much work it is, to work up a star chart and do a horoscope? I did that for free, I did it out of love, and none of you little jackasses took it seriously!"

"Hey, things happened," Olson said. "You gotta go with the flow."

"No, you don't. We were held up by a good ninety minutes, maybe more. By then, things had *changed*. We weren't in the optimum position for success anymore. We should have bagged it, we should have called a rain date. We should have gone home to our hovels and waited until I could work out the next time we'd have a *chance* of success."

"A lousy hour and a half," Don said.

"Even an hour makes a difference, Don."

"Spencer had some doubts about that, you know."

"To his sorrow," she said.

When the group finally reunited, Mallon refused to listen to her. Well, he didn't actually *refuse,* he just dismissed her worries and ignored her advice. He blew her off, was what he did. The actual situation, the one he should have known enough to care about, was that by the time they assembled in the wreckage and puddles left behind by the cops and the demonstrators, it was past eight-thirty, and the light was going fast. All of her calculations had been thrown off, and from what she remembered of the astrological signs, from here on out things looked pretty grim. If you missed the window that had just slammed shut, it was best to wait a couple of days. That was how she interpreted the chart, anyhow. But as they stood and talked about it on a water-darkened sidewalk covered with soaked, pulpy leaflets, Meredith understood that her warnings meant nothing to Spencer. He was in forward gear, and he was going to stay that way.

If you're looking for someone to blame, pick HIM.

The students had fled, and the cops and firemen had finally wandered back to their stations to file statements and process arrests. Mallon and the high-school kids had emerged from behind the cement walls of the parking garage where they had sheltered during the uproar. Meredith could see that with one exception, their group as a whole was rattled by what had just happened. Keith Hayward, the exception, seemed exhilarated by the free-for-all they had just witnessed. Violence perked the guy right up, Meredith observed, it lightened his step, it brightened his eyes. When he was in this fresh, lively mood, she also observed, Hayward wasn't so horrible looking any more. You could almost think he was kind of attractive in some really eccentric way. This transformation spooked her a little bit, but more than that, it interested her. It spoke of some vital, previously unsuspected force within Hayward—a force that would almost certainly be connected to the "private room," obviously some sort of sex pad, he had mentioned to her in private a couple of times.

He was playing it as cool as he could, and the way he met her eyes when she gave up on Mallon and turned away toward the devastated street— Keith Hayward, actually meeting her eyes!—suggested that the sex pad was in his mind again. So why not? Maybe she'd have a look. Meredith had no doubt that she could control Hayward, no matter what he had in mind, and if she allowed him to think he was taking her out, that they had a "date," Spencer Mallon would take notice, all right.

She sent Keith Hayward a little smile to cherish and fold up into his pocket, and saw it zing straight to the center of the target.

Mallon made a short speech to them all, asking them to calm down and gather their thoughts and put away all the bad energy ("Even you, Keith," he said, which make Hayward sulk and Milstrap chortle, causing her to realize that Milstrap *liked* Hayward's bad energy, what a creep), and think about the task ahead of them. Out there in the meadow, they had to be straight. Could they do that? Could they put this unfortunate delay behind them? (Total bullshit, of course. He'd already made up his mind.) He looked at Donald and asked, What about it, Dilly-O? Can we get ourselves together? A shock, in a way, because he was showing that he thought Donald, not that "Boats" boy, was the leader of the little group. And Donald said, do you remember, Donald?

"I said, We're already together," Don said, looking grim.

That's right. Donald spoke up, Donald gave him what he wanted. Spencer loved that. It got his juices flowing. He said, Okay, let's get our wagon train on the trail, all right? He wasn't looking at Hootie and the Eel, but Meredith was, and she had to say, they seemed to be what people used to call a little peaked. A little *drawn*. Especially Hootie. All through her life, Meredith seldom had anything like a maternal impulse, she wasn't built that way, sorry, but something about Hootie made her almost want to pick him up and carry him out to the agronomy meadow. And funny thing, although Meredith knew Hootie was as love-struck with her as those other boys were, from then on right through to the day's horrible finish, Hootie kept his eyes glued on the Eel. She *meant* something to him, you could see that.

Along they went through town, and the farther they got from University Avenue the more remote all the excitement back there became. Everything looked so normal, you almost couldn't believe how savage the world had become. Some residential parts of Madison, you could be in New England or the Bay Area. Great-looking houses on tree-lined streets, places where you think you have a handle on life. Through these kindly, professorial streets they walked, moving deliberately—thanks to their knot-headed leader—toward death and ruin. Then the professor-style streets dropped away, and the houses got smaller and farther apart, and after that they were walking past foundries and machine shops and auto-parts stores and chain-link fences that blocked off filthy windows no one would ever want to look through anyhow, and after that they strode, wandered, or strutted, according to their individual styles, into Glasshouse Road.

Instinctively, they drew closer together. Spencer dropped back to protect them from the rear while issuing remarks such as—Just keep moving forward, me buckos, me hearties, there's nothing to be afraid of here, unless Eel's Dad wants to come out for another round of fisticuffs—

Which proved he wasn't as confident and upbeat as he was pretending to be, didn't it, because since when did Spencer Mallon ever say cornball junk like me buckos me hearties, right? Hootie whispered something to the Eel, too. No wonder, after that stupid crack. Not that Meredith was feeling especially sympathetic toward the Eel in those days, since she'd gone out with Spencer just a few nights before—did Lee Harwell, supposedly the girl's twin, know that?

Does that come as a shock? It was a shock to Meredith, you can bet on that—her lover, her Master, her guide betrayed her, in a sense, by taking out this *high school girl* after they'd had a nasty argument, about guess what, that same *high school girl.* The rat, her lover, whom Meredith had hoped was going to stay with her or at least take her with him if he actually did take off after the ceremony, as he said he would, had gone out on a *date* with this girl, this child, who, let's face it, was pretty cute, kind of an Audrey-Hepburn-in-the-larval-stage thing. Not only that, he took her to the best restaurant in town, the Falls.

Didn't know that, did you, Harwell? The Falls.

I turned to Donald Olson and saw on his face the answer to the question I had yet to ask. "I didn't, no. You did, though."

Olson hesitated, then said, "Yes. Spencer felt close to her."

" 'Spencer felt close to her,' " Meredith said, mocking the words. "Is that right? He felt *closer* to me."

"Hmm," I said. "He took her to the Falls? She never mentioned that to me."

Olson's lips tightened, making him look as though he had just bitten down on a tough little seed and heard a crunch that might have been a tooth.

"All this happened a long, long time ago," I said, rejecting the sleepless hours of the previous night. "I mean, I guess I'm surprised, but it's totally meaningless, after all."

"I'm curious about something," Meredith said. "Did your girlfriend say anything to you that night after she got home, or maybe the next day? You must have asked her about it."

"I didn't even see her that night. In fact, I barely talked to her all day. That night, nobody answered her phone at home. It turned out, she ran out of the meadow with Boats, Jason Boatman, and spent the night on his couch. When I went over there, Boats wouldn't let me in. He said everything got screwed up, he couldn't talk about it, and Eel was just conked out and didn't want to see anybody, not even me."

"But when you and she were finally together, and you were able to talk to each other in private, what did she tell you?"

"Nothing. She said she couldn't tell me anything. It was no use, because if she didn't understand it, I sure wouldn't be able to, either. Lee was really angry at Mallon, that much was clear. I thought it was because he had taken off and left them all to deal with the mess—and because he more or less stole Don, her best friend, apart from me. Our best friend, come to think of it."

"That's nice," Olson said. "But Meredith, keep going."

"Yes, please don't stop," I said. "I want to hear what happened during the ceremony."

"Good luck," Meredith said. "It got completely crazy out in that meadow. People say nutso stuff about piled-up corpses and millions of dogs, and monsters flying out of orange clouds . . . I didn't see anything like that. The truth is, I kind of liked what I saw. It didn't scare me at all. That was where and when I started to figure things out, right there. A queen gave me a gift, and that changed everything."

Now that they were getting close to the meadow, they were really getting together, too, like Donald said. You could feel something happen, on the way down Glasshouse Road. Hard to say what it was, exactly, but for the first and last time in her life Meredith felt like part of a *unit*—like a participating member of a group that informed her identity. Like a bee in a beehive, or the shortstop on a good baseball team. Teams had captains, bees had queens, and they had Spencer Mallon. Total trust, total faith. How often do you feel that way? Spencer Mallon collected innocence, all right, but Meredith would never have guessed that hers was part of the package.

What a sap.

Anyhow, there she was, a dewy young thing madly in love with her handsome adventurer/philosopher/magician, moving down Glasshouse Road with these people she suddenly felt tremendously connected to, and there's this feeling of threat, small at first, barely noticeable, but it got stronger with every foot of ground they cover. Something, maybe a lot of somethings, was watching them. Then subtle noises began to reach them from behind, and these noises got closer and closer while the group, breathing as one, moved forward, Mallon in the lead. Those things that were following them didn't sound like bikers. Didn't even sound like anything human. Nobody looked back, not even Hayward, not even Milstrap, who for once seemed to have forgotten how to sneer. He glanced over at Meredith to see how she was doing, or maybe just to see if her shorts were riding up, and his face looked as white as cottage cheese.

Eventually *someone* looked around, she couldn't remember who, and after that they all did. Except her. Meredith wanted to keep moving, which she gathered was what those *things* wanted her to do, so everything was cool on that front, no need for anyone to get upset. She was walking along behind Mallon and Don and Eel, and it looked to her like they looked back at pretty much the same moment—the Eel snapped her head forward in less than a second, but Spencer and Don kept looking a while longer, and their faces went as pale as Milstrap's. Both of them looked her in the eye to check her out . . .

"I wasn't checking you out," Don said. "I needed to see you."

. . . or because they needed to see her, whatever that meant. Mallon said, Keep moving, troops, they aren't really there, and that's not what they really look like, anyhow.

She again broke away from her narrative. "But what *did* they look like, Don? I never knew."

"Biker dogs, like dogs in biker jackets," he said, almost chuckling at the combination of threat and absurdity in this image. "Big, savage-looking, snarling dogs, standing up. Walking on their hind legs. I was too scared to look at them for very long, but I thought they had feet instead of paws. They were wearing motorcycle boots."

"Mallon kept going," she said. "I can't believe it. Wouldn't you think that would be enough to tell him to stop? But no, he thought he was going to change the world, he thought he was going to see what was on the other side."

"They wanted him to keep going, and you know why? I finally figured this out. They had no more idea what was going to happen than he did."

Mallon held them together, he got them to do what he wanted, which was to reach the end of that street, slide over the concrete barrier, and walk into the meadow. Never thinking that he was being pushed by forces he did not understand and could not control—not Spencer! He thought he was one of the lords of creation, and everything he did was going to turn out well, especially that night. Because it *was* almost night now; it was dark and getting darker. Meredith wouldn't have been able to find the spot they had picked out, but Donald seemed to have a good memory of where it was, and Mallon went right alongside him. He looked back just once, and his face relaxed, so Meredith could look back, too. One lonely drunk wandered out of the House of Ko-Reck-Shun and went staggering down the middle of now-empty Glasshouse Road. *That's the old world,* Meredith said to herself, *the one we're leaving behind—so sad and lost. What will the new world be like?*

Mallon said, This is it, guys, you have to concentrate and do your part. In the meantime, let's find our spot.

And Donald led us right to it. You knew where it was, didn't you? Right there, and your voice was full of triumph when you said, It's here, right here, down this swale or dell kind of thing. You were so proud of yourself! I'm not picking on you, it's just worth saying, that's all. They had this little moment of vanity, of egotism, and it was all his—Mallon's. Anyhow, Donald was right, of course, they were standing at the edge of this fold that went down into the meadow, and even in the bad light and everything, they could see that white circle Donald and his friend had painted, well, poured onto the ground on the right side, where it went up.

And you know what? It looked pretty good, that circle! Shining, actually shining! What was that, do you think, the reflection of the moon? Reflections of the stars? Whatever the hell that was, it worked, it made them feel like they were in the presence of something, like they were *ordained,* and right where they were supposed to be. *Come down, come on in,* that gleaming white circle was saying, *let's get started.* Up until then, Meredith had not even noticed that Mallon was carrying this big briefcase with him. Up until then, she hadn't even known he *owned* a briefcase.

"He didn't," Don said. "Later on, he told me he 'borrowed' it from that kid with the red beard. 'Everything is everything,' remember?"

"As if I could forget," she said.

That group feeling, the interconnected thing, got stronger, and it was really magical, the way things felt there for about fifteen minutes or so before everybody started freaking out.

We're on the verge of something here, Mallon said. I can sense it. Nobody say any more about that because we might jinx it.

Just before they went down into the fold in the earth, everything, everything around them, especially the moon and the millions of stars, looked absolutely gorgeous. Even the headlights of the cars moving down the highway off in the distance, like jewels but alive! Meredith hardly wanted to move along with the others, but Brett and Keith were giving her that hungry, besotted look again, the one that suggested they were hoping a runaway horse would come galloping along so they could wrestle it to the ground before it disturbed a honey-colored strand of her hair. Eel and the high-school boys, they had eyes for no one but Mallon, and Hootie, he caught Meredith's eye once and went back to studying the Eel like before long he was going to be tested about her.

They went down in there and stood around Mallon while he got down on his knees, opened the briefcase, and passed out the candles and the matches. Then they did the thing with the ropes, looping them in front of the circle in case something happened along and they weren't able to just jump onto its neck.

You know how you can suddenly feel that things just got kicked up a notch? That's how it was after the ropes went down. Like the air got tighter, and the moon and stars got brighter. Like the spaces between all of them standing there shrank. Meredith's breathing got tighter, too, as if her lungs were being squeezed.

One after another, they lit the candles and held them up. You know how they were standing, don't you? Mallon at the center, facing the white circle. Boats and Donald stood on each side, maybe six feet from him—closer than before. To the left of Boats, Hootie, Eel, and Meredith stood together, with Hootie in the middle. Eel and Meredith didn't want to stand side by side—when you get right down to it, they didn't like or trust each other at all. They wound up in the same group because they didn't want to get close to Hayward. He and his roommate were off to Donald's right. The two of them looked more relaxed than the others.

Boats, he broke Meredith's heart, the way he wanted so much to be Mallon's favorite, the one to be with him when the tide rose. He would have stolen the dome from the state capitol if he thought Mallon would have applauded. Hayward, though, that boy was thinking about something else. He kept sneaking glances at Meredith.

When Mallon called for silence, even Hayward settled down. Raise your candles in your right hands, Mallon said. Concentrate on your breathing. Keep your mind empty. We will spend a lot of time emptying our minds and watching our white circle. Then I will begin to speak the words that will come into my mind. They will be in Latin, and I think, I pray they will be the right words. Those words, and what we bring, all of what all of us, bring to the meadow, this moment, will determine what happens here.

Off to his side, Hootie mumbled, They're here again. I don't like 'em, I don't want 'em here.

Mallon said, Nothing is with us yet, Hootie, please hold your silence.

That crazy little Hootie, he said, *Must I sink down there, and die at once?* If memory serves.

Silence, Mallon said.

Little Hawthorne, said Hayward.

Shut up, Mallon said. Please.

You may close your eyes, Mallon said.

Meredith did as he said. The silence went on a long, long time. Funny thing, after a minute or two, inside her head Meredith could *see* them all with total clarity. But the way she saw them, they were all, all, close together, and she could hear their breathing, and there was this rank, terrible smell that was Keith Hayward's skunky breath. In her head, she could see Hootie clamping shut his beautiful little rosebud mouth and forcing himself to stare at the gleaming circle; and she saw the Eel open wide her eyes and open wide her mouth and tilt her head back and bend her spine so that she was gazing not at the white circle but the blazing stars above, the Eel *watching,* and Meredith thought, *What's that brat watching, and why can't I watch it, too?*; and inside her head, where her vision was true, she saw the Eel gradually straighten up and stare forward, not at the white circle but about nine, ten feet to the right of it, at some nondescript part of the rise that was half dirt, half grass all baked and brown, and even that getting harder to see as the light faded and dimmed; and Hayward, breathing fumes as he stood with his candle jumping and his eyes gently shut upon some spectacle that made his mouth flicker into a smile; beside him Milstrap, tilting his head and narrowing his eyes as if contemplating some curious phenomenon that had just appeared before him; and Mallon, precious, treacherous, Mallon with his candle aloft and tears rising in his amazing eyes, his total handsomeness like a charged field around him, lifting his beautiful magician's head and preparing to speak or sing.

The world changed in that endless moment before Spencer Mallon began to chant in Latin, that time during which the glowing words embedded in the unreeling chant hovered near as pure possibility, spoken though as yet unspoken, present nonetheless. In the suspended silence, Meredith could feel the change in every element of the world present to her: the simultaneous tightening and relaxation of the air, now revealed for the first time as an actual membrane wrapped about them all, here loose and yielding, there firm and ungiving. In the long, long moment when Mallon hung fire and waited for his deepest self to give him words, Meredith felt the ground quiver under her feet, then immediately began to smell the fragrance trails of something raw, hot, sweet, and sexual. Crushed mandarin oranges, cane sugar, sliced habañero peppers sizzling in a pan, the flesh inside the juicy lower lip of Bobby Flynn, her first serious boyfriend, new blood spurting from a wound, sweat, thick white lilies, semen, a freshly sliced fig, all these odors and fragrances and stinks coiled around each other, rubbed flanks and floated toward them from the expansive, greedy world Meredith sensed behind the membrane of the air itself, a world she wished both to flee and to embrace.

In that long moment, Meredith still saw them all: the high-school kids beside her radiant now with terror (no, that was just Hootie, whose fear she could smell, separate from the sexy hot pepper/lily/Bobby-Flynn's-lower-lip odor building up behind the bulging membrane that wrapped them round), Hootie charged with terror and little Eel for some reason radiant with, well, *radiance*, a phenomenon Meredith Bright found striking, more than that, more than striking, yes, amazing, with her eyes wide open, her soul visible to any who cared to look, a tomboy on fire, which, more than striking as it was, Meredith chose to behold no longer just at the moment it began to change and darken; poor Boats staring at the circle as though his life would pour through it, also as though he suspected he would one day have to steal that, too; then Mallon with the words beginning to spill into his throat from his mysterious inner source, eyes clamped shut, candle aloft like the Statue of Liberty's torch, Mallon higher than a kite, higher than a *cloud,* so excited the guy had a hard-on, every vessel and nerve in his body quivering with anticipation, alive with the sense that everything was about to change *now, now* the moment before the moment, the most beautiful, the last drop and essence of *what had been,* of everything that was to be lost—

Then you, Donald, with her eyes closed Meredith saw you, so handsome, attending to Mallon the way the Secret Service attends to the president, with your secret hopes sizzling in your heart and those talents you didn't know you had just beginning to come into bud, poor thing, and a few feet beyond, the frat boys over there, so unappealing—how in the world had Meredith for as much as a second found Keith Hayward appealing?—looking trapped, looking uncertain, no conviction in the way they held their candles aloft, Hayward cutting his eyes toward Meredith, his dull animal lust so ugly when stacked against the weird strange sexy sweet power beginning to barrel toward them from some distant point beyond the coiling membrane of the air, the distant point which had just now snagged doomed Brett Milstrap's attention and curiosity, and which he was now really doing his best, his damnedest, to make out and peer into, his neck bent, his head tilted, and a little sweat leaking out of the dark sharp point of his widow's peak . . .

Only then had Meredith fully taken in the oddness of being able to see in such detail with her eyes clamped shut.

So, at the exact moment that Mallon's words began to pour from his throat, at the very moment she heard his beautiful voice and realized that he was *singing,* and what's more singing *in Latin,* she opened her eyes and beheld what was taking place in that meadow.

∎

It wasn't anything like one thing, that was what first struck her. Little dramas, each of them in equal parts deeply disturbing and completely fascinating, were taking place all over that low rise in front of them. The circle could hardly be seen, and the ropes, Meredith saw, would be useless. You couldn't tie down these visions, you couldn't *bind* them. They weren't solid, not really, and they were more like scenes than mere beings or creatures. The only one she could see clearly, however, was the one playing itself out before the Eel, Hootie, and her. In front of their little group, an old man with a long beard and an old woman leaning on a cane (but it wasn't a cane, whispered a cool voice in her mind, that length of wood was called a *staffe*) stood on dead-white soil before a great juniper tree. An enormous pig and a small, scaly dragon with drooping wings lolled on the white earth beside them, staring with hooded, suspicious eyes at Mallon, as if awaiting instruction. As soon as the old couple saw that they were being observed, their heads revolved to reveal at the backs of their heads second faces with long, beaky, inquisitive noses and shimmering eyes.

"Wait," Don said, his voice a velvet bruise. "You actually saw all this shit? What about the dogs, you know, the dog-things?"

"Can't you be patient enough to hear what I have to say? Anyhow, the dogs weren't important, no matter whatever Mallon deigned to share with you."

"Of course they were *important*," Olson said, a little too loudly.

Could she continue? A little bit along the rise, and in front of Boats, it looked like a big, red-faced man in bloody rags was waving a sword, but Meredith couldn't see him very well. Some kind of animal was rearing behind him. Maybe a deer, too, with antlers. These things, they were like on the other side of a plate-glass window, all of these scenes were like that, separated from them by big windows, so the students couldn't hear them. Each scene had its own weather. Lightning kept flashing behind the big guy with the sword, but Meredith's people, that horrible old couple, they came from a completely white world disturbed by a strong wind that twisted the man's beard and tore at their hair.

In front of Mallon she glimpsed a naked woman, isn't that a surprise, but only for the moment it took her to see that the naked woman was a greeny whitish color. He had an animal, too, something weird, she couldn't tell what. A dove was lurching through the air all around the white-green woman, that woman the color of a corpse . . .

Do you know, when she thinks about this now, it's like they were in a museum? These scenes were like dioramas in front of them, only the dioramas were alive, and the things in them moved. All she could see, way off to the side where Don and the frat boys were stationed, was this crazy world like a wild party. A king was riding on a bear, waving his arms and thrashing every which way, and a queen, an angry queen, was shouting and pointing here and there with a long stick—the Bear King and the Roaring Queen, Meredith called them. They had a big dog, like a hound of some kind, and all of them were made of shiny silver, or something like that, and none of them had faces, just these smooth shiny liquid surfaces. In back of them all sorts of other figures were cavorting away, and you knew it was really noisy in that world—

Donald was running around in circles, and Mallon was staring straight ahead as if he was about to go into shock, and Keith Hayward, he wasn't paying any attention at all to this amazing *stuff* going on right in front of their faces, and neither was Milstrap. Keith was staring right at Meredith, and Hayward's terrible face—because it was terrible, anything she might have once thought to the contrary was dead wrong—looked like a cement mask hung in front of a blazing fire. Meredith said to herself, *That guy better stay where he is, because he's completely off his rocker.*

The world of the Bear King and the crazy queen spilled from its diorama and rolled through all the others, filling their spaces and the spaces between. All the silvery people reeled around, declaiming to themselves with drunken, oversize gestures. Meredith thought this scene had a wild, spooky charm. It delighted her, especially when the mad queen swung in her direction and leveled the staff at her head.

Some kind of light, grainy beam flew from the end of the staff and struck Meredith's forehead with an impact like that of a flying moth, then passed through the wall of her skull and entered her brain, where it became a short, cool wand. The wand pulsed once, then evaporated into her brain tissue.

The great blessing had been bestowed and received.

The Bear King waved a beer stein and slapped his mount on the head, and the Roaring Queen swung her arm a couple of inches and aimed her distaff (it seemed to Meredith) at the Eel. Then Meredith paid no more attention to anyone or anything else, be it visionary royal personage, visionary animal creature, or ordinary everyday human commoner, because all of her attention was focused on the three great principles that had begun to take root in the center of her brain and just then were clearing their throats and getting ready to sound off. When they spoke, however, it was not in the southern-politician, ham-bone tones she had expected from this windup, but in a slender, cool female voice.

And that, gentlemen, was when Meredith Bright finally began to figure things out. The great blessing was, you could say, a vision of a new heaven and a new earth. Only the new heaven and earth were not at all what people imagined they would be, no no no. Meredith giggled at the disparity between the world as it truly was and what almost everyone, including her former addlepated self, imagined it to be. What came from the point of that distaff was wisdom—the wisdom of those three great principles.

Yes, Meredith knew, Meredith understood, the men before her wanted to hear more about this wisdom that had been passed on so efficiently from a realm beyond all understanding, but they'd have to wait, because they still had more to learn about the events of that all-important evening.

A whole lot seemed to happen all at once. The crazy scene in front of them began to move forward, as if to surround them, which would have meant they'd be lost forever in some eternal horror show, but it had moved only the tiniest part of a centimeter, say, the tiniest distance possible, which no one but Meredith and maybe the Eel even noticed, and the dog-things were just beginning to perk up, when two things happened at the far end of their row. The first was that Keith Hayward, of course not noticing the peril he was about to be in, that idiot, jumped out of position and started to sprint toward Meredith. He wanted to pick her up and snatch her away—Hayward wanted to kidnap her, she understood that: she was *really* clear about his mission. It was in his terrible, terrible eyes, that intention. Or desire, or whatever you call it. He'd starved long enough, and he was going to make his move.

At the same time, Brett Milstrap finally got his hands on that weird point in space he had been looking at and puzzling over so long. He was concentrating so hard he never even noticed that his partner had taken off and left him by himself. While Hayward was barreling toward Meredith, Milstrap bent over and tugged at something like a seam on the edge of the eternal diorama. When he got his fingers through the crack he had spotted, he closed his fists and pulled, hard. Muscles Meredith hadn't known the kid possessed popped out on his forearms, and he leaned into his work. A four-foot section of the diorama peeled up like a flexible screen, and both the Bear King and the insane queen turned to gaze at what he was doing. The king banged his heels into the bear's sides, the appalled queen roared and flailed her long stick, they wanted him to stop—

But then Meredith could see no more, as some big dark form slipped in front of her and blocked her vision. At first, she thought it was one of the dog-creatures, for all of those things were beginning to move forward in order (Meredith realized) to shield their group from the happy campers in eternity, or whatever it was. But it was not a dog-creature, it was too big, and besides it had a really weird smell, so awful it was almost beautiful. Honestly, if you made that odor into a perfume, some women would wear it all the time, and a lot of women would wear it maybe once a year, when a little serious business had to be done. That smell, that weird fragrance, made Meredith dizzy, which meant her vision lost a little reliability, since it's hard to know if you're seeing things accurately when the ground is wobbling and your knees don't work and a funny floating sensation has taken over what used to be your head.

Right? I mean, *you can't really be sure.*

However, while Meredith was coping with the effects of that odor, which she realized was much the same as the raw hot sexy crushed-mandarin-orange-inside-of- Bobby-Flynn's-lower-lip smell she had enjoyed earlier, only dialed way up, it seemed to her that the creature before her slowly, slowly turned to her and gave her a beatific smile only slightly undercut by the fact of the smiling lips being red with the blood of Keith Hayward, and the parallel fact that Keith Hayward's limp and utterly dead body, minus its head and right arm, drooped from the great creature's hands. She couldn't really describe this thing. It appeared to shapeshift from something like a short King Kong to a terrible naked old male giant with streaming white hair, its maw filled with flesh and shattered bone, and from that to an almost cartoonish purple thing that spat out red and white bits of Keith Hayward even as it graced her with its smile. Actually, all of them smiled at Meredith Bright, the big ape, the naked giant, and the cartoon—all of them smiled, and leftover bits of Keith Hayward dribbled and oozed from all three of their mouths, which were really all the same mouth.

■

At this point, I had the odd sensation that while Meredith was telling me the truth about all this smiling, she was, although she may not have even been aware of it, also lying, and about something I could define only as obscene. Meredith Walsh, I advised myself, inhabited a dizzying moral realm. I asked her a question.

■

No, the smiling didn't surprise Meredith, why should it? In those days, and for a good long time after, decades actually, everybody who crossed the path of Meredith Bright, including even the people who looked at her from the other side of the street, not forgetting even the men driving pizza wagons through the streets of Madison, Fayetteville, Greenwich, Connecticut, and so on, all of these people, these stupid men, they smiled at her until their faces ached. That was how it worked. If the Bear King and the Bellowing Queen had possessed faces, they would have smiled at her, too. In fact, although they did not have actual faces, visible ones, they smiled at her anyhow.

Meredith smiled back, of course, being polite, and as she did so, the creature vanished. Through the empty space he had just finished occupying, she happened to catch a glimpse of Brett Milstrap making an irrevocable decision, if that's what it was. It might have been a whim, even an accident. Milstrap had managed to peel back a long section of the Bear King's chaotic world, exposing a deep blackness pieced by one laserlike white light. That's all she could see back there, anyhow. Milstrap leaned into the gap and was sucked in, instantly gone. The gap sealed up, and for a couple of seconds, Meredith caught sight of him far back in the riotous world of shiny people and shiny things. He was waving his arms. He knew Meredith had seen him, and he wanted her to help him escape! Brett Milstrap lowered his arms, leaned forward, and began to run as fast as he could, as if he thought he could outrace his destiny. Before he had taken three long strides, he winked out of sight and disappeared.

Meredith checked her fellow travelers, wondering if they had witnessed these two extraordinary events, and to her amazement discovered that they were all on separate wavelengths. Now, she wasn't sure *how* she knew these things. Empathy had never exactly been her strong suit. But looking at Boats, she knew instantly that he found himself in a field of corpses, rising to his feet near a great tower made entirely of the bodies of dead children. Both Donald and Mallon saw billows of downpouring rose-orange light and upright dogs in human clothing, except Mallon saw more dogs and nastier ones. Mallon's dogs wanted to kill him for his audacity and his incompetence, and he had to take off and get out of there in a hurry. The hurry was crucial for another reason, that Mallon had also seen Keith Hayward ripped to pieces by some huge and ferocious creature he could not identify, but which he knew he had summoned to the meadow.

When Meredith turned her gaze to Hootie, what she saw, a mighty blazing sun crowded stuffed crammed jammed with words and sentences, nearly flattened her. She thought it may have been the face of God *burning through* all those humming writhing coiling sentences and paragraphs, all of them making their claim and all of them sacred . . . Hootie was too much for her. She knew that if she looked a moment longer into God's massive, sentence-packed face she would crack and fall asunder, a broken vessel, so she did what she had to do and took off running. Because Mallon and Donald were still fighting through the pouring neon light, she could have been the first to leave. The first who wound up alive and on earth, anyhow.

And now, Meredith imagined Donald undoubtedly wanted her to tell him something explanatory about the dogs. He'd heard something, hadn't he? A long time ago, he'd heard one of his friends mention a "dog"—or heard little Eel say something he didn't understand about "dogs," right?—and he had been smart enough to figure something out. Well, here's what she had to say. The creatures that these men called dogs, and Lee Harwell wrote about in his entertaining book—no, of course she hadn't read it, but she'd heard enough about the novel to know what he had done—were not dogs or "agents" or anything of the kind. *They were what kept us from seeing that which we are not equipped to see.* All these Mallon people were marked now, and the "dogs" kept an eye on them, not to keep them safe, because they cared nothing for human beings—Meredith thought they saw people as garbage—but to ensure that none of them got so far out of line again. Meredith had seen the dog-things advance toward the eternal, chaotic realm, and she knew what they really looked like, but she could not, not ever, describe them. It wasn't possible. Our words don't go that far, sorry.

■

"Oh, the three great principles?" Meredith Walsh asked, enjoying her moment even as she detested those with whom it was shared. "You want to know what they are? Are you interested in learning what the loony-tune queen sent to me, which changed my life entirely?"

"If you'd like to tell us, please do," Lee said.

"You're dying to hear what she said. And you will. The three principles are:

"One. If something is free to be taken, take it.

"Two. Other people exist so that you may use them.

"Three. Nothing on earth means anything, or can mean anything, but what it is."

Meredith Walsh checked to ensure that these men had taken in her wisdom. Evidently, what she saw before her was satisfactory. She stood up and gave them a chilly smile. "And now our appointment has come to an end. Vardis will let you out. Good-bye."

Obeying a mysterious summons, Vardis Fleck crept into the anonymous room, caressing his hands and nodding in agreement to some proposition only he had heard. He indicated the door with creepy servile gestures, and they moved toward it.

"Donald," came Meredith's voice. Both of them looked back. "It will be a very long time before you ask me again for money."

the dark matter

She's empty," I said to Don as we turned toward I-94 and the journey back to Madison. "The emptiest human being I've ever met. There's nothing there but hunger and the desire to manipulate."

"What did I tell you?" Olson asked.

"When she first came into the room, I swear, I fell in love with her. Twenty minutes later, I thought she was an unlikable hag with a great plastic surgeon. By the time we left, not that it wasn't interesting, because it really was, but by the end I couldn't wait to get away from her. And she was still hiding something."

"Well, yeah. Always. What do you think she was hiding right then?"

"She didn't tell us what she saw when she looked at Lee."

"To tell you the truth, I don't think she did look at the Eel. I don't think she could. Too much hatred."

I gave him a perplexed look. "Isn't that a little over the top?" Olson did not respond. "Anyhow, what I really meant was that she was hiding something about that crazy king and queen. It might have been something she didn't really *know* she was keeping back."

"She kept back a lot she didn't know," Olson told me. "All those figures in her dioramas represent spirits that Henry Cornelius Agrippa claimed could be called up by invoking certain specific rites. The Bear King and the Bellowing Queen with the distaff, the ones that gradually took over, are the Spirits of Mercury, which, according to Agrippa, create horror and fear in whoever summons them. Meredith says they smiled at her, but according to Meredith, Jack the Ripper would smile at her, too. The naked green girl and the camel and the dove in front of Spencer were the shapes of the Spirits of Venus, which were supposed to be seductive and provocative. The red guy and that other stuff in front of Boats were the shapes of the spirits of Mars, which cause trouble."

"Maybe this is a stupid question, but why would anyone call up these characters?"

"First, because they could—it demonstrates their power, their knowledge, their command. Second, because you're supposed to be able to make the characters do things for you. All of the characters Meredith saw were evil spirits, and when you summon them, you should have Pentacles and Sigils ready to contain them. Pentacles and Sigils are basically written symbols or sacred pictures shown in a double circle and surrounded by Bible verses and the names of angels. All of this magical juju is specially chosen for whatever effect you're trying to create."

"But Mallon didn't do any of that. He just had ropes."

"Oh, he had spells, too, but he didn't know anything about what I just told you. It all comes from Cornelius Agrippa's book *Of Magical Ceremonies,* which didn't appear until 1565, thirty years after Agrippa died. Mallon and the few other people who did research on Agrippa really only dealt with his *Three Books of Occult Philosophy,* because everyone thought the later one was fraudulent. Well, not Aleister Crowley, but no scholar ever took Crowley seriously."

Now we were already out of Milwaukee on I-94, and the sun was shining on the wide fields on both sides.

"Until you mentioned him, I'd never heard of Cornelius Agrippa. In the sixteenth century, was he a big deal? A famous philosopher?"

"I guess you could say that. To everybody like *us*, Spencer and me, he was the greatest of all the Renaissance magicians, but Agrippa had a tough old life. He was a soldier, a scholar, a diplomat, a spy, a doctor who never had any medical training, a lecturer, and he was married a bunch of times. He didn't get paid very often. To secure the patronage he needed to do his work and disseminate his ideas, Agrippa had to keep jumping around Germany, France, and Spain. High point of his life may have been when he was made a professor of theology at the age of twenty-three.

"Of course wherever he went the conventional clergy accused him of heresy, because he was, you know, interested in magic, Raymond Lully, the kabbala, astrology. He had to keep scrambling to find ways to publish his books. The guy was thrown into a Brussels jail because he couldn't pay his debts, and the Dominican monks at Louvain accused him of impiety. People were executed for that offense. Other monks claimed he had manufactured gold, which would put him in the devil's party. Actually, he said he had seen it done and knew how to do it, but could not do it himself. When he was forty-nine, the emperor of Germany condemned him as a heretic, and he fled to France, got sick, and died. The guy had written about a million words and lived five or six lives."

"God, he must have been Mallon's hero."

"Pretty much. Mine, too. His *Three Books,* and the fourth, are the most important books of occult wisdom in the Western world. And either despite that or because of it, Agrippa died broke and alone, surrounded by his enemies. In the long run, it looks like that's what our kind of magic gets you."

I uttered a noncommittal grunt. Donald Olson did not appear to be offended. I stuck my elbow out the window, got the needle up to seventy, and managed to keep it there for most of our long and strangely calm return to Madison. Outside the village of Wales, the column of black smoke had disappeared from the fields and the sky.

"Damn," Don said. "I'd pay a million dollars to know what text Mallon was quoting out there. Want to know the funny part? He didn't know what it was, either! He told me it just came to him, and afterward he couldn't remember what the hell he'd said."

"Thank God," I said.

■

At the steady rate of seventy miles per hour, we entered Madison and before long were rounding the Square and driving down into the parking garage. After we had freshened up and reconvened in the lounge, I pulled my iPhone from my pocket and enjoyed a long conversation with my wife. The Eel, for so I had begun to think of her again, was full of news about her friends and colleagues in the ACB, her experiences in the city (a Tina Howe play, Mahler's Ninth by the National Symphony Orchestra at the Kennedy Center, dinner with old friends in their apartment at the Watergate), and her plans for the next few days. The Rehoboth Beach people, plus Missy Landrieu, were asking her to come down to chair their meeting the following Wednesday, and she thought she would do it. She'd been gone so long, another few days wouldn't make much of a difference. Lee would get a ticket for Saturday. Besides, Missy was a great character, a hoot, and as he had always said, you got the best crab cakes in the world in Maryland. He wouldn't mind, would he? She supposed Don Olson was still sponging off him.

"He's staying with me, yes, but he's not exactly sponging. I loaned him some money when he first showed up, but he paid me back right away. And he's been very helpful to me with this new project of mine."

Lee Truax had some doubts about this new project.

"We met the former Meredith Bright this morning. She's a horror, but she had an interesting story about what happened that day."

Lee Truax imagined that Meredith Whatever-her-name-was would be like the beta versions of some of those word-processing systems for the blind, the ones that garbled every third word and transformed boring reports into surrealism!

"Well, when we both get back home I'll tell you what she said. For instance, I didn't know you ran into an anti-war riot on your way out to the meadow."

"Oh, that was no big deal. We hid behind a wall in a parking lot, and no one ever noticed we were there. Meredith made a big deal about being behind schedule, but no one else thought it was important. Now, what's this in your messages about Hootie?"

Everything about Hootie, Howard as he was known now, was amazing, I said. His apparent crack-up on the day Don and I had taken him outside for the first time in decades had actually led to a stupendous breakthrough. For four amazing days, Howard Bly, good old Hootie, had taken one giant step after another.

"It all started with him lying on the hospital floor, saying something very simple. He said, 'Don't do that. Take it back.' First words he'd spoken that weren't quoted in thirty-seven years, ever since he's been here. Then this girl who works there came up to him—we didn't know it, but she'd had lots of conversations with him—she came up and knelt down, and he whispered something. You'd never guess what he said to this girl."

The Eel supposed that was correct. Since she could not guess, why not tell her?

"Hootie whispered, 'She is our skylark, and I know it.' When Pargeeta told me, she asked if it made any sense. 'A lot,' I said."

"Yes," my wife said, sounding reluctant. "It does make a lot of sense, and only he would know that. *Really* know it, I mean."

I paused before asking her the question she once had batted away with a wounding dismissal. "I'm going to talk to Howard today about what happened in the meadow. He knows, and he's prepared. One day, will you tell me what *you* think happened then?"

She also hesitated, and for a longer time than I. "After all this time, I could try. Will Dilly be there?"

"He might be. I don't know yet. Do you think I'll understand why you waited so long to speak?" I meant one thing by this question; by her answer, "You certainly will," she meant another.

"What you're going to tell me can't be as flat-out crazy as Meredith Walsh's story."

She chuckled. "Mine is so beyond flat-out crazy, I think it breaks new ground. Remember . . . I'm the Skylark."

"I *know* that, but I don't know how I know."

"There are times when I think you've had a very strange marriage."

"All marriages are strange. Just give them enough time."

"Or maybe you just had a very strange wife."

Within me, words arose from the place where they were connected directly to feelings, and I said, "The truth is, I'd marry my wife all over again."

"Oh, Lee. That was such an incredibly nice thing to say."

"Do you have to go back to Rehoboth Beach?"

She inhaled, and I knew what she would tell me. "No, of course not, but I'd like to. It's not far from Washington, and I won't be long."

"You plan to be there Wednesday to Saturday of next week."

"Yes, if you don't mind. I'll probably get a room at the usual place."

Exactly as I had heard her deciding what to do, I now could hear her desire deliberately to change subjects. "I think I'd like to see Hootie, too. He was always such a beautiful boy."

"Over the last forty years, he's changed a bit."

"He'll still be beautiful to me. If he really does get out of that hospital, could he come to Chicago? In time?"

"Are you serious about this?"

"I owe him something. In the days when I could have visited him, they refused to let me see him. Then we left for New York, and life got so busy, and I let him become part of the past. And there he's been, all this time, in that terrible place. Could he function in the outside world? Is he too damaged to ever be able to live on his own?"

"Well, he's certainly come a long way, and in a very short time. I have to say, he is kind of charming. In fact, this young woman who works in the Lamont, Pargeeta Parmendera, loves him. They're pals! Even when he could talk only in quotations from *The Scarlet Letter* and a romance novel that was lying around the ward, they had long conversations about everything under the sun."

"Pargeeta is undoubtedly very attractive."

"She's a knockout. At first, I thought she was the head psychiatrist's mistress, but instead she was the guy's old babysitter."

"And what does Hootie look like now?"

I groped for something telling, and the perfect description came to me. "He looks like a character from *The Wind in the Willows*. He could be Mole."

"He sounds darling."

"He is darling. It's amazing. He's been in here his whole life, but he feels no resentment. He thinks it was the right place for him. He says he was waiting to get well enough so we could show up and make him even better."

"Do you believe that?"

"I hardly know what I believe anymore."

"You intend to stay in touch with Hootie, don't you?"

"Eel, I'm not going to walk out on him now."

"You called me Eel!"

"Sorry! Don really tried to use your name, but he kept backsliding. Before long, I was doing it, too."

"I don't mind, actually. The Eel was a good kid, if I remember correctly. But you can only call me Eel in front of Hootie and Don."

"Agreed."

Lee Truax waited a second before saying, "You seem to like Don more than you did at first."

"We've spent a lot of time together. You know how after you've had someone's company for four or five days, you start wishing he'd leave? That hasn't happened. I like having the guy around, and I have to say, he's been very helpful to me."

"You mean, helpful to this new project."

"Well, yeah. He was a decent guy back then, and I think he still is."

"Are you sorry now that you didn't come along with the rest of us?" She was silent for a moment. "Do you wish you'd met Spencer Mallon?"

I think I might have done that this morning, I thought, and said, "No."

"You can't be telling the truth."

"If I'd been there with the rest of your gang, I wouldn't able to think about everything from this angle. I like being at my own little angle. It's like standing on the sidewalk, looking in through someone's picture window, and trying to make sense of what you see."

She thought about what I had said, and I could picture her with the phone in her hand, staring blindly ahead in the darkened hotel room, her features half in shadow. When finally she spoke, it was with a degree of warmth that surprised me. "One day, I'll try to help, too, but I'll have to work up to it."

After I disconnected, I realized that I had told her nothing about our miraculous rescue from death in a plane crash. It was better that way, I thought. She need never hear of that incident.

◼

When we drove into the Lamont's parking lot, a slim dark shape moved from the shadow of the great walnut tree. The tremor of unease that visited me disappeared when the gliding figure moved into the sunlight and became Pargeeta Parmendera.

"Hi," I said, although I could see that Pargeeta was not in the mood for social niceties. As she marched up to the car it was clear that speaking to Howard Bly's friends had been uppermost in her mind for some time.

"Yeah, hi," she said, and came to a halt directly in front of me. "Sorry. I just have to say this. I waited out here because I was pretty sure you'd be getting here around this time."

"How long were you standing there?" I asked.

"It doesn't matter. Twenty minutes?"

"You were standing under that tree for twenty minutes?"

"It might have been more like half an hour. Please. I was sure you'd come here sooner or later, and I wanted to explain something before we get inside. I don't want you to think I'm a horrible person."

"Nobody could think that, Pargeeta."

"Okay, but you saw my face, the expression on my face, which I don't even know what it was. Only you *saw* it."

"I don't know what you're raving about, sweetie."

"I saw you notice. When Howard was sitting on the floor, and Dr. Greengrass was talking to him."

I did know what troubled her, I realized. In Pargeeta's face I had seen something troubled and conflicted, and she was right to think it had disturbed me. "Ah," I said. "Yes."

"You *do* know what I'm raving about."

"Well, maybe *he* does," Don began, but fell silent when I flicked an irritated glance at him.

"It's not serious," I said.

"To me it is! I went crazy, worrying about what you thought. I'm not a bad person. Howard's wonderful, and I adore him, but I don't want to make him stay here forever."

"You understood right away that he was going to leave."

"He talked without quoting! And he said 'Farewell' twice!"

"You're right." She thought Hootie's farewell had been for her.

She threw out her arms, and her face twisted. "Why am I the only person who ever *hears* him? Howard will tell you everything, you just have to understand the way he talks."

"You don't want to lose your friend, do you? Now that it's easy to understand what Howard is saying, he'll be able to move into a halfway house."

"Well, duh," she said. "You see my dilemma."

"And to make it worse, you're really proud of him, too."

"Wouldn't you be? It's fantastic, how he could let himself talk again. And it was because of the two of you. You showed up, and he just blossomed!"

"You do all the work, and we turn up and get all the credit."

"Yeah, there's that. Only it didn't feel like work." She raised both hands and flicked away tears I hadn't seen.

"Howard owes a lot to your friendship. He knows that."

"Howard wants to see the Eel. That's your wife, isn't it? Her nickname was the Eel, and his was Hootie."

"You've been having long conversations with him."

"While I still can," she said. "But I do want him to see your wife again, I really do."

"Then we'll have to make sure you're there, too, one day."

"Is it time to go inside yet?" Don asked.

■

Dr. Greengrass beckoned us into his office and invited us to sit down. The progress of everybody's favorite patient continued at its astounding pace, though he had showed some signs of backsliding today, in his friends' absence. Some moodiness, loss of appetite, and a couple of instances of his "quote mark" arm gestures to indicate that he was selecting his phrases from a wider context.

"In a sense, though, I gather that everything Howard says now comes from the much wider context of multiple sources. A near infinity of sources. That's his contention, anyhow. I can't imagine how a human memory can hold so much, and in fact, I wonder if it's humanly possible. Howard never seems to need to search through these mental documents of his for an expression, he just comes out with it, whatever it is."

"You think he's cheating?" I asked, smiling.

"I think he may still need the comfort of an underlying text, even if it's an infinite patchwork that is . . . more theoretical than actual."

"Or it may be that we just don't understand how his memory works."

"Point taken," Greengrass said. "In my view, you understand, it would be preferable if Howard is merely pretending to be quoting from an infinitely available multiplicity of texts. As a practical matter, of course, it makes little or no difference. I just want you to be aware that Howard appears to be significantly more secure in his progress when he knows that you're in the vicinity."

"He was unhappy that we left town?"

"It affected him, let's put it that way. We're open to the idea of moving Howard into a residential treatment center, but right now our first concern is that we refrain from doing anything prematurely, or anything that has even the faintest chance of undermining Howard."

"We share your concern," I said. Don nodded. "And I'm glad you're open to the idea of a treatment center."

"Well, they're very different from halfway houses, aren't they? I can't pretend that Howard is likely to get anything new out of staying on at the Lamont. Actually, I have been thinking for years that he would very likely experience considerable benefits simply from being in a new environment, but Howard never found that idea even faintly acceptable. He just shut down on me. Until now."

"That's very interesting," I said.

Greengrass cocked his head and stuck a ballpoint pen in his mouth, apparently considering some matter. "You remember promising to share any new information you might acquire about the sources of Howard's pathology?"

"If I had anything you'd find explanatory, you'd already know about it."

"Surely you have discussed the incident involving Mr. Mallon."

"We had kind of worked out that we'd start on the meadow today."

"In that case, let me detain you no longer." Greengrass smiled at them and began to stand up.

"First let me make a suggestion," I said. "You can tell me if it's any kind of possibility."

Greengrass settled down again. "Please."

"Our presence in Howard's general vicinity seems to have a positive influence on him?"

"On his progress, yes."

"Are there any special limitations or conditions pertaining to the treatment centers you would be exploring for Howard?"

"What a question! Yes, first, availability, of course. Suitability. The general condition of the unit."

"Is location an issue?"

Dr. Greengrass tilted back in his chair and gave me a careful look. "What is this suggestion of yours, Mr. Harwell?"

"I wondered if it might be helpful to Howard to be placed in Chicago. I'm completely ignorant about this kind of thing, but through my wife's work, she would know any number of people who could be helpful in finding Howard a good placement there."

"In Chicago."

"The first thing Howard told Pargeeta was that he wanted to see my wife."

"He referred to your wife as the Eel?"

"It was her high-school nickname. Her name is Lee, which backwards is. . . ."

"You and your wife have the same given name?"

"So it seems. Do you draw any psychological conclusions from that?"

"None. Why do you ask?"

"Someone we met this morning implied it meant something unpleasant."

"People's names have very little to do with their romantic attachments," Greengrass said.

"Also, back in those days, we looked like twins."

"No wonder you fell in love!" The psychiatrist tilted his head and grinned. I thought he looked a bit like a *Wind in the Willows* character, too. As Greengrass's mind returned to our earlier topic, his smile faded. "I don't believe there is any serious obstacle to placing Howard in Illinois. If we were a state hospital, of course, it would be impossible. However, those codes and restrictions do not apply to us. As I explained to you, I'd be entirely willing to see Howard pass into a good center. For me personally, and I want to be completely frank about this matter, the central issue here concerns your involvement in Howard's ongoing treatment. How committed are you to Howard's case? I am asking both of you. How do you see your wife's involvement, Mr. Harwell?"

"We'd both do everything we could."

"So would I," said Don. "It's long past time I settled down, and Chicago would be a great place to do it. I don't want to die broke and alone."

I turned my head and regarded him in amazement.

Don shrugged. "I mean, man, I'm getting too old to keep living like this. What I could do, you know, is find a little apartment and advertise for students. All the time I been staying with you, Lee, I been thinking about this. Mallon got off the road, so can I."

"Could you make a living that way?"

"Hell, yes, I can make a living. It'd be a small one, bro, I'll never buy any fancy townhouses on the Gold Coast, but it would be enough for me. D'you know why?"

"Why?"

"If you sell wisdom, you'll always have customers. I'll print up a couple of pamphlets, leave 'em in bars and drugstores and libraries, inside a month I'll have fifty, sixty queries." He swiveled in his chair to face Greengrass. "I'd consider it an honor to maintain contact with Hootie—Howard, I mean. Damn, man, I'd go over and see him once a day, until he got sick of me, anyhow."

"And I would need good, reliable paperwork for this patient. Monthly reports, say, for at least the first twenty-four months."

"You want monthly reports?" Don asked. "Whoa, Nellie. I think I'll leave that to the writer over here."

"I don't believe the doctor meant us," I said.

"Correct, Mr. Harwell. I would expect monthly reports from any treatment center that admits Howard. In a sense, Howard will always be my patient. It's essential that I be kept informed of his ongoing condition."

"Shouldn't be a problem, should it?"

"No," Greengrass said. "It should not be a problem." He looked up and placed his hands on his desk. "Our biggest problem is that we'll all be so brokenhearted when and if Howard actually does move on. Pargeeta especially."

"I promised her she could visit us," I said.

"That was kind of you, Mr. Harwell. What do you say we drop in on our patient?"

■

In a room as brightly colored as a preschool classroom, Howard Bly was seated on the edge of his neatly made-up bed, dressed in a red polo shirt slightly too small for him, striped bib overalls laundered so often the denim folded on itself like cashmere, and shiny yellow Timberland work boots. He looked splendid. His sparse hair had been combed back and flattened against his scalp with water, and his ordinarily placid blue eyes glowed with pleasure and excitement.

"You're wearing your birthday shoes," Greengrass said, smiling, and turned to us. "We gave them to Howard last year. He saves them for special occasions."

"Yes, I do," Howard said. "I love my Timbs."

"Today, you could go back into our garden, sit at the picnic table. That's a good place to talk."

"I'm going to talk today," Howard said, glowing at Don and me. "I'm going to *tell* you things. It won't be like that other time."

"You're feeling better now," Greengrass said.

The three of us stood there, lined up at the side of Hootie's bed like doctors doing rounds.

Hootie nodded. "Dill and Illslie are back again, and safe."

"Dill and *who?*"

A wide smile from Howard Bly.

"Howard, what did you call Mr. Harwell?"

The smile extended ever farther. "Illslie. Because that's what he is. He used to be Twin, but now he's Illslie."

"Oh," I said. "Yes. I get it. I'm Eel's Lee."

"Of course that's who you are," Hootie said. "And I feel better because you and Dill are back in Madison. But now I would like to go outside with my friends, please."

"Are you concealing something from me, Howard?"

Howard blinked, then smiled. "No more than a dark shimmer in the air."

"What's that a quote from?"

"*Mrs. Pembroke's Wager*, by Lamar Van Gunden. Permanent Press, New York, New York, 1957. I found it behind a sofa in the Game Room, but the next time I looked, it wasn't there."

"I think you gentlemen should take your friend into the back gardens," said Dr. Greengrass. "When he starts making books up, he's had enough of me."

■

"He thinks I made it up, but *Mrs. Pembroke's Wager* was real," Howard said. "I never make books up. To make books up, you have to be an author."

257

They were moving, at a deliberate pace, through soft, mild sunlight toward the picnic table just inside the canopy of shade cast by a huge oak with a wide crown.

"Were you worried about us?" Don asked.

"Of course I was worried. You almost could have died." Howard slipped into the shade, moved to the back of the table, and sat where he could look out at the whole of the Lamont's back gardens.

Don moved around beside him. Together, they looked like a farmer and a cowboy momentarily occupying the same picnic bench: a sly, humorous farmer; a leathery, sun-baked old cowboy with something on his mind.

"*Almost could have* died?" he asked.

"Yeah, what does that mean?" I asked, sliding into the opposite bench and planting my elbows on the table.

"It means you almost could have, but you didn't, because you couldn't. It's not the same as 'could almost have,' though. Right, right?"

"I think I see your point," I said, "but how did you know? A little bird told you?"

"The dark shimmer in the air," Howard said. "Once I found it in back of the Game Room sofa, but after I took it away, it wasn't there."

"All right," I said. "No more 'almost could' as distinct from 'could almost,' and no more about whatever was behind the Game Room sofa. All right?"

"It is, with me," Howard said. This time, I could almost *taste* the quotation: a ghostly book seemed to form itself around the words, humming with language of a remembered flavor that flowed out through details of every kind, and through these specificities into the characters. The whole experience was like a warm taste in my mouth.

I turned away from the men on the other side of the table and gazed out over the hospital's gardens.

Before me, long descending terraces unrolled like a flawless green carpet. On these wide, serene terraces, men and women in wheelchairs rolled along smooth, black asphalt paths beside tidy four-foot hedges. Through the middle of every terrace ran a long, brilliant bed of flowers bracketed at either end by smaller, circular beds. Just enough oaks and maples cast just enough shade. Fountains played, and beads of water scattered in a slight wind. It would be a nice place to end up, I reflected. Inside, of course, the hospital was less comfortable. Given their context, the gardens were a surprising fact—it came to me that they had been added later on, by someone who had understood that extensive gardens like these would aid the healing of the patients at the Lamont.

Without looking back at the other two, I said, "Hootie, was it like this when you first came here?"

"Back then, it was really ugly out here, Sarge."

"Sarge?"

"Never mind," said Hootie. "Never mind, never mind anything at all. I don't."

"Is everything you say still a quote from a book?"

"Everything I say," Hootie started off, then for a moment like the flicker of a bird's wing, seemed to search his remarkable memory, "is made up of a variety of quotations. As if in a . . . blender. Get it, Jake? Sentences that have never met become joined at the hip! My doctor does not want this to be true, but it is true, and that's that. He would prefer me to have access to entirely original language, whereas I would prefer not to. Nobody's language is really original. The way I talk is infinitely free, anyhow."

"It's wonderful that you let yourself move on from Hawthorne, though I suppose he's still in there, somewhere."

" 'In the way of literary talk, it is true,' " Hootie said, grinning with pleasure.

"What let you do it?" Don asked. "I mean, I know this sounds egotistical, but was it us?"

"I remembered my old English classes." He closed his eyes and pulled his brows together. "I mean to say, I remembered that I remembered them. And all those amazing books we read. Do you remember? Do you?"

"I remember most of them, probably," I said.

"I only read half of them," said Don. "Being a more typical high-school student than you guys."

"*The Catcher in the Rye,*" Hootie said. "*To Kill a Mockingbird. The Lord of the Flies. Tom Sawyer. Huckleberry Finn. The Last of the Mohicans. The Red Badge of Courage. My Ántonia. Hamlet. Julius Caesar. Twelfth Night. Great Expectations. A Tale of Two Cities. Dombey and Son. A Christmas Carol. The Red Pony. The Grapes of Wrath. Of Mice and Men. The Sun Also Rises. A Farewell to Arms. A Separate Peace.* 'The Bear,' 'A Rose for Emily,' 'The Rocking-Horse Winner,' 'The Celestial Omnibus,' 'Up in Michigan,' 'The Big Two-Hearted River,' and about fifty other short stories. *Black Boy. Death of a Salesman. Pygmalion. Man and Superman. Rebecca. Fahrenheit 451. The Call of the Wild. 1984. Animal Farm. Where Angels Fear to Tread. Pride and Prejudice. Ethan Frome. Emma. Vanity Fair. Tess of the d'Urbervilles. Jude the Obscure. The Great Gatsby.* The beginning of *The Canterbury Tales.* A lot of poetry—Elizabeth Bishop, Robert Frost, Emily Dickinson, Tennyson, Whitman. There's a lot more, too. Just for pleasure, I read five James Bond novels, and I remember every word of every one. And *Harrison High,* by John Farris. Our whole gang read that."

"All those books are inside you." I felt something like reverence.

"All that and more. L. Shelby Austin. Mary Stewart. J. R. R. Tolkien. John Norman. E. Phillips Oppenheim. Rex Stout. Louis L'Amour and Max Brand."

"I forgot how much stuff we read in high school," Olson said.

"To state the obvious, I did not." Hootie was grinning again.

"Just out of curiosity, what was that from?"

"*The Moondreamers,*" Hootie said. "A great novel. Honestly. But you asked me a question, and I'd like to answer it. Yes, I think it was you. The two of you. After you came to me, and I cried, and we talked, I remembered what I knew. I remembered what I had known all along, all during every minute of those long years, those dear, foolish years, those long, vanished years."

"Don't quote from that one anymore," I said. "Writing like that drives me up the wall."

"Sorry," Hootie said. "I thought you'd enjoy that. Anyhow, you were asking about the gardens. The good doctor and his fair wife are responsible for all that you see before you. They planted a lot of it themselves, but they hired gardeners, too."

"Where did 'gardeners' come from?"

"Right off the bat, at least five or six books. If you go on asking me about that, you'll drive yourself around the bend."

"I don't believe you," I said. "I'm with Greengrass. Sometimes, yeah, you're quoting, but more than half the time you're talking the same way as everyone else."

"Split the Lark and you'll find the music, bulb after bulb in silver rolled. The sun rose upon a tranquil world, and beamed down upon the tranquil world like a benediction."

"Emily Dickinson, meet *Tom Sawyer*," I said. "I know you can do that. You don't have to prove it to me."

"I don't care if he quotes from books or not," Don said. "The important thing is, it's not all in *code* anymore! He sounds like a normal person, most of the time anyway."

He turned to Howard and placed a hand on his shoulder. Hootie looked over at him with an expectant smile, as if he already knew what Olson was going to say. Howard Bly had become capable of meeting the unknown with perfect composure.

"Hootie, before you start telling us about the meadow, Lee and I wanted to ask you about something."

"The answer is yes," Hootie said, nodding.

"Hold on, wait until you hear what I have in mind."

"If you like, but the answer is still going to be yes." He caught me with a darting glance. "That one was all mine. So was that one. And ditto."

"God bless you," I said.

"This is the deal, Hootie. We were talking about you with Dr. Greengrass. The three of us wondered if you might be feeling as though pretty soon you'd be prepared to move to some new environment."

"I told you. Yes. I think I could . . . Where you are? Where's that?" He looked back across the table, an impish flame in his eyes. "And where do you live? What are you?"

"Come on, you're quoting again," I said. "I live in Chicago. So what was that?"

"*Tess of the d'Urbervilles.* If I go to Chicago, could I see the Eel? Could I see you together?"

I nodded.

"And Dilly? Where do you live? What are you?"

"I live on the road, basically, but I might settle down in Chicago," Don said. "I think I really might. Hell of a good town."

Hootie nodded. "I have heard of Chicago."

"A man can't be a teenager forever."

"Or a little child, neither."

After speaking this lovely phrase, which may or may not have been a quotation, Hootie turned his head once again to me and uttered another astonishment. The pale, peaceful blue I remembered from forty years back still hung in his eyes. "The Eel is blind, isn't she?"

I regarded him for a long time. Howard Bly did not blink.

"How do you happen to know that, Hootie?"

"It was the shiny lady with the stick. I saw it all. You don't know what I saw. *I* don't, even."

"But you're going to try to tell us."

"That's why we're here." Another dancing gleam at me. "That's why the little *Nuhiva*'s bumping along astern there."

"Joseph Conrad."

Hootie giggled and pressed a hand to his mouth. I was a real comedian. "Jack London. Are you ready?"

"If you're willing."

Hootie closed his eyes and tilted his head back. In time, and at Hootie speed, his story emerged.

| Hootie's Tale |

It was the best of times, it was the worst of times; it was intensely dark and radiantly bright. What you knew was only what you thought you knew, nothing more. It was about Oneness. It was about Allness. When Spencer stood before them, when Spencer opened his golden mouth and *spoke*, Hootie Bly heard angelic choirs. But with Keith Hayward, who was actually there on the actual first day Meredith Bright had in their presence gloriously enhanced the Tick-Tock Diner by the simple act of walking in, who had come in minutes after Hootie's radiant goddess had departed . . . with Keith everything got yanked upside down to display the wriggling bugs and writhing snakes. Keith had something to do with that terrible god-and-demon show at the end, Hootie knew that much, that Cornelius Agrippa business Mallon loved so much.

Not everyone you meet in the nuthouse is nuts, you know. And if you're in a place like Madison, even the nuts in the nuthouse can have some interesting things to say. You don't have to be a professor to read a book. Those shiny mercury-people weren't total mysteries to the kind of person who went nosing around the same library stacks that Spencer Mallon used to haunt, that is, whenever he wasn't seducing girls of college age and even younger.

Hootie *always* knew.

Some say old Cornelius Agrippa opened up something that shook him—terrified him—so badly that he backed away altogether and became a devout Catholic.

And we were afraid a lot in those days, weren't we? All of us, the whole country. Someone like Mallon, he could feel things ticking toward an explosion. That's a heck of a gift, let me tell you. He foresaw that all those big people would be shot down, he knew insanity was roaring toward us all . . . JFK, MLK, RFK, Malcolm . . . Every time one of those things happened, Hootie Bly thought of Keith Hayward, and said to himself, *I have been here before; this is not my first time.* John, Martin, Robert, Malcolm, plus whatever else you want to throw in there. How about the time they blew up that building on the campus right here and killed a grad student? World bursts into flame, smoke pours upward from the blaze, wounded people are screaming. This is how it feels, you get me, even if everybody's just standing around poleaxed. This is how you feel inside yourself, in the middle of a war. You get that end-of-the-world feeling. You don't need weapons and uniforms to have a war.

On that terrible day, Spencer was jumpy as a grasshopper. He took his merry band of children to the old movie theater to see the ancient organist and a crummy movie, and he left them there! To do one of his secret things. And when he finished that and the movie was over, he met them on the sidewalk and led them straight into combat! Did he think it was an *accident* that the world was blowing itself up on the same exact corner where he was supposed to meet Hayward and Milstrap? Did Hootie's leader and beloved ever think about that at all? No, he just got them behind a cement wall and waited it out! And then finally it was over, vastly to Hootie's relief—because Hootie wasn't like Keith, he hated violence and commotion and everybody yelling like madmen—finally there was something like quiet, if not actual silence. Sounds of dripping water and retreating crowds, and no more thrown stones, and beer bottles smashing into walls. They came creeping out into the waterlogged mess, and who's bopping around across the street? Good old Keith. All jazzed up. Eyes glowing.

The Eel, that's the main thing, though. Later, Hootie Bly saw her *travel* like no one has ever traveled before or since. And Spencer Mallon saw it, too, and it was nearly too much for him. For poor Hootie, though, there was no "nearly." For Hootie, it *was* too much. He couldn't stand up under it. Not even that. Worse. Not only could Hootie not stand up under it, what he couldn't stand up under wasn't even the whole thing. He didn't come close to the whole thing. He folded, he crumpled, he was knocked flat.

Just then, though, when they were gathering together in the center of the ruined street, Hootie looked at the Eel, and the Eel looked back and smiled, and this whole world came out of her eyes and surrounded him . . . warm and dark and lovely, able to hold him up and get him walking along . . . don't mind if I cry, it won't be the last time, that's for sure. She did that for Hootie, and it was only the first amazing thing she did for him that day.

So they walked and walked, and eventually they got to that scary road, that Glasshouse Road, where the trolls and goblins lived all the livelong day, and on Glasshouse Road they were not alone. Hootie kept his eyes on his darling, the Eel, that whole time, but Eel looked back over her shoulder, and Hootie was pretty sure Mallon did, too, and the way Eel's face tightened up and got kind of *dry* the second she looked back, that told Hootie all he wanted to know. As long as she could keep walking, he could, too, but no one could make him look. He could hear these leathery whispers of fabric and the sound of boots . . . it was not-dogs, he knew that. Un-dogs. Sad truth is, after everything that happened that day, it took Hootie a long, long time to get halfway used to dogs again.

People in Lamont, some men on his ward, they used to have these animal *companions,* they called them?

Why did that happen? Didn't they *know? Anything* can make itself look like a dog, didn't they understand that? These things, these un-dogs, these idea-dogs, Spencer hated them, and they couldn't stand him, either. Some days, Hootie didn't think they liked anything at all, that they hung around like a bunch of angry cops, ready to pound the shit out of somebody. Other days, he thought they didn't give a shit about human beings, we were just part of some job we'd never understand because it was totally way beyond us.

Hootie, now . . . Hootie would be looking out of the window in his room, one morning, any old morning, and he'd see one of those *things* out on the lawn, staring up at him . . . it was saying, *maybe everybody else forgot all about you, but we didn't.*

The rest of a day like that, Hootie wouldn't be able to eat. That night, he wouldn't get any sleep, either.

He'd rather have held Keith Hayward's hand than look behind him on Glasshouse Road.

■

So up they get into the meadow, and already everything was all screwed up because it was getting dark. Meredith Bright was in a snit about her horoscope. Hootie felt bad about that, because it was his belief that wonderful Meredith Bright should always be happy. But once they got close enough, they could see the white circle really easy. It was shining. Shining? Hey, that circle almost led them straight to it. Okay, Meredith was in her snit, and she wanted to stop everything, but everybody else, man, they were *on board,* even Keith and Milstrap.

Actually, you couldn't even begin to see that white circle when you first walked into the meadow. In order to really *see* it, you had to get up into the little swale, the fold, and then it was smack dab in front of you on the grassy rise. Only, this was the funny part, before they got there, they sort of *could* see it. They could see something, anyhow, a dazzle like a ring of white sparks above the dark, half-visible ground—a sign! They were being told where to go!

Then they had to do the thing with the ropes. Next, holding their candles, they had to arrange themselves opposite that glowing white circle. Meredith and Eel were angry at each other, so Hootie was forced to stand between them like some kind of barrier, not that he minded. Standing next to the Eel made it easier to keep an eye on her. And the Eel, man, she was watching *everything*: Mallon for sure, and Boats and Dill, but she checked in on Hayward and Milstrap, too.

Those guys, they were *off*. It was like—you do your thing, and we'll do ours. We got a private thing going on over here. That was how it looked. Everybody was excited, everybody was all caught up in the ceremony, only these two looked like they were sharing a joke. Funny, when you think about what happed to them—they practically *smirked* at Mallon. It made Hootie feel sick to his stomach, because contempt had no role in this ceremony. What they needed from each other was love and respect, and instead you got . . . smirking! The roiling in his lower regions said to Hootie, *You'd better get your skates on, because nothing is going to turn out right here, just look, it's already wrong.* Never ignore warnings that come from your troubled innards. That he did ignore it means that little Hootie accepted all the terrible crap that was waiting for him. He said, *I won't I can't I'm staying here no matter what happens, I will NOT leave Spencer Mallon!*

And just like before, the minute Spencer told them to take out their matches and light their candles and hold them aloft, those other things came crowding in. Like a host of moths, all glimmer-gray and shadow-brown, but they weren't moths. In brief, vivid images, the flares and spurts of light illuminated paws and muzzles and pointed teeth and buttons glinting on vests and suit jackets. A satin hatband captured a flare of match light, then slipped back into the teeming obscurity. And others came, too, hidden amongst those upright not-dogs. Bad things. Eel knew about them, but no one else did.

I don't like this, he said. They're here again.

Mallon hushed him, and for some reason a sad, bitter line from *The*

Scarlet Letter unfurled in his mind and rolled from his mouth: *Must I sink down here, and die at once?*

Mallon hushed him again, and Hayward swore at him, and Mallon hushed Hayward, too.

Keith Hayward aimed a smirk and a dip of the head at Meredith, but her face settled into a mask of distaste, and she flicked him away. Meredith didn't know of the Others, and neither did Keith. Did Eel? He thought the Eel knew everything, for she was already in another realm, yes, he could tell, the Eel had taken a step away, a step *out*. His poor heart folded and creased with pain, for he knew he could never follow her. Yet at the same time, his creased and folded heart expanded with love for wondrous Eel, who could know such freedom. Her boyish head went tilting back, her dark eyes shone wide open, a smile lightly touched her mouth. This is what happened: for Hootie, right then the Eel became the Skylark, just as Mallon had said. She was taking flight, and she was singing, though he could not hear a note, so earthbound and coarse were his ears.

Then what did fill his ears was the inside-out sound of Mallon on the verge of speech. It was a grand, grand moment. Electric. Sizzling. Like an invisible flash of lightning, a deep, unheard roll of thunder. Spencer Mallon breathed in, and the *air* changed. In one second, when Mallon was standing on his spot with his candle raised, eyes closed, handsome mouth just beginning to open for the release of the inspired words, the air tightened up and wrapped itself around them. Around Hootie Bly, for sure! Like cloth, like a sheet, soft, slippery, cool to the touch. Because it was still merely air, elements and beings could continue to traffic through it, but not without some effort.

All around them, shadowy forms glided through the atmosphere on the other side of the membrane that wrapped them around, and Spencer inhaled more deeply, trembling with the power of what would momentarily spill from his mouth, and the world around them darkened, and little Hootie began to realize that some of what lay waiting out there in the world beyond their membrane was purely hostile. Immediately after he registered the dim presences of those beings that were *laying in wait,* he began to smell their hot, sharp, rank fetor. This bright stench drifted toward him, curled into his nostrils, wandered stinging into his sinuses, and dripped acidlike down his throat.

Mallon was already singing. Maybe the word is chanting. Surrounded by music, words burst from him and exploded into the atmosphere—Hootie never noticed the transition from the rampant inside-out silence to this blaring, bronzy glory: he felt as though a pertinent second or two had been cut from the film of his life. Then they broke in.

He had time to glimpse them only, a red giant with a sword, a giant swine, an ancient man and woman, a drunken king made of wet mirrors. Terror made him close his eyes. Fear for Eel, fear for his beloved Mallon, made him open them again. He could not push his head down into the sand while these two were in danger.

It was as though they had, all of them but for Eel, gone to hell. Though it was actually night, the red sun had reappeared, huge and too close to the earth.

On the dark rise ten feet to the right of the painted circle, something vague, dark, and mightily pissed off was flickering in and out of sight. A few flies spun dizzied about it, transported by its terrible stink of goats, pigs, sewage, death, both all and none of these—the stink of total emptiness, total absence. The filthy creature did not *want* to be seen; it was not like the terrible god-demons that capered all about it; they demanded attention, and the twisting, flickering thing wished to escape all notice. It did its work unseen, Hootie understood. Despite its ever-constant activity, it had been created by some dire hand or agency to pass beneath the human radar.

When this recognition came to him, Hootie endured another that was much, much worse. It stopped him where he stood. It was as though a supernatural hand had loosened a valve, and all the blood had drained from his body. Hootie had been dropped into the paralysis of a confrontation with utter entire blankness, in which no action, no combination of words, no emotion however powerful or refined, had any meaning, could make a bit of difference. All was leveled flat by the flick of this creature's tail, if it had one; by the movement of its eyes, the passing through the resistant air of its blasphemous hand. All was flattened, turned to salt, turned to shit.

His legs weakened, and he sank to his knees, at which surrender the demonic thing underwent a violent spasm and succeeded at last in wresting itself from sight. The movement of the spinning flies and a pattern advancing through the grass told Hootie where the terrible obscenity was going. Like the roaring sun, it appeared to be coming his way. Hootie could no more have moved than he could have translated the molten bronze of Latin phrases pouring from Mallon's mouth. The demon of midday, the Noonday Demon, for such it was, slid another two feet toward him. He and the Eel saw it, no one else.

Only a very few seconds, Hootie thought, were left to him. On the other side of Spencer Mallon, whom he now understood he would lose by the simple expedient of death, no, not death, *erasure,* the condescending, ruinous roommates were yielding to separate impulses: vile Keith Hayward was running toward Hootie's group, with great lunging strides that would take him straight to the Eel. His eyes were black stones, and his hands reached out like claws. Brett Milstrap, still somehow capable of looking as though everything about him was faintly absurd, managed to wedge a crack into the fabric of the madhouse scene taking place before him. Hootie glimpsed a great darkness and a single, hideously mechanical light.

Then he became aware that the nighttime sun's giant sphere, tinted yellow, then red, then yellow again, pulsing with what he understood to be a kind of consciousness, had swung from the depths of the sky and approached even nearer to the meadow. In what should have been Howard Bly's last second of life, and precisely simultaneous with Brett Milstrap's disappearance from our realm, Keith Hayward's forward progress intersected that of the creature steaming toward Hootie. Through the sudden fountain of blood that abruptly replaced the psychotic frat boy, Hootie looked, for a moment only, at the pulsing, flagrant ball hurtling toward him and realized that it was entirely dangerous. At only the last possible second, he grasped that this sphere was not one thing, but was instead made of many, many words and sentences: *hot* words, *boiling* sentences, many, many thousands of sentences, thrashing and coiling like monstrous, endless, interconnected snakes. And he knew all those sentences; they were within him.

He could never describe the jumble of contradictions that followed. The moment the boiling sentence-sun struck him, he was absorbed into its substance and disappeared from this realm. He slipped out of his body, which was consumed, and threaded into a comforting subject-verb-object sequence; thence into a concatenation of independent clauses that scattered him amongst a hive of semicolons. He became an Indian in a great forest, and his name was Uncas. At the same time, bored and indifferent functionaries in the guise of upright dogs clothed in old-fashioned garments half carried, half supported him into a barren room with one high window, and there they permitted him to slip onto a thin pallet unrolled along the far wall. Someone he could not see brought him soup. Something unseen so frightened him he urinated into his trousers. Several complex sentences took him up, carried him into winter, and dumped him on the back of a wagon pursued by wolves. He said, *I need no medicine,* though his cheek was paler and thinner, and his voice more tremulous than before. A trout leaped from a Spanish trout stream and dropped into his rush-lined creel. A ferocious, formal woman in black spun from a great window opening onto the rocky, surging Cornish coast. Would he, now a nameless she, care to leap? Spencer Mallon broke his heart for good by taking off, without a glance, without a word, into a billowing orange-yellow cloud that stank of corpses, sewage, and eternity. A woman with a dirty face castrated a screaming pig and tossed its pizzle at him. A rabbit died. A puppy died. An emperor died. He was in love with an Italian nurse, and after her death, he walked home in the rain. A bookcase fell on an unpleasant and impecunious man, and it killed him. A man in a handsome uniform threw a book on a pyre made entirely of burning books. Weeping, Hootie Bly again pissed his pants and crawled he knew not where, overseen by idea-dogs, scarecrow-dogs, coat-hanger-dogs.

Eighteen hours later, a suspicious groundskeeper found him in a welter of faded gum wrappers and cigarette packs, dusty old condoms, and broken half-pint bottles beneath the bleachers at Camp Randall Stadium. He had no memory of covering the considerable distance between the agronomy meadow and the football stadium, and in fact had possessed only a very general idea of the stadium's location. It seemed likely that in a blind search for shelter he had come upon it by accident, and entered the structure without any recognition of its function. When the groundskeeper prodded his shoulder and told him that whatever the hell he was up to, he sure as hell had to get out of there now, Hootie blinked and quoted Hawthorne to the effect that by sticking to the shadowy bypaths he was going to keep himself simple and childlike, with a freshness, and a fragrance, and a dewy purity of thought.

The stadium's groundskeeper dragged him into the office and called the city police.

■

A little after six o'clock, Don and I returned to the Concourse and stopped off at our rooms for a few minutes before meeting again in the lounge. During the business of greeting Don at the bar when he walked in, ordering a glass of wine, spending a minute gabbing with the bartender, and taking our drinks down the length of the room to reclaim our little round table, I gave the half smiles and anticipatory glances that indicated I was suppressing, with some difficulty, vital new information.

We sat, and Don said, "You'd better tell me, or you'll burst."

"I know, I know," I said. "It's like the ultimate coincidence. You're not going to believe it."

"I already don't."

"But you will." I hesitated for a moment. "There was a message on my room phone. It was from Boats. He called my house, and my assistant, who just got back from Italy, told him where we were. Do you care to guess where Jason Boatman is living now?"

"Sure," Don said. "Madison, come to think of it. In his little hideout."

"He might have moved. These days, Jason lives about ten to fifteen minutes away by car. On the east side, in the Willy Street area, whatever that is. He says he has big news, and he wants to tell us in person."

"How did he sound?"

"He sounded . . . I'd have to say . . . he sounded happy."

"That is big news," Don said. "How did he know we were here? How did he know where we were staying?"

"That's what *I* asked him. But when you think about it, there's only one way he could have learned about us."

"You mean . . . the *Eel* called him? Well, why should I be surprised? She called me, didn't she?"

"I guess she e-mailed him," I said, and added that I had never realized the extent to which she kept in touch.

"You really don't get it, do you?" he asked.

Boatman's directions brought us to a wide two-story frame house on Morrison Street. It may not have been beautiful, but it certainly was no mere hideout. A tilting walkway of cracked pavement led to three wooden steps and a long front porch in need of a sanding, some screening, and several new coats of paint. The entire house, once a nice, leafy shade of green, now looked a bit jaundiced. Limp, dying ferns drooped across the cement facing on both sides of the steps. On the right side of the house, a tire-track driveway led to a garage that appeared to be trembling on the lip of collapse. Opposite the house, on the other side of Morrison Street, an overgrown bluff dropped fifteen or twenty feet to the shore of Lake Monona. This structure and its neighbors, in fact the entire neighborhood, I supposed, had declined from an original middle-class respectability to the steady deterioration of student housing. In need of a small income, a widow or a single mother had rented a couple of rooms to graduate students—the area was too distant from the campus for undergraduates—and eventually thousands had followed, burrowing into the houses while they established food co-ops, homeopathic storefronts, acupuncture centers, bad ethnic restaurants, health food stores, and cafés with cute names. What was Jason Boatman doing in a place like this?

We picked our way over the broken paving stones, went up the few steps, and pressed the bell alongside the screen door. Soon, the door to the porch swung open, for a moment exposing the dark silhouette, blurred by the mesh of the screen, of an ample, grandfatherly figure. The figure moved forward and reached for the handle of the screen door, in the process emerging far enough into the evening light to be revealed as Jason Boatman. He was smiling, and for both Donald Olson and me, the ease and friendliness of the smile indicated that some central element in the man had left him. A fire had gone out. He was too relaxed to be Jason Boatman, also he was too old and too fat: only a few gray hairs were swept back over his scalp, harsh lines sectioned his alarmingly pale face, and he had grown a small but distinct belly that rolled through the world before him.

As he swung open the dusty screen door, he said, "Hey, guys, it's great to see you! Come on in, willya?"

Even this did not seem like the Jason Boatman of old, who had been tense and often morose. The old Jason would have said something like "Okay, you're here. Finally."

Before passing through onto the porch, Olson gave me a look that said, *What's with this guy, and what did he do with the real Boats?*

"God, you're both here together, this is great." Exuding affability instead of anxiety, Boatman stepped over to his front door and thrust it open, making a sort of "at your leave, gentlemen" gesture with a sweep of his free arm. "Inside, my friends, inside. Welcome to my castle."

The door led directly into a large living room where a row of coat hooks and a section of floor tiles marked off an entry area. Beyond was a hallway to a series of smaller chambers that separated off from the big room itself, where comfortable old brown furniture sagged around a wooden coffee table. A big-screen television took up much of the front wall. Dark wooden bookshelves empty of anything but a few CDs and some small figurines and a few hand-thrown pots covered the wall to the right and the half wall separating the living room from the dining area and the kitchen. Despite its large front windows, the living room, where Jason beckoned us toward his sofa and chairs, was permanently darkened by the porch roof, which blocked the sunlight.

"Siddown, siddown, guys. Geez, I can't believe I got the two of you. What are you, both staying at the Concourse?"

"Yep," Don said. "We came here to spend some time with Hootie."

"Yeah, I think she told me that." Jason slipped into a chair to the side of the coffee table, again indicating the sofa, then, before I could speak, almost immediately bounced back up. "Boy, what happened to my manners? You guys like anything to drink? It's around that time, isn't it? I got some beer in the fridge, some vodka, that's about it."

Both of us asked for vodka. "If you have enough," I said. "If not, beer is fine. It's great that Lee e-mailed you, and that we can get together like this. I didn't know she stayed in touch."

"She doesn't, not really. I get an e-mail once a year, maybe. The Eel could always figure out where I was, I don't know how. Don't worry about the vodka, I have plenty. I'm gonna have me a beer, though."

We settled onto his sofa, and he took two steps toward the back of the house and his kitchen. "So how is Hootie, anyhow? You know, it never occurred to me to visit him out there. I thought he couldn't talk, or something."

"That's not quite right," I said, and explained Howard Bly's former communication technique. "But now, he doesn't have to quote Hawthorne anymore. Because he has one of those freak memories, every sentence, every *word* of everything he ever read is available to him, and he can combine them in any way he likes. So he has complete verbal freedom, really. And I think he fakes it about half the time—I think he just speaks, and pretends he's quoting something."

"But that's a huge breakthrough. I guess I could visit him, too, couldn't I?"

"Sure you could," Don said. "But you'd better act pretty fast. Chances are, before the end of the year he'll move into a treatment center in Chicago."

"Holy moly. Did you guys have something to do with this?"

We looked at each other, and I said, "We did have a positive effect on him, you'd have to say. I'm really glad we went to the Lamont, and I'm sure Don is, too."

"Absolutely," said Don.

"Big changes all over the place," Jason said. "Kind of makes you wonder. Anyhow, I'll be right back with your drinks, guys."

We could hear him rattling ice cubes and putting glasses on the counter and doing other things in his kitchen. While all this was going on, I realized two things about this other old friend from my high-school years. The first was that the most rootless and unmoored of all my old friends, more homeless even than Donald Olson, had settled down. Olson had at least often shared accommodations with his followers, but Boatman had shifted from one dingy hotel room to another.

The other recognition that came to me was that I had been right: something had gone from Boats, and that quality was passion. In our high-school years, we had all been passionate about a great many things, our music, sports, our books, politics, each other, our mostly awful parents . . . Spencer Mallon! But Jason Boatman's passion had been made chiefly of anger. His needs had been unassuageable, his hungers beyond fulfillment, his desires all forced inward, where they could not be met. At least to people his own age, the magnitude of his suffering had made him appealing. (We were young, is all I can say.) His passionate anger had left Boatman, and the results had been entirely beneficial. The only drawback was that Boats now threatened to be an overstuffed bore.

Jason came out of the kitchen and skirted his dining room table, holding just above the bulge of his paunch an oval metal tray with three glasses, a bottle of Budweiser, and two small bowls. When he set the bowls on the coffee table, we saw that one contained black, shiny Greek olives and the other roasted peanuts and cashews. Boatman shopped at the students' health food store; maybe he even belonged to a food co-op!

"Figured we should have some goodies," he said, and raised his beer bottle. "To your good health, gentlemen!"

We mumbled reciprocities and sipped from our brimming glasses.

"This is real nice," Boatman said. "You know, Lee, there were times I thought about seeing you, maybe, talking to you, having a little get-together, a little reunion. I thought about that. It went through my mind."

"Why didn't you do anything about it?"

"Well, for one thing, until we ran into each other in Milwaukee that time, I didn't know how to get in touch with you. I mean, you're not listed in any phone books, are you?"

"No, but there are lots of publishing and writers' directories that have my address or my agent's. Some of them have my telephone number. You could have looked me up in *Who's Who*. That's got everything."

"People like you are in *Who's Who*. People like me don't even know where to find one. What does it look like, anyhow?"

"Like a fat, red, two-volume encyclopedia."

"I never as much as laid eyes on a copy of that."

"You might have tried the local library. But look, Boats, when I gave you my card, didn't I say you could call me anytime you felt like it?"

"Sure, but I didn't think you *meant* it. And there was the other problem. Before that time, the I last time saw you, you and the Eel were getting ready to drive to New York for college and all that. Since then, you got famous. You had your face on the cover of *Time*! And you made all kinds of money! Why would anyone like that want to talk to someone like me? Man, when I thought about you, I got intimidated."

"I wish you hadn't." In my secret heart, however, I was not entirely unhappy that Boats had been too intimidated to approach me. Then something else occurred to me. "Anyhow, you had my phone number from Lee, didn't you? You just didn't want to use it."

"No. The Eel never gave me your number, only your address. I never wrote her any letters, though."

"Why didn't you?"

"Why? She didn't want me to." He said this as though it should have been obvious, even to a dullard like me.

Jason turned to Don Olson, "How did you find him?"

"I was in the joint. Lots of times, prison libraries have those writers' directories. It didn't have his phone number or anything, but it had his agent's address. So I wrote the agent, and he called Lee, I guess, and Lee said, 'Yeah the guy is legit,' and the agent wrote back to me with all the info. And that was that."

"Well, I'm glad I could do it today, man. And you guys probably don't even know that I went straight like five, six years ago."

"You went straight?" Don said. "Amazing."

"I got sick of stealing shit, and I started to get the feeling that my perfect record was going to get broken pretty soon. So I gave myself a little test."

"What kind of test?" I asked.

"I went to a little shop and tried to lift a stapler, because my old one broke. I almost got caught. If I hadn't seen the manager staring in at me through the window, I *would* have been caught. And that was how I learned I needed another line of work."

Boatman explained that after a short period of misery spent casting around for ideas and reading the want ads, he realized that he possessed only a single marketable skill. Surely he could earn an income demonstrating to chain store owners and managers of warehouses and retail outlets how to keep people like Jason Boatman from stealing whatever they liked whenever they felt like it. He could show people how to plug up the holes through which he and those like him had crawled, sometimes literally.

"So that's what happened," Boatman said. "I started down at the university co-op. Told the manager, Stand there and watch me. You won't goddamned believe what you're going to see. I park him on the second floor near the registers, remind him to watch me carefully, and I go into business mode. He keeps his eye on me while I mooch around, pick stuff up, and lay it down again. I have a backpack, but it doesn't look like I'm putting anything in it. Fifteen minutes later, I come up to the guy and say, Well?

"Well what? he says. You didn't do anything.

"That's real interesting, I said, seeing as I just swiped about five hundred bucks worth of your shit. At which point I unload my pockets and take stuff out from under my shirt and out of my pants, out of my socks, out of my *shoes,* and finally, out of the backpack. Art books, accounting textbooks, fountain pens, Badger scarves, Badger desk diaries, a Badger lamp, halogen bulbs, you name it, out it goes onto the counter. Maybe I didn't have the Spencer Mallon magical voodoo cloak over me anymore, but nobody could say I wasn't a good thief.

"Jesus, the guy says. You stole all that right under my eyes?

"I didn't steal any of it, I said. I just showed you I could. In the old days, now, many times I walked out of this store with twice what's in front of you right there, starting I think three managers back and going on right up to you. And while I was robbing your eyeteeth out of your head, I saw two kids doing the same as me only not as good. Also, one of your cashiers is getting hinky with the cash drawer.

"Then I showed him what I was talking about. We scared two little book thieves out of the shelves, and twenty minutes later, the creep doing the register scam is on his way to a holding cell, and I have a new job at six hundred dollars a week. The manager is so happy with me, he writes a letter of recommendation that gets me consultant work at a warehouse and a grocery chain, and now I'm the president of It Takes A Thief, Inc.

"So what are *you* working on now?" Boatman asked me. The most innocent of all questions, the least answerable, the words people utter to writers when they barely know them and have no idea what to say to such odd creatures. "If you can talk about it, that is," Boatman added, redeeming himself.

What to say, how to respond? I chose to offer a simple, pared-down version of what felt like the truth. "For a while, I thought about writing a nonfiction book about those Ladykiller murders in Milwaukee. Then I tried to work on a new novel. It went really slowly. Finally, something happened that sort of brought Hootie back to me, and my whole past sort of flooded back to me. Whatever happened in that meadow seemed so crucial to all of us, that I had to work it out. I had to *see into it.* You know? I had been so left out, which is something I did to myself, granted, but for some reason I couldn't *take* it anymore.

"Right at that time, Don showed up, freshly sprung from the jug. My wife pretty much arranged that, too. We agreed that he could stay with me for a while, long enough to get himself together, if he told me whatever he could remember about that day. About Mallon in general."

I blinked. I took a swallow of my drink. These actions felt faintly robotic. "And Don was really helpful. He made it possible for me to talk to the former Meredith Bright."

"Oh, God," Boatman said. "I can still get a little starry-eyed, thinking about Meredith Bright."

"Make sure you never meet her again," I said. "Or if you do, cut the encounter as short as you can. And yet, she still makes a terrific first impression."

"She told you what she remembered, from back then?"

"In detail," I said.

"And Hootie, too?"

"He had some interesting things to say."

"Well, I wish I could remember a few more things about it all, but there isn't any point. I told you everything I could remember that day we bumped into each other outside the Pfister."

"Yes," I said. "The dead children."

"Dead children all over the place. A whole tower of them . . ." He grimaced and flapped a hand in front of his face. "Don't remind me. It was always so hard, trying to keep that picture out of my head. It's funny, now that I think about it. What I thought I'd get after I gave up being a criminal and went into the anti-criminal business actually came to me. Peace, you know? My whole life, I never even thought it existed, I thought it was some kind of rumor they fed to suckers, and after I started to turn into an old guy, and stopped breaking into warehouses and hotel rooms—actual peace!"

"Let's buy dinner for this here old pussycat," Olson said.

"Good idea," I said.

As if he had not heard this exchange, Jason Boatman slumped in his chair and stared down at his lap, where his hands cupped his glass on the curve of his belly like a begging bowl. In the now-darkening air, the scant hair skimmed back over his pale scalp looked silver.

"Hold on. I used to be tremendously worried about this one weird experience I had," Boatman said, speaking to his hands, his glass, and his belly. "Not always, but off and on. There was something really terrible in it."

He looked at us without raising his head. "My name for this thing was . . . well, what I called it . . ." He shook his head, raised his glass, lowered it without drinking. Then he shook his head again. A strange, trembling spirit had moved into him, changing his features, stopping his tongue.

"What did you call it, this thing?" I asked.

The trembling spirit shifted its eyes to me, gulped a mouthful of its drink, and once again became Jason Boatman. He said, "The dark matter."

"Dark matter? The scientific thing, the invisible stuff?"

"No, not that." Boatman squirmed in his chair and looked slowly around the room, seeming to reassure himself that his little pots and his six-inch row of compact discs were in the proper places. "I can't exactly be sure of anything when it comes to this, uh, topic. It's something that happened to me on Lake Michigan, and then later on the shore. Somewhere, I for sure never knew where. It wasn't just that it was weird, it was way beyond that."

He turned to me. "This experience came from the same place as the tower of dead kids, but from further *back* in that place—the end of it, the bottom, where everything, everything we know about or care about dribbles away and nothing means anything anymore. That's what threw me. I saw that nothing meant any more than anything else."

Boats swung his head to Don. "It was about you. You and Mallon. You know how much I wanted what you got. I would have done anything to have Spencer pick me. This one night when I was in Milwaukee, it felt like I could almost, no, that I really *could* have a second chance. Would you like to hear what happened? Lee, this came from the meadow, I'm sure of that. It took a lot longer to get here, that's all."

"Please," I said.

"What I got wasn't all that easy to live with," Don said. "Just so you know."

"Shut up and listen," Boats commanded.

| The Dark Matter |

The first thing you had to understand, *Boats said,* was that his relationship to Lake Michigan wasn't like most people's. For Boats, the lake was all bound up with his father, and not in a good way. Lake Michigan was where his father went to work, while his wife and son stayed behind in Madison—it was one of the things that took his dad away from him. Plenty of nights, Charles Boatman called to say he was too tired to make the drive back home, he was just going to crash in his shop. Sometimes, his dad was drunk when he made those calls, drunk and high both, the old man was a real swinger. Sometimes, when Boats answered the phone, he could hear music and laughter drifting behind his father's slurred voice. Naturally, from time to time Jason was permitted to come to Milwaukee and hang out in the boathouses his father was renting, and that was usually a special time. Away from Shirley, his dad got a lot more relaxed, and he could be fun to mess around with. The problem was, apart from building boats and selling them to rich people, messing around was about the only thing Charlie Boatman actually cared about. So Lake Michigan stood for his father's absence but also the wild, careless stuff the old man got up to when he was on its shores.

And the lake was different all by itself, Boats thought. It didn't look like Lake Mendota or Lake Monona, the ones he grew up with—no, it looked like another species of thing altogether. Lake Michigan looked like an ocean. From the campus side of Lake Mendota you could see the fancy houses across from it, but Lake Michigan didn't look like it even had an opposite side. The thing just stretched on and on, mile after mile of moving water, starting out as a kind of pale green near the shoreline and getting deeper and deeper into a cold, flat blue the farther you went. Way out, Lake Michigan stopped pretending to be a nice, friendly body of water like Mendota or Random Lake, and showed you its real face, brutal, without any feelings at all beyond a blunt insistence. *I am, I am, I am.* That's what the lake told you when you got far enough out to lose any sight of shore. *I am, I am, I am. You're not, you're not, you're not.* If you didn't pay attention to that, you were a goner, you didn't have a chance.

There was a kid in Milwaukee who died of exposure out in a sailboat on Lake Michigan overnight in spring, 1958, 1959, Boats remembered his dad talking to him about it, telling him to act smart and never get caught like that kid. Only guess what. The same damn thing almost happened to Boats Boatman at the age of eleven, a couple of months after his dad, Charlie Boatman, broke the news that he was in love with this girl, Brandi Brubaker, so he was going to live with her from now on and would be coming back to Madison only now and then. That was quite the message. It had quite the effect. Shirley stayed pissed off and drunk for a couple of years, and little Boats bobbed up and down in the backwash.

One night he did a really dumb-ass thing, got out on the road and stuck out his thumb. God took pity on fools yet again and got him to the east side of Milwaukee in two quick, easy rides. Trouble was, Boats didn't know exactly where his father's boathouses and workshops were located, so he started looking for them miles to the north, around the lakefront marinas in

Milwaukee itself, instead of in Cudahy, which wasn't so fancy. Eleven-year-old Boats had just supposed if he got to where the boats were, he'd either see his father's sheds and boathouses or ask somebody where they were. Everybody knew Charlie Boatman, didn't they? Hey, the guy was the life of the party, and a first-class boatbuilder, too. Except, Boats couldn't find anyone who knew his dad. It started to get dark, and hunger was beginning to make him desperate. He decided to "borrow" a little boat from a dock somewhere, sail it out into the lake, and move along the shoreline until the familiar huddle of buildings came into view. He mooched along the side of the big lake for miles—going the wrong way, it turned out—and eventually came across a Sunfish tied up at a private dock at the foot of a great bluff with a tall flight of stone steps.

Boats jogged out onto the dock, untied the little boat, ran up the sail, and quickly caught a mild breeze that puffed him out into the deep water. After that, everything went wrong. Although the boy was a good sailor, he went out too far and lost the shoreline in the gathering dusk. For a time, the lights of the city told him roughly where he was, but after a couple of hours of aimless drifting, tacking he knew not where, he began to imagine that he saw small bright lights twinkling at him on all sides. A fog came in. He knew he was far out on the lake, but had no idea of how far he had sailed. Like an idiot, he had neglected to bring a compass. Eventually he reefed the sail, lay down on the uncomfortable bottom of the boat, and passed out from anxiety and exhaustion. Cold and hunger whittled him away, slice by slice. Every time he awakened, he hallucinated. It seemed to him that he had been locked at night within a great department store, and as the Sunfish floated him down its handsome aisles, he tore shirts and sweaters, lamps and serving trays, colanders and cook pots from its shelves.

At ten the following morning, the ship that saved his vanishing life came hallooing out of the dense fog, following the circular, tracerlike beam of a searchlight and broadcasting resonant alarms he had failed to hear until the rescue craft bore down upon him. A harbor patrol officer climbed down into the little sailboat, wrapped him in a fog-colored blanket, and handed him up to his partner, who said, "You little shithead, I hope you appreciate how lucky you are."

Two nights in the hospital, and the feeling of having had his strength somehow drained from him in a viscous stream, like oil from a car. His father bellowed; his mother took the Badger Bus to Milwaukee and brought him home on the flip-flop. He did appreciate the extent of his good luck: the family who lived in the mansion above the bluff with its carved steps down to their dock pitied him his ordeal and did not bring charges for the theft of their sailboat. When asked about the motives for all he had done, he always replied, "I just wanted to see my dad again, I guess."

■

"And that's still the only way I can explain it," Boatman said. "But the second time I went out on Lake Michigan in a stolen boat, I wasn't planning to surprise my dad. I thought I was going to have a reunion with you, Dilly, and Spencer Mallon. I thought I was going to get a second chance!"

He stood up. "If you're going to buy me dinner, let's go now. I'm hungry, and there's a little place I like on Williamson Street called Jolly Bob's. Caribbean food, and we can get a little exercise if we walk there."

■

Jolly Bob's, I remembered as we passed through its front door, was the very place that had made me add "bad ethnic restaurants" to the list of establishments that sprouted up in areas like this. The graduate-student waitress beside the desk grinned at our approach, and I had the disconcerting notion that she had read my mind. Still smiling, she led us to a table at the back of the restaurant.

Boatman gestured for us two to sit facing the large window and the entertainment of the crowded patio.

"Can I get you guys some drinks? This looks like a thirsty group to me."

We had amused her because she had smelled alcohol on our breath. She thought we were three comical old lushes meandering through our sunset years. We took our chairs, and the window behind Jason Boatman turned him into a dark silhouette.

"Just water for me, please," I said. "But pour some vodka in it."

Brightly, making a show of acquiescent submission that in no way implied that she had found any humor in this performance, the waitress tilted her face to Boatman.

"A Purple Meanie," he said.

"*What?*" asked Don.

"It's what you drink here," Boats said. "Fruit drinks. They're really nice. I like the Painkiller, too."

"Thank you, kind sir," said the waitress. She thought we were idiots, one and all.

I said, "If that's what you drink in Jolly Bob's, I'll change my order and have the same as my friend. A Purple Meanie. Can you do that?"

"Certainly, sir." Her smile grew a little fixed.

"Same thing here, then," Don said. "Except I'd like a Painkiller."

"I'll be right back with your menus," she said, and spun away.

"At least you didn't handcuff her by the wrist and demand to know her name," I said.

"Around me, don't even mention handcuffs," Boats said.

"I have come a long way," Olson said. He turned to the stark shadow Boats had become. "As soon as I got to Chicago, I called Lee and asked if he'd meet me at Mike Ditka's place. So this was my first day out, and I came on a little too strong with our waitress. She was one pretty woman. Come to think of it, so's this kid."

"You know what I realized just the other day?" Boats asked. "Everybody young is beautiful." That his face was still only half visible made his pronouncement sound oracular.

"Nice thought. And true, besides."

The young woman returned with drinks and menus, and a little while later, we ordered conch fritters, fried catfish, coconut shrimp, and jerk pork.

"Now that we're settled and all is well, Jason, maybe you could tell us about the second time you stole a boat and went out on Lake Michigan. Why did you imagine you were going to see Mallon and Don? Were you drunk?"

"Nope. Though back in those days, my drinking sometimes got out of hand. Not this night, though. I was staying at the Pfister, working there, too, but this night I thought I'd just walk down to the lakefront after dinner. It was summer, so the days were long, and we still had about an hour of light. I walked up Wisconsin Avenue from the Pfister, went past the War Memorial and through the parking lot, and turned toward a marina I could see off in the distance. Even before I got there, something funny happened to me."

Jason Boatman's voice, almost that of the young man he had been, floated out from his indistinct form. Particular features became truly visible only when he turned to look at one of his listeners, or when he leaned forward. I thought he almost looked as though he were wearing a shroud and tried to suppress the unhappy image.

| The Dark Matter, II |

Voices seemed to come to him from out on the water, *Boats said,* as though an ocean liner had anchored just out of sight, and all the passengers were out on the decks, whooping it up. Definitely the noise of a big crowd, definitely the noise of a party. Some things you can't mistake. It was all wrong, though; it was impossible. Sound carries over water, everyone knows that, although not that far. He could not see this ship, so it would have to be at least a mile out on the water. At that distance he might hear some noise, faintly, but it would hardly be so distinct. Voices threaded through the uproar, and he could almost make out individual words. One high-pitched female voice was screaming with laughter, and a man with a resonant tenor repeated the same thing over and over. It sounded like an order, a command. Everyone else jabbered and gibbered, some at the top of their lungs. The scream of laughter flared out, as if the liner had drifted much nearer. Boats heard the man with a ringing tenor voice pronounce the words *"I need what you need"* before his voice retreated back out onto the water.

The party ended; the liner sailed on; whatever the explanation, the sound of many voices abruptly vanished into silence.

I need what you need?

He walked on. The marina seemed a great distance away. The aural hallucination, if that was what it had been, troubled him. He settled on the explanation that the wind, or some strange property of the water, had managed to blow voices ten or fifteen miles across the lake. He had heard a party on a ferry, not an ocean liner, and the people at the party were having fun while losing their minds. That happened at a lot of parties, but, now that he had time to think about it, this one had sounded almost hellish. Really disorderly, and a little demonic. He was glad he was not out on that ferry.

Now he had reached the narrow, far end of the enormous parking lot behind the art museum. A series of gardens lay before him, leading to a greensward with a duck pond. Beyond that lay the marina, a complex series of long curving piers shaped like breakwaters and studded with hundreds of pleasure boats, some with thin, upright masts, some more massive, broader, wearing wheelhouses like stiff white hats. The boats bobbed before a breeze he could not feel. To his right, Lake Michigan sent in roll after roll of ruffles and foam sparkling with the light that glinted, far out in the deeper blue, on its massive hide. Boats stepped over the low concrete barrier at the end of the parking lot and planted one sneaker-clad foot on the springy grass.

An uproar of voices bloomed in the air to his right, a woman screamed with hysterical, dangerous laughter. A tenor voice like a trumpet rang out, *I need what you need.*

He froze, and the sounds vanished. His thief's protective instinct told him to go back to the hotel, pack his bags, and get out of this city.

He placed his right foot on the grass. Jason Boatman was not going to be spooked by a trick of sound over water. The look of the big marina pleased him. It reminded him of his dad, a little, in a nice way: Charles Boatman sailboats were beautifully made, each one (Boats now understood) a work of art, like a guitar handcrafted from mahogany and walnut, every gleaming inch of it the product of assured and careful labor. It would be a kick to spot a couple of them bobbing beside the dock at that undoubtedly private marina. Why not have a look?

At the same time, a fearful instinct within him told him to return to the hotel, check out, and get on the first train leaving the downtown station. Isn't that weird? Some bizarre snatches of sound come off the water, and he almost let this *phenomenon* drive him away.

Everybody is made of two people, you know, the guy who says no and the one who says yes, the one who says, Oh, Jesus, don't you go in there/You can't ever touch that stuff, and the get-along, riskier lad who says, It'll work out fine/Come on, a little wouldn't hurt. Boats generally sided with the second guy, though maybe four or five times the other one had kept him from walking into what might as well have been quicksand. His long career on the dark side of the law had reinforced a conviction held in his youth, that you jump into no situation without being at least 80 percent sure you will be able to jump out again. Play the odds, and don't get greedy about your chances.

This time, though, because he was putting nothing at stake, he had nothing to lose. Some odd noises had managed to awaken Mr. C'mon-let's-get-outta-here, and the guy's anxiety was in overdrive. It didn't make sense. Boats decided to override these hysterical warning signals and figure them out, if he could, later.

It was true, however, that the blaring trumpet-like voice and the screaming laughter rolling out of that hubbub had unsettled him, almost as though these horrible party noises reminded him of something his more cautious and perhaps wiser self had wrapped up and shoved to the back of a cupboard. For a second, for less than that, something else, another element, an odor, put his confidence in check: ozone and wet granite, yet a smell suggestive of vast strange places, a whiff of electricity flowing through the darkness of deep space, a whiff of rotting flesh . . .

In the last moment of the day when he would have any choice about what he did, Boats thought, *Man, there's something funny out there in the lake.* Yet, even then, before he found himself once again walking toward the distant marina, it had all been set in place. He was going to steal a boat made by his father, sail it out into Lake Michigan, which had once nearly succeeded in killing him, and there, in its distant shores or reaches, encounter whatever waited for him. As if in objection to an agreement already in force, Boats looked back over his shoulder and watched a quick, sudden whirl in the air freeze and solidify into a man of a type once familiar, at least from the party at the Beta Delt house and Lee Harwell's most famous novel, accompanied in the usual manner.

And this appearance from nowhere and nothing, a twist of the air's fabric, from the same vast dark space whose odor he had just caught, of an alert-looking fellow in a neat gray suit and a buzz cut served only to reinforce what had just taken place. Beside the man, a big dark dog with a thick black ruff and a tail like a curved sword jumped to his feet and swung his head to capture Boats with his shining, attentive eyes. He could think all he liked about packing his bags and catching trains to fat, sleepy, little towns, but he could not go back to the Pfister. That way had been barred.

So now one of those agent guys, they might as well call them that, was watching Boats from behind, and the dog wasn't anything like a real dog. If you asked Boats, that made him scarier. That agent and his mutt were from the same place as those noises that might or might not have been from some big private yacht where the drunks were whooping it up.

If a person shouts *I need what you need*, is he saying *I need you*? Is he saying, *Your appetites fill me up*?

Boats had to walk around the duck pond. The grass felt stiff, like bristles. The ducks swept their wings over their heads when he approached, and when he looked back after he had passed, they stayed floating that way, wings over their heads, looking like so many folded envelopes, inanimate things without consciousness. The agent guy trolled along forty feet behind, not paying nearly as much attention to Boatman as the fierce-looking dog.

The sky darkened. The clouds ceased to scud through the air, and at once looked as if they had been painted on the flat, hard surface above them. The remaining light, so pale it was almost blue, held no warmth. The atmosphere around the marina had a neutral, dead quality, the quality of the inert and unmoving. The grass beneath his feet, no longer yielding, felt dry and crunchy, as if it had turned brittle, yet its vibrant green had not changed. After taking two more crunching steps, Boats felt curious enough to lower himself and inspect the paradoxical grass.

Each identical stalk had been embedded, as if by an assembly line, into a raised cone of dark brown plastic. With their perfectly rounded edges, the cones resembled tiny volcanoes. Boats tried to pull a stalk from one of the molded cones, and was forced to give it a sharp, hard pull he feared would snap it in two. Instead, the green stalk separated cleanly, followed by a little puff of air from the crater and the sound of tiny metal parts locking together. He held up the stalk he had extracted from its fitting and watched it shrivel in his hand. When it resembled a sagging toothpick, he dropped it, stood up again, and continued crunching across the grass until he reached the white concrete at the edge of the marina.

He stepped off the grass, noticed that the impression he had left behind was turning a pale brown, and looked back. All along the side of the duck pond, his footsteps recorded his passage in prints of dead, sand-colored grass. On the sidewalk, the man in the gray suit opened his hand parallel to the ground and raised it a few inches. The big dog, already upright and alert, lifted its tail, bared its pointed teeth, and trotted out on the grass. As if scorched, the false grass died beneath its pads, and rows of tidy paw marks followed the creature in its course toward Jason Boatman. The animal paused twenty feet away. Flat, inert blueness filled the air. Forcing himself to hold his ground, Boats inspected the dog. It resembled a stuffed thing on a wheeled cart. The ruff of bristles looked artificial, and he thought he could see that each of the dog's fearsome and perfectly white teeth emerged from a small, molded, pink mound that looked nothing like actual gum tissue.

At that moment, wing beats and birdsong awakened the air, and Boats looked up. Overhead, a skylark sailed, wheeling in its course. It was blatantly, gloriously present, burning with life, pouring out a fresh, ardent, unending melody that nearly stopped his heart. Boats thought: *This painful goddam life is full of blessings.* Then, as abruptly as it had appeared, the lark vanished.

How, you ask, did he know it was a skylark? Anyhow, you say, he must have been mistaken. The guy's a washed-up criminal, not a birdwatcher, isn't he? Doesn't he know that skylarks have never been seen on this continent? That they don't *exist* on this continent? The guy saw a barn swallow. Well, guess again, pals, because when Boats finally managed to get home from his encounter with the dark matter, he looked up "skylark" in the encyclopedia. And there it was, a longish brown bird streaked with black above the wings and with dull white below. There was a picture, and it was the bird he saw, all right, the same exact bird. Let me tell you, that song, that melody, of the skylark . . . well, all he can say is, he heard it, and it's something, all right.

(*I should have been there,* I almost said.)

In the blue air, beneath the coruscating sun, the memory of the skylark already growing dim, he walked out onto the long, curving slip and within a few minutes spotted one of his father's boats, a little sloop with a bright yellow nylon spinnaker that hung limp and raglike from the mast. Just to make sure he was right, he hunkered down at the edge of the dock and looked at the topmost section of the hull. Exactly where he had expected it to be, he found his father's lightly burned-in mark, C. BOATMAN, 1974, along with his logo, the letters C and B placed together with no space between them, so that it looked like a letter from an unknown alphabet. But really, he had not needed to see the logo: the sloop had the tidy, *Alles im Ordnung* air common to Charles Boatman's products. As soon as you saw one, you knew it would be fast as hell, too. It was pretty funny, when you thought about it. This guy whose life was a funky mess, who stayed as stoned as possible for long stretches of the day, detested authority, and had a lifelong, sentimental connection to the working class, made these perfect vessels that were essentially playthings for rich people. The poor could learn to sail, if they grew up in the right places, but you had to have a lot of money to buy a Charles Boatman product.

A single line wound around an iron staple tied the sloop to the dock. The spinnaker should have been taken down and folded into the little bag called the turtle, but instead it drooped like a dead thing from the mast. The owner must have rushed back to the marina, jumped out, tied up, and run off to a meeting, intending to return to his boat as soon as possible. But where was the mainsail? The harried owner was nowhere in sight. Neither was anyone else, but for the creature with the attentive dog. Both of them still gazed at him, waiting for whatever he would do next.

The world looked *wrong*. No cars swept down Memorial Drive, no joggers or runners moved along the path, the ducks cowered frozen under the abrupt angle of their wings, and what he could see of the city looked dead. The stop signs all glowed red. Out before him, the entire lake had turned the flat dark blue of a bruise.

The thought of sailing away, of escaping, brought with it the memory of unhooking a Sunfish from a private dock and voyaging out in search of his father.

As if a window in space had flown open, the raucous uproar of the floating party blasted toward him as if from thirty feet away: the terrible scream-like laughter, the blaring voice with its mystifying, aggressive statement. The second the speaker had trumpeted his message, the whole thing was cut off again, as if the window had blown shut, or as if a giant radio had suddenly lost the signal from the Party Channel. What followed was not pure silence, but silence threaded with two voices. Although he could not make out the words they were speaking, the voices seemed familiar to him, more than familiar, as dear as the voices of tutelary spirits from his childhood. Long before he identified these voices, he understood that he knew them intimately, and that at this stage in his life, nothing they said could be pointless or unnecessary. That they had returned meant that they had returned *for him,* that they had *sought him out.* He needed to hear what they were saying.

Then the dog stepped forward, and the dying sun turned rusty, and the deeper of the two voices could be heard to say, *Don't you think . . .* (indistinct muttering) *. . . think we need . . . ?* To which the second voice replied, *. . . I need what you need . . .*

Great movements as of iron walls sliding forward and huge sections of concrete blocks fitting perfectly into place achieved intricate mental alignment, and he knew who was talking, out there on the lake. The first voice belonged to Spencer Mallon, and the second voice was Donald "Dilly" Olson's.

He's somewhere new, Mallon said.

We are what he needs, said the Dilly-voice.

Without pausing to think for any longer than it took to visualize the actions, Boatman unwound the rope from the staple, stepped from the dock into the boat, and pushed himself away. He saw himself do it, then he did it, step by step, with no regard for the consequences. Just as he was about to drift to a dead stop, the one and only breeze in the strange little world around him puffed out the yellow spinnaker and, astonishingly to Boats, spun the boat out into the lake.

It wasn't that he was a terrible sailor, for he was good enough to stay upright and get where he wanted to go, and he knew all the basics, but he now labored under two great handicaps. His feelings about his father had kept him from loving sailboats and sailing, so his instincts were crude and sometimes faulty; and he had never been out in a boat equipped with only a spinnaker. As far as he knew, neither had anyone else, at least by choice. Losing the mainsail made the whole enterprise trickier, more difficult by an exponential factor. A spinnaker was an extra sail that let you go faster downwind, and it was not rigged or positioned to do the job of the mainsail.

He had to steer using both the rudder and the spinnaker pole, but first he had to trim the sail, an impossible task when there was no wind. Upon the instant a nice breeze struck up, and he had to scramble to hook up the halyard and sheets to the three corners, and while he tugged at the sheets, the boat listed and hawed, circling around on itself so violently it nearly dipped the deck into the lake. It came to him that three people were really needed, one to steer, one to trim, and one to handle the pole. One guy alone had to battle to maintain a barely minimal level of control. By the time Boats was leaning back and pulling on his lines, the marina had disappeared, and he had no idea where he had drifted. The air had grown bluer and bluer, though it was still transparent. The sun had vanished, and the water looked almost black.

Abruptly, the party noises blared out at him from around what would have been a corner, had corners existed on lakes. The screaming woman, the shouting madman, the tumult of jabbering voices: he welcomed their return. He considered them a summons, a noisy call to arms. As a fresh wind filled the sail, he pulled in the sheet, and like a greyhound leaping from the gate, the boat took off in the direction of the invisible party. In moments, the din ceased, permitting two familiar voices to furl through the silence. He caught their intonations and the cadences of their phrases, but not their words.

Then he saw a length of sandy beach ending at a line of trees. It looked like a cartoon of an island. A dark fog floated like a low cloud through the tree trunks and along the beginning of the sand. Unless he acted quickly, he was going to run aground and do irreparable damage to the boat. Boats thrust at the pole and hauled on the tiller, and the boat swung sideways to the wind. The yellow sail collapsed. Everything stopped moving.

Over the drumming of his heartbeat, Boats heard Spencer Mallon say, *The tiger IS the lady, and the lady IS the tiger, and that's the part that nobody . . .*

Understands? Thinks about?

Boatman slid into the water. His skin went numb and shriveled, and he felt his penis retract. He touched down on a squirmy, slimy substance like rotting weeds that wrapped about his ankles and burned the soles of his feet. Only great effort extracted his feet from the grip of the weeds, and he had to repeat the effort with each step as he moved, guiding the boat toward the beach and the gliding fog. When the keel rasped along the bottom, he pulled himself free of the weeds, stepped up onto sand, and moved to the front of the boat and dragged it three-fourths of the way out of the water.

Boats was almost certain the voices had come to him from within the woods. Subtle low sounds that easily could have been the voices pitched at a lower volume continued to drift out from between the trees.

As soon as he moved forward over the sand, the low-lying fog swept over and engulfed him, obliterating everything before him. He cried out, "SPENCER! SPENCER MALLON! HELP ME!"

No voice came to him, and he stumbled forward, his mood falling with hideous speed from expectancy into despair. He had been lured to this part of the shore, which must have been an island because it certainly did not exist anywhere on the shoreline of Lake Michigan between Milwaukee and Chicago, no, it did not. The world had turned sour and dead, and the dead world had captured him within it. His arms outstretched, he took a step forward, then another.

Knowing it was useless, he cried out, "MALLON? CAN YOU HEAR ME?"

The fog chilled his skin and threaded into his nose and mouth. He had never felt more lost in his life. What had happened to him?

Ever since the insane voices had come across the water, the world around him had warped and darkened. Grass that was not grass died at his footstep, the lake became a giant bruise, the sun cooled and turned the color of rust, one of the awful dogs was merely an unliving animated thing. The darkening world had coaxed him into a boat without a mainsail and blown him to its wretched heart, this maybe-island where he could see nothing because of fog that smelled like ammonia and tasted like chlorine when it trickled down his throat.

He told himself to keep moving, at least. Groping with his hands, coughing, Boats stepped forward and felt his fingers touch the tree bark. He was a fool, and he had come to the end of the line. That he had stolen one of his father's boats seemed like part of the cruel joke.

The unmistakable timbre of Spencer Mallon's voice came to him from deeper in the woods, and he swung toward it. A thick branch scraped his face, and a fistful of twigs dug into his hair. Boats forced himself not to scream, though screaming was what he most felt like doing. While he fingered his hair free of the twigs, he could hear Mallon going on, obviously conversing. Holding his hands about his head like a cage, he took small steps toward the unspooling voice. He squinted through his burning eyes and saw only the fog's heavy wool.

Mallon's voice said, . . . *picked up that severed hand and threw it into the corner . . . dog . . . carried the hand outside, the wounded man's wrist . . . having a drink from a glass . . .*

"Sticky with his own blood!" Boats shouted, remembering what his hero had said in the downstairs room of the Italian restaurant. "The glass was sticky with his own blood!"

The scene in the lower room had come back to him complete and entire, as if fixed beneath a bell jar. He could see vulpine, ridiculously handsome Mallon at his table, flanked by those gorgeous women. As Boats looked on in the clarity of returned memory, Mallon snapped his head to the left and squinted at something visible only to him: a figure that had flashed into being and almost immediately disappeared.

Boats said, "You saw one of the dog-things, didn't you?"

Dilly's voice floated toward him from between distant trees that seemed to clothe themselves in the fog, thinning its substance as theirs increased.

. . . what he needs, what we all needed, what we need now . . .

"DILLY!" Boats shouted. "MAN, YOU TWO ARE EXACTLY WHAT I NEED!"

. . . Sticky with his own blood, kiddo . . . while the dog tore that hand to shreds . . .

Boatman's eyes still stung, and his throat felt raw from the fog he had swallowed. He could see fog twining around the stout trees before him, hanging between them like spider webs, thinning out as he moved deeper into the woods.

. . . shreds . . . knuckle and gristle . . . dripping down the black muzzle . . .

Boats felt himself gripped by two contradictory, utterly paradoxical feeling-states. He was elated, nearly joyous; and he felt like vomiting. All his elation seemed mocked by some underlying falsity, a cynical darkness momentarily epitomized by the image of a mutilated human hand dripping blood from a terrible muzzle.

"HEY! I'M HERE!" Boats shouted, wondering why they seemed not to hear him. Whipped by thin, low-lying branches, he took two steps forward, and had to stop moving, open his mouth, and bend over. His stomach convulsed, but nothing came up. It was the poisonous fog, he thought (and immediately said to himself, *no, it wasn't, fog isn't poisonous, and it doesn't make you want to puke*). His nausea passed.

. . . this foolhardy young idiot, said the Mallon-voice. *. . . wisdom, some of it just came through.*

"No," Boats said, "that's not what you meant."

Violence is woven right into the fabric of our time . . .

Birth is violence.

"The divine sparks yearn to be reunited," Boats quoted. He ducked beneath branches and the thinning fog. "That's right, too, isn't it?"

Mild light, tinted a faint blue, filled a clearing about twenty yards through the woods. In that clearing, visible only in the flashes granted by the intervening trees, moved a man with blond hair who was saying, *We live in a time of profound transformation.*

Boats's heart expanded with love. "Spencer! Spencer Mallon! Look behind you!"

Though he must have heard his voice, Mallon paid him no heed. Boats moved faster, more recklessly, bumping into tree trunks and stumbling over raised, snakelike roots. He scraped his forehead on a branch, and quick blood slid down past his eye and over his cheek. The swipe of his hand smeared the blood across the entire side of his face. He wiped his hand on his shirt and left a ragged stain. Boats moved to within ten feet of the clearing and saw the source of all the meaning in his life, Spencer Mallon, turned away from him in jeans, a chambray shirt, a safari jacket, and Dingo boots. His hair, rough looking and a touch too long, tended to bob when he moved. Even from behind, he looked shockingly young. Jason "Boats" Boatman had reached the weary age of forty-five: some long and equally weary years later, he would run into Lee Harwell, the once-famous author, on the sidewalk just outside the side entrance of the Pfister Hotel. Donald "Dilly" Olson was even more shockingly youthful. Seated with his back against a tree, a cigarette, most likely a Tareyton, dangling from the first two fingers of his right hand, and clothed in his high-school uniform of T-shirt, worn jeans, and moccasins, Don Olson looked youthful because he was only eighteen years old.

Boats had forgotten what a handsome kid Dilly had been. Really, he should have gone into pictures, or something.

"Yeah, sure," Olson said. "By the way, this stuff never happened."
"Not to you," Boats said. "To me, it did."

Making a more concerted effort to wipe the blood off his face, Boats moved up to the edge of the clearing and stood between two maples. Blue sunlight devoid of warmth fell in spangles on his arms and legs. He pressed his dirty handkerchief to the wound pulsing on his forehead.

"Hey, guys," he said. "You know what? I'm pretty weirded out by all this shit. What did we do, go back in time?"

Dilly looked across at him and raised the smoking cigarette to his lips. He inhaled and blew out a thin, fast-moving stream of smoke. His face was a mask of boredom.

Mallon turned around, slowly, with an almost balletic self-awareness. Now that Boats was much older than the Spencer Mallon who had so entranced him, he could see in the man's face all the qualities that had escaped him in high school—laziness, vanity, selfishness, and a willingness to deceive. Something else, too: the innate watchfulness of the true show-off. All these traits were visible in him, but they were not all that was visible. As Mallon crossed his arms and tilted his head, causing his hair to dip charmingly to one side, Boats saw that Mallon really did have the *extra* quality, the aura of being in possession of *more,* also of being slightly larger than his body, that he found he now remembered with a helpless love. The man was a born magician.

"Well, no, actually, Jason," said smiling Mallon. He had registered every one of Boats's instant perceptions. "It's good to see you again, too. But that isn't possible. No one can go back in time. Time isn't linear, not at all. Instead of going backward and forward, it goes *sideways.* Time is a vast field of simultaneity. One member of my happy little band has learned this lesson, well, I could say the *hard* way, but perhaps it is best to say that he has learned it *profoundly.* That would be Brett Milstrap, of course, Keith's roommate. Keith had a spectacular amount of promise, I thought, being so wicked, but I never much cared for Brett. I imagine you've seen him now and then, as you make your rounds."

"Yes," Boats said, "I have. But . . . so this is me now, where I am, and you're the you and Dill of 1966, which would flip me out if I already weren't so flipped out, and to tell you the truth . . . Jeez, I'm sorry I'm bleeding like this, I hit my head on a branch back there . . . well, what I was going to say is, I always hoped I would see you again, because I thought you could explain everything to me."

"Just you wait," said Dill, bored and hostile.

"You want to stop bleeding? No problem." Mallon thrust his index finger at Boats's forehead. The wound stopped pulsing. "All better now. Throw that disgusting hankie thing away, will you?"

Boats felt funny about doing it, but what the hell, it was 1966. Pollution had not yet been invented. He took the handkerchief from his forehead and tossed it behind him.

"Feel better now?"

"Not really. What's going on?"

"Jesus, kid. You finally see us again after all these years, and that's all you can say? All right. I'll explain again."

He stepped forward and thrust his right arm out straight before him. "Think of this as a highway. In time. A big highway, running through all of time. Okay?"

He thrust his left arm out sideways and held it rigid, making himself look like a demented traffic cop. "And this is a smaller, narrower road, a state highway, not an interstate. They intersect at me, I'm the crossroads here. When you get to me, you can turn off, you can go anywhere you like, because these intersections are all over the place."

"And that's how I got to you?"

Mallon lowered his arms and smiled in a way that looked neither warm nor friendly. "Well, it's more like how we got to you, Boats."

He turned away and made an actorish flourish with his right arm. "The blood ran down over the dog's jaw. Stained his muzzle red. Blood ran across the entire surface of the bar. You don't think that was a *message*?"

"You're giving me a message?" Boats asked.

The party noises exploded all around him, very near, jeering, insane, and hostile. The unseen crowd bellowed and giggled, the invisible woman screamed her laughter. As if commanded to his score by the din, Dilly scrambled upright, opened his mouth freakishly wide, and in a dense, insistent tenor voice that drilled through the surrounding cacophony, blared, *I NEED WHAT YOU NEED I NEED WHAT YOU NEED I NEED WHAT YOU NEED . . .*

Mallon faced Boats again, flapping his hand in dismissal. In a quiet voice half suffocated by the din, he said, "Weren't you listening? Go back and start over."

■

The deafening noise ceased; the blue light dimmed. The world went dark for the space of three frames: a moment only, almost not noticeable, yet nonetheless a cessation, a total, if however brief, erasure.

■

The last of the maple trees interrupted Boats's view of the clearing, yet he still had the feeling it was empty. At this distance, he should have been able to glimpse the figures whose voices had led him this far, but all he could make out through the trunks of the maples was a sunlit oval of tall grasses backed by another thick grouping of trees.

"SPENCER!" he shouted. "DILLY! WHERE ARE YOU?"

. . . picked up that severed hand and threw it into the corner, spoke Mallon's voice*. . . . dog . . . carried the hand outside, the wounded man's wrist . . . having a drink from a glass . . .*

"Sticky with his own blood," Boats whispered. "The glass was sticky with his own blood."

How did he know those words?

From the ground beside a large exposed root like an imperfectly buried fire hose, a red and white rag caught his eye, and he bent over and picked it up. Impossibly, it much resembled one of his own unusually large and exceptionally soft handkerchiefs, for which he had a variety of uses. Boats would almost have sworn the handkerchief was his, but it had been left here, wet and discolored with blood, by someone else. He had never been on this island—this shore?—before in his life. Boats dropped the sodden handkerchief next to the bulge of the root, and it folded down into itself, like an origami replica of a duck hiding its head beneath an outspread wing.

Then he remembered where he had heard Mallon's words. "You said that at La Bella Capri, in . . ."

Dilly's voice silenced him before he could say *the basement there.*

. . . what he needs, what he needs, that's all he knows, it's all he thinks about, he's been like that since he was a teenager . . . I need, I need, I need, it's enough already, other people have needs, too, and they don't go around stealing for a living . . .

Mallon's voice broke in, canceling Dill's: *. . . the dog tore that hand to shreds . . . knuckle and gristle . . . blood dripped over that goddam black muzzle . . .*

Boatman stepped through the last of the trees and looked wildly around, though he knew the clearing was empty. When the illusion that he might glimpse his tormentors snickering at him from behind the trees on the other side of the open patch faded, there swept through him a bitter disappointment that was both specific and familiar. Boatman felt as though he had been wearing it around him like an old coat most of his life. Now, Spencer Mallon's voice sounded from some invisible source, but that source was not Mallon.

Mallon was not present, Mallon was the absence that turns itself inside out.

Mallon's voice said, *Violence is woven right into the fabric of our time . . .*

"So you keep saying, but what *good* is that?" Boats asked, moving closer to the place the voice seemed to be coming from.

The tall, mustard-colored grasses thinned out, creating almost a miniclearing within the clearing. From this hole in the yellow grasses came the voice of Spencer Mallon, saying, *this foolhardy young idiot . . . wisdom, some of it just came through.*

Boats leaned over the circular parting in the grasses and looked down.

Seven or eight inches beneath the fuzzy tops of the grasses sat an irregular tree stump with a ragged edge where the trunk had snapped off. A small black tape recorder was propped against the raised part of the edge. The voice of Spencer Mallon emerged from the little machine, telling him, *Instead of going backward and forward, time goes* sideways.

Boats reached down and picked up the tape recorder. It had been made in Germany, and it worked perfectly. Long before it would fail to perform its function, it was going to be obsolete, a historical novelty, a toy no one any longer would want to use for the purpose of transporting sounds through time.

Throw away that disgusting hankie, will you? Mallon asked.

"I already did," Boats said. He looked around the stump and spotted a good-sized rock nestled in the grass about four feet away. Flecks of mica speckled on its sharp angles. Boats took a single stride and raised the black machine over his head.

Before he could smash the German recorder into the rock and forever destroy its useless perfection, Mallon's voice said, *Last chance, you dope.*

■

Another cessation; another erasure into absolute darkness.

■

This time, he emerged from the darkness in utter confusion, addled, feeling as if he had just been shot from a rifle and flown, like a bullet, a great distance at incredible speed. His entire body ached, especially his legs and his chest. His arms felt like noodles, and his head throbbed. Only gradually, he became aware that he was using a wire hanger to drag a thin triangle of polished wood, roughly five feet long at its base, across a dusty concrete floor that had recently been painted a hard, dark blue. The hook of the hanger fit into a hole drilled into the triangular thing, and his fingers were hooked into one of the hanger's corners. Baffled and weary,

Boats stopped dragging the wooden triangle and tried to figure out where he was.

A great deal of the concrete floor had been painted the dark blue he stood upon. Where the blue ended, the floor had been painted a light, khaki brown that extended perhaps ten feet before yielding to a long section painted a dark, forest green. Of the three painted areas, the blue was by far the largest, and the khaki brown the smallest. Boats didn't get it. He had been on some kind of island, he was almost certain of that, and Spencer Mallon had sent him away to . . . a huge basement? An abandoned factory?

Boats dropped the wire hanger, and the heavy wooden triangle clattered to the floor. At the center of the polished wood, he saw a familiar set of letters and a symbol he knew well. His father's trademark, the joined C and B. A short distance away was a sheet torn from one of the notebooks he had used in high school. He walked away and picked it up from the blue floor. On it was written *Lake Michigan*.

"Lake Michigan," he said, and dropped the paper.

Boats turned around and looked at the broad tan stripe perhaps twenty yards distant. He had been trying to pull the wooden triangle out of the blue and onto the brown. A second sheet of notebook paper lay on the brown paint, and another, far distant, on the green. He trudged onto the brown paint and leaned over the limp sheet of notebook paper. Printed on it in large block letters were the words *Beach or Shore*.

"Okay," he said. "I sort of get it."

It took him only moments to move across the painted beach and enter the green sector, and after a little more limping along he picked up another sheet of notebook paper. It said, of course, *Woods or Forest*. He straightened up and saw that the room, already enormous, had enlarged. A long way ahead of him three folding chairs formed a rough circle around some small object he could not distinguish. Previously, he had registered the presence of walls, probably of cement blocks, off to the sides and at the front and back of the basement; now, he saw no walls, nothing that defined the space he was in.

Actually, it was nothing at all, he understood. It was the place where nothing was anything, and everything was everything.

Jason Boatman had a sudden flash of Keith Hayward's face out in the agronomy meadow, appearing and disappearing, looking sick with anticipation in the flicker of candlelight. Had he noticed that, back then? Boats didn't think so, but there it had been, the image of Hayward staring at something, sick with hunger, starved, waiting for this dreadful moment. Boats thought he knew who it was Hayward had been staring at, wearing that expression on his face. And it wasn't who you thought it was, no it was not.

Boats gathered that he was supposed to walk to the chairs. His legs felt as though they could not move a single step, and his head had settled down into a nice steady throb. His chest hurt as though an enraged strongman had struck him there several times. He didn't feel like going anywhere, but in the place where everything was everything, there was no anywhere, because all places were the same.

He took an unhappy step forward, and an invisible branch struck him in the forehead, opening a wound that throbbed and bled. A white card on the floor said HANDKERCHIEF.

"Yeah, thanks," Boats said, and pressed his sleeve against the wound.

Dripping blood onto the painted concrete, Boats left the tan stripe and entered the green area, which seemed now to go on to the horizon. He looked over his shoulder and saw the same was true of the blue section of the floor— like the lake it represented, it exceeded the eye's capacity to take it in. Then he pushed his aching legs toward the chairs.

A note on one of the folding chairs said MALLON. The other two notes said DILLY and BOATS. Immediately behind Dill's chair was another note card that read TREE. Looking at what the chairs circled, Boats sat down on his card, crossed his knees, and folded his hands together. Six or seven old, well-worn dolls had been stripped of whatever clothing they had worn and stacked on top of one another. In the round heads, most of the eyes were closed, but two of the dolls stared upward open-eyed, both observant and blind for eternity. None of the little bodies had any more gender than was suggested by their ambiguous faces. Dirt that seemed baked on darkened the plastic faces; cracks and fissures threaded the ceramic heads. Most of the doll hair had been either pulled out or burned away.

"That's nice," he said. "A child is the same as a doll. They both mean nothing. It's a shitty old world."

And that was what it was about, he supposed. An aching body, an empty room, a stack of beat-up old dolls. Notes left behind by an absent and irritated god. It was a parody of meaning, an empty mockery—mockery completely without humor. Nothing meant any more than the wire hanger he had used to pull his "boat" to the "beach or shore." The wire hanger spoke of a death-in-life. Stretching to infinity on all sides, Death-in-life surrounded him.

On impulse, knowing that he could not be permitted the last word, Boatman leaned forward across the stack of dolls to inspect one of the note cards, and saw that while he had been musing, the battered old dolls had been transformed into dead babies. What was now directly beneath his outstretched hand was a diminished version of what he had seen in the meadow. Too shocked to breathe, too shocked even to gasp, he snatched back his hand. Blood from his hand dripped onto the little heap of bodies that lay with their mouths open, heads lolling, fingers limp, little rows of teeth white against the dull red of their mouths, the bruised, crusted, dead-white skin, the tiny white penises, the small, folded slits . . . For some reason, it was the teeth that horrified him most: so inert and exposed.

In an instant, the transformation reversed itself, and he was back with the pile of naked dolls in the flat, dead world of the wire hanger. Even his relief was a dire, humorless mockery.

Boatman once again extended his hand over the sprawling, dead-faced dolls, more slowly than before, and leaned forward until he could touch the card that said MALLON. He closed his fingers on the edge of the card and brought it toward him. Through the name on the card he could see the shadowy traces of something written on its other side.

He slowly turned it over. On the back of the card a single word had been written in squared-off, careful block letters. CONGRATULATIONS.

the phenomenon of flight

A Week Later

S carcely believing what I was doing, I rented a blister-red Honda Accord at the Salisbury-Ocean City Wicomico Regional airport, to which I had taken an uncomfortable and unreasonably delayed series of flights, and in that vehicle I traveled up Ocean Highway to US 13, now and then saying to the gospel singers and salvation merchants delivered to me by the Accord's radio, "I know I shouldn't be doing this, it's the stupidest thing I've ever done," thence into Rehoboth Beach. I drove, searching for a municipal parking lot, along the one-way streets past gift shops, bed-and-breakfasts, and cafés. I coasted down Lake Avenue and Lakeview Avenue and Grenoble Place. Twenty minutes later, thoroughly lost, I stopped alongside a policeman who was eating an ice-cream cone while seated on a bicycle and asked him if there happened to be a parking lot anywhere near the Golden Atlantic Sands Hotel and Conference Center, wherever that happened to be. The policeman said, "You're in luck today, sir, and welcome to our town," and pointed toward an empty parking spot across the street. "That big, long building right in front of us happens to be your destination, the beautiful Golden Atlantic Sands."

"Can I make a U-turn, officer?"

"Just this once," the policeman said, and abetted the lawbreaker by propping the bike against a lamppost, strolling out into the middle of the street, holding out an imperious hand (while still consuming the ice-cream cone), and halting the sparse oncoming traffic. Quickly, I cranked the wheel and crossed two empty lanes, then backed up until I could slip into the parking spot. I got out, dealt with the metering system, and yelled, "Thanks!"

I looked up at the long stretch of the hotel and regretted the impulse that had brought me to it. There was a sense, I knew, in which Jason Boatman had brought me to this pass: Boats's story had helped spur me into setting up my tickets and actually going through with this stunt. In 1994, eroded by a lifetime of theft, Boats had seen Meredith Bright's universal cynicism taken to its ultimate point. If the things of this world at all existed as physical entities, it was as no more than the gestural emptiness of a wire hanger. George Cooper had moved toward the same bleakness, and it had laid waste what remained of his life. In such a world, very few things counted, and the best of them was truth.

I wanted to understand what my long marriage had really been: I wanted to know its true shape. Was it the narrative of cooperation and accommodation I had imagined it to be, or had my own role in it been only secondary, because long ago—perhaps from the beginning!—usurped by another? Even after so long a time, wasn't that a point you had to make clear?

After Olson and I had returned to Cedar Street, I debated with myself, then called the reservations desk of the hotel now before me. When a clerk picked up, I asked to speak to a guest named Spencer Mallon. The clerk informed me that while Mr. Mallon was indeed expected at the Golden Atlantic Sands, his arrival was not scheduled for another twenty-four hours. Yes, Mr. Mallon was a frequent guest at the Golden Atlantic Sands, the clerk was happy to say. Mr. Mallon was a fine gentleman who cut quite a figure in the informal world that was Rehoboth Beach.

"Aristocratic," I said.

"I'd say that's an excellent description of the gentleman," said the clerk.

Could the clerk also check to see if a Ms. Lee Truax was expected around the same time?

"Oh! Ms. Truax!" the clerk exclaimed. "Everybody here knows her, she's a fabulous person! We all just love her, honestly we do. Well, listen to me, chattering away like a magpie. Well, she *is* special. You know it, too, if you know her."

"Oh, yes," I said.

"We like to say our hotel is Ms. Truax's second home, she's with us so often . . . Let's see, now. No, I can't find any reservations in her name, I guess it'll be a while before we have the pleasure of her company again. Is there some other way I can be of help to you, sir?"

No, but thanks for asking.

Where would the Eel be staying while she sojourned in this beachfront community, if not in the hotel where everyone loved her so profoundly?

Actually, there was a reasonable answer to that question. I called back and asked if the ACB had taken accommodations of any sort over the next few days. No, sir, came the answer, the ACB had requested no accommodations until their meeting in May of next year. So that door slammed shut. The Eel had told me she would "probably" stay at the usual place: the question that animated me now was whether or not she would be staying there with someone else.

I had called her cell phone, but she did not answer. Three hours later, I called again, with results only slightly more satisfactory. She was too busy to talk, she would call back later. Where in Rehoboth Beach was she staying? No, she wasn't there yet, she'd leave Washington tomorrow. Well, where was she staying in Washington? *Where?* That was a question I seldom asked. But if I really wanted to know, she was staying in the guest room of her ACB friend Heidi Schumacher, who owned a beautiful house in Georgetown— she was being to Heidi what Dilly was to him! As for Rehoboth Beach, there were a couple of possibilities. What was happening, was I worried about her?

Just curious, I said. I'm a little old blind lady, I can't get too wild, she told me. Don't worry, don't worry about anything. Hold tight, do some work, she'd be home after the weekend, and then they could make arrangements for Hootie.

Call me when you get to Rehoboth Beach, I'd asked. She promised, and she did call, but the reception was so foul I scarcely understood a word. Since then, nothing. Unable to keep from doing so, I had told Don I had to go out of town on a business matter, and would be back in a day or two. My accountant, my business manager, it was too boring to explain, but I had to go. And after that I got on the phone, packed a bag, and, despairing, went.

I *knew* I was being crazy. The one saving grace in my ridiculous scheme was that if Lee Truax should happen to walk down the Boardwalk when I happened to be lurking there, she would be unable to witness my shame. This reflection was not without a private shame of its own, namely that I had thought of it at all. I stood beside the ugly little car, looking at a hotel where my wife was a beloved guest, and told myself it was not too late to turn my back on both the hotel and my witless scheme. All I had to do was get back in behind the wheel, start it up, and drive back to Wicomico Regional Airport to wait for the next flight that could begin the process of returning me to what seemed now the land of the sane. Why was I here, anyhow? Because I thought my life might have been saved by a man motivated by guilt over cuckolding me? Because my wife had scarcely bothered to invent a good reason for coming to this little beach town? Because I knew Spencer Mallon was still alive and had good reason to keep on visiting the place?

I locked the car and walked past the hotel's sign to take a path around the side and get on the Boardwalk. If I saw them, I thought, it would be there—and for the first time realized that although my wife would be incapable of seeing me, Mallon certainly would not.

No sooner did I enter upon the Boardwalk then I was faced with the day's second awkward recognition, that it was early June, and although the Delaware shore had been hot, hazy, and as humid as New York City in mid-July, the season had not yet begun. Although some tourists and pleasure seekers were strolling in and out of the shops and fast-food outlets, they were far fewer than I had anticipated. I felt exposed, as if a spotlight played upon me. If I were to remain unseen, I needed a disguise.

In the first likely-looking store I examined a shelf piled with caps and hats and paid $32.99 for a wide-brimmed straw number with a bobbing fringe of untrimmed straw around the brim. In the same shop, I passed twenty dollars over a different counter and purchased a bug-eyed pair of sunglasses so dark I could barely see the way back to the door. A little way further down the Boardwalk, I bought a copy of the *Cape May Gazette* from a vending box and carried it to a bench near the railings over the long beach. A few deeply tanned couples, some of them equipped with books they were not reading, lay sprawled on towels and loungers.

I perched myself on the bench's inside edge, opened my newspaper, leaned back, and through my inky shades and beneath the screen of the dangling straw fringe, cast a long look in both directions before concentrating my attentions on the wide glass doors that led into the hotel where my wife had become such a beloved figure.

That, with many rattles of the newspaper and long sideways looks, also a few swift inspections of the long beach and a single pee break, was what I did for the next five hours. At six o'clock, starving, I folded the paper under my arm, got my overnight bag out of the car, and went through the hotel's main entrance to check in.

I was given a room on the fifth floor, which awakened some dim echo, not of something I had seen or heard, but something once described to me, some part of a tale, an anecdote. I had heard this said: *You watch the needle swing up and see it stop on the fifth floor . . . The next elevator comes down and opens its doors, and you jump in and push 5 and the Close Door button before anyone else can get on.* The anecdote, the story, had to do with Spencer Mallon and some "mind-blowing" nonsense he had passed off as wisdom. Its fragmentary mental reappearance now was a completely meaningless coincidence.

The elevator took me to my floor without incident. In absolute peace, comfort, and silence, I followed the directional arrows around several corners and gained my room, 564. Where a bellman once turned on lights, opened closets, and located the bathroom, now the weary guest does it all for himself, thereby spared the expense of a handsome sum in the neighborhood of five dollars. In the continuing state of peace, comfort, and silence, I removed my hat and glasses, zipped open my overnight bag, arranged my clothes atop the dresser, and carried my toiletries kit into the bathroom, where an incurious glance into the mirror put an end to peace and comfort, also silence. What the mirror displayed made me groan, "Oh, God."

I seemed to have aged at least ten punitive years. A shrunken, defeated old man was looking back at me. The old man was Lee Harwell, but not in an incarnation I ever wanted anyone to see. My eyes seemed sunken and as red as if filled with blood. Wrinkles carved my face, and my hair was dull and lead-colored. My entire head seemed to have shriveled, and my teeth looked yellow and enormous. My shoulders hunched over the suggestion of a concave chest. Whatever appeal or charm had once been visible here existed now as a ghastly parody of itself. That I had felt so fine only seconds before astonished me. Clearly, I was tottering on the far edge of exhaustion.

The mirror, I realized, had given me a moral shock: Here you are, this is what you have made of yourself.

To avoid looking any longer into my blood-filled eyes, I splashed cold water over my face and rubbed it in. Under my hands, the contours and planes all felt familiar and unchanged. When I lowered my hands, that depraved and dying animal was still gazing at me from the opposite side of the mirror. I fled the room, picking up my sunglasses on the way and slipping them on before I reached the elevator.

On the way down, I hunched in the corner, wondering how long it would be before I would need a cane. The elevator stopped at the third floor, and two slim blond girls in their early teens walked in, followed by their mother, also slender and blond, and like her daughters attired in a tight-fitting T-shirt and jeans. Their flip-flops revealed the small, scarlet nails of fresh pedicures. I withdrew deeper into my corner and avoided displaying my teeth. The girls cast haughty, peeved looks at me, and the mother ignored me completely. At the lobby, they bolted as if from a foul stench. I cast around the lobby until I noticed a set of stairs rising to a dark wooden arch, investigated, and discovered the hotel's main restaurant, the Ocean Room.

The restaurant featured low lighting and paneled walls mounted with giant stuffed fish. The opacity of my lenses made it difficult for me to see even the hostess at her podium, who, lit from beneath, bore a passing resemblance to a floating severed head. She spared a curious look for my glasses, but was too polite to ask. I felt like an elderly vampire.

From the waiter's endless recital I ordered French onion soup, roasted chicken with mushroom and pine-nut sauce. With a glass of pinot noir. Discreetly, I scanned the room for two faces I was certain would burn through the murk of my optics like spotlights. Though the restaurant contained any number of gray heads, none belonged to either Lee Truax or the wizardly creature who had addressed me in the Dane County airport. My soup arrived.

After the better than acceptable soup came an uninspiring chicken. When arrayed on the breast of a dry and overcooked chicken, mushrooms and pine nuts do not join hands and sing. Because I was still hungry, I labored through the meal, then signed the check, and pushed myself away from the table.

From the top of the steps, I surveyed the lobby. I was bored, and the pine nuts were still irritated with the mushrooms. A priest in a soutane swept through the lobby, followed by a sobbing woman. What was *that* about? In an envelope of laughter-spilling babble, a group of teenagers moved out of an open elevator and swerved toward the Boardwalk exit. A line of frustrated-looking men and women waited to check in at the registration desk. A knot of people moved into the elevator the teenagers had left, among them a striking silver-haired man in loose black clothing who turned to face the front of the car just as the doors began to slide shut. I had time only to notice his prominent cheekbones. Had his hair been unusually long for a man of his age, did his eyes penetrate the darkness? Three or four women I barely took in had been standing near the man. I moved rapidly down the stairs, watching the glowing red numbers track the ascending elevator.

Had one of those women in the elevator been small, white-haired, astonishingly lovely? Did the desk clerks and the maids adore her?

At precisely the moment when the numeral 5 appeared in the LED window, I remembered the entire context of the memory fragment that had visited me at the registration desk. It had been part of a story the Eel had told about Spencer Mallon. Mallon had described an unnamed disciple—a *you*—following him to a fifth-floor corner where he had to be concealed behind one of two doors. You had to choose one, then decide whether or not to knock. If you had the right room, Mallon rewarded you with wisdom; if you had chosen wrong, hideous curses afflicted your beloved. You chose; you knocked, it did not matter on which door, for you had already admitted the evil into the equation. Something like that, anyhow. The story ends at the point you'd assume it really begins, when the door opens.

Back in my room, I felt too agitated to go to bed. I picked up the telephone and asked to be connected to Mr. Mallon's room. Then I listened to the harsh, distressing sound of a phone ringing and ringing. Finally, a recorded voice requested me to leave a voice-mail message. I hung up.

I went into the bathroom and switched on all the lights. I did not look normal, not exactly, but I was younger and healthier than I had seemed before. My eyes were bloodshot, but not filled with red, and my cheeks were not sunken and bisected by fissures. My hair looked healthy, too, the color of pewter, not of lead. My teeth were a long way from Moby Dick, movie-star whiteness, but they looked like normal teeth, not fangs. I splashed cold water on my face again, then turned and pulled a towel from the rack. After I had dried my face, I looked as ruddy as if I had been hunting grouse on a Scottish moor. My shoulders still seemed hunched. I made myself stand up straight. The improvement was slight, though definitive—I no longer looked like a vampire. I decided to reward myself for my physical renewal with a trip to the lobby bar. I'd had only a glass of wine with dinner, and it was still before nine o'clock. Anyhow, I had always liked reading in bars, and it had been months since I'd had this pleasure.

Alone in the elevator, I checked my hair and posture in the smoky mirrors. Yes, there I was, back again, live and wide awake.

The lobby bar, the Beachcomber, was tucked in behind the steps up to the Ocean Room. A windowed wall fitted with batwing doors led into a long dim rectangular space scattered with tables and sofas and anchored by a shiny, light-emitting counter at its far end. Couples in play clothes sprawled on the sofas, waving their arms and pointing at things as they spoke. At two of the tables, athletic young men attempted to charm attractive young women. A few single men with expectant faces nursed beers at other tables. They were pausing in their journeys, awaiting the arrival of the next adventure. I wished them well.

At the bar I took a stool, placed my book beside me, and when a chipper fortyish blonde wearing a blue chambray shirt and a black vest with THE BEACHCOMBER embroidered on its breast approached me and, smiling, asked for my order, I named the first single-malt whiskey that came to mind. Neat, water back. Appreciatively I watched her move down the rows of bottles stacked in tiers, slid my book before me, and opened it.

When the bartender returned with my drink, she said, "Good book?"

"It's been good so far," I said. "Never bites, doesn't smoke, always puts the toilet seat down."

"And yet, it likes sitting in bars," she said. "You never know, it might have a wild streak."

"Probably it does." I showed her the cover. "Consider the source."

"My mom's a big fan of Tim Underhill's."

"Good. Tim's a friend of mine."

She stepped back, feigned wide-eyed amazement, then grinned and leaned in toward me. "So . . . what's he like?"

"Weird, weird guy," I said.

Wondering how inventive I should be about Underhill's imaginary weirdness, I swallowed whiskey and turned my head to look at the glass wall, the ugly batwing doors, and the lobby beyond. Striding past the glass and just moving out of view was the silver-haired man in black clothing I had seen from the top of the stairs. A smaller person, a woman, bustled along beside him.

I slid off the stool and fished out a twenty-dollar bill. "Whoops, I gotta go, sorry."

When I got out into the big, empty lobby I saw the couple just entering one of the elevators. The woman faded out of sight at the side of the car before I could get anything like an adequate look at her. A family of three in shorts and T-shirts piled in, and I caught only a flash of the man as he leaned forward to push a floor button. He then disappeared to the side and joined the woman who had been with him.

The man in the elevator could have been Mallon; just as easily, he could have been a gray-haired stranger. I had a feeling it was the latter, but that feeling incorporated an uncomfortably large area of doubt, 25 percent, maybe 30. Of the woman, I had seen next to nothing.

I moved through the spaces of the lobby, watching the mounting LED numbers above the elevator. It stopped on three. The tourists, or the gray-haired man? The numeral 3 hung in the display window for far longer than I expected it to. The elevator at the end of the row opened up, and a small, suntanned tribe emerged, lively and talkative and young, probably on their way to a club. No one else waited for an elevator. Deciding to move at the instant I did so, I rushed into the elevator, stuck out my elbow, and pushed

5 and Door Close. Why did I use my elbow? Ever since I had checked into the Golden Atlantic Sands, I had been opening doors with my forearm or the back of my hand. Until now, I had not even been conscious of this odd behavior. It was as if a hidden part of me were making secret plans to destroy some enemy, and labored in the dark, awaiting its moment.

The doors swiftly glided together, and I began to ascend. My heart shifted into overdrive. Whether these physical transformations actually took place or not, I thought I could feel the following changes take place in my body: my shoulders bent forward over my concave chest, my eyes filled with blood, and the life and vitality drained from my face. My lips shrank back from my teeth. Within my linen suit, my body seemed to dwindle and weaken.

The doors opened on the fifth floor. A crisp, dark voice receded down the hallway. I hurried out just in time to see the hems of a black coat and a silver dress flicker around the turning of the hallway. They were going in the direction of my room. Every time I went there and back, I probably passed their room. I moved up to the turn in the corridor and rounded the corner at exactly the time two doors, halfway down to the next turning and side by side in the hallway, slammed shut.

Appalled, I crept down to stand between them, rooms 515 and 517. Did they sleep in separate rooms, Eel and Mallon, or whoever they were? It occurred to me that despite appearances, the three people who had shared the elevator with the couple may not have been a family after all, and the older couple had a room on the third floor, the young woman up here. Or the other way around.

I did not want to move close to each of the doors, perhaps to pick up something revealing from within, no, but I did exactly that. Disappointment followed. I heard nothing. More precisely, I heard the rumble of a low male voice from behind the door to 517, and something birdlike, catlike, something brief, high-pitched, and animal from behind the door to 515.

Excuse me. I thought a friend of mine was staying in this room. Excuse me, I guess I got the wrong room number. I'm sorry, my friend told me to come, well, I thought it was here. Please forgive me, I'm sorry to disturb you.

I just wanted to see if it really was you. I just wanted to find out how much I've been lied to over the years. Lee, this began when you were in *high school* and it has lasted *ever since*?

I raised a hand to knock, it mattered not at which door. All right, it was 515, because of that strange noise. I brought my hand close to the wood; I lowered it. Again I raised my hand and this time noticed that my skin seemed papery and fragile, so thin it was almost transparent. Splotchy discolorations, unnoticed until now, here and there stood out like giraffe spots on my bony hand.

"Oh, no," I said, and fled down the hallway to the next turning, and the next, and on until I reached the relative safety of 564, where with trembling fingers I inserted the magnetized plastic card, then half fell into my room. In darkness, groping, I splashed water on my face. The heavy curtains had already been pulled across the window, so the room itself was crypt-dark, tomb-dark. There was no need at all to consult the mirror. I felt my way to the bed, sat down, and dialed the bedside lamp to its lowest setting. Then I opened the minibar, inspected the contents, found two airline-sized bottles of a single-malt scotch only slightly inferior to the one I had abandoned at the bar, and emptied their contents into a convenient glass. Then I flopped into the room's one comfortable chair and considered my situation.

I had driven into a vast desert and run out of gas. In a couple of minutes, vultures would be circling overhead. Vividly, I had imagined my body had become that of an elderly vampire. In the murky light, I held out my left hand. Here and there, my skin looked a little shiny, but it bore no unsightly, giraffe-like discolorations. Shame had produced these distortions. In my all-too-active imagination, a third-rate wizard had saved me from death in a plane crash out of guilt for having carried on a long, long love affair with my wife; this will-o'-the-wisp had propelled me halfway across the country and encouraged me to act like a foolish parody of Lew Archer. A fake shamus in pursuit of my wife's infidelity, could you get any stupider than that?

I was in danger of following Jason Boatman out into Lake Michigan in a stolen sailboat. One more day of camping out on the Boardwalk behind a fringe of straw and a newspaper would push me away from the dock and send me searching out into the fog.

I took my cell phone from my pocket, looked at it for a couple of seconds, then punched in the numeral 1, the speed-dial number for my wife. Her phone went instantly to voice mail. I said, "It's me. I just called to say I love you." I disconnected, switched my phone off, and took a sip from the glass in my hand. Then I poured the rest of the whiskey into the sink.

Before I checked out of the Golden Atlantic Sands, I placed the sunglasses and the straw hat on what had been my bed, and slid a Hamilton between them.

Lee and I had many intense conversations during the first weeks after her return. I wanted to believe her, so I did, at least as well as I could. These are some of the things Lee Truax told me:

—Yes, I had sex with him, once and once only, when I was seventeen years old in October of 1966. That's the reason Meredith Bright was so huffy with me.

—Technically, it may have been child abuse, but it certainly was not rape. I was fully consensual. I *wanted* it to happen.

—Yes, I loved him then, and yes, I still do, though in a completely different way. No, you *do* know what I mean. Don't you have people you love in lots of different ways?

—Of course I don't mean romantically.

—Yes, ever since then—1966. With long gaps while you were at NYU and I was a bartender, and after that, when you were a graduate student and I was at NYU.

—Yes, there were other long periods when we didn't see each other.

—I mean something to him. Something important.

—You know what we do? We talk. Sometimes we have lunch or dinner. Every five years or so, we go to a bar. A nice one, not your kind of bar.

—He talks, mainly. He likes the way I listen, and he trusts what I say back to him. The way I respond to what he says.

—He wants to know what I think about the things he tells me.

—Why didn't I? Because you were always so suspicious about Spencer, and what we did was so harmless. Besides. He was mine. You wanted to be kept out of it, and that's what I did, I kept you out of it. You didn't belong there. You don't belong there.

—Dilly—Donald—knew about a couple of the times, yes. I never saw him, though.

—I can't say. He didn't tell me about it, but he wouldn't, he'd never tell me about anything generous that he did, especially anything like that. He'd think it would sound like boasting. From what you say of the man in the airport, it could have been Spencer. But remember—he loved Don Olson, too. They were partners for years.

—No, he wouldn't save your life out of guilt. He would save your life because you are married to me, and he knows I love you.

—Well, there were two other reasons I went to Rehoboth Beach, actually. I realized that one of those women I talked to about the stolen money had told me a terrible lie, and I wanted to confront her with it. The other problem was that someone had started stealing from them all over again.

—The lie? I'll tell you about the lie. You'll like this. Do you remember the woman who told me about the man who blinded her, and how she had killed him accidentally after he dragged her into a ravine? I realized one morning that the whole thing had been the other way around. *She* got in touch with the man after he was released from jail, and *she* invited *him* to visit her. That boy from the café, Pete, was waiting in the ravine—he was mad for her, he would have done anything she asked. She got the man to lie down with her, and Pete smashed his head in with a rock and concealed the body. Then she had sex with that boy. She admitted the whole thing. I just wanted to hear her say it.

And the new thefts, that was easy. I went right back to the woman I had identified the first time, and she confessed all over again. Cried her eyes out. We called the police and had her arrested. It was absolutely what she deserved.

—Spencer trusts me so much because of what I did that night. Because of what he saw me do, and what he guessed I did later on.

—What did I do? I traveled much farther than he could. Believe it or not.

—What did I do? I skylarked, skylarked, skylarked all over the place. Hah!

—Yes, I'll tell you. I told you I would, and I will. But I don't want to talk about it more than once. It will be hard enough to do it once, but I also don't want to make it any easier to talk about it. Do you understand that? *Do* you? Good. But when I talk about all this the one time I ever will talk about it, Howard Bly has to be here, and so do Don Olson and Jason Boatman. Hootie, Dill, and Boats. They have to be able to hear me, too, and they have to be okay and settled, they have to have *lives.* Because it's about what happened to them. About what happened to all of us, our little group.

—Okay, then, find Hootie a residence here in the city, and then we'll get him ready to live in the world again. And we'll let you, Donald, get settled, too, as much as you can be settled.

—So it takes years. Fine. I'm not going anywhere, and neither are you guys.

■

Three months after that last conversation, I drove back to Madison and picked up Howard Bly at the Lamont Hospital. On his way out of the institution where he had spent the major part of his life, Howard carried everything he owned in a new Samsonite suitcase purchased for him as a good-bye present from Dr. Greengrass and his wife: five unread paperback books, a toothbrush, a razor, a comb, two shirts, two pairs of trousers, five pairs of underpants, five pairs of black socks, a pair of Timberland boots, and a container of dental floss. The entire staff and attendants were lined up outside the door to say farewell to their favorite patient and wish him God-speed. Pargeeta Parmendera clung to Hootie as they processed to my car, and released him, with trembling arms and visible reluctance, only when I promised to invite her to Chicago very soon. In turn, Howard, also weeping, promised to call her weekly, if not daily.

Before I drove Hootie to Chicago, I took him on a tour of Madison, and showed him our old high school and the neighborhoods we had known. Dilly's old house, Boats's old house, the tumbledown shack where once the astonishing Eel had dwelt. At the end of the tour, which had made Hootie shiny-eyed, I led him to State Street. Automobiles were no longer permitted, and we walked down one side and up the other, remarking on the ruthlessness of change. The little corner store was still there, still performing its old function, but nearly everything else we had known was gone. No more Aluminum Room, no more Rennebohm's Rexall Drugstore, no more Brathaus, no more used bookstore.

"I wonder what Glasshouse Road looks like now," Hootie said. "I don't want to go there, though."

"I never even heard of Glasshouse Road," I told him.

Hootie giggled and pressed the tips of his fingers to his mouth. "That's good," he said. "That's ripe. That's rich. That's royal."

I thought he was quoting from some book, I knew not which. "What makes it so wonderful?"

"Glasshouse Road is where every bad thing goes," Hootie said. "And you don't know how to find it."

"*Now* you tell me," I said.

"Stop stalling and take me to Chicago, please," Hootie said.

On the drive south, Hootie betrayed his anxiety in small ways. He ruffled his fingers on the knees of his trousers. He smiled and moved his head from side to side without actually seeing anything. He said, "I like your sunglasses. I wish I had some sunglasses. Sunglasses are neat-o. Can I get some, Lee? Can I get some sunglasses? Do they cost five dollars? They cost more? I didn't think sunglasses would cost more than five *dollars*." When I broke the news that most things cost more than the grand sum of five dollars, I then had to assuage Hootie's terror of poverty. In his new home, everything would be taken care of, and the meals were included. He would get a small allowance to buy things like cookies and shaving foam at the on-site store.

Would he like his new home? Would he have a private room, or would he have a roommate? Did it look nice? Was it pretty? Was it comfy? Could Pargeeta get a job there? Did they have a garden, did they have flowers? And a picnic bench? What was the name of his new home, again, could Lee remind him of that name?

"Of course, Hootie. Would you like me to write it out for you, too, along with its address and phone number? You'll have your own telephone, too. You are going to be living at the Des Plains-Whitfield Residential Treatment Center, which is just a little bit out of Chicago, and a very, very nice place. To tell you the truth, it's nicer than the Lamont."

I had learned that when Hootie was anxious, the only way to keep him calm was to speak to him as if he were a child. He needed primary-color conversations and simple answers.

Was the Eel going to be there, when they arrived?

"No, Howard, she can't be. Today, we'll make sure that you're comfortable and know where everything is, and we'll meet some of the staff. I'll bring Lee out tomorrow. She's very eager to see you again."

"Of course she is," Hootie said. "I'm the same way. But I'm a little scared, too."

"Of meeting her?"

"Are you crazy?" A roar of startled laughter, with the scratchiness of laughter long unused. "Of her meeting *me*."

"Oh, Hootie. She won't even be able to see you, you know."

"I know," Hootie said. "But she can see anyhow. She always could. And do you know what she's going to do, the first time she sees me? She's going to put her hand on my face."

"Actually, she doesn't do that."

"That's what you think."

■

Howard Bly's introduction to Des Plains-Whitfield went smoothly. He met with his doctors, he was led to his room, which was spare and white and sunny, he was introduced to three fellow patients who seemed interested and kindly, he had a tour of the facility and its grounds. In appearance something like a combination of a small college campus and a clean, well-run hospital, the center was the nicest of all the possibilities Don Olson and I had seen. A good-sized staff of experienced doctors, therapists, psychologists, and social workers managed and oversaw the progress of sixty to seventy men and women toward moving into group homes and finally locating themselves in the out-side world. I knew I had been lucky to find Hootie a placement at Des Plains-Whitfield. Lee had been crucial. A series of gears had interlocked in the right sequence at the right moment, and warm hands had delivered Hootie to a soft nest. He missed the Lamont's gardens and his view, but the new garden was extremely nice, if more functional and less purely decorative. If his new view (a field, a highway) was not as handsome as the old (an azalea bush and a stand of maples), his new room suited him far better than his cubicle at the Lamont. Here he had bookshelves and pictures on the walls and a braided rug on the floor. The room came furnished with a handsome wooden desk, three comfortable chairs, and a spacious coffee table; he was given the use of a cof-feemaker and a television set; he had the luxury of a bathroom all his own.

On his first day in the new circumstances, Hootie seemed dazed, but not unhappy. Even when crying, and during his first two or three days in Des Plains Hootie spent many minutes either weeping or wiping tears from his face, he did not appear to be devastated. He cried for what had been lost, he cried with recognition or because he was suddenly confused, he cried in gratitude.

As promised, I drove my wife to the center on the day after Howard Bly's "intake." Hootie had been prepared for this great event, and in clean overalls, a Cheesehead sweatshirt Pargeeta had given him to remind him where he came from, and his yellow Timbs, he was perched on a sectional sofa in the reception area and staring at the entrance when Lee and I came through the door and paused at the desk to explain ourselves.

"He's here," Eel said, backing away from the desk.

"Is he?" I turned my head, and saw Hootie slowly getting to his feet. The psychiatrist assigned to his case, Dr. Richard Feld, stood posted behind him. A look of wonder irradiated Bly's round face. "Yes, he is. How did you know?"

"What's coming at me pretty much has to be from him," said the Eel, smiling.

She turned in Hootie's direction as if gifted with sight, and I kept glancing back and forth between my wife and the transfigured man making his way with slow steps toward her. Looking proprietary, Feld padded after him, now and then nodding at me, whom he had met the previous day. In his turtle-like progress, Hootie seemed not to want to hasten the moment that would come. He wished to appreciate everything offered to him along the way, including his own emotions. Lee Truax, too, settled into an attitude of patient expectance, her hands folded loosely before her, her head lifted, her smile deepening. I found this admirable, impressive, moving. They were giving the moment its due. The Eel of course would do this instinctively, but Howard Bly, I would have said, was no Lee Truax. Yet here he was, taking obvious pains not to rush the moment of reunion: in fact, stretching out his approach to underline its role in that moment. Tears rose within me. It was like being at a wedding, all this crying.

"Hello, Eel," Hootie said from a foot and a half away. "You sure look good. I can't believe you're here with me in my new home."

"I'm glad we're both here," she said. "It's wonderful to see you again." She took a small step forward and raised her right hand as if to take an oath. "Would you mind?"

"Don't go fainting dead away," Howard said.

Amazing, I thought. *These two people really are something.* It came to me that despite Don Olson's claims, the pair in front of me had loved Mallon the most, and the most purely, without Boatman's neediness, Don's ambition, and Meredith Bright's tendency to keep score. Eel and Hootie had wanted nothing and pursued no agenda.

Lee Truax placed her hand on the side of Hootie's face. "You're warm," she said.

"I'm embarrassed." He giggled. "You make me . . . I don't know."

She moved her hand, a pink, amiable spider, across the front of his face, over his forehead, under his chin, around his other cheek. "You're different, but you're still beautiful," she said. "I can see you very well, and everything I see is dandy."

"'Lo, Eel," Bly said, and the Eel said, "Yep, hello, Hootie," and they put their arms around each other and cried for a little while.

"I'm sorry I never went to see you even once in all those years."

"I wasn't ready then. And there was always a lot to do, anyhow."

"Like what, Hootie? What did you do in there?" She stepped back, wiping her eyes. Briefly, she placed a hand on his shoulder, then let it drop.

"Read books. Work on the big jigsaw puzzle. Sit in the pretty garden. Talk to Pargeeta. Have my evaluations and my sessions and my group work. Clean up. Think about things. Remember things. *Really* remember, like going back to back then. And lots of times, I was so afraid, I had to stay away from the dogs." He pointed at me. "And I read his book, *The Agents of Darkness*. He got it all wrong."

"I know. He couldn't help it."

"It's only natural to be afraid. I was scared for a long, long time."

"Don was, too," I said, breaking into this duet.

"But they're like traffic cops."

"Or crossing guards," Lee said. "They're not supposed to hurt us."

Dr. Feld stepped forward and rested a hand on the same shoulder where Eel had placed hers. "This is all very interesting, but right now I have no idea what anyone is talking about. None at all. Dogs are like crossing guards? Crossing guards never hurt anybody."

"They're not *supposed* to," said Hootie, darkly.

Feld swung his body toward Hootie and leaned forward. "Howard, don't forget our meeting at three. At that time, we can go into dogs and traffic cops and crossing guards as much as you like."

During the period of Hootie's residence in Des Plains, Donald Olson began to put into effect the plans he had described in Madison. He printed up cards that offered his services as an experienced teacher of higher psychic truths who had just come off numerous years on the road and wished to settle down in Chicago with a small number of serious students. Long-term commitments preferred, reasonable rates. After Lee Truax had come back to the house on Cedar Street, Don tactfully withdrew into his quarters, which amounted to a small guest suite that lacked only a private entrance to be truly self-contained. He took most of his meals alone and acquired the cell phone with the number he printed on his cards. Don and the Eel got along extremely well, but he knew better than to trade on or exploit her old affection for him. He was not he, she was not she, and it was understood that our three-way friendship would be best served by the former Dilly moving into his own place as soon as he could. Olson and I had lapsed into certain male roommate habits and patterns, among them pizzas and Chinese food ordered in, frequent late hours, and the tendency to postpone doing the laundry, which had to be curtailed after my wife returned. She introduced a certain snap in the routines of the day, and the installation of a brisker schedule permitted Olson and me to get through more work than had been possible when we lived alone. Lee Truax spent four or five hours every day in her office, too, dealing with ACB matters or using Microsoft Narrator or Serotek's Freedom Box to write on her computer.

After a couple of months, Olson had managed to put together enough money to rent a small one-bedroom apartment in the 600 block of Webster Street, in the section of Lincoln Park near DePaul University, and I helped him with the payment on an old Accord that still ran remarkably well.

Jason Boatman reported that It Takes A Thief, Inc. had opened branches in Milwaukee and Racine. He was busier than ever before in his life. "Before this, I never understood how lazy most crooks are," he said on speakerphone to the Eel and me. "Burglars and thieves lie around their rooms all day until it's time to go to work, and the job only lasts about an hour or two." Boats would come to Chicago anytime we invited him: after having forced Don and me to listen to his sorry tale, he said, it was the least he could do.

Dr. Feld reported that Dr. Greengrass, to whom he been sending regular reports, was now on the administrative staff at the state hospital in Madison. New ownership had taken over at the Lamont, and he'd been forced out. "He's reasonably content, as far as I can tell. His only lingering sorrow concerns that young woman who befriended Howard, Miss Parmendera. Wasn't she once a kind of intern, or something? She has become second-in-command at the Lamont, and he still has hard feelings about his treatment by their board."

"I don't blame either one," I said. "They'll probably be able to repair their friendship."

"I like your optimism," Feld told him.

Soon after that, Howard Bly was released from residential supervision into the world at large and the care of his friends.

I had been watching the gradual transformation of the old Cedar Hotel across Rush Street from a down-and-dirty flophouse into a more respectable long-term rental prospect for the working urban poor. Its owners had been guaranteed substantial assistance from the city, state, and federal governments. (Anything but civic-minded, they had seen that a good deal of money could be made from poverty.) In April of 2004, the new Cedar Hotel had just opened its doors, the interiors gleamed and sparkled, and only half of its rooms were occupied. Howard Bly, now on steady disability payments that to him seemed astoundingly generous, was accepted upon receipt of the application I had helped him complete. He moved in on the day he left Des Plains-Whitfield. Many times over, he said it was the happiest day of his life.

Hootie nested in as if he had been waiting all his life to set up on his own. On his first day at the Cedar Hotel, he went to Michigan Avenue and its wealth of side streets and picked up cheap sheets and towels, a secondhand sisal rug, lightbulbs, a strange lamp shaped like a nude woman doing a backstretch, some unmatched silverware and two plates, and a sturdy chair and not-so sturdy chest of drawers he found on the sidewalk. Later that afternoon, the streets and sidewalks yielded a framed bullfight poster and a framed watercolor of a red barn that reminded him of a photograph at the Lamont. The following day he bought a cast-iron pan, a medium-sized pot, a colander, a spatula, a chef's knife, a ladle, and copies of *The Joy of Cooking* and *Mastering the Art of French Cooking.*

Initially, Hootie took every lunch and dinner with either the Eel and me or Don Olson. (He learned to cook in our kitchen, and used his recipes to help prepare some of our meals.) Before two months had passed, he had worked out a more independent schedule. Twice a week, he walked up Cedar Street to share the evening meal with us. On Sundays, Donald Olson came over to our house for drinks and dinner with Hootie. Hootie drank Welch's grape juice, and Olson drank large quantities of tequila over small quantities of ice.

The Eel herself called Jason Boatman, and Boats made a date with us all on Cedar Street for a Saturday at the end of August. He sounded both expectant and hesitant at the thought of listening to whatever the Eel might have to say. In high school, he remembered with shame, he had so greatly not wished to hear her point of view on the question of Mallon's ceremony that he had avoided speaking to her, avoided even looking at her. When they had approached each other in the corridors of Madison West, he used to turn his head and scan the facades of the lockers.

On Saturday, the twenty-eighth of August, Hootie Bly came ambling up sun-struck Cedar Street just as Jason Boatman swung his panel van, blazoned IT TAKES A THIEF SECURITY & PROTECTION SERVICES, into a parking space and got out. Because Boats had visited Hootie twice in the Lamont before his transfer to Des Plains, they exchanged a warm, backslapping hug of welcome. (That is, Boats slapped Hootie's back, twice; Hootie never slapped anybody, back or front.)

"If that slogan drove past me anywhere in the world," Hootie said, "I'd know it was you."

"That's the idea," Boats said. Then his face fell into the furrows that had been carved by his long habits of pessimism and anxiety. "You know, I haven't seen the Eel since we left high school. And we weren't speaking to each other at the time."

"Don't worry about any of that," his old friend advised him. "It certainly isn't going to bother *her*." (I'm reconstructing here.)

"Pretty special, huh?"

"Just you wait, Henry Higgins, just you wait."

"She always was pretty darn cute."

The imp of the comic perverse awoke in Hootie Bly, and he made an elaborately deadpan face. "That was then, this is now."

"Meaning what?"

As if in sorrow, Hootie looked down and shook his head.

Boatman rotated his shoulders and shook out his arms. "Let's get it over with." He gave the doorbell a delicate nudge.

From within came the sound of a pealing bell. Footsteps approached the door.

Boats glanced at Hootie, who returned a solemn, commiserating nod.

"Oh, Lordie," Boats said.

"Don't be such a Charlie Brown, Charlie Brown."

The door swung open to reveal a smiling me, who of course had as yet to hear of Hootie's wicked game. I shook hands with Boats and threw my arms around Hootie. "This promises to be an interesting day, doesn't it?"

"All shall be well, and all shall be well, and all manner of thing shall be well," Hootie said.

Boatman said, "Lee, is everything really . . . ?"

I raised my eyebrows, entirely puzzled.

"I'm sorry," Boats said.

"Don't worry about it, whatever it is," I counseled. "Come on in, both of you, please. Boats, you've never been here before, have you? After we're done, maybe I'll give you a little tour, if you're interested."

Boatman visibly roused himself into something like his conventional demeanor. "And maybe I could tell you how to burglar-proof your house, if *you're* interested. I know you think you have, but believe me, you haven't even begun."

"Is that right?"

"You have no idea."

"We'll combine tours of the house," I said, shepherding them both across the pretty vestibule and into the living room.

Don Olson stood up from his place on the sofa and held his hand out to Boatman. "Here you are, at last," he said. "Have an easy ride down?"

"Until I got close to Chicago, when it was bumper to bumper all the way. How you people put up with that traffic, I'll never know."

Boatman was casting glances around the room, checking the door, then glancing back at his host.

"You all right?" I asked. "Can I get you anything?"

"I could use a pit stop. Would you, um . . ."

"Right over that way," I said. "Lee will be with us in a couple of minutes. She is very eager to see you again."

Boats took off toward the bathroom with a hint of alacrity.

"Is he all right?" I asked.

"Charlie Brown, Charlie Brown," Hootie half-sang.

"You're making great strides in the popular culture area," I said.

"*Peanuts* has the answer to everything."

"Tell me something, Don," I said. "Has our Hootie discovered irony? There's something about him today . . ."

"I think he invented irony on his own," Olson said. "The way primitive communities had to invent fire, or horseshoes, or whatever."

Soft noises on the staircase caused the three men to glance toward the doorway. "Ah, good," I said.

The footsteps reached the bottom of the staircase. I pushed my hands into my pockets and leaned forward, unable to keep from grinning. The two men not married to the Eel revolved toward the door like weathervanes.

Small, slender, in a sleeveless black tunic and black linen trousers, a long colorful scarf wound around her neck, Lee Truax moved confidently into the living room. As was usual at home, she did not carry a white cane. Her steady internal flame, illuminating from within, rode as always with her, like a familiar spirit.

"Lee," I said, giving her a reference point.

"Hello, dear ones," she said, floating up before us. "Sorry to be a little late. I had to come to a decision about this scarf."

"You made the right decision," Hootie said, and at the same time, Don said, "Good choice."

"You look beautiful," I said, stating the obvious, and the other men murmured assent.

I wondered how she did it. Though I had seen it happen a thousand times, I had never understood the mechanism that allowed her to move from being good-looking to radiant without human or supernatural assistance. She barely used any makeup, and she never fussed. She wound a scarf around her neck, pushed her hair one way or another, applied lipstick, and the miracle had occurred all over again.

"You guys are like puppy dogs. Where's Jason Boatman? I heard the bell ring, and I heard voices. I thought Jason would be here."

"He'll be back in a moment," I said.

"And he's in the security business now?"

"It Takes A Thief is the name of his company," Hootie said.

She laughed, then caught herself. "Tremendous. He made a complete turnaround. I'm proud of him."

"Why don't you tell him?" Don asked. "He just came back in."

Jason Boatman had just entered the room from the other side, and he seemed riveted by the spectacle presented by his hostess.

"He isn't moving," the Eel said. "What's going on?"

"The poor old blind lady claims another victim," I said.

"Shut up, you. This is different."

Deep in his throat, Hootie made a low, gravelly sound expressive of mirth.

"Don't laugh at us, Hootie. What's he doing now? Ah. He's coming toward us, isn't he?"

"How do you do that?" Don asked. "I mean, is it something you feel, or something you hear?"

"Let me poke out your eyes. In twenty or thirty years, you'll know all about it."

"Sorry," Don said. "Anyhow, here he is, our old pal and reformed bad guy, Jason Boatman. Looking a little strained, a little hornswoggled, if you don't mind my saying so, Boats."

"How could I mind," Boats said, his eyes fixed on the Eel's face, "when I don't understand what you're talking about?"

Hootie regarded the handsome ceiling.

"It doesn't matter, pay no attention," said the Eel. "*I'll* decide how you look, Boats."

"And I wasn't a *bad* guy," Boats said. "I was a professional thief."

"A fine distinction," said the Eel. "But let me get a good idea of you, okay? It's wonderful to have the pleasure of your company again, and I want to take you in."

"Eel, you can take me any way you'd like," Boats said.

Lee Truax simply stood before him, her feet in flat back shoes planted on the floor, her head lifted, neither smiling nor not. Eventually she said, "Yes, I see. Hello, Jason."

"You could always call me Boats."

"I was just saying that I'm very proud of you. It's almost a little bit funny, that you went straight."

"Being crooked put too much wear and tear on the system."

"Say what you will, *I'm* never going straight."

I put my arm around her shoulders. "Thank God, that would spoil everything for the rest of us. But what do you think, shall we get started? Now that we're all here?"

"Go for it," said the Eel.

"All right, everybody. Drinks, coffee? Whatever you'd like, fellows. Let's get started. Honey, are you ready?"

"Absolutely," she said. "Would you please let me have some water?"

"I'll have a tequila, rocks."

"Coffee."

"Welch's grape juice, please," said Hootie.

When I returned with the drinks, we took places on the chairs and sofa facing the woman at the center of our attention. She was waiting with an air of deep personal calm. From her posture, from the level angle of her head and the musing expression on her face, the Eel seemed as transparent as the cool water in her tall glass.

"We're all set now," I told her.

"I know," she said.

If Lee Truax had possessed the power of sight, the way she swept her face from one side of the room to the other, taking us in, would have suggested that she wished not be interrupted in the course of her account.

"I'm set, too." This time, her sightless glance left no doubt as to her desire for every bit of our attention.

"Don, Hootie, Boats, and you, Lee, please understand what is going to happen here. I'm going to describe, as thoroughly as I can, what I witnessed and experienced before, during, and after Spencer Mallon's ceremony out in that meadow. No matter what happens, please do not interrupt me. Don't ask questions. Don't do or say anything that could make me stop talking. I *mean* that. Even if you are alarmed in some way, or if you hate what I'm saying, or are offended by it, please put your emotions aside, and let me go on as well as I can. I can only do this once. I'm not going to repeat myself, and I'm not going to try to explain things nobody could explain, so don't ask me to try. You understand, guys? You got me?"

"We understand," I said, and the others chimed in.

"I'll begin, then." The Eel put out her hand for the glass of water and wrapped her fingers around it with no apparent groping or hesitation. After taking a sip that might have satisfied a hummingbird, she replaced the glass in exactly its former position. Her hands came to rest in her lap, and she gave all of us the reassuring hint of a smile.

"And I want to start where *we* started that day, in the Coliseum Theater. I wonder if any of you remember the bizarre comment Spencer made before that organist sank down beneath the stage again, and the lights faded, and the curtain folded back. I bet you don't—I bet you all forgot it."

"Can we answer that?" Don asked.

"This once, yes."

"I can't remember anything he said, except that he'd meet us across the street after the second screening. You don't mean that, do you?"

"No, I mean what he said about movies and secret messages. Spencer thought that certain movies contained hidden communications that were intended only for the few who were capable of understanding them. That morning, he wanted to tell us about a secret hidden in the ending of *Shane*. *Shane* was one of his favorite movies."

| Skylarking |

Apart from Lee, *the Eel said,* probably they could all remember how Spencer walked them down the aisle to the second row, but how many of them knew why he did that? The screen shed a light of its own, that's why, and even when the rest of the enormous theater was in total darkness, the first three or four rows were illuminated by a thin, silvery glow that looked like moonlight. Mallon wanted them to be *visible.*

Years afterward, the Eel thought Mallon wanted to make sure they would stick to his game plan. He was slipping them into a pocket until it was time to take them out again and set them on their way. The Eel had no proof of this, but it seemed very likely to her that their great leader had given an usher five bucks to make sure they stayed in their seats.

An entire invisible world, Spencer thought, had become aware of his band of youngsters, and he wished to shield them from the denizens of that world until all was in proper alignment. And besides that, he had private business to take care of. His supposedly number-one girlfriend, Meredith, was furious with him over a certain wrong he had done her, and he had to make it up to her the best way he knew how, by screwing her until her brains dribbled out of her ears. Pardon my French, as the boys say. That's the way Mallon talked when he got onto this subject. Pardon my French, please, young lady. What were her ears supposed to be made of, anyhow? Crystal?

Eel Truax knew what was going on, she was no idiot. She didn't like it—she didn't like anything about the deal, if you want to know the truth. He put her in a crummy position, and there was nothing she could do about it. And what Mallon chose to tell them—all of them, really, but mainly her, the Eel—didn't help, not one bit. He wanted to explain something about death.

So death was there right at the beginning. Mallon put it right in front of them. Only they all thought he was just talking about this Western movie from ten years ago, the one with the kid that looked like Hootie. They'd all seen it on TV; they knew what he was talking about. Alan Ladd, Van Heflin, and Jean Arthur, that blond woman who was in a million movies. Jack Palance, the ultimate snaky bad guy. Man comes to town, helps a sodbuster, makes friends with his family and this whole community that's being threatened by ranchers. Finally the man reveals he's a famous gunfighter and does battle with the other team's gunfighter. He wins, everything is fine again, and the gunfighter rides off into the sunset. Only, Mallon told them before he ran out to hump his girlfriend back into a good mood, the gunfighter, Shane, dies at the end of *Shane*.

In the last shot, Alan Ladd slumps over his saddle. The other guy put a bullet in him, and he's dying, only he didn't want the boy, Billy, to know that. The movie is about the mystery of death in our culture, how that mystery is hidden. Shane is a killer. That's what he does. If Shane isn't a killer, the movie doesn't work, get it? If he's just another hired man, Van Heflin, Billy's dad, is going to be shot down in the muddy street. And if that happens, evil wins. But for most of the movie, this wandering killer, Shane, comes across as just a nice, friendly guy . . . so his death has to be passed off in a kind of code, in a gesture most people will never even see . . .

Mallon knew, the Eel now thought. (At the time, she had come to a different conclusion.) He knew what Keith Hayward was, and thanks to her husband, Lee Truax now knew a lot more than she wished she did about *that* subject, and it seemed to her now that Spencer also knew that Hayward was going to be killed out in that meadow. He *told* them all, too, only he told them in code, like his version of the movie.

After that, they sat through two showings of that stupid Alan Arkin movie and stuffed horrible movie-lobby candy into their mouths.

Finally the second showing was over, and they were allowed to troop outside, where good old Guess Who was waiting for them, big big grin on his face. Wonder of wonders, Miss America, Miss Badger Beauty, was nowhere in sight. Which meant that he had ditched her to pick them up by himself.

Of course Mallon had just climbed out of her bed, that much was obvious no matter where she was at this moment, and poor Eel felt like a big stupid knife had been stuck in her guts, but something came to her as their little band filed across the street to join the other two. It was a sudden insight about the Golden Girl, Meredith Bright, everybody's ideal woman, and probably it could only have come to the Eel when its subject was nowhere in sight. When Meredith was around, she was too distracting! You know what it was, Eel's insight? That there wasn't much *to* Meredith, and she'd be trading on her looks way into middle age. All she had was this strange combination of innocence and greed, and once the innocence was taken away from her, as it undoubtedly would be, the greed would be all that was left: greed, wrapped in a pretty package. Meredith didn't even know that she was going to hate Mallon one day, but she would, all right, because Spencer Mallon was never going to satisfy all that need, all that *desire* . . .

In a way, Meredith reminded the Eel of Boats, but Boats lusted only for *things,* stuff you could pick up and jam into a sack. The things that got Meredith all hot and bothered were on another scale altogether. Power and money, the ultimate American package, that was what she was after.

While Mallon was taking them to their rendezvous point with Hayward and Milstrap, they walked straight into a hellacious protest riot, with cops on horseback and fire hoses, and kids getting clouted in the head with nightsticks, people yelling into bullhorns, complete chaos. Total uproar.

The cops had gone out of control by the time their group got close to the scene, and they were all about busting heads and throwing kids into paddy wagons. It *infuriated* the cops, that the protest leaders had dared to stage an action off campus. Taking it to the citizens broke the fragile contract that had been the only thing keeping the cops to some sort of standard of behavior. They were pissed off and didn't mind showing it, and that made the protestors more and more outrageous. The clamor they had been hearing came from the students screaming and yelling up University Avenue, not to get away from the cops and their shields and horses but to provoke them into the brutal excess and lawlessness that was their true condition as agents of the state. And, boy oh boy, did it work! By the time Mallon and his core group had made it to North Charter Street through the running crowds, the place was a battleground.

Except for one last-minute stroke of luck, whether good or bad is up to you, they would inevitably have been drawn into the maelstrom, struck with clubs, trampled by horses, assaulted, beaten, and dragged off to jail. But Mallon looked over his shoulder and saw a big new parking garage, and that was all he needed. He pointed, he turned and ran, and the four of them followed him, a second before the firemen arrived with high-pressure hoses and began bowling the students over and sweeping them away. They got out just in time to avoid being turned into waterlogged refuse.

Of course it wasn't all over when the firemen went into their act. Plenty of students were still primed to do battle, and most of the police were having too much fun to quit. You can only aim a hose in one direction at a time, after all. So once they were all safe behind their concrete wall, there was still a lot to watch. Only, the Eel saw more than she wanted to, and it all seemed to flow from what Spencer Mallon had told them about the end of *Shane* after they had taken their second-row seats.

At the beginning, though, she saw Keith Hayward and Brett Milstrap, and for the first time really took in how strange they were, both as a couple and individually. When the Eel caught sight of the frat boys, they were slipping along the fronts of the buildings on University, staying as far back as they could from the sidewalks and the street, where all the action was taking place. They were making their way toward the intersection on the same side of the street as the parking garage, so the Eel was able mainly to see the boy in front, Hayward. Behind him, Milstrap appeared in flashes and snatches. They were creeping along like spies, their hands flattened on the walls at their back, slightly bent at the waist, eyes on the commotion. Hayward was *loving* what he saw—the Eel should have known how he'd be, but when she saw his reaction to chaos, she was shocked.

It was so inhuman, that joy, so perverse . . . so innately wicked. His eyes were alight; he was grinning and bobbing his chest up and down in an unconscious, delighted chicken dance. Hayward didn't even know he was doing it, the Eel thought. Probably he was chuckling, too. The strangest part of it was the cold, terrible impersonality of his body's movements.

Which was the moment a dire perception snapped into focus. Mallon said, Shane dies at the end of the movie: wasn't Mallon their version of Shane? It seemed so obvious to the Eel, she could not imagine why she had not understood him immediately. He had given her the message, and she had fumbled it in her hands all the while they had trekked after him through the streets of Madison into this grinding chaos. Mallon had told her that he was going to lead them into the moment of transformation and pay for it with his life. That was why he had been so explicit about leaving them after the end of his ceremony, and they had one and all misunderstood him. Mallon was not just leaving town. When he said leaving, he meant *leaving*.

Horrified, the Eel twisted against the white concrete wall and stared at Spencer Mallon, who had jumped onto the seat of a convenient metal chair and propped his elbows on the top of the wall. His leather jacket, his boots, his perfect hair, and his lightly sunburned face, these aspects of his being took on an abrupt iconic weight, as if the image before her now had been reproduced on a thousand posters: the handsome creases in his face when he smiled, the crinkles at the ends of his eyes, one hand raised in greeting to an unseen rioter.

"Don't die," she said, and her words were instantly lost within the roar and rumble of the street.

He could not have heard, but he turned toward her and smiled down.

Rocket shells should have been bursting in the sky above, white loops and spirals should have printed themselves on the pale upper air. His beautiful mouth shaped words she could begin to make out, and he jabbed a finger toward the street. Whatever it was, he wanted her to see it, too. She dropped to her knees and scooted along to the edge of the wall, where she could peer out in relative safety.

And there, in the violent street, the Eel saw the first real sign that this day the world was going to turn itself inside out. And even in the midst of the craziness and chaos rioting out there, what she saw was so unexpected, actually so *impossible*, that she thought she had been mistaken. Because, to begin with, she saw a flash of bone.

But what cleared the street for this vision was extraordinary in itself. It was like watching some behemoth launch itself into view with a plunging demon on its back, a figure so large and terrifying that everyone in sight, students, cops, and firemen, dropped what they were doing and ran for cover. The creature was simply the largest, most enormous horse the Eel had ever seen, an ink-black horse that resembled a heroic, rearing statue brought to massive life. And the face-masked officer mounted on its back, the muscles in his thighs and arms bulging, might have been a general of monumental frame who had raised his huge sword only that he might slash it down again. Together, they seemed superhuman, supernatural, a joined figure of savage retribution called out of an uneasy slumber to enforce the civil order.

The giant horse *did* rear, and the massive assault cop in the saddle *did* raise his long riot stick like a sword, and on his great mount swept like an avenging angel down the length of University Avenue, scattering students and policemen alike, then rearing and wheeling to charge slashing back. None could stand before him, and yet the protestors kept re-forming in his wake, then scattering all over again before his next charge. It was in that context that the Eel saw the flash of bone.

It appeared, then vanished, and where she looked to find it again, she saw only a smudge of dirty khaki as a soldier inside an old uniform whirled away from the horse and its implacable rider. An old uniform, still stained from the battlefield, its insignia obscure . . . she looked again and saw a skeletal arm, then a skull to which some limp hair and rotting flesh still clung. The skeleton of a dead soldier had come to join the protest, and a few of his fellows had joined him. Rifle in hand, a tall, broad man with three stripes on his arm ran toward the plunging horse, unimpeded by possessing only half a head and intestines that followed him like a silver rope. The skeleton jigged and jittered, and the dead sergeant slipped out of the way a moment before the horse could run him down.

No one else saw the dead soldiers, Eel knew.

Had Mallon taken in the rotting dead men, did he rejoice at their presence? The capering dead meant that a veil had been torn, the customary rules overturned . . . She looked back up at her beloved on his chair and realized that he had not after all seen the dancing corpses; he was looking at her and pointing somewhere farther off.

The Eel glanced in that direction and spotted Meredith Bright: of course. Who else would Mallon be looking for, who else would be all that he *could* see, really? She looked a bit frightened by the disturbance before her but not as scared as Eel would have thought she'd be—instead, she seemed frustrated, eager but irritated, in a hurry to proceed to their destination.

Her doomed calculations had been thrown off by at least an hour, probably more. The horoscope was her great contribution to the venture, and she was going to be miffed if it became irrelevant. It seemed likely, thought the Eel with a savage splash of joy, that very soon Meredith would be forced to discover that from the beginning her hero/savior/philosopher king had been merely humoring her.

Spencer was waving at Meredith, and Meredith was looking back and forth between Mallon and Keith Hayward. Neither one of them had seen the dead soldiers. Maybe only she thought it made sense for the spirits of dead soldiers to join protests against the war that had stolen their lives. It seemed plenty sensible to the Eel. Under their circumstances, she'd do the same, if she could. They didn't *like* being dead, these poor guys. They thought they'd been cheated, which she found completely reasonable. It seemed strange but not unsettling to Eel that she did not find these aggrieved ghosts frightening. Keith Hayward, though, *that* was scary. He had arrived at a hysterical pitch of joy that made him jig in place—of course, she should have understood it before, Keith had seen the ghost-skeletons, too. Had he ever! How had she missed it, it was so completely obvious. What Keith was looking at, what he was *drinking in,* was driving him out of his mind with happiness. Death turned the guy on! Spencer had no idea what he had invited into their circle.

Spencer was playing a game, the Eel recognized. She wondered why she had not always known it: from the beginning, he described everything as one kind of game or another. The worst game of all, the most destructive, was "the reality game." He and Meredith actually talked this way.

"He didn't know what he was doing?" asked Jason Boatman.

"The answer is no, but I requested that you do not interrupt me, especially with questions," Eel said. "If anyone else jumps in, I'm done, I'm outta here."

"Sorry," Boats said.

So far, we've had only prologue, *continued the Eel.* The prologue has to do with death, and the story of what she did that day revolves around death and evil, evil and death, with appearances in featured roles by two completely different demons, and they are both frightening, but there is something else, too, something greater and wiser and better in every way, something she could dare to approach no more than any of them could, which is not at all, because it was the scariest of all. Her experience wasn't all one sided, far from it, only the two sides don't turn out to be what you think they are. The Eel is still trying to work it out.

After the cops and the firemen wandered off, their little group re-assembled itself from its various hidey-holes, and the Eel saw that she had been right about Meredith. The girl was insulted and angry. She felt betrayed. Mallon didn't even pretend to care about the effect of a long delay on their horoscope. He didn't believe, no matter what she said, that this was one of the very few times when a delay would have serious consequences. Spencer, she told him, I think our window just shut. Fine, he said, we'll open another one.

People should be careful about the things they say.

Furious, Meredith turned away from Mallon and deliberately made goo-goo bedroom eyes at Keith Hayward, who came close to levitating. Meredith thought it was romance, and love, and young lust, or whatever, and sure, it was partly those things . . . but mainly it was something else, the side of Keith the Eel had first noticed for really the first time just a little while before. Eel still had no idea of its shape or dimensions, she just knew that he was even sicker than she had thought. A good deal of her experience that evening was going to consist of becoming familiar with the nature and scope of Hayward's illness.

Mallon cranked them up with a few words and broke Jason's heart by asking Don if he thought they could pull it off. In spite of screwing up the horoscope, he meant, but Don didn't get that, and neither did Boats. To them, it felt as though Spencer had anointed Dill as his apprentice and suc-cessor. The Eel wondered, *What is poor Dilly going to do if Spencer dies today? What do we all do?*

Anyhow, Don said what Spencer wanted him to say, and they set off. Hootie kept his eye on the Eel all through the rest of the night, right up until the moment he lost consciousness—Hootie knew something, he had seen something, and the Eel thought he had probably taken in the moment when she had seen the dead soldiers. She was worried about all of them, but he was worried about her. They were so connected, he had almost seen the walking dead himself . . . so she had to put him back together, which she did with a smile and a look filled to the brim with love. The Eel loved Hootie, and with that look she declared her intention of protecting him all the way through to the end.

On Glasshouse Road, she kept him focused and moving forward, and after she had glanced around at the source of the strange noises that followed them, she silently let him know that he should not turn his head. That was a funny experience, Glasshouse Road. Most of the boys looked around, and what they would have seen, she knew, was the spectacle of those oversized dogs, dressed like men and upright on their hind legs, dogs that might have stepped out of that dumb painting her father brought back from the saloon except they weren't friendly or harmless anymore, were they? They would have looked savage, like Hell's Angel dogs, biker-thug dogs that would have attacked if Mallon and his little band had done anything but go forward. That's what they all saw, and the Eel saw it, too, but it wasn't *all* she saw.

Brett Milstrap was moving forward with the lock-step, barely contained fury of the insane. When she looked forward toward the end of the street, she could see Brett Milstrap up there, too, mooching along with a sideways smirk on his almost-handsome face at the right hand of Keith Hayward. The Brett up front knew nothing of the enraged Brett stumping along behind, but the one back there hated his position and wanted to swap. Somehow, Eel understood that this exchange wasn't supposed to be in the cards. It was an impossibility. Brett had been the victim of one of those mistakes, those errors, that can never be made right again.

Here we come to another really strange part of the evening. In the troubled journey up Glasshouse Road they had cohered into a true unit—she had felt it happening, and she knew the others had, too, even Hayward and Milstrap—and at the center of that unit, she recognized, stood Eel Truax. Not Spencer, for Spencer, whom at this moment she loved entirely, was going simply to be the mechanism that launched her. He only half knew it, because his vanity recoiled before any such knowledge; his own centrality to whatever took place around him was a great foundation stone of his existence, but he did at least have a half knowledge of his true role. That was what permitted him to fulfill it.

And Spencer's role was going to be great, the Eel knew. It all depended on him, really, since she would never be able to do her part if he failed in his. And *look* at the guy! Even before Don led them into that little folded-in part of the meadow, even before they all saw that white circle shining out at them like an invitation, Spencer had been absolutely glowing with his conviction that he was doing the right thing.

Mallon's vibrant conviction that on this night they would all achieve the extraordinary swayed them all, she thought. After a while, even Meredith seemed to relinquish her desire for control. And even the fraternity boys stared at her in a way that suggested their ideal woman had moved into a realm beyond the merely sensual. That realm, filled with hints of transcendence, seemed to lie all about them. By the time they were really getting ready to kick things off, it had become the most beautiful evening the Eel had ever seen. The moon and the stars came out, shining pale and growing brighter and brighter as the evening went on. Hootie was still keeping track of Eel, who could see that he thought the stars and the glowing points of light from the traffic had become twice as beautiful because they had passed through her—Hootie saw them as she did, and he was determined to miss nothing.

As for the Eel, she had a feeling about Spencer Mallon: that he was going to be able after all to reach down into himself and produce the key that would allow her to spring free and do whatever unimaginable things she was meant to do. The man was humming with purpose, focused, electric, joyful. He was so beautiful, it almost hurt to look at him. The Eel could at least persuade herself that this man had become so in tune with himself and his goals that he could not possibly die in the execution of his task. This ceremony *was not* going to kill him. Which could mean only that he would after all simply take off for some other part of the country. This version of the future made the Eel no happier than it had when Mallon had first revealed it, but as an outcome it was a million times better than death.

So mixed in with her pleasure and admiration of the much-loved Spencer Mallon as he helped the boys loop the ropes in front of the white circle and passed out the candles and matches, mixed in also with her sense of brimming transcendence, was the painful awareness that no matter what the two of them managed to accomplish that night, he would soon be lost to her forever. Think about it—wouldn't that have some effect on what happened afterward, exactly the same way as Keith Hayward's terrible illness? The Eel had death and loss in her mind, too, even while she could feel herself humming and trembling toward this . . . *consummation* that hung unseen before her.

Once they had all their equipment laid out, they seemed almost to start breathing together. Inhaling and exhaling at the same time, all of them. The Eel was intensely aware of the intimacy of that moment. It didn't matter that she and Meredith had been grouped so closely together, they seemed almost of the same substance. Their mutual detestation endured, but weightlessly.

When they got to the part where they raised their lighted candles and waited for Mallon to begin, Hootie tightened down into himself and complained about "them" having arrived, and everyone who was thinking supposed that he was talking about the dogs, didn't they, Hootie?

Please don't answer, I know you saw something else around us, too, something that had come in with the dogs. Something hiding amongst them. It's what you saw on that day last year when my husband and Don took you outside the Lamont for the first time. By that time, you understood them so well you knew it was saying good-bye, and you felt a terrible pity. Jason Boatman is going to be amazed that what you pitied so much was what he called the Dark Matter, but that's what it was.

Hootie, who could feel compassion for something like that, must have one of the purest hearts in the world. The Eel knows. She saw one of them, too, before she went on her long journey and wound up in the most amazing of all the places she visited, the most despairing . . . at the end of the journey that began with such a sense of richness and fullness, almost of luxury, she found herself faced again with the filthy piece of shit that started moving in and out of vision the second Mallon drew in his breath to speak, to *sing*: the creature that told her how misguided Spencer had been, how foolish, yet at the same time, how close he had come to the breakthrough he had been seeking all his life. A red-bearded demon with a ponytail, bad teeth, and an old-time Noo Yawk accent . . .

First, though . . . first, she became the skylark. The most wonderful moment she ever had or ever will. It was like getting dessert before dinner, or getting the reprieve before the punishment.

Hootie, watching, knew something had happened that he couldn't share. It had come to her too quickly, too massively, to be shared. She was on the inside of an experience that had locked him out. The only reason she wasn't devastated, Hootie, was that she knew you could love what was happening to her. And in his own way, Spencer Mallon could love her, too, for the same reason. He understood that she had gone beyond him, and if he felt envy, it was only for a second.

The air got thicker somehow, more like a membrane. Unseen things, unseen lives were shooting and spinning around—she became aware of them for a second only. Because then Mallon found his words, or his words found him, and his head fell back and his chest expanded, his fingers spread apart, and this great *sound* came out of him.

Right then, crazy as it sounds, she became two people, or one person and one soul, or something like that. Her soul lived in her imagination, she knows that much. Hootie saw it happen, and Spencer did, too.

■

Spencer didn't know, and neither did anyone else but Hootie, about the final thing that sent the Eel on her way. It was the terror, revulsion, and shock that shot through her immediately after she noticed a strange motion happening in the scrubby grass about ten feet to the right of the circle. This motion, this *activity,* meant that the circle had been drawn in the wrong place. Mallon wasn't even looking in the right direction! Hootie was the only other person out there who saw what really happened.

A terrible being woke up, that's what actually happened out there. Not only had Mallon awakened it when it did not wish to be awakened, he missed the entire thing. The Eel wished she had missed it, too. The creature struggling to its feet on the worn-out grass might have been invisible, but it terrified her—it made her want to fall to the ground and press her eyes into the dirt. She could tell by the movement of the sparse grass that the thing was twitching with irritation, that it wished to remain unseen. No one was ever supposed to see it as it made its way to and fro in the world, causing men to fall off ladders, and babies to stiffen and die, and corn crops to wither, women to lose unborn babies in a bloody flux, drunken drivers to steer into oncoming lanes, husbands to beat wives, women to roast their husbands alive in their beds like cockroaches, old friends to quarrel and separate. It moved through its boundless territory, bringing chaos and disorder, bringing despair.

A few flies spun away from its reeking hide. The Eel could sense the creature shifting its ugly head and moving a step forward, a step sideways. Her hopes had curdled inside her—the others were all seeing whatever they saw, but what they smelled was *it.* In the midst of her revulsion and terror, it came to her that the demonic monster before her was the famous Noonday Demon, rumors of which her father and his corpselike pals had whispered after the slaughter of miserable afternoons at the House of Ko-Reck-Shun: the savage demon of the second rate, the demon of everyday evil. It had entered through a door Mallon had opened without knowing how to close. This was the pure demon of the vengeful, of envy-unto-sickness. As the demon of what was grasping and inferior and unappeasable, it could never be sated, satisfied, pacified, or put to rest. Probably she had breathed its fumes all of her life.

Mallon was staring at her, barely able to see her through the stinking orange cloud he had created out of nothing.

The Eel ascended a notch or two up a narrow passage that had taken shape around her. It rose to intersect other, larger passageways she intuited more than saw. From her new position, Eel was permitted to understand what had had happened six years earlier in the stacks of the Columbia University library: drawn to the carrel that was the source of the same glowing color now engulfing them, Spencer Mallon had knocked, answered an array of questions, and been reluctantly admitted. It came to her that she knew all of this because Don "Dilly" Olson had once dared to ask his mentor about it, and his mentor had dared to tell the truth.

On that day, Eel entered the great course of time and observed something that, although it was not to happen for another ten or eleven years, was taking place close at hand, which she could see by turning her head. What Mallon said to you, Don, was *Want to know what that asshole in the carrel told me? I never understood it, so I might as well give it to you, kiddo. What that freaky-looking jerk said to me was, I feel sorry for you. I have control over what I do, and you probably never will.*

The Eel watched it take place though she stood in the door of the hotel room where mentor and pupil shared a pint bottle of Johnnie Walker Black, no ice, no water. Then she spread her wings and lifted off. In the meadow, Hootie and Spencer Mallon watched the Eel's soul in its flight until it was lost in the darkness. The Eel's body sipped the momentarily foul air, trembled before impersonal evil, and took in the antics of the other beings Mallon had succeeded in welcoming into our world. This Eel, the physical Eel, witnessed Milstrap's stupid, bull-headed disappearance into the riotous world of the gods and avatars. But the rest of Eel, her essential self, soared up into a dazzling expanse of sparkling avenues and wandering byways linked to roads broad and narrow, and she understood that Mallon, all unknowing, had given her access to the heart of time, which lay like a huge map on all sides, neither two-dimensional nor three, but both simultaneously. With the addition of breathing, static time, the fourth dimension had been set in place. Across its great map she was free to travel as she wished.

The Eel was putting this the only way she knew how. She thought that she separated into two equal parts, one of them a skylark. That happened. Yes. It *happened.* Even if the entire amazing episode came directly from the imagination of the Eel left behind in the meadow.

With Mallon's song filling her ears, ecstatic Eel soared in giddy flight through many skies:

At recess in 1953, Milwaukee schoolchildren ran panting through the concrete schoolyard in a game of tag, ignoring one small boy seated alone beneath the jungle gym. He followed them with his eyes, but he never moved his head. Alone on the playground, this boy set apart looked up at the passing skylark. In her flight, Eel knew that the boy was Keith Hayward, and her heart ached in sorrow and pain;

with a brief skim down an avenue and a twirl into a narrow lane, the skylark was ascending at a steep angle, pouring out her song, over the garden of a Camden Town pub, London, 1976. Amongst the people at round tables scattered through the potted trees, a smiling dark woman prodded the shoulder of a man in a black sweater, who amazed and joyous shot to his feet and pointed, grinning, at the first skylark he had ever seen or heard;

in 1958, she whirled over the heads of Indian villagers who gazed up in slow incomprehension while the lean, leather-jacketed American who had been the center of their attention placed one hand atop his rough blond hair, tilted his head, and for a moment appeared to go into a swoon;

then it was the summer of 1957, and she was soaring over a handsome backyard pool in Fox Point, Wisconsin, where a sullen-looking twelve-year-old boy with a prominent widow's peak pushed his right hand into his bathing shorts and fondled himself as he raised his left, pointed the barrel of his index finger at her, and twice lowered the hammer of his thumb;

then the skylark wheeled through a shining passage and entered the future, in the form of a soaring, high-summer whirl above the Great Lawn and

Belvedere Castle in Central Park, New York City, for the sake of middle-aged men and women strung out like a necklace along the paths. The bird-watchers gasped and fumbled for their notebooks, their cameras, their cell phones, that they might document the appearance before them of the never seen, the impossible, the soon-to-vanish;

after that blatant bit of exuberance, a wheeling turn into a darkening lane and a cold, dead diorama from a corner of the future, where under a painted sun in a painted sky a skinny, aging Boats Boatman, soon to have the worst experience of his life, looked up at her baffled from the strip of concrete between a marina and a long artificial lawn pocked with artificial brown foot-prints in two straight lines. The prints were his and those of a huge non-dog with pointed white plastic teeth that shed the bare moonlight of exposed bone; for a terrible second, she saw *herself*, a small brown bird with outspread wings, from the perspective of an eye placed beneath the dog's ugly, inert muzzle; at the heart of a strident tumult of voices a steely tenor voice trum-peted *I want what you want*;

the Eel shuddered away, her outpouring song interrupted so brusquely that back in the meadow, Hootie cast her a look of terror and alarm.

Her shock and dismay at the painted sky and the dead world beneath it, the plastic teeth of the stuffed dog, Boats's distress, the deadly tenor voice and its invasive assertion, and Hootie's fear for her sent Eel tumbling through frame after frame:

standing before his useless "workbench," her father dropped a shot glass, which shattered against the floor and sprayed whiskey across the Eel's infant feet;

in the next room, the invisible, fly-haunted Noonday Demon lounged up to a secondhand crib, and Colby Truax, the Eel's baby brother, twitched once and died;

Roy Bly's head exploded into hanks of hair and bloody brain matter on a jungle trail in Vietnam;

sprawled across chairs, in a year when the Eel could still see, she and

Lee Harwell, unthinkingly happy there at the beginning of the great problems they would face together and apart, she home from her bartending job, he away from his desk for the first time that day, read aloud to each other from a book called *Rivers and Mountains* on East Seventh Street;

the last frame was of a sun-streaked State Street in early autumn and the large, unclean window of the Tick-Tock Diner through which the fallen Eel, now a skylark no longer but merely a transient speck drifting across the sidewalk, could dimly see herself and her companions of the little band all leaning toward the scrawny figure addressing them, in this frame visible only in one-quarter view but clearly identifiable as Keith Hayward,

to whom, the fallen Eel understood, something truly terrible was going to happen; but not before she learned a great deal more about him.

■

In the darkening meadow from which a soul-portion of her had ventured forth, the Eel stood close to Hootie Bly and watched Mallon's lunatic spirits riot before them. That these spirits had taken him by surprise, that he was absolutely stunned by what he had called up and brought into being, could be read both in the expression on his face and his posture. Now, at what should have been the moment of his greatest triumph, he stood stock still and cursing. He looked exhausted and unprepared: an actor who had been thrust onstage before he learned his lines.

The Eel, though still concerned with Keith Hayward, understood that Mallon saw himself engulfed in the foul orange-red fog and beleaguered by hundreds of savage dogs. Of the reckless panorama before them, he took in only glimpses. He had no idea of the actual majesty of his failure. Over in front of Don and the fraternity boys, a kind of drunken circus roistered away, a wild party on some cold and distant planet where all the inhabitants were made of shiny wet metal. In an atmosphere of lunatic festivity, a mad king rode around teetering atop a bear; a bellowing queen aimed a long stick at various people, directing curses at them in the way the ten-year-old Brett

Milstrap had aimed a pretend bullet at the skylark-Eel skimming above him. The mad, faceless queen gyrated toward Eel as if wound on a spring, leveled her silver rod, and made a simple check mark in the air. Painlessly, a small cold capsule struck the surface of the Eel's right eye and slipped within like a diver into a pool. Instantly, the capsule was absorbed.

My eye! thought the Eel. Then, in the odd, harrowing rush that followed, she managed to forget this event until the darkening vision of her early thirties returned it to her.

In front of Mallon a naked woman who looked nearly green posed listlessly before a dead landscape with a slow-moving camel, a floating dress, a white dove . . .

An extraordinary hubbub came from these scenes: hooting and yelling from the mad queen's blank world, loud groans from the territory behind the green woman. In a crackling thunderstorm, a red-haired giant with a raised sword screamed at Boats. In the scene before the Eel, an ancient couple, he with a long Don Quixote beard, both of them with streaming white hair, leaned into a fierce wind and twisted their necks around, viciously, to expose the ugly faces with enormous, pointed noses on the backs of their heads.

They were nothing to these figures. Insofar as human beings entered into their notice, they existed to be tormented and dispatched. These things had the transparent, empty viewpoint of gods. (The actual deity is another matter.) Mallon had called them up, but now that they were here, he barely saw them, and had no idea what to do with them.

At that point, the Eel saw Brett Milstrap bend down and tug at something, an edge, a seam with a break in the thread. She had the feeling that this idea was so terrible that he should forget about it immediately. On the other hand, Brett Milstrap seemed to have been created to invent terrible ideas.

The biggest problem with the world over there on the other side of the tough air-membrane gliding around her, Eel gathered, was that it was both lunatic and poisonous. Being crazy and toxic, according to some sources it had frightened Mallon's beloved Cornelius Agrippa right back into Christianity. If it hadn't, it should have. These faceless kings and queens, wilting girls, floating shirts, giant ranting warriors, and the rest, these camels and dragons and curious pigs, failed to make sense because they were utterly incapable of logic or coherence. Rationality had no place in their world. They could not make sense; sense wasn't in them. Meaning had come late to the world, and they had no use for it.

■

In the meadow, Brett Milstrap was standing in front of the seam he had opened, revealing a single, inhumanly bright light surrounded by darkness. The Eel saw him bend toward the opening, probably in hopes of getting a better view of that strange, blank realm.

Alongside him, Hayward seemed to have forgotten all about his frat brother, nor did he demonstrate much care for the spirit world. From the fixity of his glance, evidently he had been staring at the Meredith-Hootie-Eel trio for some time. Eel could not tell if the object of his gaze was Meredith or herself. All she knew for sure was that he was not staring at Hootie. According to everything she had intuited about the sorry Keith Hayward, he had some kind of punitive crush on Meredith. Yet his eye seemed to flick back and forth between them, a matter that disturbed her, profoundly. The Eel did not desire the attentions of Keith Hayward.

Sweat shone on his face, and his eyes looked hot, almost poached. Distracted by the thoughts jittering across his brain, he took a hesitating forward step, then another, more decisive step. On the other side of Hootie Bly, Meredith subtly rearranged her stance, a shift in the angle of one hip and one shoulder, in a way that claimed Hayward for herself alone. She was welcome to him, that idiot. With his third step Hayward burst into a run, and maybe Meredith couldn't or didn't want to see it, but he was looking straight at the Eel. He was the Unappeasable itself—she didn't know how she had failed to see it before, that Hayward out-Boatsed Boats—and he *wanted* her.

Because he knew, too! He had seen something. Hayward had taken in some portion of Eel's journey, and what he had taken in had unhinged him. The Eel wished she could transform herself into a real skylark and take off into the night sky, because her terrified body refused to move. She had become an inert, passive thing, a statue.

And she really did think she was going to die. So do you know what she learned? She learned that she would be all right when her time came. The Eel would not surrender her hold on life sweating and trembling with fear. Standing in the meadow at that extraordinary moment, she thought, *if that asshole psycho is actually going to murder me, at least I have seen what I have seen today, and at least I have had love, and at least I didn't let my father ruin my life. A life is a life, and this one was mine.*

Now, she wasn't claiming that at the age of seventeen or eighteen, whatever she was that night, she said these exact things to herself in this exact way, but she was going in that direction. She thought she had been a tremendously brave, savvy girl, and she wished that she could be more like that now. Over time, she thought, the Eel had softened up. She thought it was too bad it didn't work the other way around, so you could get braver and smarter as you move up in years.

But obviously, she didn't die, did she?

Now she's getting close to the part that is going to be really difficult to talk about.

Well, before they got to the really *hard* part, they had to deal with Keith Hayward. From *inside* Keith Hayward.

All this time, however, two other things were happening. Behind Hayward, the Eel was vaguely aware that Brett Milstrap was leaning closer to the opening he had forced in the fabric between this world and theirs—like a cat that could not keep from poking its head into an inviting bag. Brett moved even closer by a crucial half inch, and then he was *gone,* sucked right in. It happened so quickly that all Eel saw was only a pair of brown Bass Weejun loafers flying through the entry point, which instantly zipped itself shut—then, just before his roommate blocked her view, Milstrap appeared far back in the cold world of the lunatic spirits, running hard toward the foreground, his face a mask of panic.

Determined to sink his claws into the Eel, Hayward clattered forward, all knees and elbows. If it had not been for the second process then taking place before her, the Eel would have been snatched up and carried off, soon to be a goner. However, the demonic being Mallon had awakened was whirling in their direction, and it fixed her and Hootie Bly in its sights. Of Mallon's band, only they had seen it! Hayward wanted Eel, but the *thing* wanted both of them. As it launched itself—and it was a lot faster than Hayward—it helplessly moved into partial visibility. What very briefly had appeared to be a bristly pig with a faintly manlike head and an air of aggrieved entitlement was stretching out and putting on bulk as it raced toward them. As if in strobelike flashes, the Eel saw dark gloves that had burst their seams, and a dusty, stained, black swallowtail jacket. A few lazy-seeming flies continued to describe circles around its upper reaches.

When this industrious being had nearly drawn parallel to Hayward, and was in fact only a single stride from overtaking him, Keith glanced to his side and—the Eel supposed—took in what was gaining on him. Without losing a beat or slackening pace, Hayward went through what was evidently a complex mental process. Then, with a strange, questioning glance at the petrified Eel (in the few seconds since last we checked in, her serenity had shredded), he threw himself into the path of the demonic creature that was the primary result of Mallon's work.

So what did Keith Hayward do? Attack the thing beside him? Sacrifice himself so that Eel, or Hootie, or both (but not Meredith, though like them she came in for the benefits) could live through the night? Hayward died, and if Eel and Hootie hadn't survived, they wouldn't be in Chicago this night, but what actually happened in the moment? And what happened in the moment just *before*?

■

Well, here's one thing that happened, or might have happened.

In the sliver of time between Hayward's puzzling glance at Eel and his leap into the creature's trajectory, the Eel traveled again, skylark or not, at incredible speed into HaywardWorld, you might say. She said she "traveled," but there was no sense of flight or transition—she was skimming over what appeared to be small backyards in a city like Milwaukee, but the light was a strange blue-purple, and the air was of no temperature at all, and nothing moved or grew or breathed. She understood that she had come to an interior world, a world held in memory. This time around, she had not been released, and she had not chosen to embark. She had been plucked from her space and thrown here. This was another thing Mallon had done unaware: he had given her access to Keith Hayward, the last person to whom she would have desired any such thing.

But here she was, and there *he* was, the same sallow-faced child with the head that looked subtly misshapen whom she had seen as a playground outcast, now a few years on, lying on his back on the worn-out grass, clearly turning something over in his mind. The musing boy looked up and seemed to notice her in the same second that she saw he was holding a long kitchen knife in one hand. This was merely a memory, she reminded herself, but the idea of being *seen* sent sparkles of alarm through her chest and stomach.

Of course she was not seen. His eyes moved across the sky, tracing some odd Haywardian thought—or, she wondered, tracking a skylark?—and he sat up and sprang to his feet. The boy was out of his yard and into the alley before she could move, and she floated over the fence and saw him already down at the end of the block, turning the corner.

Then she was at the end of the block following close upon him as he trotted up the street and ducked into an overgrown empty lot, where he slid in behind a brick wall and hunkered down in a thriving stand of Queen Ann's lace. Keith tilted left to dig into his right pocket, from which he tugged a small plastic bag containing eraser-sized nibs of cooked brown meat that looked as though they had been worried off a couple of hamburgers. He reached in, withdrew about half of the nibs and gobbets, and deep within the flowering weeds arranged them into a miniature ziggurat. With a final pat to the heaped-up hamburger pellets, Keith scooted backward and leaned against the wall. With both hands, he anchored the base of the knife on his groin and held the blade upright.

Sweat poured out of his hairline and bloomed on his cheeks. His eyes twitched. He tightened his mouth into a single downturned line.

Long minutes later, a scrawny cat padded into the nest beneath the white canopy of Queen Ann's lace. Hayward said, "Nice kitty, kitty, kitty. Don't you want this nice new lunch I made for you, kitty kitty?"

Purring, the cat flattened lower to the ground and slid creeping up to the mound of hamburger meat. Its nose fluttered. The cat dipped its head toward the food and licked.

"Yeah, that's right," Keith said, "you skinny, funny-looking little creep." He slowly extended a hand and began to stroke the animal's spine. When the cat opened its jaws and took a real bite, Keith's hand tightened around the cat's neck and jerked it upright. He slammed the spitting, clawing animal against the brick wall and thrust the knife into the middle of its back. A thin stream of blood spurted out and soon dwindled. The cat's paws curled inward; its tail curled up. The boy drew the knife down the cat's midsection, slicing it like a melon, and the whole thin body went limp.

The expression on the boy's face was that of a ten-year-old barrister listening to the Crown's arguments.

When Keith lowered his victim to the ground and bent over it, the Eel flicked away. *No more of this,* she thought, but there was much more. She was present for the lurid memory of Uncle Tilly's crucial slow drip of a small number of words that poured a world of depravity into his young disciple's willing ear. In Keith's mind, above the impossibly handsome head and Roman nose of Tillman Hayward the sky blazed blood-red, purple, bruise-blue, gorgeous as an orchid. A dozen dogs and cats fell before Keith, and after the acquisition in high school of a friend/slave named Miller, a dozen more. Miller, two years younger than his friend/master, looked like Pinocchio, and had a good mind and an ingrained despairing passivity that made him, another starving skinny, funny-looking little being, perfect for his role as Keith's sidekick. The Eel visited Hayward's memories of his private room, one grotesque animal mutilation after another, and saw that a variety of tenderness and connection, a sick love, did bloom in that awful place.

At last she was obliged to watch, as though on a private screen, Hayward's memory of the Christmas of his junior year and the wicked exchange of gifts between uncle and nephew. Around Uncle Till wavering lights always played, a cold but brilliant sun always hung in the daytime sky, and nights were always the deepest, richest, most breathing blacks. His smallest gestures threw out immense shadows. Till gifted his nephew with a Sabatier chef's knife, and informed him that it was going to be his centerpiece, his show pony. Uncle Till accepted his nephew's gift, that of Miller, with a smile like the glint of steel razors, and his nephew grew faint with loving admiration.

Even before the three of them entered the abandoned building on Sherman Boulevard, Miller clearly felt alarmed and fearful about having been given to Keith's dangerous uncle. His knees jigged in his blue jeans, and his pores seemed to exhale an odd, metallic smell. After they had gone downstairs into Keith's secret place, he announced that he would prefer to live through the experience, and Keith's uncle informed him that he could rest easy, as he had never killed, nor ever would kill, anyone with a dick. ("Unless maybe by accident," he added.) Then he ordered trembling Miller to undress and asked if he was hung pretty good. When Miller replied that he didn't know, Uncle Till said that they would find out soon enough. There were a lot of things they were about to learn, he said, all kinds of things. And nephew, he added, if he were to enjoy himself in the deepest possible way, he feared he would have to be left alone with his Christmas present.

Through Keith Hayward seemed to move the wayward spirits of resistance, defiance, regret, and reluctance, a surprising matter given his love for his uncle, but he acted in the spirit of Christmas and remembered aloud the existence down the Boulevard of a certain diner. Try their cherry pie, said Uncle Till. Fit for a king, it was.

Keith's memory of his hour's penance in the diner was a nightmare of huge, grotesque faces, the company of men and women enduring a horrible death-in-life, a monumental struggle with a cardboard pie smothered under an excess of poisonous cherries. The world about him had grown seedy and poisoned. Down the counter, a repulsive giant named Antonio with a disfiguring stutter let the waitress know that he had just landed a good job at a mental hospital in Madison. Hayward did not understand why he saw things as he did.

He had given one of the two people he loved permission to kill the other.

Of Miller's last moments, the Eel knew she could bear to watch none, and dreaded what was to come, only to discover that neither did Hayward wish to keep these moments clear, and had buried them beneath layers of smoke and chiaroscuro, where they existed only as hints of movement polluted throughout by guilt. Reluctantly catching sight of a twitching foot here, a flopping hand there, eventually she glimpsed Hayward squatting behind his carved, beaten, bleeding friend and guiding, under Uncle Till's instruction, his Sabatier show pony to the side of Miller's neck. Words came garbled through the visual static: . . . *use your arm muscles and sink it in . . . a good hard pull all across then . . .* On the instant Eel tasted a dark, bitter venom flowing into her, staining her tongue, her palate, and the inside of her throat. Teenaged girl, bird, or a dot of consciousness swimming through another's mind, she could not bear what was happening to her, and twisted around, eyes clamped shut, and coughed and spat, hoping to retch.

Then her feet met some solid surface, and the unspeakable taste rinsed itself from her mouth and throat. The nature of the space about her had undergone a great change. Eel risked opening one eye halfway and peering out through the slit. From other forms of sensory evidence—primarily the absence of a choked, overheated underlying emotional atmosphere—it was clear that she had been translated out of Keith's dreamscapes. What was reported by the half-opened eye reassured her: a tufted red-leather sofa against a wall hung with a row of graphics, a tall reading lamp, a neatly crowded bookcase, a Persian rug on a polished hardwood floor.

These impressions and reflections required no more than a second and a half.

Eel opened both eyes fully and observed that the graphics above the handsome sofa depicted the tortures of hell.

In what she did not recognize as an old-time, grade-A New York accent, a voice behind her said, "Hiya, kiddo, how ya doon?"

She whirled around to see a man with a neatly trimmed red-brown beard and a cap of short curly dark hair smiling at her from behind a desk. His cheeks had sunken, and his eyes hid far back beneath hedgerow eyebrows. The man was standing up. Suspended between his hands he held a row of books.

"You still okay?" he asked, and lowered the books into a cardboard box, where they fit exactly, as if measured for the space. The bookcase at his back was half-empty. Stacks of cardboard boxes with folded tops covered the rug beside the desk.

The Eel said that she was okay, yes. She thought.

He smiled, showing teeth as white as dentures. "No prollem, no prollem. Hey, yawanna know ya few-cha?"

She shook her head.

"Smawt. That's pretty smawt."

His sunken eyes turned color as he spoke. When she first saw him, they had been as brown as a cigar wrapper, but when he asked if she wanted to learn about her future, they had become an innocent and playful blue. His eyes had turned a glowing golden yellow while he admired her intelligence.

"Most pee-pul wanna know dere few-chas, but dey don' like it much when dey heah abouddit. You got nuttin ta worry abaht, lemme say dat. Maybe a liddle trubble heah and deah, you'll get troo it. An in style, ya know? First class, dat's you."

From here on out, the Eel was going to stop trying to imitate this pungent accent and just use her own voice. It could have used any accent it wanted to, anyhow. The accent wasn't important.

She asked where they were, and what sort of being her kindly new companion might happen to be. Eel thought she knew the answers, but she asked anyhow.

"Oh, you're still inside my boy Hayward," answered her new friend. "And you know exactly what I am."

She guessed she did. Did he have a name?

"Doesn't everybody have a name, sweet thing? I'm Doity Toid."

Thirty-third? They had numbers instead of names?

"No, kiddo, no, you have to listen up. I'm not Thoity-thoid, I'm Doity Toid. 'D' as in demon. Toid as in you know what."

Was there a whole Toid family, with a Granddad and Grandma Toid?

"It's not an unusual name for us. We don't have parents, and we don't have children. We don't reproduce because we never die, we just sort of wear out after five or six thousand years. Anyhow, when the world out there changes, all of a sudden one day we find out we have new names. Takes a little while to adjust, natch. Until about six hundred years ago, I was called Sassenfrass. But I don't care what my name is. My name doesn't make any difference."

He turned away, pulled another two feet of books from a shelf behind him, and with the same confidence of having calculated within a tolerance of a millionth of an inch, slid them in them beside the first group of books.

"Gotta get packed up pretty damn quick. It's all over here, and I have to go. I don't know where yet, but it doesn't matter a good goddam. In this line of work, you're never really out of a J-O-B."

The Eel supposed they weren't. Could she get out of here, too, please? And what was going to happen Keith? It looked like—

"What it looks like is what it is. Good-bye, Hayward, and farewell. Too bad, you know, because this kid, he was one in a million. They don't turn out Keith Haywards every day, you can bet on that. Rare. Very rare. But you got a glimpse of the big guy?"

Unfortunately, yes.

"You said a mouthful. That guy, his name is Badshite, and he doesn't like anyone to see him. Winds his crank, you know? Means he's got to dole out some heavy-duty punishment, and Keith just put himself in the way. Sort of volunteered, the damn kid. Pisses me off, he was coming along so well. We could have gone a long way together, him and me."

He volunteered?

"Sure looked like it to me. Of course, he has no idea what Badshite is going to do to him. People really don't understand demons at all." He sighed. "You guys don't get it, and probably you never will."

Don't get what?

Doity Toid's eyes turned a hot red. He plucked a brass paperweight from the desk, and for a moment Eel feared he was going to peg it at her. An expression of contempt passed over his face and faded into what looked to Eel like a mixture of weariness and acceptance.

"You ready for this? You need us. That's the deal. That's why we're here."

She wondered—if there were demons, didn't that mean that angels existed, too?

The demon shuddered with distaste. "What are you, a sap? You don't need big protective cops with wings, you need *us*. People are angels, get it? (*Pee-pul ah angels, geddit?*) But without us, you got nothing really worth having."

Eel thought that was completely crazy, sorry.

Doity Toid slid the paperweight into a space exactly its size and came around the desk. He was scratching his curly head and giving her sideways glances. His sudden fit of ill-temper had vanished completely. With him came a whiff of feces, almost too faint to be detected, which dissipated as quickly as it had come. The demon perched himself on the front of the desk, crossed his legs at the ankles, and ran his long fingers through the rufous beard.

It came to her that as frightened as she had been at various moments, she had never been in fear of her life, nor was she now. They—whoever they were—wanted her here because they wanted to teach her something. Her only real fear was that she would not be capable of fully understanding it, seeing it from all sides: she feared that in telling other people about it, she would mess it up.

Doity Toid didn't sound anything like a college professor of his era, but in his khaki trousers, rumpled blue blazer, and blue shirt, he looked like one. His feet were shod in cordovan Weejuns, like Milstrap's. His considering, patient air also struck her as professorial.

"You guys, you people, you all run on one big engine, all the same for everybody, the whole world over. Know the name of that engine?"

Love? she speculated.

"Good try, but completely wrong, sorry. (*SAH- ree.*) The name of the engine is story."

He gestured behind him, where a green chalkboard had appeared in front of the half-emptied shelves. When he rotated an index finger, the word *story* wrote itself in nice cursive letters on the board.

"If you want to get fancy, we could use the word *narrative*."

He wiggled the finger, and *narrative* wrote itself across the board beneath the first word.

"And what does a narrative need? The presence of evil, that's what. Think of the first story, the one about Adam and Eve and the Garden. The first human beings decide—they choose, out of their own free will—to do the wrong thing, to commit an evil act. And because of that, they are driven from the sinless Garden into *this* place, the good old gorgeous (*GAW-juss*) fallen world. Turns out, what do you know, this world of ours only came about *because of* an act of evil! The first demon, who appeared in the form of a sexy, sexy snake, more or less *created* your goddam world, you could say. And how do we know this, how is the information given to us? 'Unto' us, as the other team likes to put it? In a story, a neat little narrative packed into a few short pages of Genesis."

Okay, said the Eel. I think I got it.

"Then try this one on. *We* give *you* free will, so we are responsible for your entire moral life. You can't have a story without including a bad deed or a bad intention, you certainly can't have redemption without you got some bad behavior to make it juicy, and decent behavior only exists because of the tremendous temptation provided by its opposite."

Doity Toid hitched himself closer to her on the top of the desk. He leaned forward. Deep in their caves, his eyes shone unsettling amber.

"And here comes a real biggie, little sweetie. When you think about evil, you have to think about love, and vicey-versy. Love love love, you people love to love, you love to talk about love, you even sing about love, over and over, all the time. It gives me gas. It makes me feel nauseous (*NAW-shus*). It gives me a royal pain in the tuchis. I could puke ground glass and razor blades for a week, all this crapola about love. Because, what is the opposite of love? Come on, tell me, you got a tongue on you, I know that much."

The opposite of love was hate, said the Eel.

The demon tilted back his head and laughed. The laughter of demons was rich and dark, and contempt invariably honed it to a nasty edge.

"Oh, that's what you all say. And that's what all of you actually think, one and all. From presidents and kings to bums in the gutter, who by the way are almost all gone. Used to be, you couldn't walk down a couple of blocks without seeing some poor ruined jobless homeless clapped-out lush booze-hound glue-sniffing coke-snorting junkie meth head stretched out in the gutter and stinking to high heaven of piss and shit. Even the cops didn't want to handle these guys, but they had to, it was their job to throw them in the vehicle and drag them off to jail where they could sober up until the next binge. Those guys are almost all gone now, and I can't figure it out. What happened? Where'd they go? Did they all die of their bad habits, and no new ones got made? Why not? Where are the new down-and-outers, the *new* old guys with bad teeth and stinky breath and bad B.O. and filthy, ripped clothes and bruised, dirty faces and bare footsies all bruised and swollen?"

The world changes, said the Eel, who had rather enjoyed the last part of his rant.

"Yeah, you got that right, kiddo. They can't ride the rails anymore, Skid Row is done for, the Bowery is middle-class, gentrified all to hell, public tolerance is over, it doesn't exist anymore—turns out, to have lousy shiftless self-destructive bums, first you have to have a generous society, go figure."

But what was the right answer?

"The right answer to what? You're beginning to get on my nerves. I was told, you know, hey, take a little confab with this girl, and here we are, but I have to pack up my stuff now, because this here is like the Bowery—it isn't going to exist much longer, you know?"

What is the opposite of love? asked the Eel.

"Oh, yeah, I forgot the topic."

Engaged again, the demon drew up one leg and knitted his fingers around its knee, making him look more than ever like an eager academic in front of a class. He was grinning at her.

"Hate can't be the opposite of love, dummy. You still don't get it, do you? Hate *is* love. The opposite of love is evil. Of course, evil does *include* hatred, but it's only a small subset. When love goes bad and wrong, that's when evil is created."

He released his knee and leaned forward and threw out his arms. For a moment, his eyes flashed a traffic-light red. His craggy, bearded face moved forward, pushing toward Eel through the stale air.

"You stupid human beings, the whole thing is right in front of you, but on you go, debating whether evil is internal or external, inherent in everyone or created by circumstance. Nature or nurture, I can't believe you're still debating that dim-witted opposition. *The world is not divided into two.* You have evil within you, you *contain* evil, that's the basic idea. When you open the door, what do you get, the lady or the tiger? Whoops, sorry, you get both, because the lady *is* the tiger.

"Let's not even get into death, okay? Millions of dumbbells believe that death is evil, as though they thought they should be immortal. Without death, you would have no beauty, no meaning . . . and when you try to work around death, or when you act as though you can avoid it, right then evil is set free."

The Eel told him that she did not think she really understood what he was saying. As she spoke, she was surprised to feel tears on her face. She had not known she was crying, nor did she know for how long.

"It will come back to you, in bits and pieces," said Doity Toid. He pushed himself off the desk and gave her a kindly, brown-eyed look. "Just make sure you remember the part about the lady and the tiger. It might help you out, when you get to the last stop."

The last stop?

"Walk up those stairs and open the door. We have to leave our lovely Mr. Hayward before Badshite gets his teeth into him. Walk over to the bus stop and get on the bus."

The bus?

"It's waiting. Hurry up, now. None of us have much time."

She wiped tears off her face with the palm of her hand and realized that what had made her cry was the demon's kindness. That was all, nothing more. Then she gasped. No, there was one more thing. She did not know how she could have left it until now.

Keith was going to save her life, and maybe Hootie's, too, by throwing himself before Badshite, was that right? He *volunteered*, wasn't that what her new friend had told her? So evil didn't have to stay that way, did it?

"Stay what way? You're still thinking either/or, you dummy, when there is no either/or, it's both. Mallon, the poor dope, he was right about that part, at least. And maybe Keith was more interested in something like Badshite than he was in you and your little towheaded buddy. It could be as simple as that, you know."

He really did say *towheaded*, as if his favorite author was Booth Tarkington or someone like that. Later in her life, the Eel remembered all those books he'd been packing up, and she thought that many of them had probably been novels. Demons like Doity Toid, they were a sort of literary bunch.

Anyhow, he had dismissed her and turned back to his packing, so the Eel looked to her left, saw against the wall a steep flight of stairs that looked like the steps up to an old attic, and waved good-bye. He did not see the gesture. The fecal smell she had noticed earlier reached her again, and she fled as quickly as she could.

The narrow white door at the top of the stairs opened out onto an empty urban street late into twilight. Exhaling puffs of white exhaust beneath a harsh yellow sodium arc light, a double-decker bus containing only the driver and a conductor waited at a bus stop across the wide sidewalk. Tall, dirty brick buildings lined the street. Lamps burned in only a few windows, a couple of inches of light shining beneath pulled-down shades. It seemed that she was in London.

The conductor bent to peer at her through one of the side windows, and she trotted across the sidewalk and stepped up onto the open back of the bus. Immediately, the driver dropped the transmission into gear, and the bus set off with a jolt that nearly sent her sprawling into the street. The conductor, a beefy man with deep wrinkles in his forehead and a permanent frown, grasped her arm and tugged her firmly into the body of the bus.

Where should I sit?

Turning his broad back to her, the conductor asked, in an accent she would have guessed was perfect Cockney, "Why should I bloody care where you sit?"

Sir, could you please tell me where we are going?

"*We* are not going anywhere," the conductor said in a choked, indignant voice. Still he would not turn to face her. "*I* am going to White City. *You* are going elsewhere."

Do you know where?

At that, he did swivel his upper body and again revealed his face to her. Tiny, caramel-colored eyes peered at her out of a ruined moonscape. His mouth slid to the left and twitched open into a smile crowded with broken teeth.

"TAKE A SEAT, IF YOU PLEASE."

She walked up a few rows and dropped into an empty seat. Then she moved over to the window and watched the empty city roll by. Wherever she was, it was a long way from the agronomy meadow, Mallon, and Hootie. Twin was even more distant. A moment of profound doubt claimed her: she was lost in an unknown and unreal world, and instead of trying to escape it, she was speeding deeper into its territory. The driver accelerated down the avenues and thoroughfares, blowing past the bus stops that were almost always empty. Twice, and at widely separated stops, a man in a long gray coat, a gray fedora, and sunglasses attempted to stop the careering bus by raising an arm punctuated with a black-gloved hand, and both times, to the Eel's immense gratitude, the driver ignored the summons and rocketed past. The men in gray, Eel felt, wanted to throw her off the platform, or pull her off—they wanted to thwart her mission, they wanted to keep her from arriving at the last stop.

Intending to jump onto the back platform, the second man had run after the bus, but the reckless driver picked up more speed and left him stumbling down the middle of an avenue called (she thought) Indignation Heights. So fast were they moving, Eel was unable to make out most of the street signs they passed. Every time they zoomed around a corner, the bus seemed to tilt into the curve like a motorcyclist.

A long straightaway named Climber's Corner? A wide, reeking avenue called Wherewithal Way?

From a neighborhood of great public buildings filmed with soot and pierced with blackened windows they sped into broad streets (Warlove Terrace? Blooded Place?) lined with solid, respectable residential buildings, each with a massive bow front and a great Georgian door.

Without a sideways look, the burly conductor clumped up the aisle and dumped himself into the seat immediately behind the driver. Around another corner they wheeled, into a sunken, down-sloping region of three-story brick commercial buildings where immense stone churches with towers, arches, and darkened columns sprouted like giant toads at every other corner.

To get farther from the conductor, Eel slipped out of her row and moved well back. When she sat down again, the conductor leaned toward the driver and whispered something. When he straightened up again, he turned his head and looked straight at her, brimming over with hostility and something else, something like resentment. He blamed her for having to work this endless route as evening fled into night. The simmering conductor and the stolid but reckless driver were her chauffeurs, piloting her through this endless city.

The shops and churches fell behind them, and the streets narrowed. The buildings grew shabbier, smaller, huddled side by side instead of arrayed in ranks like soldiers. The dark, unclean windows shrank. Dodger Place, the Hatters, Mandolin Terrace. A tight, rackety corner yielded to Slightly Street, then Crumbledun Row.

Street after street of dark tenements flew past the rocketing bus, with never a light in the scanty windows. The Eel slumped in her seat and rested her head on the bar of the next row forward. The tenements grew smaller and meaner. The bus rolled past a sign that announced either Mysterium or Mysteriac (graffiti had obliterated the final letters) Place. The sodium lights had dimmed and stood only one to a block.

At Tremens Passage, the bus hurtled around a corner, rolled twenty or thirty feet, and jerked to an abrupt halt. The driver swiveled in his enclosure; the conductor heaved himself to his feet and, with the expression of an executioner setting off for the scaffold, advanced down the aisle. The bus had halted before the meanest tenement on the meanest of all the streets down which they had flown. The dark, narrow building looked as though its neighbors propped it up.

I can't get out here, the Eel said. Please, don't make me.

Implacable, the conductor moved forward until he reached the Eel's row. She scooted sideways to the last seat.

How do I get home? What am I supposed to do?

"I'm sick of your whining," said the conductor, and reached forward and trapped her wrist in his enormous hand. "And I'm sick of you."

What am I supposed to do?

"You could always curl up and perish in the street." He pulled her from the seat and into the aisle as if she weighed no more than a kitten.

Up in his enclosure, the driver cackled.

She tried to shriek, but only a dry, barely human moan came out of her mouth.

The conductor dragged her to the platform and threw her off the bus. In less than a second, long before the Eel could have gathered herself and tried to jump back on, the conductor had whirled around and hooked a pole with his elbow, and the bus was racing off, dwindling as it disappeared into the night.

The weak arc light seemed to turn its idiot head toward her. Maybe the stupid light was curious about what she intended to do next. As if in guidance, a whisper of sound, more the suggestion of sound than sound itself, an exhalation without air, seemed to reach her from the repulsive, unsafe-looking building before which the bus had dropped her. Eel regarded the tenement for a while.

To get a closer look, she took a step toward it. On the instant, the front door clicked open. Her heart gave a quick extra beat. At the top of the steps, the door moved forward in its frame by no more than a subtle quarter of an inch.

Something wanted her to go up those steps and through the door. In a window on the top floor, a curtain seemed to flicker. Was she being invited in? Stupid, stupid question. Of course she was being invited into this wretched building, this site of an endless succession of tears and sorrows and murdered hopes. But why in the world would she . . . ?

Then it was as if all the joy and sweetness that had ever existed behind the door at the top of the stairs had come coiling down, as invisible as a fragrance, and wound itself around the Eel. A great impersonal beauty spoke from the center of the joy, and a great, exquisite pain pierced her heart with awareness of the loss at the heart of all the world's sweetness. The Eel felt as though a great curtain had been rolled away from before her emotional life, and that for a long second she stood within an ultimate meaning: the meaning that beat at the center of the piercing sadness within the extravagant beauty and joy of every moment on earth. Then almost as soon as it had been experienced the sense of a revealed meaning slipped away, and even then she knew she would not be able to remember that astounding, slippery moment in all its interlocking, swooning parts. It did not leave her; it *fled*.

That's the way it was, thought the Eel, you did what you could with the little bit you managed to keep. The next thing that came to her was that, no matter what it might cost her in the long run, she had to get into that amazing house as soon as she could move her legs.

"Sorry about all these tears," said the Eel, who had sobbed during this latter portion of her account.

"Lee?"

She held out a wad of wet tissues, which I took from her and replaced with dry, folded ones.

"Oh, this is hard," she said. "Please, stick with me."

"We're not going anywhere," I said. "Can you go on?"

"Oh, yeah." She smiled in my direction. "If you can take it, I can."

Her coward legs didn't exactly feel like moving, *said the Eel,* but she forced them to carry her forward onto the bottom step. The sense of a great revealed meaning still clung to her.

The Eel moved up the front steps and paused in front of the door. It hung open by maybe half an inch. The crack revealed only charcoal-colored darkness. For a moment, her enterprise showed itself to her as doubtful and riddled with danger. A thug in a bus conductor's uniform had thrown her into the street before an evil-looking building on the verge of collapse: now she thought she should go inside? On the advice of a *demon*?

Her trembling hand met the rough surface of the cracked paint at the edge of the door.

The paint seemed to be of no color at all. She did not believe in the existence of a non-color, yet here it was, neither gray nor white, nor green, nor yellow, nor alabaster, nor ivory, nor any of the actual colors it suggested in its nothingness. Though dead, in the gray light and the hint of a reflection from the sodium lamp, it seemed to shimmer, the shade of a raindrop as it squeezes from the underside of a cloud.

For a sliver of a second Eel thought she hovered on the lip of an abyss, like Brett Milstrap but worse. Then she said to herself, *I have been brought to this place, however roughly, and it will all be for nothing if I do not go in.* She grasped the edge of the door, opened a two-foot gap, and slipped inside the old building.

Her first impression, that nothing happened, came to her on a grim tide of disappointment. A part of her mind had expected a revelation, a key to the grand puzzle about beauty, sweetness, and pain the building had sent to her. Now she stood between a peeling, off-kilter door and a dark, unsafe-looking staircase in a gritty entryway. Even the dust seemed tired. Generations of thwarted lives had traversed that staircase.

The Eel stepped carefully across the filthy floor. When she settled her left foot on the first step, the dust-gray remains of the stair carpet, once a gay color and now of the same raindrop nullity as the paint on the door, crumbled into particles and sifted down. Touching the banister with the tip of a single finger, she lifted her right foot and placed it beside the left, causing identical destruction to the wasted fibers. She moved up to the second step, looked up, and called out a greeting.

Hello?

Silence responded with more silence.

Is anyone up there?

Silence again. She thought of her voice floating up the stairs, coiling through the rooms, closets, bathroom, and moving through the third floor, announcing itself in every chamber, large and small. If Eel could follow her voice as weightlessly and as fast, she wondered, what might she see? A top-floor curtain had flickered, a door had opened. Some force had invited her to enter, or so she had imagined. More than imagined, *felt*. The second she had moved toward the building, a bolt of insight had practically lifted her off her feet and carried her forward. Had all of that come from the tenement, or from some being inside it?

Before she had even finished asking herself the question, the conviction that the answer was a being, not the building, slammed into her with a rough, undeniable authority. It was like being slapped by the giant hand of a monstrous creature impatient with her doubts and fears.

Of course I am here, you idiotic child. How could I summon you if I were not?

If demons existed, then, presumably, so did a Deity. Even before the Eel had worked out what this involved for her, she began to tremble.

Knowing only that the attempt was necessary, she found that her body was willing to move up another two stairs. Then she realized that her knees, like poor doomed Miller's, were trembling, so violently that soon she would be unable to stand. The tenement wavered around her. Eel stopped moving, lowered herself, and flattened her upper body against the steps. The wall to her left turned to liquid, to a gas, to nothing, and the short hallway beyond the banister shredded away like the stair carpet beneath her feet.

Unmoving cold air hung about her. Beneath her hands, her cheek, and her hip burned the icy touch of cold marble. Directly to her right, where a moment ago the banister and a dead, colorless wall had been, hung a vast, dark three-dimensional space pierced with pinpricks it took her a moment to recognize as stars. This was so far beyond being too much to take in that she closed her eyes and for a moment concentrated on the unusual experience of feeling her pulse beating in her brain. Before she risked opening her eyes again, she turned her head forward to look at no more than what was directly before them.

The great, though dread, temptation was to peek sideways, but she could not allow herself to take such a risk until she had anchored herself in the near at hand. Flattened against a slab of dark green marble shot through with white and gold tracers, her fingers seemed small, pale, and only barely useful. That freezing marble had replaced the staircase became her immediate focus. Everything else would fall into place as soon as she had worked out the question of the unstable staircase. This was pretty feeble, but it would do. The Eel raised herself up onto her knees and saw that the flight of steps inside the fragile tenement had indeed been transformed into green marble. Strange, yes; bizarre, certainly. Oh, we can all agree on that point, can't we? Yes, we are in agreement here. But it is everything else that is the problem.

Because the minute we let our eyes wander from this handsome if puzzling marble staircase, categories such as *bizarre* and *strange* dwindle into cold, hard pebbles; they become nothing, poor things. It will be a long time before the word *bizarre* stirs anything in the Eel but a dim wonder at its insufficiency. The marble stairs were floating unsupported in midair, in fact not only in midair but apparently in deep space: unsupported, hanging there like a satellite. On both sides was nothing but frigid, unmoving air; beneath and behind, the same. In all her seventeen years, the Eel had never felt so frightened, so dislocated and imperiled. She was stuck between planets and surrounded by the cold, pinprick lights of stars. The real problem, however, was what lay at the top of the stairs.

Earlier that day, what seemed several hours earlier but had been actually only a couple of minutes, she had seen a partially opened door at the top of the tenement's front steps. Superficially, this was also true of her present situation. At the top of the marble stairs to which she had been transported hung a partially opened door. It was taller and broader, altogether grander. Unlike the front door of the tenement, this door, *her* door, spilled out a dazzling light.

The light undid her.

No, not just the light. Everything about the room above her unstrung the Eel. Occasionally, the light varied in such a way as to betray the presence of something *moving* inside the room. A man walking back and forth, a woman pacing. Something that was neither man nor woman moving slowly, deliberately within its chamber, letting her know it was there. Of this presence within the room, Eel could not think. The saliva dried in her mouth; the small blond hairs on her arms bristled straight up, like quills.

The room, she thought, would be small and still, almost barren. Whatever its physical size, the being within it was neither small nor still. Love and indifference, the civilized and the savage, compassion and cruelty, overwhelming beauty and shattering ugliness, every possible human and natural quality teemed within it, seethed there, expanded beyond our capacity for understanding, therefore unbearable—it was too beautiful, too glorious, also too furious, too destructive, and too utterly unknowable to be contemplated for longer than a nanosecond.

As an example of the millionth part of what it contained, the waiting being at the top of the stairs surrendered to her these images, strung end to end until she could take no more:

A bellowing king swept his sword downward and severed the infected arm of a weeping peasant;

a bartender with coarse black hair and a peasant's impassive face brought down a cleaver and severed a thieving patron's hand;

a surgeon in a white operating room cut off a patient's hand with a clean swipe of a bone saw;

a naked lover cut off his nude lover's pale hand with the brutal kiss of a chef's knife;

in an empty equipment room, a grim-faced schoolboy pulled a long knife from his waistband and detached the hand of a looming, red-faced gym teacher whose other hand fumbled in his fly;

a thug in an alley hacked off an old woman's hand with a swift blow of his knife;

a machinist bit his lip and thrust his hand into a die-cutter;

an Arab in a sweeping robe brought down an ax and severed the hand of a thrice-convicted pickpocket.

At this ninth iteration, the Eel cried out for release: and was given:

a golden field of mustard-flower;

a bright, dancing mountain stream;

a shaft of sunlight between the skyscraper canyons of a Manhattan avenue;

a radiant face glimpsed at a window;

a candle guttering, then flaring;

a little girl in a princess outfit treading barefoot across a sparkling green lawn;

a glass of water atop a table in an empty room;

and knew that, seen one way, the presence in the room above was the glass of water, and that pure, transparent entity was abiding and unendurable; and that the purpose of the non-dogs had been to protect human beings by keeping them from close contact with that abiding and unendurable presence.

Assailed by both love and terror, an unbearable combination, the seventeen-year-old Eel, who had been weeping uncontrollably, cradled her head on her forearms, urinated into her blue jeans, and wept some more. Warm liquid rushed down her legs, cooling as it intersected the marble platforms of the steps. Her back heaved, her eyes overflowed, her stomach trembled. To the extent that she could think at all, she thought, *So the Great Mystery and the Final Secret is that we cannot tolerate the Great Mystery and Final Secret.*

When she finally reached an interruption in her hiccupping, weeping, and moaning, Eel found that her hands were splayed on grass, not marble, and that stone treads were not digging into her thighs and hips. With a huge, disbelieving gasp of air, she struggled to her feet. Five feet away along the rise, Keith Hayward's mutilated body lay at the center of a pool of blood soaking into the grass. Hootie had vanished. Meredith had vanished. Boats was squatting on the ground, sobbing and clutching his head.

Dazed, Spencer Mallon wandered around in a loose, irregular oval, obviously unable to see most of what was actually before him. The capering spirits and godlets had sunk back into their realm, and through the pink-orange mist that had marked the limit of his vision, Mallon spotted Dilly Olson, who was looking straight at him in adoration, poised to do whatever he wished. That Mallon could see the Eel, too, was obvious in his returning gaze, which told her that after all he had witnessed at least some of what she had done. Her face was a mess, and urine darkened both legs of her jeans. These defects had no effect on Mallon. Burnished by his actual modesty, everything she loved in him glowed like a campfire. Yet no matter how greatly he admired her, Mallon was going to leave; with Dilly attached to him as if by a leash, he was going to take off at a dead run.

He turned from her and began to trot toward Glasshouse Road. The golden leash already taut, Dilly ran with him. In a moment, they had fled. The surprising weight of her misery pushed the Eel back into the afternoon of the previous day, where she had become a ragged white scrap blowing forlorn across the meadow, unseen by all but Hootie Bly.

■

"I saw that!" Hootie burst out. "You have to be telling the truth. I never talked about that with anybody. Oh! I interrupted you. I'm so sorry, Eel. Sorry, sorry, sorry."

"You didn't interrupt me, I was finished. I'm pretty sure I am, anyhow. After what I just went through, I'd better be."

The world beyond the windows had turned dark. Boatman had switched on a single low lamp during her account, and its glow left large shadowy spaces at the periphery of the room.

The Eel wiped her face with a clutch of tissues, blew her nose into them, then walked to the wastebasket beside the fireplace and dropped them. The wad of tissues missed the wastebasket by a couple of inches. In the dim light, the four of us in the room regarded the slowly unfolding tissues and decided to pretend that they had gone into the basket.

"Wow, what do you know, I missed," said Lee Truax. "The sound the basket makes is really different. You'd hear it yourself, if you paid attention to anything. Thanks, guys. Now, of course, I'm embarrassed by your tact."

She lowered herself, and reached out for the tissues. On her second try, she found them. "Seems I'm a little off right now," she said, taking care to position the wad over the basket before she dropped it.

"Why don't you sit down?" I asked.

"Because I don't feel like sitting down right now. If I stay on my feet, I have at least a chance of maintaining my composure. Really lost it back there, didn't I? Well, I just . . ." Her face went loose with a sudden wave of emotion. "I just . . ." Her eyes clamped down, she shook her head and made abrupt waving-away motions with her right hand.

"We'd be exactly the same," I said. "Cry all you like, Lee. And really, get off your feet."

"I'd be a million times worse than you are," Hootie said. "Eel, you're awesome. That's what you are, awesome."

She ignored these compliments and, in one of those moments that discomfit and unsettle the guests of a couple that begin to snipe at each other in public, spoke directly to me. "I don't want to get off my feet, all right? I just said that to you. There's something I still have to say."

"Well . . . good. Please, go on. Are you going to sit down again?" I stood up and moved a step toward her.

"We're both going to sit down. I don't need any help. I'm in my own house. Please, Lee."

"Okay," I said. "Of course you are. Sorry."

"Everybody keeps apologizing to me today. Please, guys, don't keep doing that."

She walked in the direction of her chair, obviously feeling her way with her foot at only the last minute. After she sat down again, Lee Truax closed her hands on her armrests and drew herself up straight in the chair, her back easily six inches from the back of the chair. She looked like the queen of a small, rather bohemian realm with a good deal of gold in the treasury. My eyes misted, and somehow the Eel seemed to know it, for she turned her head to me and said, "Oh, I'm not all that special, you know. Don't make a fuss."

"Noted," I said, remembering not to apologize.

"I didn't know I had any more to say," Lee told them, "and then I found myself fumbling with that Kleenex, and I realized that after making you listen to so much crazy stuff, I owed you this much. So I'm almost done, but not quite. I want you to know as much about all this as I do. That seems fair, doesn't it?"

We muttered sounds of assent, and the Eel leaned forward and settled her elbows on her knees. "All right," she said.

| Final Thoughts from the Eel |

So the main question about everything she had said, *the Eel continued*, was whether or not it all happened, wasn't that right? Or put it another way: did the Eel actually believe that all of that wild stuff actually took place? Did Spencer Mallon peel back the material of our world at least far enough for a horde of spirits and demons to come tumbling out? Did she zoom inside Keith Hayward and enjoy a chummy conversation with a literary demon who affected an old-fashioned New York street accent? Had she been thrown off a London bus, had she pissed herself on marble stairs before the Godhead? Every single thing she witnessed and did could have been the result of stress and fear—of hormones, even, the product of chemicals firing in her brain.

But.

As goofy, as flat-out loony as it seemed even to her, she still thought that every bit of it really happened. If the only place where it actually happened was her imagination, then it still really did happen.

Lots of times, the Eel had said to herself that she had learned much more from good old Twin than she ever did from Spencer Mallon.

She wanted to tell them one specific reason why she believed that everything she had told them was the literal truth. It was about something that happened long, long after they had all been high-school students in Madison, long after the Eel and Lee Harwell got married, and so long after the onset of her blindness that she had become involved with the ACB, especially its chapters in Chicago and Rehoboth Beach.

So there was this one time . . .

"Are you all right?" I asked.

"I will be, if you let me explain this," said the Eel.

So this one time she had to go, she was asked to go, to Rehoboth Beach to see if she could straighten out an ACB problem there before they had to get the police involved. It had to do with a criminal matter, funds being stolen from the treasury, always a little bit at a time, but it was adding up to a sizable amount, an amount in the low five figures. You have to know—the Eel *loved* the Rehoboth Beach chapter. She had spent a lot of time helping them get organized, and she agreed to do whatever she could as soon as they asked.

There was no reason to go through everything that happened while she was in Delaware that time. The Eel solved their problem. She got the thief to confess, the funds were restored on a payment schedule, and back home to Chicago she went, filled with the satisfaction of having done her job well. However, there was more to the story. During the four days she spent in that beach resort, something had happened that distressed her greatly and made it extremely difficult to go on. It brought back everything that had befallen the Eel out in the meadow, and she'd had to work hard to set it aside and stick to her task. Although she was unable to betray what was happening to her, and in fact was not allowed to show any of this by the nature of her role, she had gone through a period of disgust and revulsion, a nausea that included a healthy portion of outright loathing. If she had shown any of this turmoil, her entire mission would have gone right down the drain.

You have to picture a good-sized boardroom with a big table in the middle. There were no lights burning, because all of the people who entered this room were blind. The other thing you have to try to imagine is that the surroundings were almost stiflingly luxurious. Heavy gold candlesticks, gold candlesnuffers. A couple of tapestries, a crystal chandelier. Now, none of them could *see* any of that, but it all made for a certain atmosphere—it was the air you breathe when you're setting up something massive, something dirty at the core. In that room, the Eel spent about an hour with a woman who had committed a murder.

Her story, and it was just a story, came out of the blue. It had nothing to do with the stolen money. The woman who had committed the murder was trying to shock her—she knew the Eel wasn't going to turn her in. That was part of the deal from the beginning. They could speak with impunity, no matter they might say. However, this particular woman, the murderer, told her a lie. She falsified what had happened to present herself as more of a victim than a killer.

An old lover of hers had blinded her, and her testimony sent the man to jail. She told Eel that after his release, he discovered where she was living and called her to ask for a brief meeting. She refused, but he begged and begged, and finally she agreed to meet him for coffee at a place near her apartment. On the day, things went surprisingly well, and she said yes when he asked if he could walk her home. When she got to this part of her story, the Eel felt—she was sure she felt—some other presence slip in behind her. It took her a couple of seconds to realize, or if you must, to imagine, that it was Keith Hayward, some part of Keith Hayward, that had joined her.

The woman said that the man dragged her across a vacant lot and down into a ravine, where instead of raping her, he just held her down for a while, let her go, and said that he had wanted to let her know how he'd felt every day during the years he'd been in prison. She was so infuriated, she said, that she flipped out and hit him in the head with a rock. And kept on hitting him with the rock until she'd smashed in his head. At which point a young admirer wandered into the scene and helped her get cleaned up before he went back to the ravine and disposed of the body.

When she came to the part about the vacant lot, Keith Hayward's arm slithered over her shoulder. The Eel could *almost* hear his breath in her ear, his head was so close to hers. It was like being embraced from behind by a slug. She was too afraid and disgusted to move, and of course she couldn't let the other woman know what was happening. But here's what she could feel: Keith Hayward loved this woman's story, it thrilled him down to his dirty little toes. When her story ended, he had a kind of shivery ecstasy—like a demonic version of an orgasm! It was hearing about the murder that turned him on, she thought. And she thought he knew that she owed him that much, anyhow.

Yes, owed him, that's what she said. She thought she owed him that much, at least—the squalid pleasure the woman's story gave him. On the last day of his life, she had made an extensive journey through his mind and his memory, after all. It was even possible that he had sacrificed his life for her. She didn't think that's what happened, but she could not dismiss it out of hand. She'd spent a lot of time in the inner world of Keith Hayward, anyhow, and she'd been left with enough of a sense of connection to let him join her at that appalling moment. Nothing goes one way, you know, no matter what you think.

A couple of months later, she was going over all this in her head, mainly because her head wouldn't let her do anything else, and she remembered feeling that, as terrible as this sounds, Hayward was getting too much pleasure, and that his pleasure was too complicated, for what he and she were hearing. He had heard more than she had, but she couldn't imagine what it could have been. A little while later, one day when she was working on a report in her office upstairs here, it came to her that slimy Keith Hayward had immediately understood that the woman was lying. She had set up the meeting, she had lured the man into the ravine, and her admirer had jumped out of the bushes and killed him. As much as the murder, Keith had gotten off on the lie!

"So that's why I think it was real," the Eel said. "I could feel him there with me in that room—our old friend, Keith Hayward, come back to cash in an IOU with my name on it. I don't know how I ever got through that interview. Before I could face the ACB people again, I had to go up to my room and take a shower. *But okay,* I said to myself, *now I know it was true, now I know it all really did happen.*"

She slumped against the back of her chair and let her hands drop to her sides. "I don't think I can say any more. Except I don't believe that Shane dies at the end of *Shane*. Mallon was full of bull puckey."

"Yep, I agree," Hootie said. "I don't think he dies, either."

"Of course he doesn't," Boatman said.

"There's no way Shane dies," said Don. "Eel, you got that right."

They were giving serial assent to everything she had told them. They had signed on to the party of the Eel; they were believers.

"You're with us, right, Lee?" Don asked. "I don't have to ask, I know."

"At the end of that movie, Shane is a goner," I said. "He was dead before he hit the ground."

A shocked silence filled the room.

"And at the end of *Casablanca*," I said, "Humphrey Bogart and Claude Rains walk straight into the propeller of that plane and get chopped to pieces."

Slowly, Hootie, Boatman, and Olson all revolved their heads toward me. Lee Truax snickered. The three other men in the room turned from me to gaze at her. Then Hootie pointed at me and laughed. Don shook his head, rocked back in his chair, and grinned.

"I don't understand humor like that," Jason said. "Sorry, I don't get it."

"You don't have to get it," the Eel said. "You're plenty fine as is."

■

In anticipation of a long evening, we had prepared a great deal of food, and after she had come to the end of her tale and reassured Boatman, kindly but falsely, that his lack of even a rudimentary sense of humor did not diminish him in her eyes, everyone followed us into the dining room and helped themselves to slices of rare beef from a standing rib roast, roasted chicken, steamed mixed vegetables, steamed asparagus, sautéed mushrooms, sweet potato chips, and as a nod to the ghost of Keith Hayward, a cherry pie I had brought home from a neighborhood bakery. Bottles of a Russian

River pinot noir, a Napa Valley cabernet sauvignon, a chilled Alsatian pinot gris, sixteen-year-old single-malt scotch, twenty-year-old bourbon, water from icebergs, and Welch's grape juice stood on a sideboard with glasses, an ice bucket, and tongs.

The conversation felt anticlimactic to all, and dropped into frequent silences where the only sounds to be heard were the clicking and scraping of silverware on china. Ice cubes rattled in a glass of grape juice.

I said, "I suppose there's no hope for that Milstrap kid, but can he at least look forward to dying?"

"I don't think so," Don said. "I don't think anything dies in that world. They don't even age. They just keep getting crazier and crazier."

"Is that some kind of release, at least? Some kind of escape?"

"From what I've seen," Hootie said, "things don't get better when you go crazy. They tend to get worse, fast."

"That may not be true for Milstrap," Boatman said. "The last time I saw him was maybe eighteen months ago. He was sitting on the curb on Morrison Street, just watching the students walk by, it looked like. You know the deal—khaki shorts, polo shirt, madras jacket. Bass Weejuns with no socks. Still dressing like a mid-sixties frat boy."

"I sometimes wonder, where does he get his clothes?" asked Don. "What is there, a dispensary somewhere?"

"No idea. But the point is, he didn't look crazy. He didn't even look so desperate, the way he used to. Man, there were times I saw that guy, I crossed the street rather than get near him. On Morrison Street, though, he just looked kind of resigned and worn out. He waved at me, only he had this unhappy-looking smile on his face."

"Maybe he was waving good-bye," Hootie said. "I'm sorry he didn't come to see me, too." He bit into a steamed carrot and chewed for a couple of seconds. "But I'm glad he didn't, too."

Soon after, the aging men who carried within them the glowing embers of Dill, Boats, and Hootie said their good-byes, hugged me, kissed the Eel, who had grown weary, and set out for their various destinations.

Eel and I closed our front door and went back to the dining room to pick up the dishes and pack away the leftover food. When she returned from the kitchen after rinsing off their dinner plates, I said, "Go to bed, sweetie. I'll take care of the rest."

"I'll just do a little more." She tucked the stems of a handful of wine glasses between her fingers and with her free hand picked up a short, fat cocktail glass that shed, as if in successive rings, the smell of expensive whiskey.

"Um, I'd like to ask you something," I said, and gave her a glance that felt so uncertain and divided that I imagined it was what stopped her in her course toward the kitchen.

No, I thought, *it wasn't the way I looked at her. How could it be? She heard something in my voice.*

"Oh," she said, her voice neutral. "Please do."

I had the feeling that she already knew what I wanted to ask her. I plunged into it anyhow. "I thought it was nice, when you were skylarking around, that you saw us in that pub garden in Camden Town. July of 1976 was a lovely month. I still remember seeing that skylark."

"I remember you seeing it, too."

She could remember that moment from more perspectives than one, I realized.

"But go on," she said, and I had an uncanny certainty that she knew what was on my mind.

"I was wondering if you also saw me making a fool of myself on the Boardwalk outside that hotel of yours."

"It's not my hotel, but yes, I did." She set the glasses back down on the table and let her arms hang at her sides. "Of course, when I was seventeen, I couldn't be sure it was you, lurking there. I only figured it out later on."

"I was an idiot," I said.

"You even knew you were being idiotic," she said. "That's why you bought that stupid hat and those terrible sunglasses."

"Can I apologize now?"

"You can do anything you like. As I said to Jason Boatman, you're fine as is."

"Do you mean that?"

"As much as I did then. Maybe a little more."

I smiled, and understood with absolute certainty that she was aware of it. "We don't really want to know Jason anymore, do we?"

"Leading the life of a thief for better than four decades does very little for your character. He turned into a bore. But maybe he always was boring, and we didn't notice."

With that, she probed the glasses with her fingers and fitted them back into her hand. Then she picked up the whiskey glass and walked without hesitation into the kitchen. I followed after her, carrying two fistfuls of silverware. She put the glasses on the counter, and after disposing of the silver I placed the half-tumbler in the dishwasher and the wine glasses in the sink.

She leaned against the butcher-block island and waited for me.

"What you did, that was wonderful," I said.

"Do you mean back then, or now?"

"Just now. With all of us there."

"Thanks. I have to get to bed, though. I'm worn out."

I cupped one cheek in my hand and looked at her.

"But while we're on the subject," she said, "you should know that I do think that the wretched Keith Hayward actually did something great, too. Selfless, anyhow."

"You think he really did sacrifice himself? You said you weren't sure."

"Nobody wanted to hear it. Jason and Hootie, they hated the idea."

"It doesn't sound much like Hayward, you have to admit that."

"I know. But I was *with* him, I went to the diner with him. He felt miserable—he didn't even understand this, but he actually loved Miller, in his pathetic way. That he turned him over to his murderous uncle made him sick with guilt."

"But how would that . . . why would he . . . ?"

"Sacrifice himself for me? Because he knew I understood about Miller. That he wasn't completely evil, that there was at least some kind of spark in him."

"So he traded his life for yours."

"Meredith obviously thought he did it for her, to save *her* life. Maybe I'm as delusional as she is. Neither one of us will ever really know. But I saw him think. He knew I understood."

"So he . . ."

"He was making up for Miller," she said. "Yep. That's what I think."

"Astounding."

I lifted her hand and placed it where mine had been, on my cheek. She did not pull her hand away. For a moment, we stood there without moving or talking.

"Go on," she said.

"I feel . . . it's like . . . I have the feeling that we've been set free."

"Do you feel that, too? Good."

At last, she smiled at me. With a final pat, she dropped her hand. "Now that you're a free man, do you plan to write a book about Mallon and what all of us did?"

"It feels like I already wrote that book."

"Ah." She smiled again. "So?"

I couldn't help it—laughter ignited within me and flew from my throat. *So?*

Acknowledgments

Gratitude and admiration to my friend Brian Evenson, whose extraordinary novel *The Open Curtain* suggested both the material and approach of the subchapter entitled "The Dark Matter, II." Good Brian cannot say he wasn't warned. Bradford Morrow, Neil Gaiman, Gary Wolfe, Bill Sheehan, and Bernadette Bosky, early readers of this novel when it was very much in progress, offered wise, helpful, and supportive comments and advice, for which I am deeply grateful. I also owe thanks to the small press publishers who created exquisite limited editions of earlier variants of some of this material, Thomas and Elizabeth Monteleone and William Schafer. To the original "Eel," Lee Boudreaux, I sweep off my hat and bow low in admiration and wonder. My agent, David Gernert, supplied wisdom, psychic comfort, and excellent advice on the many occasions when these were needed. My editors, Stacy Creamer and Alison Callahan, were immensely helpful in bringing this long project into balance and clarity. Jay Andersen performed his usual keen-eyed amateur copyediting during the book's earlier stages. Lila Kalinich knows what she did, and it is too deep, almost, for words. Of my wife, Susan Straub, I can say only that my nearly lifelong debt of love given and returned and lived with really is too deep for words: it goes down as far as I do.

About the Author

Peter Straub has written nineteen novels and won, multiple times, every award his expanding genre bestows. He lived in Ireland and England for a decade, and now lives in a brownstone on the Upper West Side of Manhattan with his wife, Susan, the founder and director of the Read To Me program.